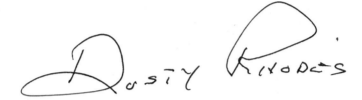

Man Hunter

Man Hunter is the Winner of the
2001 Epic Awards for the
Best Historical Western

Don't miss these other great books
by Dusty Rhodes

Shiloh

Jedidiah Boone

Treble Heart Books
1284 Overlook Dr.
Sierra Vista, AZ 85635-5512

The characters and events in this book are fictional, and any resemblance to persons, whether living or dead, is strictly coincidental. Holy Bible scriptures from the King James Version are used herein.

ISBN: 1-931742-62-6

Man Hunter
by
Dusty Rhodes

Sundowners
A Division of
Treble Heart Books

CHAPTER I

In the beginning

The blazing sun seemed unusually hot for mid-February. It cooked into Matt Henry's bare back and caused the hundred or more deep, ugly scars that crisscrossed his broad shoulders and back to itch like crazy.

His arm muscles rippled and bulged as he leaned into the heavy double winged breaking plow and felt satisfaction as the point bit deeper into the virgin ground. He liked to watch the chocolate brown soil slide off the plow's shiny silver wings and curl onto itself like the big ocean waves he had seen one time down on the Gulf of Mexico.

"Whoa, mules," he called out and the matched team of big brown Missouri mules responded immediately.

Tugging the red bandanna from around his neck he mopped sweat from his face and glanced up through squinted eyes at the noon sun. Amelia and James should be coming soon. They always brought a picnic lunch when he was working in the fields. He liked it when they came out and ate together so they could see what he had done that morning.

Looking back over the line of freshly plowed rows he had laid by that morning he was pleased. He already had eighty acres under plow. This twenty acres of new ground ought to help him bring in a good corn crop this year. Maybe even enough to pay off that little loan he had at the Waldron Bank and still have enough left over to buy Amelia that cook stove she had her eyes on at the general store.

"Get up, mules," he said, rippling the long reins to pop their rumps. He would finish out this row and break for lunch.

A man can do a heap of thinking trudging along in a furrow behind a plow from can see till can't see. It gives a fellow time to think when he's working hard and Matt had done more'n his share of both in his twenty-six years, that and trouble.

He recalled his ma reading to him and pa about trouble from her good book when he was just six. She often read to them while they sat around that old pot-bellied stove. He still remembered the words.

'A man's life is of few days and full of trouble,' she had read. Strange he could still remember that after all these years. He had asked his pa about what it meant one time when they were riding along in the wagon together. He could still see his pa's face, how it got all serious, like it did every time he was about to say something worth remembering.

'Son, trouble follows a man closer than his own shadow. It can either make a man, or it can break a man. It's what's inside the man that determines which.'

Boy he sure had seen plenty of opportunities to test the truth of that advice in his lifetime.

"Whoa, mules," he called out, reaching the end of the row.

He slipped the long reins over his head, wound them around the handle, laid the plow over on its side and headed for the inviting shade of the big oak tree where he had left his rifle and water jug.

Slouching his six foot three inch frame down against the tree, he took a long swig of the lukewarm water, rested his tired head against the tree and smiled. He always smiled when he thought about Amelia. She was the best thing that had ever happened to him. These past three years with her and his six-year-old stepson, James, had been the best years of his whole life.

The quietness was suddenly shattered by gunshots. His heart leaped into his throat as the shots rang out. One! Two! By the second shot, he had already grabbed his rifle and was racing towards the house as fast as his strong legs would carry him.

Three! Four! Five! A hot flush of fear swept through him as he raced up the small hill that separated him from the house. Topping the hill and streaking down the other side, he counted the saddled horses around the yard. Ten, twelve, fourteen, sixteen, seventeen, no, eighteen. Why would eighteen horses be at the house? From somewhere he found the strength for even greater speed. As he neared the house he levered a shell into his Henry .44 rifle.

That's when he saw James. The boy lay under the giant oak tree in the front yard, near the swing Matt had made for him. Blood still gushed from a deep gash in his throat and stained the dusty ground where he lay. His blonde, curly hair was caked and matted from the puddle of his own blood he lay in. His blue eyes were wide open and a look of terror was frozen there forever as he gazed blankly into the sky. His throat had been cut from ear to ear. He was dead.

A great sob wracked Matt's big frame and welled up in his throat, threatening to choke him. He clamped his jaws shut to stifle the scream that fought to escape his lips. A volcano of rage boiled somewhere deep inside him and surged through his whole being, erupting as a mighty explosion of energy.

One giant leap landed him on the porch. Like a charging bull he hit the partially open front door. His powerful shoulder splintered the wood, driving it inward. Someone had been standing just inside the door. The sudden force of Matt's entry sent the man flying across the room into a huddle of others, sending them sprawling.

He shot the first man he saw standing, jacked another shell into his rifle and sent another bullet square into a second man's face. Something hit him hard in his left shoulder, spinning him half around. Another sledgehammer blow struck his right side and a third found its mark in his lower chest, driving him backwards, slamming him against the wall.

He saw the floor rushing up to meet him. Even while falling, he strained to work the lever of his rifle but his hands refused to obey what his mind told them to do. It all seemed so strange, like another of those nightmares he still sometimes had. His mind told him he had been shot, but he hadn't even heard the sounds.

His face slammed into the floor. Something was wrong with his eyes; they were growing blurry. He squeezed them shut, trying to clear his vision, then opened them again. That's when he saw Amelia.

She lay on the wooden floor near the fireplace, her clothes torn completely off. Ugly bullet holes dotted her beautiful body. She had been shot five times.

A hot chill surged through him. His face flushed and felt numb. His body shook from the sudden coldness. The light was fading. Is this how it feels to die? It wasn't that he was afraid of death. He came face to face with it more than once in his life. He felt no pain, but he was so tired.

What was left to live for now anyway? Everything he cared for had been taken from him. Maybe he should just close his eyes and let death take him too.

His eyes blinked wildly, trying desperately to focus. He saw a big black man standing nearby. His head was completely bald.

There was a Mexican. His straw sombrero hung down his back by a neck cord. A knife scar ran from his left eye down to the corner of his cruel, smiling lips. Smiling? Why would he be smiling at a time like this? A long, bloody knife was tucked under his waist sash. Blood dripped from the knife to form little red spots on the wooden floor.

A big man with red hair and beard stared at him from one eye, the other hid by a black patch. The hard, cruel eye bored into him. Somehow, Matt sensed this man was the leader of this band of killers.

At that moment Matt knew he had to live. Somehow, like so many other times in his life, he had to find the strength to survive. Standing there before him were the reasons he had to make it through this. These men had to pay for what they had done.

If the God his ma had told him about was really real and was the God of justice like she said, then surely a God like that would allow him to live long enough to track down every last one of these killers and bring them to justice.

But he was so tired. . .

CHAPTER II

My flashing sword

> "When I sharpen my flashing sword and my hand grasps it in
> judgment, I will render vengeance upon my enemies."
> (Deut.32:41)

*Voices, did he hear voices? They sounded so far away. Like they
were coming from a deep cave. Then they faded away and darkness
wrapped its soft arms around him again and he drifted back into
the land of nothingness.*

"He's coming around, sheriff. Shore as shootin' he is. It's a
slap dab miracle if you ask me. Wouldn't a give a spit in the wind
for his chances of pulling through, all shot up like he was. It's
just gotta be a slap dab miracle, that's all it could be."

The strange voice seemed to be getting closer. Am I dead?
He strained to open his eyes. The bright light burned his eyes.
Vague shapes appeared from the misty shadows and floated in
front of him, gradually becoming clearer.

An old man with snow-white hair and tiny spectacles sitting
on the end of his nose emerged from the foggy world and bent

over Matt. Who is this guy? Matt tried to raise himself up and a thousand sharp needles of pain raced through him.

"Whoa there, young fellow," the old man said. "You best lie back real easy. You've been shot up worse than a watering trough on Saturday night."

When Matt forced his eyes open again he saw another man also. A big man sat in a straight-back chair near the bed. His salt and pepper hair hung collar length with more salt than pepper. He had a firmly set jaw and a penetrating look about his dark eyes, like they could see right through a man. He wore a friendly smile on his wrinkled, weathered face and a star pinned on his leather vest. Matt felt he had seen him before.

"Welcome back, son," the big man said. "You've been out quite a spell. You likely won't remember me, we've met a couple of times before, but it was some time back. I'm J.C. Holderfield, the Sheriff here in Scott County. Can you remember what happened, son?"

Matt shut his eyes and fought back the painful memories that rushed through him like a raging river, churning his insides, tossing him to and fro, flooding his mind to overflowing, sweeping all other thoughts aside like so many tiny twigs, leaving only the hurt behind. Slowly, he lifted a weak hand and swiped a tear from his cheek.

"I'm real sorry to have to put you through this again, son. I know it hurts to even think about it, but I've got to know what happened out at your place. I rode out and took a look around and think I know pretty much what went on, but I need to hear it from you."

It took awhile, but the words finally came. Sometimes barely a whisper, sometimes choked back by sobs Matt couldn't swallow back down. When he finished the sheriff leaned back in his chair and pulled out an old, wornout pipe. He produced a tobacco sack from a shirt pocket and poured the pipe full, then used a .44 shell from his gun belt to pack it down. A match struck on his britches leg put fire to it and sent a cloud of sweet-smelling aroma wafting across the room.

"If memory serves me right they call you Matt," the sheriff said, drawing deep on the old pipe. "Where you from, son? Before you married the Morgan girl, I mean."

"That's a hard question to answer, Sheriff. I always figured wherever I hung my hat was home and I've hung it in more places than I care to remember. Never had a real home, at least not since I was six.

"My family's from the boot heel of Missouri. We set out for California when I was six, didn't get far though. Apaches hit our wagon train and wiped out our whole bunch. Killed everybody except me and two other boys about my age. The Apaches raised me till I was fourteen before I managed to escape.

"I signed on with a cattle drive headed for Wichita. After that, I spent a couple of years just trailing around from here to yonder."

"Couldn't help noticing them scars you're wearing on your back," the old sheriff said. "Never seen worse on a man. Mind telling me how you got 'em?"

"Ever hear of a place called Yuma Territorial Prison in Arizona? It ain't a fit place for a man. The day I turned sixteen, a fellow in Tucson pushed me into a fight I didn't want but couldn't get out of. He drew on me and I had no choice. I shot him in self defense but his daddy was a big something or other in them parts and his money bought me five years' hard labor and a whipping once a week."

"Is that where you got them scars on your ankles, too?"

"Yes, sir. They had a contraption called the Oregon Boot. Looked like a round chunk of iron hollowed out in the middle and split in half. It had hinges on one side and an iron strap that fit under your foot. They weighed sixteen pounds apiece. They usually only put them on runners, but the day I checked in they locked one on each ankle and didn't take them off until I checked out five years later."

"Don't see how you made it, son," the big lawman said, shaking his head.

"Wouldn't have, if it hadn't been for a lifer named Duke Hatcher. Toughest man I've ever seen. He taught me a hundred ways to kill a man with your bare hands. He took a liking to me I guess, said I reminded him of his own son. That's all that kept me alive. The cons were bad, but the guards were worse."

"Sad to say but even the law's got a few bad apples."

"How'd I get here, Sheriff? Shot up like I was."

"Fellow named Hawkins brought you in, said he was out hunting along the river and heard the shooting. You know him?"

"Yeah, I met him once a while back. He's got a pretty big spread down the river a few miles. Guess I'm lucky he came along."

"Matt, when I rode out, I buried your wife and boy on that little hill behind your house. I didn't know what else to do. I put a little cross on their graves. Sure sorry about your family."

"Thanks, Sheriff. I'm beholden to you."

"While I was looking around I found your team of mules still hitched to the plow. I also found two horses I figured belonged to you. They're all down at the livery. I'm afraid that's about all that's left, though. What they didn't take, they destroyed. Good thing they didn't spot your horses or they'd be gone, too. Especially that big black stallion. Can't say I ever seen a finer piece of horseflesh."

"Don't know how or when I can repay you for all you done, Sheriff. Maybe someday I can. Got any idea who done it?"

"Oh yeah, I know who done it all right. You got two of them before they got you. They rode with the Trotter outfit. Remember the one you told me about with the black patch over one eye?

That's One-eyed Jack Trotter. Him and his gang have been robbing, raping and killing ever since the war ended. They usually don't leave any witnesses. Guess they didn't figure on you having so much bark on you."

"How come the law ain't caught them before now?"

"Well, fact is, son, there just ain't no law that can stay on their trail long enough to catch them. Take me for instance, I can chase them as far as the county line, but that's where my authority ends. We've got a few U.S. Marshals and the Texas Rangers, but they're both spread so thin and under funded they just can't do it all. After the war ended, so many took to the Owl Hoot Trail, there's just more than we can handle."

"Just don't seem right that they could do what they done to my family, then just ride off free as you please, with nobody that can do anything about it."

"It ain't right. Ain't nothing right about it, but that's just the way it is. Wish there was something more I could do. Trotter's pretty smart. His bunch rides around doing what they good and well please, then they just ride across the line, knowing we can't follow them. If things get too hot, they just crawl into a hole somewhere that nobody's been able to find. When things cool off, they slither out like the snakes they are."

"Soon as I'm able to fork a horse, I mean to find their hole and set things right, law or no law, either at the end of a short rope or in front of my gun. And I don't much care which it is," Matt said bitterly.

"Can't say I wouldn't do the same, son. Oh, I meant to tell you, the two you rid the world of before you got shot? They both had fliers on them. Five hundred apiece, dead or alive and they both shore fit that description. You've got a thousand dollars waiting on you at the bank."

Their conversation was interrupted be a pretty, young girl who burst into the room. Her long, corn silk hair hung in platted pigtails down her back with a small white ribbon tied to the end of each. She had a freckled nose and a perky little smile and wore a flour sack dress that touched her ankles.

"How is he?" she asked before realizing he was awake. "Oh, he's woke up. Daddy! Why didn't you come and tell me he was awake. You knew I wanted to be here when he come to. Is he okay? Is he hungry? Can I get him anything?"

"Whoa there, girl, just calm down a tad," the sheriff told her. "Matt, this little wildcat is my daughter, Molly. Her and Uncle Doc has set with you ever since they brought you in. She's been like a mother hen seeing after you."

"Nice to meet you, Molly. Thanks for looking out for me," Matt told the bubbly young girl.

"It's good to meet you, too," she said. "Now maybe I can call you something besides Mister."

"Well, Matt," the sheriff said, getting to his feet, "I hate to leave you alone with these two but I've got to go. If I was you, though, I'd keep a close eye, they're quite a pair."

"Thanks again, Sheriff. Sure appreciate all you've done. When I get back on my feet maybe I can square it with you some way."

The sheriff was right—Molly and the Doc were a pair sure enough. Molly spent most of every day waiting on him hand and foot. He was getting stronger every day and regaining the weight he had lost, thanks to the meals Molly brought him from the café. The weight mostly came from the fresh apple pies Molly baked him at least twice a week. The sheriff came by every day, often visiting for an hour or more.

Over the next two weeks they all became close friends. More than friends, more like family, and yet the closer they all drew together, the more scared Matt became. All through his life, it seemed like something bad always happened to everybody that he grew to care for.

Matt soon discovered what he suspected all along—J.C. Holderfield wasn't just your ordinary small town sheriff.

"Yes siree, son," Uncle Doc told him one day. "J.C. Holderfield is known in most every town west of the Mississippi as the Town Tamer. He's planted more than a few in Boot Hill with their toes pointed straight up. Folks that know say he's cleaned up more towns than most can count."

"How'd he come to be in a small town like Waldron, Arkansas?"

"Rode in about three years back, I reckon it was, just him, a sickly wife and little Molly. Said he was looking for a quiet little place to settle down. Town hired him on the spot. Elected him Sheriff the next year. His woman died right after that. He's been raising Molly by himself ever since. Doing a right good job of it, too.

"Dirty rotten shame though," he continued, "all them years doing law work, risking his life and all and he ain't got two double-eagles to rub together to show for it."

Matt learned that Molly worked part time at the general store for Mr. and Mrs. Jamieson. He asked if she would mind picking out some new clothes for him.

"Doc said he had to burn all the clothes I had on when I came in. I guess I'm gonna need everything. Pants, shirt, hat, boots and, well, everything."

"You mean long johns?"

"Well, yeah, but I didn't want to just come right out and say it."

"Silly, I wash my daddy's long johns all the time."

"Well, I ain't your daddy. More'n likely if I was I'd take a peach tree limb to you more than he does. How old are you anyway?"

"I'm twelve. Going on thirteen. Most folks say I look lots older than my age. Do I look older to you, Matt?"

"Twelve going on twenty would be more like it," he kidded her. "Some old boy's going to have his work cut out for him when it comes to throwing a loop over your head."

"I don't like boys. At least not the ones my age, they're all so silly. Besides, when the time comes for roping, I expect I'll do my own, thank you very much. I can see why daddy likes you so much."

"What makes you think your daddy likes me?"

"Probably because you're about all he's talked about for the last two weeks. He says you're like the son he always wanted and never got. Hey! That would make you my big brother wouldn't it? I always wished I had a big brother."

"Tell you what, Little Bit, if you'll make me another of those apple pies, I'll be kind of like your big brother, is it a deal?"

Molly leaped into the air, hit the floor running and hugged his neck so hard it hurt his wounded shoulder.

"Oh, Matt, would you really? It's a deal. Let's shake on it and seal the bargain. I'll be back with that pie before you can shake a stick and I'll pick out the best looking clothes in the whole store too," she hollered over her shoulder as she hurried out the door.

Finally, his coming out day arrived two days later. He must have tried on everything in the store before Molly was satisfied with both the fit and the match. He felt both relief and excitement as he slipped into his new clothes. He stomped into his black, high-heeled boots, stuffed his pants legs down into his boot tops, poked the tail of the blue shirt into his pants and tied the dark blue bandanna around his neck.

He adjusted the black, flat-crowned Stetson on his head, gazed at his reflection in the mirror and adjusted it again. The silver conches on the hatband caught light filtering through the open window and sent flashes of light dancing around the room. Finally satisfied, he playfully tipped the hat, shrugged and strode from the room that had been his home for the most part of three weeks.

The single narrow street in Waldron, Arkansas still bore deep ruts from recent early rains and the passage of untold wagon wheels. The persistent winds of the last several days had dried the ground and transformed it into fine dust. Today, strong wind gusts pushed clouds of the stinging particles between the flat board buildings that lined both sides of the street.

What few hardy souls that dared venture out, bent into the wind and ducked their heads to avoid the blowing sand. Matt did the same, holding tight to his brand new Stetson.

'The door to the sheriff's office was closed as Matt stepped up onto the wooden boardwalk. Before reaching the door, however, it was jerked open by his new friend. A smile as big as all outdoors washed across the sheriff's leathered face.

"Come on in here, boy, before you get blown away. Ain't this wind something? Don't think I'll ever get use to it. Real glad to see you up and around, son. You're a mite taller standing than you are laying."

"Morning, J.C., it's good to be up. Never spent so much time in bed in my whole life. I think I about wore out my welcome at Doc's and I could tell Molly was ready to get shed of me, too. She hadn't brought me an apple pie in two days."

"What are you griping about? She's baked a half dozen pies in the last two weeks and I ain't had the first bite of one yet. All kidding aside, Matt, helping nurse you back to health has been one of the highlights of her life. She's taking quite a liking to you. She hasn't talked about much else since you came in. Say, you want some coffee? I made it fresh just a couple of days ago."

"No thanks," Matt said, spinning a chair and straddling it. "I ain't feeling that good just yet. I was hoping you might walk with me over to the bank and see about that reward you mentioned. I'd like to settle up with some folks before I ride out."

"Be glad to, son. You still got it in mind to go after Trotter's gang?"

"Yep. I'll be leaving this morning. I want to ride out to the farm and see the graves and all. Then I thought I ought to ride by the Hawkins place and say a thank you for hauling me in."

"Matt, I know you've thought a lot about what you're setting out to do. It's a might big job. Some would call it impossible. By your own reckoning, there's still sixteen of them. They're all out and out killers, Matt—men who live by the gun—men that think nothing about gunning down anybody that gets in their way, be it men, women, or children. How you figure to take on men like that? Sixteen to one is mighty tough odds."

"My pa always said if you wanted to move a mountain, you had to do it one rock at a time. The only thing I know, J.C., this is something I gotta do. I'll stomp that snake when it rears up its head."

"There's something I want to show you." The sheriff opening a drawer of the battered old desk then lifted out something wrapped in an oily rag and handed it to Matt. "Go ahead, son, open it up."

Matt slowly peeled away the rag and gazed down at the most beautiful gun rig he had ever laid eyes upon. The holster and gun belt was of black, hand-tooled leather. Shell loops were in groups of six with sliver conches separating each group.

Glancing quickly up at J.C. with a disbelieving look, Matt saw his friend's face beaming with pride. Gently, almost reverently, Matt slid the pistol from its holster. He hefted it in his hand, turning it over and over, admiring the weapon. He laid the weapon crossways across two fingers, testing its balance and found it to be perfect. He stared in absolute awe at the blue steel revolver, amazed at its beauty. A black, striking rattler was embedded into the pearl white handles.

"It's called The Rattler," the old lawman told him. "It's an Army model 1860 .44 caliber, but it's unlike anything you've ever seen before. Whoever the gunsmith was that rigged it up was a genius. Pull that hammer back till it locks and I'll show you what I mean."

Matt did as the sheriff instructed and heard a metallic click as the hammer locked in place.

"That there is a hair trigger, Matt. You don't pull it, all you got to do is touch it. Go ahead, son, it's empty. Touch the trigger and watch what happens."

Matt swung the nose toward the wall and nudged the trigger. The hammer slammed down then immediately sprang back to the lock position, ready to fire again. Matt's mouth dropped open. It was amazing. The sheriff was right. He had never seen anything like that before.

"Try it again, boy. This time pull the trigger several times as fast as you can."

Five times Matt touched the trigger as fast as his finger could move. Each time the hammer shot forward, then bounced back, ready to fire again.

"I don't believe it," Matt said, his eyes as wide open as his mouth. "I never even heard of something like that."

"It's rigged with a special spring mechanism. Once the hammer is pulled back and locked in full cock position, it will fire and return to that position as fast as you can pull the trigger. That eliminates the time and effort it usually takes to pull back the hammer between each shot. That pistol will get off six shots quicker than most others can fire twice. It's that fast," the big lawman explained..

"Over my years of law work, I've taken lots of guns off men that didn't need them anymore. Most I sold to help supplement the starving wages a lawman draws. A while back, I took this rig off a man down in Austin, named Ben McCaskill. He thought he was faster than he turned out to be. It's the only rig I ever hung onto. I couldn't bear to part with it, least wise, till now. It's yours, son, I want you to have it."

"I appreciate it, J.C., but I can't accept that. It's too much. No telling what it's worth. It's the most beautiful rig I've ever seen, but I can't accept it. It's too much."

"It's all settled and done with." The sheriff pushed the offered gun rig away. "Strap her on and let's see how she fits."

Reluctantly, Matt slung the belt around his waist and buckled it in place. He adjusted it for height so the butt of the pistol hung just above the natural level of his relaxed hand. He buckled the leg strap to his right leg and stood up straight. The rig fit perfectly, like it was custom made just for him.

"The truth of the matter is, son, it seems to me you've been dealt some mighty poor hands in your short life. Near as I can tell, you've done the best you could do with the hands you was dealt.

"These are hard men you're setting out after, Matt. I wish I could go with you, but at my age, I'd be more harm than help. Thought maybe I could help by sharing a few things it took me my whole life to learn.

"Most of my life I've made my living, such as it was, dealing with the likes of Trotter and his bunch. I've been up and down the trail a time or two, son. I've seen some mighty bad men and some that just thought they was bad. More'n a few times I've faced men that were faster than me, but they're in boot hill. I'm still alive and kicking because I've learned some things.

"First thing I learned is that most gunfights are either won or lost before anybody ever pulls a pistol. What most don't know and don't live long enough to find out, is that a man's mind has more to do with winning or losing than how fast he is with a gun.

"Now don't get me wrong, son, a man's got to be quick and he's got to be able to hit what he's shooting at or he won't live long enough to learn the rest of it."

Matt stood, entranced by what the old lawman was sharing with him. He listened intently, committing every word to memory.

"Over the years," the sheriff said, "I practiced as hard on working on a man's mind as I did drawing and firing my pistol."

"I don't understand, J.C.," Matt said. "What do you mean when you talk about working on his mind?"

"Most times, a man's only as good as he thinks he is. You gotta do and say things to cause him to start to wonder if he can really beat you. You gotta plant a seed of doubt in his mind. You gotta get him to thinking he don't stand a Chinaman's chance in Dixie against you, then most likely he don't.

"Fear is a powerful emotion, Matt. One of the strongest a man can have and it's awful hard to hide. You can hear it in his voice, it will show up in his movements, but most of all, you can see it in his eyes.

"Sounds funny I guess, but a man's like a dog in a lot of ways. Take a dog when it's young, grab him around the throat with both hands and lift him high over your head. Stare him right in the eyes until he looks away. Right then and there you become his master. He's submitted to you. From then on he'll obey you.

"Practice what I call the death stare. Don't just look a man in the eyes, stare him down until he breaks eye contact by either blinking or looking away. Spend time staring without blinking your eyes. At a bush, a leaf, anything. At first it will burn your eyes. After a while, you'll be able to stare for long periods without blinking your eyes. A good gunfighter can kill you in the time it takes to blink your eyes.

"Watch your opponent for signs of fear: A quick sideways glance, a drop of sweat on his forehead, licking his lips or wiping his hand on his britches leg. All these are signs that fear is setting in. Never take your eyes away from his. A man's eyes will tell you when he's about to draw.

"When you have to shoot a man, shoot to kill. A wounded man can still kill you, dead men don't shoot back. The only reason to draw a gun is to kill him before he kills you. Never, never, never shoot him just once. Most times one shot won't kill a man. Just look at your own experience—you were shot three times and here you are fixing to go after the ones that done it.

"When you shoot a man, hit him right here," the one they called the Town Tamer told him, pounding his chest with his fist. "Would you just listen to me, going on and on. Go ahead, son, shuck it a time or two so you can get the feel of it."

"What's the grease on the holster for?"

"That's beef tallow," the sheriff told him. "Most gunfighters grease down their holsters to cut down on the drag. The friction of the metal gun coming out of the leather holster creates a drag. Just that split second could make the difference between living and dying."

Matt spread his legs apart to a comfortable position and dropped into the familiar gunfighter's stance he had learned when he was just a kid of fourteen and which he had practiced countless hours since. Knees slightly bent, shoulders square, eyes straight ahead, his hand hanging relaxed just below the handle of the pistol.

For a moment he stood motionless, as if frozen in place. Then, in a blur of motion, faster than the eye could follow, the pistol seemed to leap from its holster into the hand that flashed by on its lightning journey upward and outward. Like the deadly rattler from which the pistol drew its name, its mouth struck at the air in front of Matt, ready to spew its deadly venom.

"Holy Christ!" the lawman shouted, his mouth wide open in awe. "I ain't believing what I just saw. Do that again, son. I've got to see that again."

Matt spun the pistol back into its holster. Once again he assumed the position and repeated the draw again and again, each time faster than the time before. J.C. stood speechless, shaking his head in disbelief.

"Son, I've seen some mighty fast guns in my time. There was a time I thought I was pretty salty myself, but I'm telling you like it is, I've never in all my born days seen a man that quick with a pistol. Either you had an awful good teacher, or you were blessed with more natural ability than any man I've ever seen. I'm guessing it's some of both. Where'd you learn to draw like that?"

"After I escaped from the Apaches when I was fourteen," Matt explained, "I signed on with a cattle drive pushing a herd of longhorns up to Wichita. The ramrod of that outfit was a man named Chance Longley. They said he was the fastest gun in Texas. I set in on him to teach me how to use a gun. I reckon he took a liking to me or something, anyway, he finally gave in and agreed. Every day for three months we rode off away from the herd and practiced. Over the years, when I could, I just kept at it."

"Well, if that don't beat all," the big sheriff said, leaning back against the old worn out desk. "That shore explains a whole lot. So happens I know Longley. He's a fellow with a lot of bark on him. I seen him take on three pretty salty hombres down in Abilene, Texas a few years back. He left all three lying in the street staring up at the sky and dying of lead poisoning. Longley's good, no doubt about it, maybe one of the best, but I'm telling you, kid, he never seen the day he could get his pistol out as quick as you. You're maybe the fastest I ever saw."

Sauntering over to an old cabinet, the sheriff pulled open a squeaky drawer and lifted out the scariest looking contraption Matt had ever seen.

"What in tarnation is that?" he asked.

"I call it the Widow Maker," the lawman said proudly. "I thought it up myself. Had a gunsmith friend of mine down in Brownsville make it up for me. She's a twelve gauge double barrel that's sawed off to thirteen inches. She's got an oversized pistol grip and it's special rigged with only one trigger that fires both barrels at the same time.

"It throws a twelve foot pattern at about ten yards. This baby will blow a hole in the side of a barn that you could drive a team and wagon through. It's mounted permanently by a swivel to a double thick scabbard with the front cut away. You don't even draw it. You just push down on the handle. That swings the nose of this Jessie up level. Then all you got to do is touch that trigger and hold on, because she'll shore scoot you back a step or two.

"Old Widow Maker here has saved my bacon more'n a few times. She's got a way of evening up the odds, if you know what I mean. With what you're setting out to do, I figure she might come in handy from time to time."

"I don't hardly know what to say, J.C.," Matt strapped the weapon on his left hip. "Except thanks."

They left the sheriff's office and walked across the street to the Waldron Bank. They were greeted warmly by Mr. Wilkerson, the bank president.

"I'm very sorry to hear about your family, Mr. Henry," the banker said as they seated themselves in front of his desk. "Terrible tragedy, simply terrible. I certainly trust the authorities will be able to apprehend those responsible and bring them to justice."

Sheriff Holderfield signed the necessary paperwork for payment of the reward and the banker handed Matt an envelope. He accepted the envelope and peered inside. For a long moment he stared speechless. Slowly, he fanned his thumb across the edges of the bills. He had never even seen that much money at one time.

"Thanks, Mr. Wilkerson. I'd like to pay off that little loan we had on the farm. Two hundred fifty dollars, I think it is."

"I believe that's correct," the banker said, fingering through a file and pulling out a paper. "Yes, here it is, two hundred fifty dollars. You have a nice little place down there in the valley. Have you ever considered expanding? I've made the decision to liquidate some of my holdings along the Fourche River Valley. I have some very desirable land that adjoins your place."

"Just out of curiosity, how much land are you talking about?" Matt asked.

"Oh, I'd have to check my records to be sure. At one time I held fifteen thousand acres in the valley. Of course, I've sold off a few pieces. Off hand, I'd say I still have twelve thousand acres or so, maybe more."

"I didn't know there was that much land in the Fourche Valley," the sheriff said.

"Oh, there's much more than that," the banker said. "The government is opening up another five thousand acres further down the valley for homesteading. That's one of the reasons I've decided to liquidate my holdings. It's hard to sell land when the government is giving it away."

"Well, I appreciate the offer, Mr. Wilkerson," Matt said. "But I'm afraid I wouldn't be a very good prospect for you. I've got about all I can say grace over right now. If you'll just sign the release on our mortgage."

"Certainly," the banker said, signing the paper and handing it to Matt.

"Thanks, Mr. Wilkerson," Matt stood and shook hands with the banker. "If I come into a bunch of money I might be back to see you."

"When are you leaving, Matt?" J.C. asked as he and Matt walked up the street together.

"Just as soon as I can settle up some things. I want to pay the doc and I owe the café for all my meals while I was laid up. I'm gonna try to sell my team of mules to the holster at the livery, then I've got to pick up some trail supplies and settle up with Mr. and Mrs. Jamieson down at the store. Lordy, Lordy, by the time I get out of town I'll be as broke as when I came in."

"Ain't it the truth," the sheriff said. "Seems like my money runs out before the month does. Be sure to stop by before you ride out."

"You can depend on it," Matt said over his shoulder as he headed toward Doc's house.

He paid old Doc Monroe double what Doc said he owed, then went by the livery where he sold his team of mules for a fair price and bought a packsaddle. He had it in mind to use his little pinto for a packhorse.

After settling up with the lady that owned the café, he headed for Jamieson's general store. It felt good to be up and around. His wounds were mostly healed up and no longer hurt when he moved.

"How you feeling, Mr. Henry?" Mrs. Jamieson asked cheerfully, as Matt pushed through the front door.

"I'm feeling tolerably well, thanks," Matt told the nice storekeeper's wife. "I need to settle up my bill for these clothes Molly picked up for me and I'm gonna need some trail supplies too."

"What kind of supplies will you be needing?"

"Most everything I reckon. The sheriff tells me those fellows didn't leave nothing at the house that's fit for anything. I'll need a coffeepot, a skillet and a pan for beans. I'll need a couple of tin plates and cups for coffee and something to eat with. Shucks, ma'am, you likely know more what I'll need than I do, would you mind just picking out what all I'll need and I'd be obliged."

"Sounds like you're leaving the country," Jacob Jamieson said, coming in from the back and overhearing what Matt said. "I sure hope not, we need more folks like you around these parts."

"No, sir. I'll be back. I'm just going after the ones that murdered my family."

"The sheriff said as much. Well, I sure wish you success. It was an awful thing they done. We sure are sorry."

"Thanks. What have you got in rifles?" Matt asked.

"Just got a new shipment of the latest model Henry. It's a big improvement over the older model. Let me show you."

Walking over to the wall rack, the storekeeper took down a shiny new rifle, worked the lever and handed it to Matt.

"That's the improved Henry, model .44-40," Mr. Jamieson told him. "It holds fifteen shells in the magazine and has the smoothest lever action of any gun on the market."

"How much you asking for one of these?"

"They're forty five dollars and worth every penny."

"I'll take it and I'll need a couple boxes of shells too."

The storekeeper's wife was busy gathering up supplies and piling them in a stack on the counter. The pile was getting mighty high. He began to wonder if it had been a good idea to let her pick out what all he needed. He could make do with less.

"Mrs. Jamieson," Matt said. "I've been thinking I'd like to do something nice for Molly. She's been so good to me and all. Don't know how I could have made it the past couple of weeks without her help. I was thinking maybe you might know somebody I could hire to make her a pretty dress. Do you reckon she'd like that?"

"Oh, she would love it. I just got a brand new shipment of pretty calico, maybe you'd like to pick out something and I could sew it up for you."

"Ma'am, I'm ashamed to say, I'm not much when it comes to picking out clothes. Wonder if you'd mind picking out something you think she'd like?"

"I'd be happy to. There won't be any charge for sewing it though, I'll be glad to do it. Molly's a special young girl."

"Yes, ma'am, she sure is. I'd be obliged if you'd take care of that for me."

After he had paid his bill and told them he'd be back shortly with his packhorse, he strode down the dusty street toward the livery. The sheriff came out of his office, spotted him and hurried to meet him.

"Glad I caught you, Matt. I just got a telegram they sent out to all the county sheriffs. Trotter's gang hit the Butterfield stage down near Tyler, Texas just a couple of days ago. They shot the driver and murdered a whole family that was on board. I thought you'd want to know."

"Thanks, J.C. That will give me a place to start anyhow. Soon as I load my supplies I'll be pulling out."

"The sheriff in Tyler is named Lassiter. Come on, I'll help you load that pack."

"Where's Molly?" Matt asked, as he, J.C. and Mr. Jamieson finished loading and tying down his supplies on the pinto.

"I tried my best to get her to come and tell you good-bye, but you know how she is. She said she couldn't bear to see you go. She'll be okay though."

"That's okay, I understand." Matt said. "Well, adios, partner. Thanks again for all you've done. I won't be forgetting what I owe you."

"I ain't saying good-bye, son, just so long for awhile," the big lawman choked out.

Their hands clasped, their gazes met, locked, and held for a long moment. Nothing more needed to be said as their looks made clear their mutual feelings for each other.

Matt gathered the lead rope for his packhorse, toed a stirrup and swung into the saddle. His black stallion pranced in place and tossed its big head, seemingly anxious to get on the trail.

J.C. leaned against a hitching rail, his gaze intent on his boot toe scraping a line in the dust. Was that a tear Matt saw the sheriff swipe from his eyes? Mr. and Mrs. Jamieson stood side by side on the boardwalk. Down the street, Matt saw the old Doc pause to wave good-bye before stepping into his little black buggy. All along the street, folks stopped what they were doing to watch the rider as he rode slowly down the street. Little puffs of dust rose from the stallion's hooves as he high-stepped sideways. The calm little pinto followed obediently along behind.

Matt rode slowly and watched closely as he passed J.C. and Molly's little house, hoping his young friend would change her mind, but understood when she didn't.

He was well past her house when he heard a door slam and footsteps running. Twisting in his saddle, he saw Molly, her long pigtails flying in the breeze as she ran down the street after him.

Reining up, he reached down and gathered the sobbing girl into his arms, lifting her up onto the saddle in front of him.

"Don't cry, Little Bit, I'll be back before you can shake a stick, then you can make me another of those apple pies."

"Please, don't go!" she choked out. "I'm afraid if you go, I might not ever see you again. I don't want you to go."

"I know, honey." he swallowed down a big lump in his throat. "This is something I've gotta do for my wife and little boy. I want you to promise me something, okay? I want you to take good care of J.C. for me while I'm gone. I've grown mighty fond of both of you. Will you do that for me?"

"I promise," she said, moving a finger across her chest, "and cross my heart. But you've got to promise to come back to us. Is it a deal?"

"It's a deal." He kissed her freckled cheek and set her down onto the street. As he turned his horse and rode away, he could hear her beautiful, quivering voice calling out behind him.

"I love you, Matt Henry! I love you, Matt Henry! I love you, Matt Henry!"

Gradually, the tiny voice faded into the distance from his hearing, but would never fade from the memory of his heart. It would be lodged there forever. He clamped his jaw, swiped a tear away with the back of a gloved hand and set his face toward the task that lay before him.

It had been quite a spell since he had spent any time on his horse. The animal tossed its head and pulled at the reins, aching to run. Matt's mind went back to the first time he had seen the big black stallion. It was in the hills of Arizona, only days after his release from Yuma Territorial Prison. Matt had been coaxing along the broken down nag he had bought with the ten dollars he had been given on release, going nowhere and taking his time doing it.

The sight took his breath away. Standing on the top of a butte, keeping a close eye on its herd of mares in the valley below, stood the most beautiful horse Matt had ever laid eyes upon. A stiff breeze lifted its long mane. The afternoon sun bounced off the coal black coat and set it aflame, casting a golden aura around the big stallion. He knew right then and there, he had to have that horse.

It had taken two months of hard work to capture the stallion and another month of even harder work breaking him to ride, but the reward had been well worth the effort. The big stallion was the envy of every man that saw it.

The sun was well past noon when he topped a pine-covered hill overlooking their little farmhouse in the distant river valley. Reigning up, he swallowed down a big lump and gazed for a long minute at the place that held so many happy memories.

Grassy pastures where horses should be grazing peacefully, lay empty. Their chimney, which should have been trailing lazy plumes of puffy smoke, sending signals of life and activity and a welcoming invitation to all, stood lifeless and silent and cold.

Matt wiped an eye with the back of a gloved hand and kneed his mount forward to a reunion with hurtful memories that flashed to the forefront of his troubled mind.

As he rode slowly sadness overwhelmed him. Except for the smashed front door, one would never have guessed the tragic things that happened here.

A soft squeaking sound drew his attention. A gentle breeze pushed an empty tree swing in the big oak tree back and forth, as if lonely for the happy little sandy-haired boy that had spent so many hours in it.

For long minutes he sat motionless in the saddle. He stared off into the sky at nothing. Midnight stood quietly, unusual for the big stallion, as if he somehow sensed his master was waging a battle within himself. A battle whether to turn and ride away, sparing himself the hurt that would surely come, or from somewhere, finding the strength to go inside.

Setting his strong jaw in grim determination, he swung resolutely from the saddle, ground hitched his horse and climbed the three steps onto the porch. He hesitated for only an instant, again fighting off the urge to run away, before stepping through the open door.

An avalanche of painful memories swept over him, flooding his mind, reliving the events all over again. He staggered backwards under the weight of the hurt. His back pressed against the wall.

In his mind the room was again full of men, ugly men, evil men. A surprised look on their faces quickly turned to hatred at Matt's sudden entry. The tangled web of events had played out in mere seconds, but the results would last forever.

His gaze swept the room. What he saw was a picture of destruction. Just as J.C. had said, what they hadn't taken, they had destroyed. The table smashed, chairs in broken pieces, Amelia's china cabinet which had held her precious dishes, overturned, its contents broken and scattered about the cluttered room. Everything they had worked so hard for was gone.

The outlaws had taken everything of value, unless... Unless they might have overlooked the loose rock in the fireplace behind which Amelia had squirreled away their meager savings. His gaze swung toward the fireplace, but in doing so, fell upon the spot he had purposely avoided.

A large, brownish stain still discolored the wooden floor where she had lain. A sharp pain shot through him like a bullet and found lodging in his heart. His strength drained from him as he slid down the wall until he sat on the floor, his head buried in his hands, weeping uncontrollably.

Sometime later he swiped at his face with a sleeve, wiping away the wetness left by tears stored up over a lifetime of hurt. Even with all he had been through in his life, he hadn't allowed himself to cry since he was six years old. Living with the Apache, he had learned to hold his emotions in check. In their view, crying was for squaws and babies.

He struggled to pull himself to his feet and on shaky legs, made his way over to the fireplace. Unbelievably, the thieves had somehow overlooked the loose rock. Lifting it out, he retrieved the small leather pouch. He knew without looking it contained exactly eighty-two, hard saved dollars—their life savings. Amelia had called it their emergency savings.

Turning on his heels, his eyes fixed straight ahead, he strode from the room.

As he stepped from the porch, he paused and picked two handfuls of flowers from Amelia's little flowerbed she had been so proud of. Then, like a condemned man on his way to the gallows, he made his way up the small hill behind their house.

A small wooden cross stood at the head of each grave. The loose dirt still looked fresh and rounded to a small mound. Hat in hand, he dropped to one knee and gently placed a bouquet on each grave.

His mind flooded with a thousand memories. Memories of life—and love—and laughter. Memories of happy times and quiet times and times of closeness like he had never known before. Memories of dreams shared, of plans made, of small achievements celebrated.

Kneeling there, he realized, perhaps for the first time, these were the moments he must hold on to. He must cherish the good times and live in spite of the bad. Placing one hand on each of the graves, he renewed his promise to them. He would find those responsible and see that they were brought to justice.

Rising, he jammed his hat onto his head and set his jaw in grim determination. Without looking back, he strode quickly down the hill to his waiting horses, swung into the saddle and pointed the big stallion's nose downriver.

As he rode, he soaked up the beauty of the land. He never ceased to be amazed just how beautiful the Fourche River Valley really was. The rugged Ouachita Mountains where bear, deer, cougar and turkey were plentiful and available for the taking, served as a backdrop for rolling, pine covered hills. These eventually gave way to large expanses of flat, fertile bottomland, formed and nourished by the winding Fourche LaFave River.

It was a good land, an inviting land. A land that lured the farmer, the cattleman and the hunter as surely as the California gold fields lured the prospector. And they came. They came from Alabama, Kentucky, Mississippi and Tennessee. Men who had fought on both sides of the brother against brother war. Men who had somehow survived the bloody battlefields and freezing prison camps, only to return home to find nothing left.

They came by boat, by wagon, by horseback and by foot. Many with nothing except the tattered uniforms or hand-me-downs on their backs and a hope in their hearts. They came with their families and their dreams and the muscles in their backs to start a new life on a little piece of ground where they hoped to build a future for their children and their children's children.

But with the good, who were called homesteaders, also came the bad. In the Fourche Valley, these were called Bushwhackers. They were mostly renegades, misfits, deserters and local predators who ran in packs like ravenous wolves and preyed on the weak, the defenseless and the many isolated homes scattered throughout the valley.

They usually struck during the dead of night and took control of an isolated home, raping, terrorizing, killing and taking what they wanted when they moved on. Matt had long ago learned that not all predators walked on four feet, more often only two.

The Hawkins place lay about eight miles downriver from Matt and Amelia's farm. As he rode near, he was appalled at the rundown conditions he saw. Not a single head of stock grazed the rich pastures. A pole corral was in dire need of repair in several places. A barn door hung askew by only one hinge. A wagon with a wheel off and lying broken nearby a dry watering trough unfilled by the rusted pump.

"Hello the house," he called loudly, as he reined up in the overgrown yard.

The two front windows of the house were missing half the panes and Matt considered the place might be deserted until the nose of a shotgun poked through the hole of a missing glass.

"Who are ye and what do ye want?" a gruff voice demanded from inside.

"I'm Matt Henry, Mr. Hawkins, from upriver."

"Ye shore don't look like that fellow to me. Ye're packing a heap of hardware fer a dirt farmer."

"Yes, sir, but mine is where they ought to be, yours ain't. I just rode by to be neighborly and say a thank you for hauling me into town when I was shot up a while back. Now that I've said it I'll be riding on." Matt turned his horse to leave.

"Now just hold on there," the voice called out. "Now that I think on it, I reckon you might be that fellow after all. Go ahead and light and sit a spell, I'll be out directly."

Matt sat right where he was until the gun had been withdrawn and Jeb Hawkins emerged, the shotgun cradled in the crook of his arm. Unwashed, unshaven, with long, shaggy, dirty looking hair and beard, the man was as unkept as his property. His dirty, tattered britches were held up by only one suspender. He wore no shirt or socks. His untied work shoes looked as if they should have been thrown away years ago. Even before Matt climbed down from his horse, the sickening smell of body odor reached his nose. This would be a mighty short visit.

Hawkins plopped down in a rocking chair with one rocker missing and motioned for Matt to sit in a straight chair with a straw bottom, except there was more bottom than straw. He quickly chose to sit on the edge of the porch as far from that awful smell as possible.

Mrs. Hawkins appeared, but stood just inside the door. She made no effort to come outside. Matt didn't blame her. He was shocked by the contrast between the two. She wore a clean dress with an apron over it. Her hair was done up into a bun on the back of her head. A nasty purple bruise had her right eye swollen near shut.

"Get back in the house, woman," Hawkins shouted at her. "Us men got some neighborly talking to do." She cowed like a beaten hound dog, ducked her head and retreated from sight.

"Didn't know who you was awhile ago," Hawkins said. "Thought you might be one of them bushwhackers that's riding around bothering decent folks. Guess you heard what they done to old One Jones over on Dutch Creek? They come swooping down on his place in the middle of the night, tied him to a tree and put a bullet right square between his eyes. Like that weren't enough, they scalped him slicker'n a whistle. They carried that dripping topknot right into the house and hung it over the fireplace to dry, right in front of his womenfolk and young-uns.

"I kinda figured they was the ones that got your folks when I come on the house and seen what all went on. Thought you was a goner for shore. Figured I was wasting my time hauling you plumb into town. Got my wagon all bloody and busted a wheel to boot. You just come by to say a thank you, huh? Way I figure it young fellow, a thank you don't hardly seem enough for what all I done."

"What do you figure you got coming?" Matt asked, more than a little annoyed at how much gall the man had about him.

"Well, sir, I been thinking on it. Seems to me there ought to be some kind of reward or something. Them thank you's don't go fer when a man's buying beans. Way I figure it, hauling a man all the way into town, getting my wagon all bloody and bustin' a wheel and all. It ought to be worth a couple of double eagles. Yes, siree, a couple of double eagles would be a mighty small price."

Matt fished two double eagles from his pocket and pitched them to Hawkins. The man caught them deftly in midair and hurriedly stuffed them into his pocket as Mrs. Hawkins again came to the door.

"I got some leftover coffee on the stove heating if you men got a notion for some," she said.

"Not for me, ma'am," Matt said, "but thanks anyway."

"Just telling Mr. Henry here, we got our place up fer sale. We've had a string of bad luck and lost all our stock. I'm down in my back and can't work the place. Don't reckon you'd be knowing somebody looking fer a good place?"

"How many acres you got?" Matt asked, just making conversation.

"Got three hundred sixty acres of the best grazing land in the valley. I'd make a man a right good deal on the place."

"What are you asking?"

"I hear tell land not as good as mine is going fer six-fifty an acre," the man said, "you interested?"

"Who, me?" Matt laughed. "I'm afraid not. Well, I've got to be riding on. Good day to you Mrs. Hawkins, you take care of that eye."

Matt toed a stirrup and climbed into the saddle, reined his horse around and, with his packhorse trailing along behind, pointed Midnight's nose upriver. He wanted to put tracks between him and that awful smell. He figured the string of bad luck

Hawkins had talked about was at a poker table in Fort Smith. As for him being down in his back, most likely it was from laziness. He felt sorry for Mrs. Hawkins though. The man ought to be horsewhipped, hitting a woman like that.

Hawkins was right about one thing, though. This was some of the best grazing land in the whole valley.

CHAPTER III

The Ways of Death

"There is a way that seemeth right to a man, but the end
thereof are the ways of death."
(Proverbs 14:12)

Matt headed south. He figured to follow the trail across the
Ouachita Mountains to the small town of Mena, then on to
DeQueen and follow the Cossalot River to the border town of
Texarkana. From there he would strike out southwest until he
found Tyler, Texas. Riding steady, he ought to make it in less
than a week. One thing for sure, he wouldn't get far today.

The sun was already kissing the top of the mountains when
he neared a place the local folks called "Twin Forks." He decided
it would be a good place to camp for the night, cook himself a
good supper and get an early start in the morning.

Now that he thought about it, in all the hustle and bustle of
leaving, he hadn't ate a bit all day. His belt buckle was rubbing
his backbone.

He remembered a good spot up ahead where he had camped when he first rode into this neck of the woods. Pretty little spot as he recalled.

He found the place just off the road. Two mountain streams rushed down out of the rugged Ouachita Mountains and merged into one just above his camping spot and formed the Fourche Le Favre River. The torrent of water cascading over large boulders littering the streambed created a masterpiece of sound to soothe a man's soul. A carpet of lush, green grass was shaded by pine, sycamore and oak trees. Large boulders protruded from the ground and guarded the little valley like sentries assigned by its creator.

After gathering wood, he built a fire and put on a pot of coffee. He unsaddled, watered and picketed his horses so they had good graze. With the sweet smell of coffee filling the little valley, bacon frying and beans boiling, he sliced potatoes into the frying pan, then set back to enjoy a good supper. He ate until he could hold no more, then practiced for an hour or more with his new guns.

After pouring another cup of coffee, he slouched down against his saddle and soaked up the sight, sound and solitude of the night and of his peaceful surroundings. By the time he drained his third cup of coffee, his eyelids were getting in the way of his seeing. He shook out his new bedroll and folded one of the extra blankets for a pillow. He kicked off his boots and slipped his new Rattler pistol between the folds of his blanket pillow, then snuggled under the other blanket against the chill of the night. For a few minutes before drifting off to sleep he lay there, gazing up at the star-studded sky and thinking of Amelia.

A good horse, well-known to his master, can be a better watchdog than a dog. Sometime during the night his stallion gave the warning snort that woke Matt instantly and told him they had company. From his trailing days, he had learned that a heavy sleeper, traveling alone, ain't likely to live to a ripe old age.

Moving nothing but his hand, he grasped the pistol from between the folds of his blanket and thumbed back the hammer to full cock. Only then did he glance at his horses. His big stallion stared toward the road, his ears pointed forward.

The campfire had dwindled to a pile of smoldering red embers giving off little light, but the three-quarter moon lit the surrounding area better than a dozen lanterns.

Anybody with a lick of sense knows better than to approach another man's campfire without calling out "hello the camp," one that would is either a fool or a pilgrim. The three hombres sneaking through the woods were no pilgrims. They were on foot and spread out about twenty feet apart, but still a ways off.

Quickly bunching the extra blanket down inside the bedroll, Matt bellied behind the nearest boulder. Two of the bushwhackers approached with pistols drawn. The third held a pig sticker out in front of him. He seemed to hesitate for a moment, but was impatiently waved on by the other two. Slowly, pig sticker crept toward what he thought was a sleeper inside the bedroll, obviously intending whoever lay inside would never wake up.

"You boys are too late for supper," Matt said, rising from behind the waist high boulder.

From their reaction, if surprises could kill, all three would be dead as doornails. They stood frozen in stunned silence, undecided what to do. The first man that swung his pistol toward Matt died first with two, well placed .44 slugs in his chest. The next followed a split second later. Matt swung his pistol to cover Pig Sticker who still held the knife in his shaking hand.

"Drop it or die with the others," Matt said, "makes no difference to me." He dropped it.

Walking barefooted around the boulder, Matt drew close to the man and discovered he wasn't really a man at all, but only a boy, probably no more that seventeen.

"What's your name, boy?"

"Uh . . . Billy, sir, Billy McCraw. Them are my older brothers, Jacob and Jeremiah."

"You mean they were your brothers. Where do you live, Billy McCraw?"

"Other side of Abbot Mountain with our—with my ma. Pa run off about a year ago, don't have no idea where. You gonna shoot me too, mister?"

"Depends," Matt told him, "haven't made up my mind yet. What were you gonna do with that pig sticker? Tap me on the head to wake me up?"

"I didn't want no part in this, mister, honest, but I had to do what they told me or they'd whip me real bad like they always did. Please don't shoot me mister, don't know what my ma would do with all three of us boys gone."

"You got horses?" Matt asked. "Go get 'em and don't even think about riding off 'cause I'd hunt you down before morning."

While the boy was gone, Matt spread his saddle blankets over the bodies, then coaxed the smoldering embers of the fire back to life and hung the coffee pot over the flames. By the time the boy returned with their horses, the coffee was boiling.

"Take their saddles off and picket them with mine," he told the boy.

Matt poured them both a cup of steaming coffee and for a long time they sat in silence, sipping the hot liquid and staring into the fire.

"How old are you, Billy?"

"Sixteen, sir" the boy told him, "least I will be in a couple of weeks."

Billy's answer hit Matt like a runaway wagon. He jerked his head up, but said nothing. For a long time he stared into the hypnotic flames of the campfire, remembering another time, another place, another boy just turning sixteen and facing five years hard labor in Yuma Territorial Prison.

"Are you okay, mister?" the boy asked with a puzzled look on his young face. "You look like you just seen a ghost or something."

"Well, Billy McCraw, it seems we both got a decision to make here. My decision is whether I ought to just go ahead and shoot you and maybe save the world a lot of trouble, or give you a chance to make the decision you've got to make.

"Long time ago my ma used to read to me and pa from her good book. The smartest fellow that ever lived wrote one of the things I remember her reading. He wrote, 'There's a way that seems right to a man, but the end of it are the ways of death.'

"It's kinda like that road over there where it forks. If you follow one of them roads it takes a fellow one place, the other leads him somewhere else. Right now, Billy, it's like you're sitting your horse at that fork in the road. You've got to go one way or the other.

"One of them roads leads you to going home and taking care of your ma. It leads to working honest work to look out for her while she's alive. It leads to someday having a family of your own.

"That other road is the one you and your brothers have been on. It leads to stealing and robbing and killing and getting killed, just like your brothers there. Now I was just wondering, if I decided not to shoot you and I was to let you choose which of those roads you would take. You got any notion which one you'd pick?"

For a long time the boy didn't answer, he just sat there staring into the fire, looking like he was doing some mighty hard thinking.

"When you think on it like that," Billy finally said, "a fellow would have to be plumb loco not to know which road to take, wouldn't he?"

"Yeah, Billy, I reckon he would at that. When I was a mite younger than you, a fellow gave me a chance and we've been friends ever since. I'm gonna give you a chance, son. I want to be your friend. I'm sorry about your brothers, boy, but they chose the wrong road and you can see where it brought them to. Don't make the same mistake they made. Right now I figure you got some thinking to do and I've got some sleeping to do. What do you say we both get at it?"

Before crawling into his bedroll, Matt threw a blanket to the boy, then pulled his hat down over his eyes and went to sleep. Sometime later he woke to find young Billy still sitting beside the fire with the blanket pulled around his shoulders, sipping coffee and staring into the fire.

They rolled out of their blankets at the break of dawn. Billy watered and saddled all the horses without being told, while Matt built a fire, put on another pot of coffee and cooked them up some breakfast. He couldn't help noticing the pig sticker still lying where the boy had dropped it the night before.

The boy ate like he was starved. After breakfast they lugged the two bodies over to their horses and tied them across their own saddles. Before mounting up Matt handed the boy three double eagle gold pieces. Young Billy's eyes bugged wide as he stared at the coins.

"Thanks, mister, that's more money than I ever seen before."

"It ain't much, son," Matt told him, "but maybe it'll help you and your ma until you can find honest work."

"What's your name anyway?" the boy asked.

"Name's Henry. My friends call me Matt."

"Henry," Billy said, frowning. Saying it like he was testing it on his tongue. "I've heard that name somewhere before. Wasn't it your family that got killed not long ago? Honest, mister, we didn't have nothing to do with that."

"I know you didn't. Fact is, I'm riding after the ones that done it right now. Soon as I get back I'll be looking in on you and your ma to see how you're doing."

"Thanks, Mr. Henry. I never knowed anybody like you. Thanks for the money and for giving me another chance. I won't be letting you down, that's a promise."

As they reached the fork in the road Matt extended his hand to his new friend. Young Billy took it and shook it firmly before reining his horse around and leading the horses carrying his two brother's bodies, turned north. Matt watched the boy ride away. A feeling of hope swelled inside him. He had done the right thing. He looped the lead rope to his pinto packhorse around his saddle horn and headed south.

The sleepy little town of Tyler, Texas had barely begun to wake up when Matt tied his horses to the hitching rail in front of the sheriff's office. He had been on the trail for six days. He pushed through the door as a sleepy-eyed young fellow with a deputy badge pinned to his shirt was pulling a suspender over his shoulder.

"Sheriff Lassiter around?" Matt asked.

"You don't see him do you?" the deputy said sarcastically, eyeing Matt suspiciously.

"When do you expect him?" He tried to ignore the deputy's attitude.

"Hard to say." He cast a long, lingering look at the two weapons strapped to Matt's sides. "Something I can do for you?"

"Well," Matt said, more than a little annoyed, "let's try it this way then, could you tell me where I might find him?"

"Might try the little café across the street. He usually takes his breakfast about this time."

"Really appreciate all your help, deputy." Matt wheeled and strode through the door, slamming it as hard as he could to show his displeasure.

Matt had no trouble recognizing the sheriff since he was the only customer in the small café. He was a tall, rangy fellow with broad shoulders, a long handlebar moustache and a friendly look about him. A big fork full of eggs stopped halfway to the sheriff's mouth when Matt strode up to the table.

"Sure hate interrupting a man that's about to tackle a breakfast like that. I'm Matt Henry from up Arkansas way. Mind if I join you?"

"Drag up a chair, Matt. I'm Sam Lassiter. You're a long way from home. You had breakfast yet?"

"Yeah, but looking at that, I'm wishing I hadn't. A fellow you might remember said I ought to look you up. Folks use to call him The Town Tamer, name of J.C. Holderfield. You know him?"

"You bet your boots I know him. Whatever happened to him anyway?"

"He's fine, he's the sheriff up in Scott County, Arkansas. He's getting on up in years now. His wife died a while back and he's raising his daughter by himself."

"Man oh man," the sheriff said, staring absent mindedly off at nothing, "now there's a lawman of the old breed. They don't make 'em like that anymore."

"I'm looking for some men, Sheriff," Matt told him. "J.C. thought you might be able to point me in the right direction."

"You a bounty hunter, Mr. Henry?" the sheriff asked, glancing at the weapons Matt was wearing.

"No, sir, I'm hunting men, not bounty. A few weeks ago, Jack Trotter and his gang hit my little farm. They raped and murdered my wife and cut my six-year-old boy's throat from ear to ear. I'm aiming to track them down and set things right."

"I see. Yeah, they rode through here a little over a week ago. They robbed the Butterfield stage and shot the driver. They hit one of our local ranches and murdered the whole family, after they got done with the womenfolk, that is. Are you real sure you want to catch up to them? They're a bad bunch."

"Yeah, I'm sure. There ought to be sixteen of them left. I got two of them before they put three slugs in me and left me for dead. Got any idea which way they headed?"

"Yep, me and my posse tracked them as far as the county line. They were headed due south. If I was you—and I'm real glad I ain't—I'd head south. I'd head straight for Waco. I'd bet a month's wages they'll stop there."

The brilliant red sun approached the distant line of low, hazy-blue mountains slowly, almost timidly, like a lover about to say a final goodbye. It gently kissed the tops one last time before dying for the day and being buried somewhere in the crevices of the western horizon. Behind it, in one last hurrah, in a final legacy, it splashed the velvety blue sky ablaze with shades of boiling reds, brilliant yellows and glistening golds, that could only come from God's own paintbrush. Streaks of light shot across the sky as if from a great unseen cannon and careened off the few puffy white clouds, framing them in shiny silver.

Matt shifted uncomfortably in the saddle. He had ridden hard for the past three days and for a week before that. He wearily lifted his hat and swiped the sweat from his forehead and held it above his eyes, peering into the shimmering distance. The outline of buildings against the setting sun's last rays brought a deep sigh.

"Just a little ways further, big fellow. That's got to be Waco up ahead. I'm gonna get you and the pinto a nice clean stall and plenty of grain. You've both earned it."

"Rub 'em down good, double grain and water them and put them in separate stalls with plenty of fresh hay," Matt told the old holster. "You got someplace safe you could store my gear?"

"Shore do, young fellow. Mighty fine looking stallion you're riding. He be a mite tired, I'd say, but I'll have 'em both fit as a fiddle in a day or two. How long will you be staying?"

"Hard to say," Matt told him, slinging his saddlebag over his shoulder. "Can you point me to a clean bed and a hot bath?"

"Other side of the street, about halfway up."

"Obliged," Matt said, flipping the man a half eagle for the care of his horses.

The hotel was small. His room was hardly bigger than a good horse stall. But the sheets were clean and the bath the boy brought was hot. Matt spent the next hour soaking off a week's trail dust and soothing his saddle sore muscles.

"You'll find the best steaks in Texas right down the street at the Longhorn café," the desk clerk told him later, after Matt made inquiry.

He found it and made his way to the lone table near the back. The place was crowded. By the time he scraped out a chair, someone set a pot of coffee and a cup on the table.

"What can I get for you, stranger?" the waitress asked.

Matt's eyes followed the friendly voice and found it came from a pretty lady with lake blue eyes and full lips that parted in a wide smile, showing pearly white teeth. Her face was framed with sandy colored hair that was pulled back and tied with a red ribbon. She was tall, but the white blouse and flowery skirt she wore were both filled out in all the right places.

"Somebody told me you serve the best steaks in Texas." Matt smiled at the pretty lady. "Did they lie to me or what?"

"They told you like it is, cowboy. How do you like it cooked?"

"Tell you what, ma'am, I'm so hungry, whatever you got back there that ain't moving or smelling bad, just cook the bellow out of it and I'll eat it."

"Then you better loosen your belt, cowboy, because I'm going to fill you up."

By the time he finished the Texas sized steak and all the trimmings, the other customers had long since left. The friendly waitress sashayed up holding an empty coffee cup turned upside down.

"Mind if I join you for a cup before I start cleaning up?" she asked, trying to look pitiful and failing badly.

"Be right glad for your company, ma'am."

"I'll make a deal with you, cowboy," she told him, pouring herself a cup from the pot on Matt's table. "I'll stop calling you cowboy, if you'll stop calling me, ma'am. My name is Abigail, but my friends call me Abby."

"Real nice to meet you, Abby, I'm Matt Henry."

"Are you just passing through or planning to stay awhile?"

"After the meal I just put away, I might just decide to settle down in these parts. Don't recollect ever eating better."

"Now that's the best compliment I've had all day."

"You happen to know who the sheriff is here in Waco?" he asked.

"That would be big Ben Thompson, but I thought you said the food was good."

"Oh, it was, ma'am. I mean Miss Abby. No, I'm just looking for some men. I thought they might have rode through here in the last week or so. Figured the sheriff might have seen them."

"What do these men look like? Maybe they came in here. My experience is most men get hungry pretty regularly."

"There's sixteen or so of them, the leader is a man named One-eyed Jack Trotter. He's a big man with red hair and beard, wears a black patch over one eye."

"Matter of fact him and seven or eight others were in the day before yesterday. There was a Mexican in the bunch. Men like that's hard to forget. Hard men, I'd say. Come to think about it, I'm pretty sure I saw some of them ride in just a while ago. I'd say they're up the street at the Cattlemen's saloon. That's where most of their kind hang out."

Matt stood up quickly and dropped money on the table for the meal and a generous tip. He turned to leave, then paused.

"Does the sheriff know these men are in town?" he asked.

"I doubt it," she said, looking concerned, "he's been out of town most of the week. He had to take some prisoners up to Austin, He just got back this afternoon."

"See if you can get word to him," Matt told her. "Ask him to meet me at the saloon as quick as he can."

"I'll go find him right now," she said, pulling off her apron and following Matt toward the door. "You be careful, Matt, I don't want to lose a good customer."

The street was dark and deserted. The only light to pierce the darkness filtered through the windows and door of the saloon up the street. Music from an out of tune piano carried on the warm night air and reached Matt's ears as he stepped into the dusty street and strode toward the sound. Judging by the number of horses still tied in front of the saloon, there were lots of thirsty cowboys still in town.

He stepped up onto the boardwalk and paused in front of the batwing doors. His tall frame allowed him to peer over the top of the doors. After carefully studying those inside, he decided there were three types of men in the crowded saloon. There were the usual cowboys, of course, who mostly stood along the long bar together. There were the local types, easily recognizable and sitting in small groups, chatting among themselves and nursing a half filled glass of beer. Then there were the hombres that sat at a table near the back. They all wore tied down pistols and had hard case written all over them.

Five of them sat together. They were drinking red-eye and laughing loudly. Five to one odds sure weren't the kind of odds a man goes looking for, but he figured it wasn't as bad as it would be if he caught up to the whole gang somewhere on the trail.

He slipped the traveling loops from both of his guns and thumbed back the hammers to full cock, then pushed through the swinging doors and strode to an empty table within earshot of the five. He had to make certain they were part of Trotter's gang.

He scraped out a chair and sat down with his back to the five outlaws. From the corner of his eye he could tell his arrival did not go unnoticed. The five were eyeing him with more than a passing interest.

A bar girl with too much paint on her face and a dress that was too short on both ends sauntered up to Matt's table.

"What's your pleasure?" she asked in a throaty voice.

"A beer," he replied, avoiding her overly suggestive manner.

She paused for a long minute, then when he refused to look up at her, shuffled off the get his beer. He didn't like beer, but figured it would look might peculiar if he didn't order anything. In fact he had only tasted beer one time. He had never been able to understand why anybody would want to drink the juice skimmed off rotten corn.

"Well, I don't give a hoot what Jack says," he overheard one of the five men say, "I'm tired of riding. My backsides feels like it's growed to my saddle. Seems to me like we've rode clear across hell and half of Texas. This is the first time we've lit for a spell and I for one, ain't ready to leave."

"Well now, Mort," a gruff voice spoke up loudly, "why don't you just tell all that big talk to old Jack when we get back to camp? He'd likely cut your tongue out and stuff it back in your big mouth."

"Where you reckon we're headed?" another asked.

"Where do you think we're headed?" the first talker asked. "We're headed for Mexico. That's where we always head for ain't it?"

"Shhh," the one with the gruff voice said, "shut your big mouth. You talk too much."

Matt had heard enough. Pushing up and scraping his chair back, he turned to face the outlaw's table. When he spoke it rang out across the big room. The words came out hard and cold.

"You boys part of Jack Trotter's outfit?" he asked loudly.

A roomful of eyes cut a gaze his way. The piano fell silent. The five at the table nailed him with a hard glare.

"Who wants to know?" the one with the gravely voice demanded.

"Name's Henry, Matt Henry. From up Arkansas way," Matt said evenly. "Had a little farm on the Fourche River and a nice family. Your bunch rode through a few weeks back. You raped and murdered my wife and cut my six-year-old boy's throat. You put three .44 slugs in me and left me for dead, but I ain't."

"You're plumb loco, mister," gravely voice said. We ain't never been to Arkansas. Don't know nothing about your wife or boy getting killed. Come on boys, we don't want no trouble, we're leaving."

"Well, you're part right," Matt said. "You're leaving sure enough, only question is, are you walking down to the jail with me? Or would you rather be carried out feet first?"

"That's mighty big talk for just one dirt farmer. In case you can't count, there's five of us and one of you. You can't get us all and you can bet your life we'll finish you off this time."

"Maybe so," Matt said, sweeping his gaze at all five men, "but something you ought to think about, loudmouth. This double barrel here on my hip will make you boys look like mincemeat. Talking's over. Time to decide. Either stand up real slow and easy with your hands on top of your head, or start drawing and dying. Makes no difference to me either way."

For long seconds, but what seemed like an eternity, nobody moved. The saloon was deathly quiet. Somewhere, somebody coughed. Another quietly shuffled out of the line of fire. Death hovered in midair like a heavy fog, waiting to discover who it would claim this night.

Matt stood waiting, his eyes searching for the slightest movement. Knowing full well the next moment would determine who would live—and who would die. He felt strangely calm. His mind flashed back to a happy scene. His Amelia was running through the high grass and early spring flowers to meet him. Her long hair flew in the breeze. Her arms were outstretched....

Somebody upended the table and bedlam broke out. As one,

the five men leaped to their feet and slapped leather. Some came close to making it.

The deafening explosion literally shook the room. Blue-black smoke boiled from the twin noses of the Widow Maker. Two loads of double aught buckshot slammed into the wad of outlaws like a runaway wagon, lifting three of them off their feet and propelling them backwards several steps. They were dead before what was left of their bodies hit the floor. A fourth grabbed what was left of his face and stumbled around screaming. Bright red blood gushed between his fingers and covered his chest, spilling onto the floor. He let out a terrible scream, then toppled over onto his face.

Ironically, the last man left standing was none other than the loudmouth. He stood, apparently miraculously unscratched. His right hand held his pistol, half raised and frozen in indecision. His whole face quivered and great drops of sweat popped out on his forehead. He nervously licked his lips and his glance flicked from side to side, seemingly searching desperately for help from his companions.

"I got a pretty good idea what you're thinking, loudmouth," Matt said evenly. "You're thinking both them barrels went off at the same time. You're thinking your pistol is already out and mine is still in the holster. You're thinking there's no way I could beat you. Well...you might be right, then again, what if you're wrong?"

Matt stood easy, squarely facing the outlaw. Matt's right hand hung relaxed at his side. His gaze fixed upon the outlaw's eyes in a deadly stare. Never blinking, never wavering. Quietness again settled upon the room, a deathly quietness.

"Drop it or use it," Matt said coldly.

The pistol began its journey upward, swinging toward Matt. Three rapid-fire shots shattered the stillness. Three dark spots appeared in the loudmouth's chest. The man staggered two steps backwards, driven by the impact of the three bullets. An unfired pistol curled from lifeless fingers and clattered onto the wooden floor.

"Somebody ought to get the sheriff," Matt said, punching empties from his pistol and dropping two new loads into the Widow Maker, then taking a seat to wait for the lawman.

CHAPTER IV

The Ways Of The Transgressor

"Then will I teach the transgressor thy ways."
(Psalms 51:13)

The Sheriff's office looked pretty much like the one back in Waldron, Arkansas. A small office, furnished with a battered old desk, a few straw bottom chairs, a gun rack on one wall with a Henry rifle and a Greener shotgun and the spitting image of the pot-bellied stove he had seen in J.C.'s office. A sturdy looking door in the back wall obviously led to a one room jail. Matt tipped his straight chair back against the wall and waited impatiently for the sheriff to return.

Only seconds after the shooting, the sheriff had rushed into the saloon with gun drawn. After quickly sizing up the situation, the lawman talked to the bartender for several minutes before approaching Matt's table, pistol still in hand.

No wonder they call him Big Ben, Matt thought as he watched the sheriff go about his duty with efficiency that comes only by experience. The lawman looked to be a good three inches taller than Matt's own tall frame and would outweigh him at least fifty pounds. Yet, to be such a big man, he moved like a cat. This was a man to walk around.

"I'll be needing those guns until we get this all thrashed out," the sheriff said, stopping several feet from where Matt sat.

Matt had reluctantly surrendered his weapons and felt naked as he and the sheriff walked down the street to the sheriff's office. The big lawman watched Matt closely and listened intently as Matt related the whole story. Somewhere in the telling, he happened to mention the name of J.C. Holderfield. As it turned out, the sheriff had known the Town Tamer and had worked with him in years past.

"If you can count Holderfield a friend that goes a long way in my book," the lawman said. "Wait here, Matt, while I talk to a few more witnesses. I'll be back directly."

When the door opened, the sheriff's big frame filled the doorway. Matt looked up from his chair but made no effort to rise. Sheriff Thompson shucked his hat and hung it on a peg near the door.

"Well, Matt, your story checks out," he said over his shoulder before turning around. "Every man who saw it says it was a clean shoot. Don't know how much they stretched the telling, but if you're half as fast as they all said, I probably ought to charge you with murder. To a man, the witnesses all agree those five hombres didn't have a snowball's chance in hell, even if they did draw first."

"They had a choice, Sheriff, they chose wrong."

"Yeah, I reckon if they were able they'd sure agree with you on that score. You going to be around a day or two, Matt? Don't figure I'll have any more questions but I might. The undertaker said he'd never seen such a mess. That's sure some contraption you shot them with, never seen anything like it."

"J.C. had it made special and used it in his law work. He gave it to me just before I rode out after Trotter and his gang. He said it might even up the odds."

"I reckon it did. I believe that's the scariest thing I've ever seen. No man with a lick of sense would go up against a thing like that."

"I'll either be at the hotel or up the street at the Longhorn Café if you need me. If that little gal keeps feeding me like she did awhile ago, I might grow up to be as big as you."

"Oh, you mean, Abby? If a man was the marrying kind, there's a lady to take home to mother. I reckon every cowboy within a three day ride has been trying to put their feet under Abby's table, permanent like."

"Does that include you?" Matt asked, as he accepted his guns and strapped them back on.

"I'd be the first in line if I thought I stood a chance," the lawman said. "If you think her supper was good, wait until you dig into the breakfast she sets in front of a man. I used to be a ninety pound weakling until I started sitting at her table. Tell you what, if you're up and around, how about meeting me there about six in the morning? I'll buy you a breakfast you can tell your grandkids about."

"Don't recall ever turning down a free meal," Matt told him," especially from a lawman. About the only thing I ever got from them was advice. See you at six."

Matt lifted a hand in farewell as he strode from the office. The street was completely deserted now. Not a light showed anywhere up or down the street. As he made his way to the hotel, he noticed the five outlaws' horses still standing hip-shot in front of the saloon. A hair-brained notion popped into his head. He shook it off and kept walking, but then stopped and stared at the horses for a long moment. It was a crazy idea, but it was worth a try, it just might work.

He turned and headed quickly for the livery stable, threw a saddle on Midnight and rode back to the saloon. Untying the five horses, he looped the reins around their saddle horns and slapped them on the rump. As one, they wheeled and trotted south out of town. Hanging back so as not to spook them, he followed.

Outside town, the horses slowed to a walk but kept moving south. Just as Matt had hoped, they knew where they were going. It was an hour or more before he spotted the campfire. Hardly visible, the outlaw camp nestled in a sycamore grove on the far side of a small creek.

Swinging to his right, he found a good cover beside the creek in a willow thicket. Peering through the moonlit darkness, he could make out three men sitting by the fire passing around a bottle. The rest had obviously already hit the sack.

"What the—?" one of the drinkers suddenly called out, standing to his feet. "Somebody's coming."

"Most likely Jack and the boys dragging in from town," another said.

The five horses splashed across the little creek, heading for the line of horses picketed nearby.

"There ain't nobody on them horses!" the standing man shouted. "That's Jack and the boys' horses all right, but where are they?"

Instantly the camp came alive. Men, some still half asleep, grabbed for their guns and scrambled for cover.

"Saddle up you idiots," a gruff voice boomed. "Break camp! Let's get out of here! There's likely a posse trailing them horses!"

Matt would have bet his saddle that was Trotter shouting orders. Men grabbed bedrolls and dashed for their horses. They saddled up and lit out like their shirttails were on fire. As they plowed through the little creek Matt reached down to his saddle boot for his rifle. Only then did he realize his mistake. In his haste, he had completely forgotten to get his rifle he had stowed with his pack at the livery.

No use crying over spilt milk now, he thought. All he could do was sit his saddle in the willow thicket and watch helplessly as the outlaw gang, or at least what was left of them, splash through the creek and ride off into the night.

Sometime well after midnight, Matt wearily climbed the stairs to his little room. He propped a chair under the doorknob, shrugged out of his clothes, slipped the Rattler under his pillow and plopped down on the corn shuck mattress, completely exhausted.

As tired as he was, sleep refused to come. His mind raced through the events of the day, trying to sort through the maze of emotions that kept whirling around and around in his head. What had the sheriff said? That he ought to be charged with murder because those men didn't have a chance? Strangely, he felt no remorse for killing them, yet deep within something troubled him. Had he taken upon himself the role of judge, jury and executioner?

But hadn't he given them a chance to surrender? Hadn't they raped and murdered his wife? Hadn't they cut the throat of his helpless son? What kind of chance had they given them? No, those men chose to ride the outlaw trail. They chose to murder his family. He had given them a chance to surrender and that's more than they deserved. What had he told young Billy McCraw back in Arkansas? "There's a way that seems right to a man, but the end of it are the ways of death."

That thought brought peace, and peace brought welcome sleep.

The eastern horizon was giving birth to a brand new day as Matt stepped from the hotel onto the boardwalk. He leaned against a post and watched darkness being swallowed up as dawn crept silently over the small Texas cattle town. The good people of Waco, Texas were already up and stirring. Up the street a pretty lady in a flowery dress with an apron tied around her waist swept the boardwalk in front of the general store. Somewhere on the edge of town the rhythmic beat of a blacksmith's hammer beat out a tune familiar to every small town in the west. A stray dog scampered out of the way of a heavy freight wagon pulled by a three-team hitch of sturdy horses. A bright ball of fire peeked its golden head over the horizon and gave promise it would be another hot day.

Matt felt good. He stretched, adjusted his Stetson and headed for the Longhorn Café. He had discovered over the years that the trouble with being early for an appointment is you're usually the only one there. This morning proved no exception. The sheriff hadn't made it yet but it seemed everybody else had. The place was packed. He stood just inside the door and waited for a table to empty. It was immediately obvious his presence didn't go unnoticed. Quick glances, outright stares and whispered conversations told him the whole town had heard of last night's shooting.

Abby was as busy as a cranberry merchant, rushing here and there, carrying huge platters from the kitchen in back, pouring coffee, clearing away dishes, yet she took time to be friendly with every customer. As she rushed past, her arms loaded with dirty dishes from a table being vacated by four cattlemen, she spotted Matt. A big smile lit up her face.

"Well, good morning, Matt. I guess you've already noticed you're the topic of conversation this morning."

"Morning, Miss Abby. I reckon people have to talk about something, guess today is my day."

She headed on back toward the kitchen while Matt wove his way through the crowd to the vacated table. He removed his hat and hung it on a chair-back, scooted out its neighbor and folded into it. Miss Abby arrived with a pot of coffee and poured him a cup of steaming liquid.

"After the meal you put away last night, I didn't think I'd see you again for a week," the friendly waitress told him jokingly. "They say the way to a man's heart is through his stomach, so I guess there's hope for me yet. What do you feel like this morning?"

"Actually, Ma'am, I feel right good, but thanks for asking," he kidded her.

She rewarded him with a swat from the dishtowel she carried over her shoulder. Just then, the big sheriff strode into the crowded room. He was an imposing presence, sure enough. Most every eye in the place swung in his direction. Six foot five or six inches, his black broadcloth suit with matching string tie, set off his shoulder length, silver hair. Only the shiny badge and low-slung Colt tied to his right leg kept him from looking more like a banker or politician than a lawman.

He worked the room like a man running for some office. Shaking a hand here, slapping a back there, stopping to ask a fellow if his wife was still feeling poorly. All the while, working himself toward Matt's table. Abby had him a cup of coffee already poured when he scraped out an empty chair and sat down.

"This young fellow bothering you this morning, Abby?" he asked, cutting a glance at Matt and cracking a friendly smile.

"I could get use to it real easy," she said, smiling at Matt. "You be nice to him, Ben Thompson, he leaves good tips and that's more than I could say about some people I won't mention. What can I get for you two this morning?"

"He's been going on about your breakfast," Matt told her, "and since he's buying, I'm gonna let him do the ordering, but I'm giving you fair warning, I'm hungry enough to eat a buffalo."

"Oh, suddenly he's the big spender?" she said, propping fisted hands on her shapely hips. "Okay, moneybags, what will it be?"

"Reckon you could rustle up a thick slab of ham and a half dozen eggs? I'll have some fried potatoes, a pan of biscuits and a jar of honey. That's for me. My friend here will have a buffalo, well done."

"Very funny, Ben, very funny. That's two man-size breakfasts, coming right up," she said, shaking her pretty head and hurrying off toward the kitchen.

"I got some good news for you, Matt," the sheriff told him, blowing on his steaming coffee. "You're twenty one hundred dollars richer this morning. All five of them fellows had dead or alive posters on them and they definitely qualified on the first part. Three were five hundred apiece, the other two were three hundred each. When the bank opens we can walk over and make the arrangements."

"Ben, I hope you don't think I shot those men to collect the reward. I'm hunting men, not bounty."

"Nothing wrong with collecting bounty, as long as it's within the law. You done the world a favor, Matt. No telling how many people those hombres have killed, nor how many more they would have killed."

"I reckon so," Matt said, sipping his coffee. "Somehow it don't seem hardly right though, getting paid because you kill somebody."

Matt told the sheriff about turning the outlaws' horses loose and following them to their camp. He was embarrassed to have to tell about forgetting his rifle and having to sit and watch them ride off.

"I was wondering what happened to their horses. Why didn't you tell me, I'd have gone with you?"

"Figured you'd think it was a dumb idea, which it turned out to be. I guess I'll just have to take my medicine and act like it tastes good."

"I'll say one thing for you, Matt Henry, you've got a lot of sand, taking on five killers like them fellows. In all my years of law work, I've never faced down odds like that."

"Old Widow Maker kind of evened up the odds I reckon. You know, Ben, I was thinking. If you was Trotter and five of your men rode into town for a few drinks and nothing but their horses came back, wouldn't you be itching to know what happened to them?"

"Yeah, I guess I would at that," the sheriff said. "What are you getting at?"

"Well, I've got a notion he might send somebody in to nose around a bit. Somebody that ain't likely to be recognized as being part of the gang."

"Makes good sense. I'll keep my eyes peeled for a few days."

Abby walked up carrying two huge platters of food two ordinary men couldn't eat in a week, then hurried back to the kitchen to return with another load.

It took the best part of an hour but they both cleaned their plates. They lingered awhile over another cup of coffee and visited. Matt found he liked the big sheriff.

As they left Matt tried to pay for their breakfasts but Ben wouldn't hear of it. Matt curled a half smile at Miss Abby and winked when he saw Ben leave a generous tip.

"Don't want you telling folks they got a tight wad sheriff," he told her, smiling.

"Well glory be," Abby exclaimed. "See what a good influence you are on him, Matt? Hope you stay around long enough to teach him how a man ought to treat a lady."

"What makes you think he knows anything about it?" the sheriff asked.

"Some things a woman just knows."

"Come on Matt, let's get out of here. You're corrupting her," the sheriff said as they headed out the door. "I've got a couple of things to take care of. How about meeting me over at the bank in about an hour and we'll take care of that reward."

"Sounds good to me," Matt said. "I saw a barber shop up the street. I think I'll get my ears lowered a tad."

* * *

Later that morning Matt walked out of the bank with more cash money than he had ever seen in his whole life. He found a freight office that had a telegraph and wired the whole twenty one hundred back to Arkansas, asking J.C. to put it in the bank for him.

"Any other message you want to send with that?" the manager asked.

"Just say, Widow Maker works, he'll know what I mean," Matt told the man.

Leaving the freight office and walking across the street to the General Mercantile store, Matt noticed an old timer sitting on a split log bench in front of the store. He was smoking an old corncob pipe and whittling. From the pile of shavings, it was apparent the old fellow spent a lot of time sitting there. That gave Matt an idea.

The old man didn't even look up when Matt sat down beside him, but as a rider rode down the street on a bay horse, the old fellow's eyes flicked up, took in every detail of the horse and rider, then returned to his whittling.

"If I was a betting man, which I ain't," Matt said, "I'd wager my boots and saddle you spend the better part of most days sitting here whittling."

"Likely," the man replied without even looking up.

"I also got a notion you know most folks around these parts, am I right?"

"Likely."

"Tell you what, old timer," Matt said. "I'm halfway expecting a stranger to ride in sometime today or maybe tomorrow. My name's Henry, Matt Henry. I'd shore be obliged if a man were to spot that stranger and let me know about it. It would be worth a dollar to me."

"Knowed who you was before you sit," the old fellow said, never looking up. "You'd be that fellow that cleaned house down at the watering hole last night, I reckon."

"Likely," Matt said, as he rose and strode into the store.

The storekeep was a short, stocky fellow with a beet-red face and a friendly smile. He was busy stacking feed against the back wall when Matt entered. The lady he had seen early that morning sweeping the boardwalk was busy waiting on a heavyset woman with a pink bonnet on her head and a straw basket on her arm and a sour look on her face.

"I'll be with you in just a moment," she took time to tell him, adding a pleasant smile.

"That's all right, ma'am, I'm in no hurry."

Matt browsed around the well stocked store. A display of knives caught his eye and he spent some time examining them closely.

"How about some nice fresh canned peaches, Mrs. Cooksey?" the storekeeper's wife asked the lady. "We just got them in last week."

"Don't need no peaches," sour apple replied curtly, "grow my own."

"Would there be anything else then, Mrs. Cooksey?"

Sour apple didn't even bother replying, she simply snatched up her purchases, dropped them in her basket and stomped out the front door like she was mad at the whole world.

"Is she always that happy?" Matt asked.

"Aw, Mrs. Cooksey is all right. She just has a hard time finding anything to be happy about."

"My pa always told me you pretty well find the things you spend your time looking for," Matt said.

"Your pa sounds like a wise man. Can I help you find anything in particular this morning?"

"Well, yes Ma'am, I reckon you can. I'll be riding out day after tomorrow and I'll be needing to restock my trail supplies. Would it be all right with you if I picked out what I need, go ahead and pay you for it and pick it up sometime tomorrow?"

"Certainly, if you like, just tell me what you need and I'll write it down and gather it all up later. I'll have it ready for you whenever you come for it."

"That would be right nice of you, Ma'am. Let's see, I'll be needing a slab of salt bacon, a couple dozen potatoes, a half dozen tins of beans, a few onions, a tin of coffee and a dozen boxes of .44-40 cartridges. I think I'd like a half dozen cans of them peaches too."

Matt saw the lady smile at his mention of the peaches. He walked over to the display of knives he looked at earlier. He needed a new knife. The one he had was so old and dull it wouldn't cut hot butter. One particular knife stood out above the rest. It looked more like a sword than a knife. Picking it up, he turned it in his hand. As big as it was, it was perfectly balanced.

"That's an excellent choice," the lady said, "that's a Bowie, invented by Colonel Jim Bowie in 1835. So the story goes, he broke his sword in battle, later, he ground down what was left to a needlepoint. What he came up with was a large bladed, extra long and heavy knife that has become the most popular knife in the west. The one you're holding is the twenty two inch model, the longest they make. They call it the Arkansas toothpick, though I can't imagine why."

It was a wicked looking weapon, sure enough. It had a bone handle and a heavy hand guard. Matt gingerly felt the point with the tip of his finger. Immediately a small droplet of blood appeared.

"Sure wouldn't want to meet the man that would pick his teeth with that," Matt said. "How much is it?"

"With the matching leather scabbard, I can let you have it for fifteen dollars."

"I'll take it," Matt told her. "Just your sales pitch was worth that. I noticed that Sharps long gun there on the wall. Is it a used one?"

The lady took the gun down from the wall and handed it to him.

"My husband bought it from a down-and-out buffalo hunter that was passing through a while back. He was down on his luck and needed a stake. That's a .52 caliber Sharps, the most powerful long gun in the world. It holds seven shots in the tube, plus one in the chamber. My husband checked it out and says it's in excellent condition.

"He asked the old hunter how far it would shoot," she told Matt, chuckling. "The old buffalo hunter said, Well, sir, I'll put it to you this way, I was up in Colorado one time. I was shooting at a buf over in Wyoming, but I killed two in Montana with the same shot," she said, mimicking the old hunter.

"What are you asking for it?"

"It's a bargain for forty-five dollars," she told him.

"I'll take it. I'll need a half dozen boxes of shells for it too. Tally up what I owe you or I'll be broke flatter than a flitter before I can get out of here and ma'am, thanks for being so nice."

"Well, thank you, young man. It's easy to be nice when someone is nice to you."

She figured up his bill and he paid her. Just then, the old timer tapped on the window with his walking stick. Matt rushed outside.

"That stranger you're looking fer. . .wouldn't happen to be a big black fellow riding a steel gray mare would it?"

"Could be," Matt said.

"He just rode in and tied up in front of the saloon," the old fellow said.

Matt pulled a half eagle from his pocket and flipped it in the old man's direction. His hand shot out and caught the coin in midair, seemingly without even looking up.

"Thanks," Matt told him, "I'm obliged."

"Easiest five dollars I ever made," the old timer said. "You be careful, young fellow, you hear?"

Matt raised his hand in acknowledgment as he headed down the street. Walking to the livery, he quickly saddled his horse. This time he made sure to slide his rifle into the saddle boot, then rode to the saloon. Tying his stallion to the hitching rail beside the steel gray mare, Matt strode to the batwing doors.

A quick flick of his thumbs removed the thongs from his guns, another brought the familiar double click as the hammers locked in firing position. He hoped it wouldn't come down to a shoot out with the black man, he wanted to have a little talk with him first—but he had to be ready for anything.

Peering over the batwing doors into the smoke filled dimness of the saloon, he quickly spotted the man. He was sitting at a table with another fellow that had the looks of a local barfly. They were engaged in deep conversation between sips of the drinks sitting in front of them. Pushing through the doors, Matt walked to within ten feet of the two men before speaking. Neither noticed his approach until he spoke.

"Either one of you fellows move a muscle and I'll blow you right outta them chairs," Matt said in a loud and clear voice. "You got a choice, either put your hands on top of your heads, real nice and easy like, or you can die right where you sit. You got exactly two breaths to decide."

The barfly still had one breath to spare when his hands hit the top of his head. He was shaking like a leaf in a whirlwind. The black man sat perfectly still, staring straight ahead, moving nothing but his dark eyes that were now as big as saucers and shot frantically from side to side, as if desperately searching for a way out. Great drops of nervous sweat popped out on his forehead and he licked his thick lips.

His large frame sat hunched over the table. A worn out gray Confederate cap lay on the table. The man's totally bald head shone from the dim light filtering in through the front door.

Matt could imagine what might be running through the big

man's mind. His violent past had finally caught up with him as it always does. For an instant, his face revealed that he might try for his pistol, then whatever courage he had left seemed to drain from his face, leaving only the look of a beaten man. Slowly he raised his hands and placed them on top of his head.

"Good choice," Matt told him. "You! The one with the mustache, stand up real easy, if you got a gun stashed, best slip it out real slow."

"I...I don't carry a gun, mister," the man got out, his voice shaking as badly as he was.

"Who are you?" Matt demanded. "How do you know this fellow?"

"I . . . I'm John Starnes. I live here, he just offered to buy me a drink that's all. I never seen him before."

"Bartender," Matt hollered, "is he saying it like it is?"

"Yeah," the heavyset man behind the bar said. "John don't mean no harm, he just has a hard time turning down a free drink, that's all."

"Okay, John," Matt said, "you can go."

The barfly shot to his feet and hurried out the door. The black man still sat motionless with his hands on top of his head. He shifted his eyes to stare at Matt for the first time, the whites of his eyes standing out in contrast to his midnight black skin. Matt saw no fear in the man's eyes, only hatred.

"What's your name?" Matt asked, striding over to stand face to face with the man.

"Mose. Mose Jessup," he replied in a deep voice that sounded like a bullfrog.

"Well, Mose Jessup, we finally meet again."

"What you talkin' 'bout mister? I never see you before. What for you botherin' me?"

"I'm the last man this side of hell you ever wanted to run into, Mose, I'm that farmer from up in Arkansas that your bunch shot up and left for dead after you raped and murdered my wife and cut my little boy's throat."

Matt saw recognition wash over the man's face and with it came a look of terror. He remembered all right. Matt removed the man's pistol and searched him for hidden weapons, finding a knife stuck down inside the black's right boot. Sliding out a chair, Matt planted a foot in it and leaned an elbow across his leg.

"Now, Mose, me and you are gonna have us a little talk. You're gonna tell me everything I want to know about Trotter and his whole gang. Where are they headed?"

"Ain't tellin' you nothin'," the man spat out defiantly.

"Aw now, Mose, you see, that's where you're wrong. Now I'm asking you real nice like, where is Trotter and his gang headed?"

The big black shook his head stubbornly and glared silently back at Matt.

"I done told you, mister, ain't tellin' you nothin'. Jack would skin me alive."

"Mose, if there's one thing in this life you don't have to worry about it's what Jack Trotter might do to you. Now, I'm usually a patient kind of fellow, but I gotta tell you, Mose, my patience is wearing mighty thin. I'm gonna ask you just one more time, but before you answer, I think it's only fair to warn you, I was raised by the Apache. They got more ways to convince a man to talk than you could ever imagine. I sure don't want to have to show you some of them, but I will if I have to. Either way, you will tell me what I want to know. You can do it now, or you can do it later. Now would sure go a lot easier on you."

The man set his lips and slowly shook his head. Without another word Matt pulled a rawhide pigging string from his pocket and tied the man's hands tightly behind his back. Shoving Jessup ahead of him, he took the black to his steel gray mare in front of the saloon. He lifted one of the man's feet and rammed it into the stirrup, then hoisted him into the saddle. Matt was about to step into his own saddle when Sheriff Thompson came hurrying up.

"Who you got there, Matt?"

"His name is Mose Jessup. He's one of Trotter's men."

"Where you taking him?"

"We've got us some talking to do, Sheriff," Matt said. "We'll be back directly."

"Uh, Matt?" the Sheriff said, "you will bring him back alive won't you?"

"That's up to him," Matt said, stepping up into the saddle and gathering the reins to the mare. "Don't you reckon his wanted poster says dead or alive?"

"Well, yeah, I reckon it does," the big lawman said, swiping his hat from his head and mopping sweat from the hatband with a bandanna from his pocket. "But if it's all the same to you, I'd sure rather have him back alive."

"Like I said, Sheriff, that's up to him." Matt wheeled his horse and, leading the gray, headed south out of town at a trot.

As they rode, Matt stared at the man. He saw the dark, defiant look, the hard set of his jaw and a stubborn streak that more than likely had caused his poor mama lots of grief.

"Mose, I don't want to hurt you. Why don't you save yourself lots of hurt and tell me what I want to know?"

"No, sir! Ain't nothin' you can do to make me."

Matt kneed his stallion into a short lope and said no more. Another half hour brought them to a spot he had noticed the night before while following the outlaws' horses. He reined up by a small grove of saplings and swung down. Using his new Bowie, he cut four stakes about four feet long. It took only a few strokes of the razor sharp knife to sharpen one end of the stakes. He swung back into the saddle and rode a ways farther and pulled up beside a huge anthill. It rose over three feet out of the ground.

"What we have here, Mose, is the home of the Mexican red ant. They grow to near an inch long. When they get disturbed they get awful mad and will attack anything in sight. Ever been stung by a desert scorpion? Well, these little devils hurt might near as bad, maybe worse. I've seen them bring down a thousand pound steer.

"If you got something to say, now is the time to say it and save yourself a whole lot of hurt. Otherwise, I'm gonna stake you over that ant bed and believe me, Mose, it ain't gonna be pretty what they do to you."

The big black man stared straight ahead, refusing even to look down at the anthill. Without another word, Matt grabbed one of his feet and lifted, dumping him unceremoniously in a heap on the ground. Using his Bowie, he drove the stakes into the ground on four corners of the anthill then roughly threw the man down, face first onto the hill. It took only a moment to secure both of his hands and feet to the four stakes.

By the time Matt cut Jessup's shirt off, the big red army ants were already swarming over the man's dark, bare skin, stinging as they went. The outlaw bit his lip until the blood came, trying vainly to stifle the screams that welled up in his throat and couldn't be held back.

"Ain't no skin off my back, Mose, but the sooner you start talking, the sooner you get off that anthill and you ain't got a whole lot of time left to think about it."

The man was either the stubbornness man Matt had ever run into, or he was awful tough. He bit his lips and groaned pitifully, but still refused to talk. Matt sat down straddle-legged at a safe distance and watched the ordeal, reminding himself what they had done to his wife and little boy.

It took only a few more minutes for the man to reach the point Matt knew all along he would come to. No matter how big and tough a fellow might be, there comes a point when he just can't take any more. Mose Jessup was there.

"Okay! Okay!" the big man screamed, "get me off'n here. I'll tell you what you wants to know!"

"Sure took you long enough," Matt said, cutting the rawhide strips holding the man down. "Might help if you trotted down to that little creek yonder. The water might help some, then we'll talk."

Mose didn't trot, he ran as fast as his legs could carry him. Matt heard the splash when he jumped in. Matt took his time picking up his pigging strings, gathered the reins of the two horses and led them down to the creek. Squatting on the bank, Matt watched the big black in the water, trying desperately to find some relief. His big dark body was already swelling.

"We better get you back to town to a doctor," Matt told him, "we can talk on the way."

Matt helped the man into his saddle and took the reins.

"Okay, Mose, who's still riding with Trotter?"

"Well," the black man said between groans, "there's Jack and his two boys, Luke and Luther. They's a cousin from up in Illinois, name of Hank Trotter. Oh me, mister, I'm hurtin' somethin' bad."

"Keep talking," Matt told him.

"There's that Mex that cut your boy's throat, Luz Rodriquez. They's an Apache called Two Bears," the man said, starting to shake all over like he had a chill or something.

"They's two brothers named Bishop, I think they's from Oklahoma territory. Then they's the gunfighter they call, Reno. Then they's the woman."

"A woman?" Matt asked, his head popping around, surprised to hear a woman rode with that murdering bunch.

"She be Jack's woman," Mose said, "She don't do none of the killin' and stuff. She mostly cooks and takes care of Jack."

"Where are they headed?"

"Mexico," Mose said, beginning to droop in the saddle and barely able to talk. "A place 'bout two days other side of Laredo called Anahuac. Jack, he pays the head of the army to let us come there when things gets too hot."

"What's the woman's name?" Matt asked.

"Miss Lilly," Mose said, "she be a right nice lady."

"Come on, let's kick it up a bit," Matt told the suffering man, "we need to get you to a doctor before you go cheating the hangman."

Sheriff Thompson stood in front of his office as they rode up. He took one look at the black man and hollered to one of several gawkers standing nearby.

"Somebody go get the Doc and be quick about it."

Between Matt and the sheriff, they managed to get the man out of his saddle and inside to the jail cell. He was swollen to near twice his size and was moaning and groaning with every breath as they eased him down onto the small bunk.

"Good Lord, man," Ben said to Matt, "what happened to him?"

"He got stung," Matt replied.

"Yeah, I reckon he did."

"What went on out there, Matt?" the sheriff asked, as he and Matt walked back out into the office after the Doctor came and started working on Mose.

"Told you, he got stung by some ants. That big fellow is as tough as saddle leather," Matt said, "it took awhile, but he finally came around. Been talking a blue streak ever since."

"Forget I asked," Ben said, shaking his head, "I think I'd be better off not knowing all the details."

"We still on for supper?" Matt hollered back over his shoulder as he walked from the office. "It's my turn to buy."

"Yeah, but after seeing that fellow, my appetite ain't working real good right now," Ben hollered after Matt.

He walked to the stable and cinched the packsaddle on his little pinto, then led it up the street to the store where he loaded his supplies. While he was there he bought himself a new pair of pants and a pretty black shirt that caught his eye. After taking his packhorse back to the livery and unsaddling her, he went back to the hotel, ordered a hot bath and spent the rest of the afternoon soaking and resting up. He had it in mind to hit the trail at first light the next morning.

"Well, well, just look at you," Abby greeted him as he sauntered through the door of the Longhorn café late that afternoon. "Don't you look handsome. All spruced up like you're going courting or something. You're too early for supper but just in time for a cup of coffee, have a seat and I'll pour us a cup."

"Never turn down a cup of coffee with a pretty lady," Matt said, sliding out a chair and settling into it.

"Well, until she shows up, I'll just have to do."

"To be honest about it, Miss Abby, that's why I came so early. I was hoping we could talk some," he told her as she poured them both a cup.

They both sipped their coffee for long, awkward seconds, neither saying a word. From the look on her face, Abby looked like a woman with something on her mind.

"Matt," she finally said, staring down into her coffee cup, "Ben came by for lunch. He told me what happened to your wife and stepson. I'm awful sorry I didn't know, I mean, I've been kidding and flirting with you and all. I'm really sorry."

"Thanks, Miss Abby. Those men I shot last night were part of it. I caught another one of them today, he's over in the jail. There's still ten of them left and I've got to find them. I'll be riding out at first light."

"Sure hate to see you go, Matt. I've only known you one day but it seems like longer. I was kind of hoping you might settle around here close."

"Wish I could, Miss Abby, but this is just something I've got to do. I've got a gnawing inside me that won't go away until this is over and done with. It just keeps eating at me."

"Believe me, I know. I lost my husband in the war. He was captured and then froze to death in a prison camp in Camp Douglas, Illinois in February of 'sixty three. There were a thousand prisoners in the camp. Three hundred eighty seven froze to death just in the month of February. They didn't even have a blanket to keep warm. You don't forget, but after awhile, you realize you have to get on with your life. My husband died for what he believed in."

"Can't ask more of a man than that," Matt told her.

"For a long time I was bitter," she went on, "I hated everybody that wore a blue uniform. I blamed them all for what a few did. Finally, I took a hard look at myself and didn't like what I saw. I had allowed my hatred to consume me, to make me into something no one, not even myself, could like. Sometimes it helps just to talk about it, Matt. I'm a pretty good listener."

So he did. He told her the whole story. Not just about his wife and boy, but from the time the Apache captured him. He told her about spending five years hard labor in Yuma Territorial prison for shooting a man in self-defense. When it was finished he felt drained.

"You're a good man, Matt Henry," Abby told him, speaking softly. "I wish we could have met when things were different. I know you aren't ready right now, but someday you'll meet someone and she'll be a lucky lady."

"Who's a lucky lady?" Ben asked, surprising them by his presence. Neither of them had heard him come in. "Unless it's the lady that gets the pleasure of cooking my supper. I sure hope you brought plenty of money, Matt, 'cause I'm one hungry critter."

"I think you were born hungry, Ben Thompson," Abby told him. "I doubt there's enough steak in Texas to fill up you two men, but I'm sure gonna try. You boys just sit there and have some coffee while I fix you a supper you won't ever forget."

She poured them some coffee, then hurried to the kitchen. Both men watched her admiringly until she had disappeared from sight.

"She's quite a woman," Matt told his friend. "Don't see why you haven't already asked her to marry you."

"Me?" Ben asked, seemingly shocked at the suggestion, "she wouldn't have an old codger like me."

"You might be surprised," Matt said, sipping his coffee. "How's our prisoner?"

"He's got a bad case of hurt. When I left he was screaming bad things about your mama and papa. The doctor says he'll recover in time for the hanging. Right now, that noose might not look too bad to him the way he's hurting. Oh yeah," the sheriff said, scooting a wanted poster across the table, "I found a flyer on him. Just like you said, five hundred dollars, dead or alive. I wired Austin for authorization. I heard back awhile ago so I took it on myself of getting your money for you. Five hundred dollars in U.S. Treasury notes."

The sheriff laid the stack of cash money on the table in front of Matt.

"Thanks, Ben, that ought to just about be enough to buy your supper. Jessup told me Trotter is headed for Mexico. Ever hear of a place called Anahuac?"

"Can't say I have. Wonder what's so special about that place?"

"According to him, Trotter's got the local Captain of the federales in his pocket. Likely pays him off. I hear that's the way business is done in Mexico."

"Where is this place?"

"Mose says it's about two days ride south of Laredo. I'll be riding out first thing in the morning."

The big sheriff cocked an eye in Matt's direction. A frown creased his forehead.

"You ain't thinking about crossing the border and following them into Mexico are you? Seems to me that would be quicker than suicide."

"I found out a long time ago, Ben, there's worse things than dying. Like going back on my word I give over the graves of my family. I got it to do, Sheriff, I can't rest till it's done."

"I'm half a mind to lay down my badge and ride with you."

"I appreciate that, Ben, but I got to stomp my own snakes."

"Never met a man like you, Matt. You might hail from Arkansas, but in my book you stand Texas tall."

"I'll second that motion," Abby said as she walked up carrying their supper.

For the next hour they visited between bites of the delicious supper. When they finished they pushed back and lingered over another cup of coffee and visited until Miss Abby joined them for a cup before closing time.

It was near midnight when the three friends parted, each knowing it would likely be a long while before they would be together again, if ever. There was no better feeling than to have folks like Abby and Ben to call your friends.

Matt climbed the stairs to the second floor and reached for the doorknob before noticing that familiar tingling on the back of his neck that usually meant trouble. Funny how a man's intuition can save him an awful lot of grief, that is, if he's apt to pay a mind to it. Thankfully, this time he did.

It's probably nothing, he thought, but better to be safe than sorry. He thumbed the loops from his guns and drew back the hammers of both to full cock. Pressing his back against the wall beside the door, he turned the knob and pushed the door open with the toe of his boot.

In the closeness of the small hotel, the deafening sound of two .44s going off near the same instant shook the thin walls. Even as the slugs tore through the wall on the far side of the hall, Matt dropped to his belly and chanced a quick glance around the edge of the doorframe in time to see two bouquets of red still blooming from the darkness. He snapped two quick shots from his pistol toward where one of the shots had come from, heard the familiar soft smack when they both struck flesh, heard a muffled grunt and a body hit the floor.

Matt knew at least one more had fired, but where was he? Except for the slight grayness of light that filtered in through the open window, the room was pitch black. He couldn't see his hand in front of his face. Somehow, he had to flush this fellow out.

He lay perfectly still and, remembering his Apache training, held his breath. He could clearly hear the man in the room breathing but he couldn't pinpoint his location. Noiselessly, he pushed to his knees. Returning the Rattler to its holster, he swiped the brand new Stetson from his head and gently laid it on the floor. Pushing down on the handle of the Widow Maker, he slid the hat across the floor into the room.

The fiery explosion from the shooter's .44 lit the room for the briefest instant and sent Matt's hat flying back through the open door. At the same instant the man fired, he made a dive for the open window. He didn't make it.

The roar of both barrels of the .12 gauge going off at the same instant sounded like a stick of dynamite. It was deafening. The walls of the hotel shook. Twin loads of buckshot caught the man in mid stride and literally blew him through the window, across the small balcony and sent him crashing through the railing and onto the street below.

"Matt? Are you hurt?" the sheriff's voice called from the bottom of the stairs.

"I'm all right, Ben, come on up."

"Thank goodness you're okay," his friend said, taking the stairs two at a time. "Who was it?"

"Don't know. There's one in the room. He's hit but don't know how bad so be careful."

As it turned out they wasted their worry. Both of Matt's shots had struck home. The wounded man was still alive, but just barely.

The acrid stench of gunpowder and smoke filled the small room and burned their lungs. Ben lit a lamp and knelt beside the wounded man. A rattling noise from deep inside the man's throat with each struggling breath told them he didn't have long.

"You ain't gonna make it, son," the sheriff told him honestly. "What name should I put on your marker?"

The dying man struggled mightily to say the word, like it was the most important word he had ever uttered. His lips moved but nothing came out but a bloody froth. A scared look masked his face. He choked, coughed and finally in little more than a whispered gasp, "B...Bishop."

Then, drawing one final long breath, he sighed peacefully as life left him.

Matt delayed his leaving. He spent the better part of the day visiting with both Ben and Abby. It was hard to leave. He had found it so most of his life. He collected another three hundred apiece for the two Bishop brothers from Oklahoma territory and wired another thousand dollars back home to J.C.

"Keep the coffee on and the skillet hot," he told Abby, as they said another good-bye after supper that night. "I'll be putting my feet under your table again right soon."

"Reckon I ought to check out your room tonight before you go up?" Ben asked as they left the café together. "We ain't had this much excitement since that young gun slick, Wes Harding rode through awhile back. There wasn't any posters on him at the time so I couldn't hold him, but it sure give the folks something to talk about for awhile. They'll be telling tales about your visit till the cows come home."

"Do you happen to know who the Sheriff is in San Antonio? Don't know if I'm gonna stop there or not, the town's so big I doubt Trotter and his bunch would chance it. I've got a friend that supposed to have a ranch somewhere in that neck of the woods, thought I might stop by and say a howdy. Haven't seen him in since I was fifteen."

"The man you'll want to see is a fellow named Dan McAllister, he's the United States Marshal and a good man to boot. I'll send him a telegram and let him know you're coming. Matt, if you ever need me just send me word, I'll drop my badge and come riding."

"Thanks, Ben, I believe you would. I'm right proud to count you a friend. Be seeing you around, pard."

Their hands clasped in a firm handshake, then each turned their backs and went their separate ways, both knowing there was a better than good chance they might never see each other again. But that was the way it was.

CHAPTER V

To Whom Honor is Due

"Render honor to whom
honor is due." (Roman's 13:7)

Waco, Texas still slept. Matt held his big stallion tight reined to a fast walk and headed south out of town. Susy, his smaller pinto packhorse, struggled to keep pace with Midnight as he swallowed up the ground with his fast gait.

Darkness still held the land hostage. A million twinkling stars and a quarter moon broke an overhead canopy of black. It gave one the feeling of vastness. Somehow, the sky seemed bigger in Texas, but then, so did everything else.

Somewhere a rooster crowed, announcing the approach of a new day. A dog barked as he rode past a lone farmhouse. A single light showed through the window. It gave Matt a lonely feeling. He envied the man who lived there. He had a home and family and someone that loved him.

The sound of the barking dog faded into the distance and the only sound was the muffled crunching of his horses' hooves in the soft sandy soil and the steady creak of saddle leather.

As he rode the darkness gradually surrendered to the grayness of a promised dawn. A soft pink, then orange, then golden eastern sky gave birth to a new day.

He picked up the outlaws' tracks at the camp by the creek and followed them all day. Just before sundown he found where they had camped the next night. Stepping down from his horse he squatted and fingered the tracks. Taking his time, he read the signs as easily as most would read a book. He closely studied every detail. How they set up their camp, how far away they picketed their horses. He examined whether they slept bunched or scattered and how close to the fire. Two had slept well away from the actual camp. Matt assumed it was Trotter and his woman. What had Mose said her name was? Lilly, Lilly Sawyer.

By the footprints in the soft sand he could tell one of the outlaws limped on his right leg, another had a hole in the sole of his left boot. One of their horses had a chip out of his right front shoe and one of the horses was unshod. All of this was valuable information to a tracker.

As a young boy growing up with the Apache, he had listened and watched and learned to read signs from the best trackers the world has ever known. By the time he was thirteen, it was spoken about the camp that he was one of the most skilled hunters and trackers in the whole village. Chief Elkhorn had told him many times that nothing nor no one passes through a land with leaving signs of his passing. One only has to know what to look for.

He found prints of the two Bishop brothers as they rode out of camp and headed for town and their mission of murder. Little did they know that would be their last ride.

He was about to mount up when something puzzling caught his eye. A single unshod horse had left camp, headed down their back trail and returned sometime much later, likely the next morning. He thought on it a spell and decided it had to be the Indian. Trotter had sent him out to make sure they weren't being followed.

The ashes of the fire and the softness of the horse droppings told Matt they were only one day ahead of him. Having learned all he could, he used their former campsite for his own. He watered and rubbed down his horses with some dry grass, cooked himself a good supper and spent his usual hour practicing with his guns.

He slept well and by the time dawn broke, he had several miles behind him. Clouds were beginning to build back in the west and it looked like rain. He held his horses to a fast pace hoping to gain ground on his quarry. Knowing the Indian was keeping an eye on their back trail, Matt rode more cautiously. He stuck to lower ground when possible, careful not to skyline himself. He kept well off the actual trail, riding parallel to it, using trees, bushes, or even dry washes to give him as much cover as possible. It was clear Trotter was being more cautious, having lost eight of his men so far.

The gentle rolling hills and vast, seemingly endless expanses of grassland had cattle country written all over them. Several times he rode within sight of large herds, roaming free, reviving the secret dream he had never shared with anyone, that maybe someday, he himself might own a small cattle ranch. It was a silly, childish dream. After all, he was a farmer.

By early afternoon the trail angled west, then near sunset, swung back south again. Matt figured they had skirted wide to avoid getting close to the large city of Austin, the capital of Texas. A slow, steady drizzle set in. He figured he couldn't find a dry place to sleep anyway so he kept riding. Most of the time he couldn't see the trail but he knew they were headed south. It was near midnight when he spotted their campfire.

Locating a brushy hill maybe a quarter mile away, he unsaddled his horses and tied them in a gully nearby, gave them grain from the pack and let them drink from a small puddle.

He couldn't risk a fire, even for coffee, which he wanted badly. He settled for munching on dried beef jerky and one of the dozen cold biscuits that Abby had insisted he take with him.

Lying there in the gully in the dark, trying desperately to stay dry under his rain poncho and failing, he suddenly felt very lonely. It had only been near two months since Amelia's death. Still it seemed so long ago.

He slept fitfully and rose well before first light. Climbing the hill, he found a heavy clump of bushes on the very top and crawled inside. Dawn was slow coming. A deep grayness crept silently over the horizon and sent the darkness retreating reluctantly to wherever it came from. Heavy clouds hid the stars and delayed the arrival of daylight. Ugly storm clouds gathered themselves to the west and Matt could hear the distant rumbling of thunder.

The sleepers in the camp below must have heard it too and began to stir. Matt watched as one by one they rolled out of their wet bedrolls, shook out their boots and stomped them on.

Somebody built a fire and the woman set about making coffee and cooking breakfast. Even though the clothes she wore were identical to those worn by the men, her long, red hair pouring out from under the floppy hat and the way she filled out those clothes told any onlooker this wasn't just one of the boys.

Smoke from their fire drifted lazily upward and hovered just above the sycamore trees under which they were camped. He knew it was impossible, but he could swear he smelled the coffee boiling. Out of the corner of his eye he sensed, rather than saw, a far off movement. Swinging his gaze he peered through the early morning haze. It was the Apache. He rode slowly, his head sweeping from side to side as all Apache do, always alert to their surroundings. He was returning after a night guarding their back trail.

"Well now," Matt said softly. "That's right interesting. We'll see if you do the same tonight."

* * *

After the outlaw band finished their breakfast, broke camp and pulled out, Matt rode down to their abandoned camp. He found nothing new and set out to backtrack the Indian. He found where he had spent the night less than a mile from the main camp. The Apache had chosen wisely. From his vantagepoint on top of the hill where he stayed, he could have easily spotted any campfire within miles.

Typical of his Apache training, Two Bears had left his horse tied in a dry wash well away from where he himself slept. Matt took note that the Indian slept with his back to a large boulder and with his rifle within reach on his right side.

The rain came. Just a few large drops at first, then the sky opened up and it fell by the bucket full. The wind picked up and drove sheets of rain before it, soaking everything in its path. Matt hunkered down inside his poncho and pulled his hat low. He peered out from under the brim to watch the outlaws' tracks, half expecting them to seek cover from the storm. They kept riding and so did he, careful to keep a distance between him and the gang. By late afternoon the rain let up and finally stopped.

Off in the distance he spotted a clump of green that told him of likely water.

Odds were, the outlaws would choose it for their night's camp. About half a mile away he spotted a hill from which he could keep an eye on the camp. He headed for it.

Tying his horses in some bushes on the backside of the hill, he took his rifle and canteen and climbed the hill. Bellying down between two large boulders he scanned the countryside. Sure as shooting, there they were, right where he figured they would be. They were busy setting up camp. The smoke from their supper fire reminded Matt he hadn't ate in awhile. His stomach was sending out hunger pain signals.

After the outlaws finished supper they sat around playing cards, smoking and passing around a bottle. Near dark, Matt watched as the Indian swung aboard his paint horse and retraced their back trail for a mile or so. He turned sharply at a right angle toward a large outcropping maybe half a mile off the trail.

"So that's where you figure to spend the night," Matt said out loud.

Having learned what he needed to know, Matt climbed back down the hill and tended his horses. He made do with another strip of jerky, a cold biscuit and a can of peaches. After supper he spent an hour practicing with his guns, then removed his shirt and boots. He removed a pair of moccasins from his saddlebags and slipped them on. He tied a folded bandanna, the sign of an Apache warrior, around his forehead and lay down to get some rest.

He dozed off and on but couldn't sleep. The battle going on in his mind as he lay there in the dark would be fought in reality later that night. Two Apache warriors would meet, they would do battle, but only one would walk away. Would his early training be enough?

Waiting was always hard but he had learned the lesson of patience at the age of ten. The first tests an Apache boy must conquer on his path to becoming a warrior are the lessons of patience and discipline.

Many times he had been required to stand motionless for long periods of time on top of a rock finger, no larger around than a man's waist, thirty feet in the air. One wrong move, one careless moment of inattention meant a fall, likely resulting in serious injury or even death.

He had often run for hours through the burning hot desert with a mouthful of water, unable to swallow even a drop, knowing Chief Elkhorn would require it be spat out in his presence.

Patience and discipline were part of every Apache warrior's schooling. If you learned the lessons well you lived—if not—you died very young. Matt waited patiently.

Sometime past midnight he rose, unbuckled his guns, slipped the Rattler into his waistband, took the long Bowie in hand and trotted off into the night.

Matt knew that an Apache never selects a campsite and sets up camp as would a white man. He simply stops when and where the notion strikes him, selects the safest place from his enemies, rolls up in his horse blanket and goes to sleep.

He found Two Bear's horse hobbled in a small sycamore grove near the base of the large outcropping. Moving cautiously and alert to all sounds, he deer-footed through the thick stand of saplings. A jackrabbit jumped from under a gnarled mesquite bush and sped away. An owl awakened, gave him a great round eye and scolded in a melancholy way, then, resetting his feathers, sank back to sleep.

Silently, like a cloud moving across the face of the moon, placing each foot carefully, Matt inched slowly up the steep incline. One misplaced foot, one dislodged pebble, would alert the Indian instantly.

On top of the outcropping, Matt found a flat, sandy area maybe twelve feet across. On the far side, with his back to a large rock, lay Two Bears. He was rolled up in his blanket and snoring loudly.

Sinking to his knees, Matt placed the Bowie between his teeth in order to free up both hands. Slowly, he inched forward. How long it took he couldn't even guess. Time meant nothing now. One mistake would likely be his last. He held his breath the last few inches. At last he was able to reach out and grasp the rifle, lift it carefully and place it on the sand behind him out of the Indian's reach. In doing so, however, the metal contacted a small pebble, making the slightest scraping sound.

Instantly the Indian was awake. He threw the blanket from him and came to his feet, knife in hand. Matt, too, shot upright, the big Bowie out in front of his body. Instinctively, he dropped into the familiar fighter's stance he had learned after untold hours of practice as a young boy. Facing his opponent squarely, knees bent, feet well apart, up on the balls of his feet, his left hand held far out to his side for extra balance. He held the big knife flat, squarely in front of his body.

Even at the age of fourteen his skill as a knife fighter was unquestioned and rarely challenged by the warriors of his village. But from the looks of his opponent, Matt figured he would need every trick he knew and maybe then some, to survive this encounter.

Two Bears stood upright and motionless. No trace of fear evident in his cold, dark eyes. Shorter than Matt by several inches, his bronzed body was no less muscular. He wore long buckskin leggings with a breechcloth over them and a single eagle feather in his long hair.

Matt watched the man's eyes through the dim moonlight and saw them flick to the pistol in Matt's waistband. Neither did he miss the slightest hint of a smile that lifted the corner of his lip when Matt removed the pistol and tossed it in the sand beside the discarded rifle. Only then did the Indian drop into a crouch and rise to his tiptoes, announcing his readiness to do battle with an honorable opponent.

The two warriors circled each other, sliding their feet rather that lifting, not chancing even one misstep. Light from the moon reflected off the silver blade in the Apache's hand. He held it low and flat, slowly swinging it back and forth like the pendulum of a grandfather clock.

Matt quickly stepped in, swiping at the man's stomach, not really expecting to connect, but testing him, seeing how he would react. Like a cat the Apache slipped backwards, allowing the razor sharp point of Matt's long Bowie to flash harmlessly by.

He tried a quick jab. This time his opponent slid easily to his right, the point of Matt's knife missing by scant inches. Two Bears countered with a lightning fast slash that opened a shallow gash across Matt's stomach and brought blood. Ignoring the cut, Matt continued to circle, watching for an opening, searching for a mistake, careful not to make another himself. This Apache was good.

Perhaps sensing a quick victory the Indian attacked with a fury. He shot out a forward jab, pulled it back, faked to the right, then swung a backhand slash that would have meant a quick end to the fight had it connected.

Matt skillfully parried, did a quick half step forward and swept his long blade upward as the man retreated. He felt his blade contact flesh. A nasty looking gash on the warrior's right forearm spat blood. It was a deep cut but certainly not fatal. Ignoring the cut as if it never happened, the Apache reversed the direction of his circling, now moving to his own left.

Hoping to use the man's injury to his own advantage, Matt attacked with a double slash, first to the right, then to the left, hoping to catch the man coming in. Instead, the Indian retreated backwards. Matt pressed him hard, slashing with a double, a quick jab, followed quickly by a triple slash, then a deep, straight-on thrust. Suddenly it dawned on Matt that, on each of his thrusts, the Apache always escaped by shifting to his right, never to his left. Maybe that little habit would prove to be the mistake Matt had been looking for.

He had to be sure before risking everything. If he was wrong, or if the Indian was setting him up on purpose, it would likely cost him his life. He attacked again, slashing with seemingly reckless abandon with doubles, triples, fakes, then stepped in quickly with two half steps and a deep thrust. Sure as shooting, the man slid quickly to his right to avoid the deep thrust.

Two Bears counter attacked with several thrusts of his own, then tried the backhand slash that had worked for him the first time, but would not fool Matt again. Matt circled slowly, watching the center of the man's chest. He knew one could fake with his eyes, his hands, or even his feet, but where his chest goes, everything else goes with it.

Matt's strong legs propelled him forward with three quick shuffle steps. Two, then three slashes forced the Indian to retreat backwards. Matt stepped straight in with a full step and a deep thrust, but pulled it back at the last possible second, shifted to his left and risked it all by plunging forward with yet another deep thrust.

Old habits are hard to break and sometimes can get you killed. Just as he had each time, the Indian warrior slid quickly to his right to escape the faked thrust, only to step directly in front of the real one. The needlepoint of Matt's twenty two inch Bowie buried in the center of the Apache's throat, continued through, extending out the back.

Stepping back quickly, Matt withdrew the long blade leaving a gaping hole where it had been. Matt stood silently, blood dripping from the blade in his hand. The Apache dropped his knife. Both hands went to his throat, trying desperately but in vain, to stem the flow of lifeblood squirting from his neck with each heartbeat.

Two Bears sank slowly to his knees as if he was kneeling. His dark eyes searched for and found Matt's and locked for a long moment. The slightest hint of a smile creased the warrior's lips, then he toppled over onto his face.

Dawn crept silently across the south Texas desert and drove away the blackness of night. Somewhere a mocking bird sang its haunting melody. Overhead a hawk circled lazily in the powder blue sky. The first rays of sun peeked over the eastern horizon and lit the elevated platform, transferring its shadow onto the desert floor below. Built with sycamore saplings and driven into the soft sand of the flat battleground atop the rocky outcropping, it stood like a monument reaching into the morning sky.

Lying upon the platform, wrapped in his own riding blanket, lay an Apache warrior who had fought gallantly. The Apache burial was a final tribute of honor from one Apache warrior to another.

CHAPTER VI

Give and it Shall be Given

"Give, and it shall be given
unto you." (Luke 6:38)

A tired and trail weary rider rode into San Antonio, Texas at sundown. It had been three days since his battle with the Apache. Pointed in the direction of the livery by the thumb of a freight driver, Matt guided his two tired horses through the double doors and pried himself from the saddle that had been his home for way too long.

The old holster that emerged from a horse stall with a pitchfork in his hand had solid white hair and a tobacco-stained beard. He was gimpy in his left leg and swung it outward straight and stiff when he walked.

"Howdy stranger," the old fellow greeted Matt, "looks like you've come far."

"Yep, and going further," Matt replied as he began loosening the cinch straps, "but not today. Me and these horses are plumb tuckered out. Rub 'em down good and curry 'em. Double grain for both and stall them separately with plenty of fresh hay. You got someplace safe to stash my pack and long rifle?"

"Safe as my own sleeping room," the holster said, eyeing the big Sharps, the sawed-off double barrel on Matt's hip and especially the pistol with the coiled rattler on the handle. "If they steal them they'll have to deal with me and that might be a full days undertaking. Don't mean to meddle, young fella, but we ain't got no buffalo in these parts, so it's got to be men you're after with all that hardware I'm looking at."

"Only thing I'm hunting right now is a hot bath, a thick steak and a clean bed," he told the old timer as he stripped his rifle and saddlebags from his big stallion.

"Likely find all three one street over and halfway up. I'll have these horses rested and rearing to go when you are."

"I'll be pulling out at first light day after tomorrow. Seen anything of a bunch of hard cases, maybe seven or so, leader's a big fellow with red hair and beard, wears a patch over his right eye?"

"Nope," the old fellow replied, spitting a stream of tobacco juice at a nearby horsefly and hitting it square. "Might talk to the marshal though, his name is Dan McAllister. If he nor me's seen 'em, likely they ain't been through here."

Two hours later, after soaking off a week's trail dust in a steaming hot bath, both his tired muscles and his disposition were much improved. Now if he could find enough food to hold his britches up and a gallon of coffee to wash it down, he intended to try out those clean sheets he had insisted on.

The dining room, as the desk clerk called it, was a bit too fancy to his liking. He felt downright silly following the stiff-necked waiter that was gonna show him a table.

Despite his earlier misgivings, the food proved to be good. Halfway through his big steak a long shadow fell across his table. Matt glanced up at a big man who looked to be in his early to mid fifties. He stood Texas tall and leather tough. His square jaw and cold, penetrating eyes told everybody who bothered to look, here was a fellow to walk around. He wore a United States Marshal's badge pinned to his leather vest.

"I'm Marshal Dan McAllister and you'd likely be Matt Henry I expect, mind if I sit down?"

"Nice to meet you, Marshal. Drag out a chair. Do you give everybody a personal welcome to your town?" Matt sliced off a chunk of steak and forked it to his mouth.

"Only them that's toting enough hardware to start the war all over again, or if his reputation gets here before he does. In your case, it's both." The marshal told him, motioning for a cup of coffee.

"Two questions, Marshal." Matt fixed the lawman with a stare. "How'd you know me? What kind of reputation are you talking about? I didn't know I had one."

"Last couple of hours I've had half a dozen people come telling me about a fellow wearing a sawed-off shotgun on one hip and a fancy tied-down gun rig on the other. Now you got to admit, most folks don't go around packing like that. That kind of news usually gets my attention.

"Besides that, I got a telegram from a friend of mine, Ben Thompson, over in Waco. He said you might be headed this way. He called you The Man Hunter. He didn't say why and it's been gnawing at me so I figured I'd ask."

"I'm a farmer, Marshal. My wife, my six-year-old stepson and I had us a little place in the Fourche Valley, in Scott County, Arkansas. Doing pretty well too, I guess. As good as a one-team farm can do. Then one day while I was out in the field plowing, One-eyed Jack Trotter and his gang of killers rode through. They raped and murdered my wife, Marshal. They shot her five times just for sport after eighteen of them got through with her. I heard the shooting and come running but it was too late. I managed to get two of them before they put three .44 slugs in me and left me for dead. Well I ain't dead, just almighty mad.

"Seems the law ain't able, or willing to do anything about it," Matt told the marshal bitterly, "so I'm aiming to. I'm telling you straight out, Marshal, I mean to see every last one of that bunch brought to justice, either at the end of a short rope, or in front of my guns. I aim to stay within the law, but they're gonna pay for what they done, one way or the other."

"I see," the lawman said, staring hard at Matt as he talked. "I'm sure sorry about your family. I can see why you'd be bitter. You say there was eighteen of them when they hit your place?"

"Yeah, one was a woman. Like I said, I got two of them before they shot me up. So far since then I've caught up with eight more. Best I can figure, there's still eight more left."

"Sounds to me like they picked the wrong farm to hit. Got any idea where they're headed?"

"Place down in Mexico called Anahuac, ever hear of it?"

"Oh yeah, I've heard of it. I hear it's a place where they don't take kindly to gringos. The word is the Comanchero hang out around there. You ain't thinking about following them down there are you?"

"I'll follow them till I set things right, no matter where they go."

"No wonder Ben Thompson called you The Man Hunter. Offhand, I'd say that handle fits you a whole lot better than farmer. We need men like you wearing a badge. Seems to me you've accomplished more, in less time, than all the law enforcement we've got. Can't help wondering about that shotgun rig you're wearing, never seen anything like it before."

"Friend of mine up in Arkansas gave it to me when I set out after Trotter. Man named J.C. Holderfield."

"Holderfield?" the marshal said, rubbing his chin. "There use to be a lawman by that name, fellow they called The Town Tamer. Don't reckon it'd be him by chance?"

"One and the same," Matt told the marshal. "He's the Sheriff up in Scott County, Arkansas now. He's a good man and a better friend."

"Well what do you know about that? I never actually met him myself, but I've sure heard plenty of stories about him. Most folks on both sides of the law has heard about The Town Tamer. They still talk about him around most campfires."

"I'm looking for a friend of mine, Marshal," Matt said. "He's supposed to live around here someplace. Man by the name of Cunningham. Used to own a ranch called the Circle C. Wonder if you might know him?"

"Know him? I reckon most everybody hereabouts knows J.R. Cunningham. He just owns about half of Texas, that's all. Say he's a friend of yours?"

"I rode with him on a trail drive when I was fourteen. Didn't know if he was still alive after twelve years. Is his ranch pretty close? Thought I might ride out and say a howdy."

"Well, I don't know if you could call it close. It starts about a half day's ride to the east. Once you cross the San Antonio River you're on Circle C land. Course it's another day' hard ride to the ranch itself."

"I had no idea his spread was that big." Matt was shocked to hear his friend owned a ranch that large.

"That would be old J.R., sure enough. If a fellow didn't know better, you'd think he didn't have a pot to pee in. Fact is though, right behind Richard King, J.R.'s most likely the richest man in Texas. Last I heard he owns near half a million acres and is buying everything that comes up for sale. The way he's going he might even pass the King Ranch before long. I don't know how many friends you've got, Matt Henry, but the two you've told me about so far leave some mighty big tracks."

"How would I go about finding the Circle C Ranch house?" Matt asked.

"That's easy. You don't have to find it, once you cross the San Antonio River you're on Circle C land and they'll find you. They've got the best security force in Texas."

"Marshal, what are you doing in the morning about six? I need to talk some more but right now, I'm just plain tuckered out. How about I buy your breakfast in the morning?"

"Sounds good to me, I'll look forward to it."

Matt went to his room, propped a chair against the door and shucked his clothes. He slipped the Rattler under his pillow and promptly fell fast asleep.

He slept like a log and rose before the roosters. He washed, dressed and was sipping his second cup of coffee when the marshal strolled into the dining room.

"Morning Matt, you sure look a heap better than you did last night. Looked like you'd been rode hard and put away wet."

"Felt like it too."

They ordered breakfast and visited before, during and after the meal. Matt liked the big lawman.

After they parted, Matt spent the day restocking his trail supplies, having his clothes washed, and buying himself another outfit to wear while he was at the Circle C. He figured if it was that big a place, maybe he ought to wear his Sunday-go-to-meeting clothes. He spent a couple of hours in his room practicing with his guns, and the rest in a hot bath.

He had a late supper by himself in the hotel dining room, not really wanting any company and planning on turning in early so he could get an early start in the morning. Leaving the dining room, he decided to get a breath of fresh air before turning in. He stepped out the front door and right into the path of three cowboys who happened to be passing.

"Hey! Watch where you're going!" the biggest of the three snarled at him angrily.

"I'm sorry, I didn't see you fellows coming," Matt apologized and kept walking.

"Hey you!" the big man bellowed after him, "don't walk away when I'm talking to you."

Matt stopped in his tracks, stood motionless, then after a moment's contemplation, turned to face the speaker. He measured the man and knew the breed of him. He had seen his kind before. He was a bully. One that most likely had run roughshod over weaker men most of his life. One who enjoyed making others grovel, especially in front of his friends.

He stood nearly as tall as Matt. A thick-set hulk of a man whose shoulders looked mite near as wide as he was tall. He had no neck; his head seemed to sit directly on top of his massive shoulders. His muscled arms looked like hamhocks. A barrel chest stretched the denim shirt with sleeves rolled up past his elbows. He wore a Colt on his hip, but Matt suspected this man relied on his brute strength more than his gun.

"Look, mister, I said I was sorry," Matt told him, "let's drop it, huh?"

"Ain't dropping nothing," the man growled, "don't set well with me when people turn their backs on me while I'm talking to them. Like spitting in a man's face. You need to learn some Texas manners and I'm just the man that's gonna teach 'em to you."

"Better let it alone, Bruno," one of his companions said real low. "I got a notion he don't wear them guns just for show."

"What's the matter, Rowdy? You scared of this fellow? He don't scare me none."

Again, Matt turned to walk away, determined he wasn't going to have trouble with these fellows, especially over nothing. But it seemed every town in the west had itself a Bruno.

"Hey, you lily livered coward!" the man shouted. "I done told you not to walk away from me when I'm talking."

Matt froze. He had about had his can full of this loud mouth. Matt knew a man sometimes let his mouth outrun his brain now and again, especially when he'd had a few too many, or when he was trying to convince somebody he's something he ain't, but even then, there's a line he ought not to cross. This fellow just stepped over it.

"I'm gonna say this just one more time," Matt said low and even and cold. "I don't want any trouble. Let me buy you fellows a drink and let's just forget this. It don't amount to a hill of beans." Matt reached into his pocket and pulled out three dollars and held it out to the bully.

With a backhand swipe of his left hand Bruno slapped the money from Matt's hand. At the same time he swung a roundhouse right that would have torn Matt's head off had it connected. The big man's momentum turned his body half around. Matt lashed out with a short driving right that buried wrist deep into the man's right kidney, dropping him to his knees like a sack of potatoes.

The big man crawled heavily to his feet and came at Matt in a half crouch, his arms open wide to grapple. Shooting out a strong hand and grasping the man's left wrist as he lunged forward, Matt jerked the bully off balance, at the same time lashing out with a booted foot, kicking the man's feet out from under him, again sending him sprawling.

Roaring like a wounded grizzly, he lumbered up, diving headlong at Matt's midsection, obviously trying for a bear hug. Matt shifted easily to the side as a Matador would a charging bull, allowing Bruno to charge past. As he did, Matt unlimbered a haymaker from somewhere up north that sent the bully face first into the dusty street.

Peering up through squinted, hate filled eyes, loud mouth glared at Matt. Lurching unsteadily to his feet, he lifted both fists in front of him in an awkward imitation of a boxer and shuffled forward. He swept the air with a clumsy roundhouse left, missing badly. Matt answered with three lightning fast left jabs to the man's mouth, splitting his lips and bringing blood. He followed with a powerful right smack dab in the middle of the man's nose and felt the crunch of a broken nose. Bruno hit the dirt flat on his back.

Unable to accept defeat the wounded man had difficulty getting his feet under him, staggered twice, swiped the blood from his face with a backhanded drag of his arm across his bloody face and grabbed for his pistol.

From out of nowhere a hand shot out and clamped on the man's wrist. Marshal McAllister stepped between them. The Marshal's right hand held a Colt and lashed out in a vicious arc, laying the barrel alongside the bully's right ear, knocking him out cold.

Wheeling, the Colt still in his steady hand, the Marshal pinned a gaze on Bruno's two companions who stood motionless, their hands well away from their pistols.

"You two," he said coldly, "either drop them guns in that watering trough and ride out or die where you stand. You buying in or riding out?"

They rode out. They dropped their guns in the watering trough as they hurried past and lit a shuck. Dan turned back to Bruno, who still lay unconscious in the dirt. The marshal swiped up the man's hat, stepped to the water trough and dipped a hat full, dumping it in Bruno's face. Sputtering, the man came around and rose to sit dazed and shaking his head, as if trying to figure out what hit him.

"Mister," the marshal told him, "you might be known as tough where you come from but this time you bit off more that you could chew. You're lucky I come along when I did, you don't know how close you come to getting your head blown clear off.

Now I'd suggest you get astraddle your hoss and hightail it outta here while you still can. I mean git!"

He got.

Dan fished the pistols out of the water and added them to the one he took from Bruno as he and Matt watched the bully ride out of town at a gallop.

"I'm real sorry about that, Dan," Matt told the marshal. "I tried every way I could to talk him out of it. I didn't want any trouble in your town."

"Don't worry about it," the marshal told him, "his kind is always on the prod looking for trouble, even where there ain't any. Did you say you're headed out to J.R.'s place in the morning?"

"Yep, planning on pulling out at first light. Thought I'd mosey down to the livery and tell old Willy I'll be leaving early. Thanks for the help awhile ago."

"Forget it, you didn't need my help. I was just trying to keep those fellows from getting themselves killed, that's all. Tell old J.R. howdy for me, will you?"

"I'll do it, Marshal. Be seeing you around," Matt called over his shoulder as he headed for the livery.

True to his word, the old holster had Matt's horses rested and rearing to go. Matt didn't bother waking the liveryman because it was so early. He saddled and cinched them tight by lantern light, blew it out and stepped into leather. He tight reined the big stallion, sitting easy in the saddle as the big stallion high-hoofed sideways down the dark street. Once outside town, Matt gave Midnight some slack and he slid easily into an easy short lope. He had put a good five or six miles behind him before dawn broke. Matt settled comfortably against the cantle of his saddle and stared thoughtfully at the sight that never grew old, the start of another day, another gift of life. He found himself looking forward anxiously to seeing his old friend J.R. again. Cunningham had been good to him, had treated him more like a son than one of his drovers. He could hardly believe it had been twelve years.

Twelve years, it seemed like a lifetime. He had been only fourteen years old the first time he met J.R. Cunningham.

Matt had just escaped from his Apache captors after spending the last eight years being raised as one of them. The Apache had raided a wagon train and slaughtered everyone except Matt and two other boys about his same age. They had raised him as one of their own. He had learned their customs and ways but he had always known he would one day escape and return to his white heritage. They had killed his parents and taken him captive when he was six. His escape had succeeded and he had been headed nowhere and taking his time getting there when he stumbled upon the trail herd by sheer chance.

He remembered climbing off his Indian pony and sitting on top of a hill, watching the herd for hours. The endless mass of longhorns plodded along, encouraged from time to time by cowhands swinging coiled ropes that they applied frequently to stragglers' dusty backside.

Watching the cowboys, he had found himself wishing he was old enough to hire on, but he hadn't figured anybody would hire on a fourteen-year-old kid, especially one that had spent the last eight years living as an Apache and looked more Indian than white. The cowboys would likely shoot him on sight. Besides, what did he know about cattle?

Then he had remembered something his pa had told him many years before as they worked side by side on their little farm up in the boot heel of Missouri.

"Son," his pa had said, "always remember, when you don't know how to do something, watch the ones that do, then set your mind to do it better than they did."

Why not? He decided he had no other place to go. So, every day he had followed the herd, staying well away but always watching from a nearby hillside. He had seen how the cowboys seemed to sense what the cows were going to do, even before they done it and were there to head them off. He watched how they urged the cattle along but never pushed them. The cattle seemed to just plod along, pretty much setting their own pace.

He remembered how he especially had liked to watch them bed down the herd at night. How they turned the ones in front until a large circle had been formed, finally getting the cattle to mill about, then lay down, only to get up again around midnight, bawl and mill around for awhile, then settle back down again until first light. Matt had never forgotten those nights. They had been some of the loneliest nights of his whole life.

His life had taken on a new twist one morning. He had been following the herd for the most part of a week when one of the drovers had ridden up the hill toward him. At first Matt had considered jumping on his Indian pony and running away, but something had made him stay.

"The boss wants to see you," the tall cowboy had told him simply.

They had ridden side-by-side down the hill to the chuck wagon and dismounted. The tall cowboy took two tin cups from the back of the wagon and poured them full of coffee from the blackened pot hanging over the campfire. That had been the very first time Matt had ever tasted coffee. He remembered blowing on it like he saw the cowboy doing, then taking his first swig. He hated it. If he hadn't felt he was expected to like it he would have dumped it on the ground. Instead, he had swallowed it and acted like it tasted good.

A large man in dark pants, leather chaps and denim shirt had been squatting near the fire, his large hat was pushed back on his head to reveal salt and pepper hair. His deeply tanned, weathered face told Matt this man had spent more time outside than in. His face had a chiseled look. A square, hard-set mouth gave him a look of authority. Nobody had to tell Matt this man was the boss.

"What's your name, boy?" the man had finally asked without looking up from the fire.

"Name's Henry, sir, Matt Henry. My Indian name is White Hawk."

"Why you dogging my herd?"

"I watch because I want to learn how to herd cows," Matt had told the man simply. "My father tell me if I don't know how to do something, watch the ones that do, then do it better than they."

For the first time since he rode in, the big man lifted his face to look at Matt. He well remembered the first time he looked into those piercing green eyes that seemed to look right into a fellow's soul.

"How long you been with the Apache?" the man had asked him.

"Eight years. I wait eight years to escape. I not go back."

"Sam," the boss had called out to a fat man standing nearby, "fetch the boy some grub, looks like he ain't ate in a month."

Little could the big man have known how right he was. Matt had lived off the land since escaping nearly a month before.

He had been handed a plate filled with more food than he had seen at one time in years. He still remembered how good it had been and how he had refused the spoon they handed him and scooped the food into his mouth with his two fingers.

"How old are you, boy?" the boss had asked.

"Fourteen," he had said, "but I learn quick. I watch many days, I see the hardest job is riding behind cows. That is job I want. I work hard and do good job."

"What do you think, Chance?" the boss had asked the tall cowboy.

"You're the boss, J.R.," the tall one had said. "If it was me, I'd give the boy a chance."

"Okay, son," the boss they called J.R. had said, "you got yourself a job. Twenty-five dollars a month and keep. Long as you understand, like everybody else in this outfit, the day you don't pull your own weight is the day you ride out. Sam, see if you can rustle the boy up some clothes, we can't have him riding with us and looking like an Apache, somebody might use him for target practice.

"My name is J.R. Cunningham," the boss man had told him, sticking out a big hand. "That tall drink of water that brought you in is named Chance Longley, he's my trail boss. He'll show you the ropes. What he says is the same as if I said it."

That had been the beginning of his knowing J.R. Cunningham. He had spent three months on the trail with the herd, winding up in Wichita, Kansas. In those three months J.R. had become like a father to him.

As Matt had been riding and reminiscing, the country through which he rode was changing rapidly. His surroundings were now rocky and hilly. Gnarled mesquite bushes dotted the sandy soil and bunch grass grew in abundance. Rocky outcroppings reached their fingers into the sky.

Matt squinted through the rippling heat waves at a line of steep, rocky hills ahead of him that blocked his trail to the east. The only visible access was a narrow pass through which the trail wound. It would be a good place for an ambush and as a precaution, he slipped the thongs from his guns and thumbed back the hammers.

"Let's ride right easy, big fellow," he told his horse soothingly, as if speaking to a friend. Matt knew that on the trail, a good horse was often more of a companion that another man might be and often made the difference between living and dying.

Likely the narrow pass had been cut through the rocky hills many centuries ago by the persistent waters of the San Antonio River, which he could see on the other side of the pass. The sheer walls reached fifty feet into the sky. Boulders, big as a house, littered the trail. He strained his eyes in both directions, searching for another opening, but as far as he could see, the narrow pass was the only way through.

Cautiously he approached the entrance. Every sense came to full alert, his ears listening intently for even the slightest sound that shouldn't be there. His eyes scanned the ground, searching for any telltale prints. He watched Midnight's ears for any signs of alarm. Finally reaching the opening on the far side of the pass, Matt breathed a sigh of relief and patted his big stallion's neck.

"Better safe than sorry," he told his big horse, as if trying to justify his own nervousness.

Down a steep, sandy bank lay the San Antonio River. According to the marshal, that was the beginning of J.R.'s Circle C Ranch. The river was forty yards wide at this point and looked to be belly high on his horses. They slid their way down to the near bank where Matt reined up. He stepped from the saddle and loosened the cinches on both horses, allowing them to drink their fill from the muddy water.

He glanced around, then swiped off his hat and knelt beside the stream, cupping a handful to his mouth. He removed his bandanna and wet it, mopping the sweat from his face and neck. The cool water felt good.

When the horses stopped drinking, he tightened their cinch straps, climbed into the saddle and waded them across the stream. Once on the other side, he heeled Midnight into a lazy dogtrot.

By late afternoon, a dry, west Texas wind picked up and sent clouds of dust before it. Little funnels dipped down and picked up the powdery sand sending it swirling and skipping across the desert terrain. Matt untied the trail duster from behind his saddle and shrugged into it, preferring the added heat in return for protection against the blowing sand.

* * *

He camped that night beside a small stream and was saddling up the next morning when he saw the smoke, far off to his left and on his back trail. Thin fingers trailed into the air, interrupted momentarily by empty spaces, then more puffs drifted upward. Someone was announcing Matt's arrival.

The sun rose high, near noon, when he spotted dust plumes trailing skyward from the east. He watched the sky as they drew closer and closer. He was about to have company.

There were eight of them. Their wide-brimmed sombreros tugged at their chinstraps as they rode toward him at full gallop. Most wore crossed bandoleers and carried their rifles in their hands or across their Mexican saddles in front of them. These were definitely not your typical working vaqueros. These were fighting men.

"If these ain't Circle C riders, we're in a heap of trouble." He said the words both to himself and his horse. Hoping this was the welcoming committee the marshal had spoken of, Matt nonetheless flipped off the traveling thongs and thumbed back the hammers on his guns.

While still a hundred yards off, as if by some unseen signal, the riders fanned out in a precision movement, forming a horseshoe formation, encircling Matt on three sides. They reined up and sat their horses for a long moment, eyeing Matt suspiciously.

The obvious leader rode a steel gray gelding and emerged from the formation to walk his horse forward and stop only a few yards from Matt. The ornamented saddle he sat on was a piece of work. Solid black leather with silver trim and conchos caught the sun's rays and sent blinding beams of light flashing out in every direction. His embroidered sombrero hung down his back by a neck cord, revealing long, coal black hair held in place by a folded, dark red bandanna, the sign of an Apache warrior.

He wore a pearl handled Colt in a belly holster. A greener shotgun rode in a saddle boot on one side of his horse and a Sharps. 50 caliber long gun on the other side. Matt had seen plenty of tough hombres in his time, but if he was any judge of a man, sitting before him was one of the toughest.

Through dark, piercing eyes the man raked Matt with a gaze, pausing to stare long at the two weapons strapped to Matt's legs. When his eyes shifted upward to lock with Matt's, the stare was hard and cold. Matt's hands rested crossed on his saddle horn.

"Buenos tardes, señor," the Mexican said. "Your name, por favor?"

"I'm Matt Henry. I'm an old friend of J.R. Cunningham. I've come to pay a visit. Could you take me to him, por favor?"

"Si, señor, come with us, por favor."

Wheeling their horses with military precision, they maintained the horseshoe formation in reverse with Matt in the very center. What had Dan McAllister said—that the Circle C had the best security force in Texas. Well, he sure couldn't argue the point. It puzzled him though how they had even known that he had ridden onto ranch property. The smoke signals he had seen earlier had to have something to do with it.

After they had ridden awhile one of the vaqueros broke from the formation and rode on ahead, most likely to alert those at the ranch of his arrival. As they rode within sight of the ranch complex, he couldn't believe his eyes. He wanted to rub them to make sure he wasn't dreaming. One would think they were approaching a fair-size town. Matt saw row after row of large bunkhouses, numerous individual cabins and several large barns, each of which was surrounded by sturdy looking pole corrals.

What was obviously the main house dominated everything. It sat on top of a sloping hillside that was dotted with stately oak trees. The house was a large two-story structure made of massive logs. A large covered porch completely surrounded the house. To say it was impressive was the understatement of the year. Matt had never seen anything like it.

On the front porch was his old friend J.R. Cunningham, a tad older perhaps, but Matt would have recognized him anywhere. Standing at his side was a beautiful señora.

As Matt drew rein and stepped down J.R. rushed from the porch to greet him. A smile as big as all outdoors occupied his whole face. Why did he suddenly feel like the prodigal son his ma used to tell him about, Matt wondered?

"Matt my boy, you're sure a sight for sore eyes." The big rancher threw both arms around him and enclosing him in a crushing bear hug.

"It's real good to see you, J.R.," Matt told his friend as he swallowed down a big lump in his throat. "It's been a long time."

"Way too long," his friend told him, holding him at arms' length. "Here, let me have a good look at you. You're a far cry from that fourteen-year-old boy I remember."

"Been up and down a lot of roads since then. Quite a place you've got here."

"Come on up to the house, Matt, there's someone I want you to meet."

They walked side by side to the house, the big rancher's arm around Matt's shoulder. Waiting on the porch stood one of the most beautiful women Matt had ever seen. She looked like she had just stepped out of a painting or something. She was dressed in a floor-length black dress made from some kind of shiny material. The neck and wrists were trimmed with black lace. Her coal black hair was pulled tight into a bun on the back of her head, held in place by a large silver fan comb. Her pleasant smile looked genuine and was aimed directly at Matt.

"Juanita my dear, this is the Matt Henry I've told you about so many times. He's finally come to visit with us. Matt, this is my wonderful wife and the love of my life, Juanita Cunningham."

Matt took the extended hand, bowed from the waist and gently kissed the back of her hand.

"It is a great pleasure to meet you, Senora. Thank you for receiving me."

"The pleasure is ours, Mr. Henry. John Riley has told me so much about you I feel I already know you. Welcome to our casa. I know you and John Riley have much to talk about. If you'll excuse me, I will make arrangements for dinner."

J.R. led Matt into the house and to a large, impressively decorated den. A huge rock fireplace dominated one wall. Another whole wall was filled from floor to ceiling with books. Matt had never seen so many books. A desk made from half of a flatbed wagon, with the wheels still on, sat in front of double, floor-to-ceiling windows that looked out across a wide porch to the river below.

They barely got seated when a Mexican house girl hurried in carrying a large silver tray with a silver coffeepot. She quickly poured both J.R. and Matt a cup. Over coffee, his friend insisted that Matt give him a detailed accounting of the twelve years since they had last seen each other.

After a wonderful dinner, they again retired to the den to continue their conversation. Juanita herself brought in a fresh pot of coffee and joined them for a time of visiting.

"I must apologize that our daughter isn't here to meet you, señor Matt," Mrs. Cunningham told him. "She's attending a finishing school for young ladies in Philadelphia. She'll be coming home in just three weeks. I hope you'll be able to stay and meet her."

"I'd love to meet her but I'm afraid I can't this trip. Maybe I can get back this way before long."

After Mrs. Cunningham excused herself and retired, leaving the two men to their coffee and cigars, J.R. and Matt strolled out onto the back porch. It looked out over a sloping bank down to the Guadalupe River.

"Your wife is one of the most beautiful and gracious ladies I have ever met," Matt told his friend.

"Yes she is, isn't she? I'm very proud of her. We've been married going on forty years now. Without a doubt, she's the best thing that ever happened to this broken down cowboy. She's the daughter of a wealthy and prominent hacendados. I met her down in Mexico when I was just a young buck. I was rounding up wild cows to start my ranch and saw her riding down the road in a carriage. Her beauty come near knocking me right off my horse. I knew right then and there I was gonna marry her. It took some doing but I finally convinced her. It took a while longer to convince her father.

"We've worked hard to build the Circle C. Times were mighty rough those first few years. It seemed like if it wasn't the Indians or the weather, the Mexican bandidos stole us blind. Oh, we still got our problems, rustlers mainly, but all in all, things are a lot better than they use to be."

"Looks to me like you pretty well got things going your way. I can't even imagine one ranch being so big."

"It's a handful sometimes, sure enough. We've got nearly half a million acres. The ranch stretches all the way from the San Antonio River on the west to the Colorado River to the east. Our northern border is near Austin and runs to the Gulf of Mexico."

Matt just shook his head in wonderment. It was more than he could comprehend.

"Sure wish you could stay and meet our daughter, Matt. She's my pride and joy. I'll be straight with you, Matt. I always wanted a son to take over the ranch after I'm gone. There were complications when Jamie was born and Juanita couldn't have any more children.

"Maybe I tried to make a boy out of her, I don't know, I taught her to ride and shoot as well as any man on the ranch. Juanita thought I was going overboard, I guess. Anyway, she felt like Jamie needed to attend a finishing school back east. I thought she was perfect just the way she was, but you know how mothers can be. Sure would like for you to meet her."

"I wish I could too, J.R., but I got some things that need doing and I can't rest till they're done, but I'll try my best to get back by before long."

"I sure am sorry about what happened to your wife and stepson, Matt. I can't imagine what it would be like losing a man's family like that. I can sure understand you wanting to square things, but just keep in mind that you won't be helping them any if you go and get yourself killed.

"Guess we might ought to turn in, son," the rancher said, "we've got a big day tomorrow. There's some things I been waiting twelve years to show you. You'll be staying in the guestroom, top of the stairs, first door on the left. It shore is good to have you here, Matt."

"Thanks, J.R., it's mighty good to be here. It feels, well, it feels real good."

The sun peeked in the bedroom window and found him still sleeping. It crept silently inside and inched across the floor and onto the big comfortable bed where he lay. The only evidence of its presence were the warming rays that finally splayed over his face, waking him instantly. He jumped out of bed, ashamed that he had slept so late. Washing quickly, he hurried downstairs to find the family just sitting down for breakfast.

"Sorry I'm late," he said, embarrassed.

"Morning Matt," J.R. greeted cheerfully. "I told the wife to let you sleep as long as you could, figured you needed the rest. Matt, this is Slim O'Dell. Slim's my ranch manager. This is Matt Henry, Slim, he's the same as one of the family."

Matt reached a hand to the one extended and felt the firm grip of a man who had worked with his hands his whole life. He was a tall man, thin around the middle and broad shouldered—a man with a look of authority.

"Good to meet you, Matt, anything you want while you're here, just let me know."

After they had said their howdies, they dug into a breakfast fit for a king. Two Mexican house girls just kept bringing food and the three men just kept putting it away. Between bites, J.R. explained how the ranch was set up.

"The ranch is divided into eight districts, Matt. Each district has its own foreman that looks after his district. Each foreman has several top hands that work under him and as many vaqueros as he needs to get the job done. Slim meets with his foreman once a month, then we all get together about every three months."

"How many people does the ranch employ?" Matt asked.

"Somewhere in the neighborhood of five hundred," J.R. told him. "That don't count their families, of course, most of our vaqueros are family men. We've found they're reliable and stay with us longer. I've got several that's been with me right from the start. All told, counting children, there's more than two thousand that live on the ranch. We provide a school and all in each district for the children."

"When I worked for you I had no idea the Circle C was so big," Matt told him.

"Oh, it wasn't back then. We've grown an awful lot in the twelve years since then."

After breakfast the three men lingered over a second cup while J.R. and Slim went over several things pertaining to ranch business, then Slim excused himself.

"Have Manuel throw a saddle on our horses will you, Slim? Matt and I are gonna take a little ride after a bit. I want to show him around the place."

They spent the whole morning riding the ranch and talking cattle. They rode past herd after herd grazing contentedly in the rich, grassy valleys of the vast spread. Several vaqueros rode slowly around each herd, watching and caring for them. Near noon, J.R. and Matt topped a line of low hills and gazed down into a beautiful green valley filled with fat cattle grazing on the rich, high grass along the Big Sandy River that cut the valley in half.

"Have you ever seen a more beautiful sight?" J.R. asked, looping a leg around his saddle horn and stoking up an old, worn out looking pipe.

"No," Matt said, staring down admiringly at the vast herd of longhorns, "can't say I have. That's some of the best looking cattle I've ever seen."

"Glad to hear you say that, son," the old rancher said, putting fire to the pipe, "cause they're yours."

The words didn't sink in for a long moment. When they did, Matt thought he had misunderstood what the rancher said.

"What?" Matt asked.

"They're yours. There's five thousand head of the finest cattle in Texas down in that valley, Matt and they're all yours. You've got three more herds just like them scattered in other districts. Last time I checked the books you had something over twenty two thousand head and growing every day."

"I don't understand," Matt said, puzzled by what his friend was saying.

"You remember back in Wichita when we finished the drive and I sold the herd and paid everybody off? You had two hundred sixty dollars coming with your wages and bonus. You took sixty and asked me to keep the two hundred for you? You said you'd probably just blow it if you took it all and that you'd come by for it someday."

"Yeah, but I'd forgotten all about it, but I still don't understand."

"On the way back to Texas I got to thinking about it. Instead of just holding on to your money for you, I decided to put it to work for you. I decided to invest it until you came back for it. Course, I never thought about it being twelve years.

"Back then, cows were cheap because any cowboy with a good rope and horse and a little sand about him could gather all the wild cows he wanted out of the thickets over in east Texas and along the Mexican border.

"Good stock was going for about a dollar a head. I bought you a hundred head of good young heifers and a couple of quality bulls. By that next spring you had near two hundred head. I sold off most of the steer calves and replaced them with heifers. Year after year your herd just kept on growing. Over the twelve years, that little herd has grown to over twenty two thousand head of the best cattle in Texas."

Matt sat his horse in stunned silence, utterly flabbergasted by what his friend had just told him. He dropped his head to hide the tears that welled up inside him and trickled from his eyes, washing a trail down his cheeks, finally brushed aside by the back of a shaking hand.

"I...I just don't know what to say, J.R.," Matt stammered out. "It all seems like a dream, but I never even dared to dream of anything like this. I just can't believe anything like this could ever happen to me. I'm gonna tell you something I've never breathed to another living soul. Ever since that first day when I sat on top of that hill and saw your herd, I started dreaming that maybe someday I could have a little ranch of my own with a small herd like that. It was a silly dream, I know and one that I didn't figure would ever happen, but it was a nice dream. Now this. But I still can't believe a hundred head could grow to twenty two thousand in just twelve years."

"Let me tell you a story I read one time, son," the old rancher said, "maybe it will help you understand. Seems this selfish king had a reputation for taking advantage of everybody he dealt with. One time this smart young fellow came along and made the king an offer. He told the selfish king he would clean his stables for just a penny wages the first day, if the king would agree to double his wages every day for thirty days.

"Well, being as selfish as he was, the king figured it couldn't add up to much and didn't stop to figure it all out, so he quickly agreed and put it in writing and sealed it with the official seal before the young fellow backed out.

"At the end of the thirty days the young man came to collect his wages. It all come to over ten million dollars in just thirty days. When the king couldn't pay up, the young man ended up with the whole kingdom.

"I'll show you the books when we get back to the house," J.R. told him. "In the ranching business you always have losses from predators, rustlers, disease and so on. I took out for grazing fees and to pay the vaqueros that work with your herds. After taking out all those expenses, your herds still averaged a seventy six percent increase every year."

"What in the world am I gonna do with twenty two thousand head of longhorns?" Matt asked, swiping off his hat and sleeving sweat from his face. "How much are they worth?"

"Market's pretty weak right now," J.R. told him. "There's too many cattle in this part of the country and no market for them. A man might get three dollars a head, maybe even three-fifty right where they're standing. Shucks, as good as yours are, they might even bring four dollars a head if you could find the right buyer. Trouble is, nobody's buying, at least not around here.

"You might think about a drive, them cows would bring eighteen, maybe even twenty a head at the rail head in Wichita. But nobody in his right mind is driving up the trail right now. The trail blockers from Kansas are up in arms over the Texas fever scare. They ain't letting Texas cattle in. They say the ticks some of our longhorns carry kill the shorthorn cattle they raise.

"All the Texas growers are in the same boat, nobody can get their cattle to market and the herds are backing up with nothing we can do with them. I don't know how long some of us can hold out. It's a real problem."

"Well, I'm shore beholden to you for what you've done for me. I guess I need a little time to let it sink in and try to work it all out."

"Take all the time you need, son, those cows aren't going nowhere till you decide what you want to do. Meantime, they just keep on having calves every spring."

Long after supper was over and everybody had turned in for the night, Matt strolled down to the river behind the ranch house. There he found a wooden bench built beside the quiet stream. It was peaceful there and for a long time he sat, listening to the constant croaking of frogs and the steady drone of crickets. Far off in the distance the lowing of cattle made a soothing sound, but inside him, a battle was raging.

All those cattle were like a dream come true. They could be the means to a better life, a secure future, the means to start that cattle ranch he'd always dreamed of. Yet, he could not, he would not, allow this turn of events to deter him from his sworn oath to his wife and son. No matter what, he had to see this thing through to the end. He had to track down the rest of Trotter's gang and bring them to justice. He couldn't rest until it was done. Having reaffirmed his mission, he felt a peace wash over him. He strode back to his room and slept peacefully.

At breakfast the next morning he shared his late night decision with his friends. A concerned frown plowed a furrow across the rancher's leathered face.

"I hope you can understand why I have to do this," Matt said, seeing the disappointment on his friend's face. "The way I see it, a man is only as good as his word. I swore my word over my wife and boy's graves, if need be, I'll die trying to keep it."

"Son," the big rancher said, "I can understand how you feel and

I respect you for what you're doing. I won't lie to you. I'm disappointed. I was hoping we could keep you here with us. But I can see now, that was just me being selfish. I can't help but worry though, what with the size of the job you've taken on. By your own count, there's still seven of those killers left, then there's the Comanchero roaming all over the country and the corrupt Mexican federales, that's a mighty big mountain you're facing, son."

"Yes, sir, it is," Matt said, "but my pa had a saying he used all the time. He said, son, when you're facing a big mountain you've got to move, just do it one rock at a time."

"When you figure on leaving?"

"Right after our next cup of coffee."

"Then let's make it a mighty long cup," the old rancher said sadly, "a mighty long cup."

They sipped that cup slowly in quiet conversation. Neither wanted it to end, each knowing it must, but in those quiet moments they shared together something special happened—something that would change all their lives forever. In those moments a new feeling of closeness bonded them together much more than mere friendship. In those few moments they became family.

Matt finally found the strength and determination to rise. Juanita cried and the old rancher brushed away a tear from a wrinkled cheek.

"So long, son," J.R. said, barely above a whisper. "You hurry back to us, you hear?"

Juanita choked back soft sobs and turned away, her face buried in the apron she wore. Matt went to her and with hands on her shoulders, turned her around and took her in his strong arms and held her for a long minute or more. The hug they shared brought to mind the times he and his own ma had hugged like that. It seemed so long ago.

Swallowing down a big lump in his throat, Matt turned and strode determinedly out the door and to his waiting horse, held by the old stable man. Toeing a stirrup, he stepped into leather.

"I'll be back," he called, reining Midnight around, looping the lead rope around his saddle horn, "and that's a promise."

Far down the road, Matt twisted in the saddle to see his new family still standing on the front porch, gazing after him. He wheeled his horse, tugging back on the reins and at the same time touching his toes to tender flanks, caused the big stallion to rear high in the air, his front hooves pawing the air. Matt swiped his hat and held it high in the air in a final good-bye.

It was a scorcher. The blazing noonday sun bore down with a vengeance. Matt stepped from the saddle at the edge of the San Antonio River and loosed cinch straps, allowing his horses to slake their thirst and blow. Remounting, he splashed across the river and climbed the steep bank, leaving Circle C land.

All day he rode steady, stopping often to rest his horses from the blistering sun. The country was changing fast. The plentiful bunch grass of the day before had given way to sandstone littered hills, gnarled mesquite, catclaw and seemingly an endless sea of sand.

Just after sundown, lady luck smiled on him, or more likely just felt sorry for the horses. He came upon a small, fresh running stream of the sweetest water he could remember ever tasting. He quickly saw to his horses and made camp, then cooked himself a good supper.

There are times when silence can be a beautiful sound. This was one of those times. A desert night can be almighty quiet. The tiny gurgling sound of the lazy little stream, the sound of a desert blue quail calling to a mate and somewhere off in the distance, a lone coyote yelping its lonesome call. All these sounds did their job well and soon, Matt slid down to rest his head on his saddle and drifted off to sleep.

* * *

No one seemed to pay any mind to the lone weary rider on the big black stallion and leading the pinto packhorse as they plodded down the single dusty street of Laredo, Texas. Matt had seen lots of one-horse towns in his time, but this one took the cake. He could see no earthly reason for its even being there except maybe as a last jumping off place before crossing the Rio Grande River into Mexico.

The street, if one could call it that, seemed to just run right off into the river, only to begin again on the other side where he could see a cluster of adobe buildings.

He reined up in front of the weather beaten double doors of a rundown livery. The old Mexican that appeared from a stall didn't speak English and Matt spoke very little Spanish. Between hand signals and the few words he knew, he managed to get across what he wanted done for his horses.

After four days of hard riding, he just wanted to find a hot bath and a soft bed. He had spotted a small hotel on his way in and headed for it. They had four rooms downstairs and four up. Matt chose an upstairs room and after inspecting the sheets, insisted they be changed. Somehow, he didn't cotton to the idea of sleeping on another man's dirty sheets.

"A hot bath?" he asked the fat little Mexican man at the desk. "Could I get a hot bath brought up, por favor?"

"Si, señor," the man said, showing rotting teeth with his wide smile, "Manuel will bring it quickly."

Matt had just hung his saddlebags on the bedpost and pried himself loose from his boots when he heard a soft tap on the door.

"Who is it?" he called out.

"It is Manuel, señor. I bring your bath, por favor."

"Come in."

A handsome young Mexican, who Matt judged to be in his late teens or early twenties, pushed through the door carrying a large wooden bathtub. He quickly placed it on the floor of the small room, bowed from the waist and trotted from the room. After several hurried trips, the tub brimmed with steaming hot water. The young man placed a cake of lye soap and a towel on the floor near the tub and left quickly.

An unhurried and relaxing hour in a tub of hot water can do wonders for a man's disposition, not to mention his aroma. After several hard days in the saddle, Matt badly needed improvements in both departments. He lingered in the tub, soaking off trail dust, until he felt waterlogged. He had barely climbed out, dried off and shrugged into a clean change of clothes from his saddlebags when another knock came at the door.

"It is Manuel, señor. If you are finished with the bath I will remove the tub."

"Come ahead," Matt called out.

While the young man removed bucket after bucket of water from the tub, Matt flopped down on the bed, curled an arm behind his head and watched the hard-working young Mexican. It made Matt tired just watching the young man rush around. He seemed to have only one speed, a fast trot. Finally the tub was dry and he came for it.

"I will wash those clothes for you, señor," the young man said, pointing to the pile of dirty clothes lying on the floor where Matt had dropped them.

"Si," Matt said, greatly impressed with the young man. "How much do I owe you?"

"One dollar, señor."

Matt fished two dollars from his pocket and handed it to the Mexican. A huge smile broke over the handsome young man's face.

"Gracias, señor. Muchas gracias." Manuel scooped the pile of dirty clothes and hefted the tub to his shoulder, then hurried from the room in his usual trot.

Heading downstairs and out into the street, Matt quickly found what served as the town Marshal's office. It was unlike any he had ever seen before—it was worse. The small excuse for a building, like everything else in town, was made of adobe. Except much of this one had already fallen off, leaving a crumbling, decaying, mud wall. It looked for all the world like one swift kick and the whole thing would come tumbling to the ground. Scrawled over the door in weathered letters that were barely legible were two words. TOWN MARSHAL.

The fellow in the chair tilted back against the front wall looked every bit the part. He was whipcord thin with a prominent Adam's apple and aquiline nose. His brown hair, which needed a cutting, was speckled here and there with streaks of gray. Turkey tracks had bitten deep at the corners of his blue eyes, for he habitually squinted against the glare of a sun-drenched land. He casually chewed on a small stick, whittled on another and watched from under a gray Stetson as Matt approached across the dusty street.

A tarnished looking town Marshal's badge pinned to his faded dungaree shirt was the first thing that caught Matt's eye. The Colt in a well-greased holster tied low on his right leg also drew Matt's interest. But what captured his undivided attention were the ice blue, penetrating eyes, colder than an outhouse in the middle of winter—eyes that had something burning in them that made a man instinctively step aside—eyes that seemed to rake him with a once over, twice.

"Afternoon," Matt offered in his most friendly tone. "You the town Marshal?"

"Reckon so," the man replied, never taking his gaze off Matt, "at least I have been for the last eight years. Couldn't say about tomorrow, I just take it one day at a time around here. Something I can do for you?"

"Name's Henry, Matt Henry. I'm trailing some men, One-eyed Jack Trotter and his bunch. Thought you might have seen them ride through in the last week or so?"

"Nope," the lawman replied, still whittling, "men like that don't ride through my town, never have, never will, they ride around it. Took 'em a while to learn that lesson, but they finally learned. You a bounty hunter, Mr. Henry?"

"I'm hunting men, not bounty," Matt told him. "Makes no difference to me one way or the other if they got bounty on 'em, I'm still gonna do what I'm gonna do."

"And what, exactly, might that be, Mr. Henry?" the marshal pulled a tobacco sack from his shirt pocket. . . rolled a smoke. . ..licked the edge of the paper to seal it and put fire to it with a match struck on his britches leg.

"They raped and murdered my wife and cut my six-year-old boy's throat from ear to ear. Now what do you think I'm gonna do to 'em? I aim to see every last one of them swinging from a rope, or buried with their boots on. The only thing they get to choose is which."

"I'll say one thing for you, Mr. Henry, you shore don't waste no words beating around the bush."

"My pa use to say, a man could get a lot more said, in less time, if he used half the words."

"Sounds to me like your pa taught you well. I hate it about your family. Couldn't help noticing that doublebarrel strapped to your leg. It kinda has a way of getting one's attention. Never seen anything like it, mind telling me where you come by a weapon like that?"

"Friend of mine use to be in law work. Maybe you've heard of him, folks use to call him The Town Tamer. His name is J.C. Holderfield."

"Yeah, I reckon I have. Most folks good and bad has heard that name. Say he's a friend of yours?"

"I'm right proud to say he is," Matt told him. "He's one of the best men I ever met. He's the Sheriff up in Scott County, Arkansas where I'm from. He's getting on up in years now."

"Ain't we all though?" the marshal said. "You catch up to any of that Trotter gang yet?"

"Some, there was eighteen of them when they hit my farm, there's seven of them left."

A wrinkled grin creased the corner of his mouth. He casually flipped the used up cigarette stub into the street to join the remains of countless others that Matt had already noticed.

"Sounds to me like they picked the wrong farm. What can I do to help you Mr. Henry?"

"First thing you can do is stop calling me Mr. Henry, my name's Matt. I didn't catch yours."

"That's because I didn't give it. I'm kinda careful who I throw my name out to. There's more'n a few folks that would like to see me six foot under. Some have tried. Packing all the hardware I'm looking at, I had to be sure you wasn't another they had sent to do the job. My name's Earl Tolleson. I'm right proud to make your acquaintance, Matt Henry."

"Howdy, Earl. Sounds to me like you've stepped on some sidewinder's tail and got 'em all stirred up."

"Uh huh, you could shore say that all right. They don't take to kindly being told they can't ride through my town. Course, Henry Bragg's behind most of it. I hear tell he's put a two thousand dollar price on my head. Some men will do most anything for that much money. Every now and again one of his customers takes a notion to try and collect all that easy money."

"Who's this Henry Bragg fellow?" Matt asked.

"Look yonder," the marshal, said, pointing across the river. "See that sorry excuse for a town across the river? That's what they call Boys Town. Most folks around these parts just call it the end of the street on account of the way the street jumps right off into the river and starts up again on the other side. That's Henry Bragg's town. He owns it lock, stock and barrel.

"Course, there ain't nothing there that decent folks would have use for. Mostly crooked gambling, watered down whiskey and diseased women. But it draws all the scum from both sides of the border like a cow patty draws flies.

"Those men you're looking for? The Trotter outfit? Most likely they're right over there across the river not half a mile away. Like as not, half the men I got wanted posters on are over there right now and there ain't a dad blamed thing I can do about it. My authority stops in the middle of that river."

"Mine don't. Sounds like you got yourself an impossible job, Marshal."

"Yep, should have quit years ago. Likely would have to, if they hadn't tried to run me out of town. Never left anywhere yet till I was ready to go. Don't intend to start now."

"Wonder if you could point me to the best place in town to eat?" Matt asked. "I've been on the trail and I'm tired of my own cooking."

"Best place in town is the only place in town. Right next door to Peterson's store there. It ain't got a name, most folks just call it Marie's cause she's the pretty little señorita that runs it. Don't go getting no pleasant thoughts about her though, she's already roped, tied and branded by that young fellow that works over at the hotel."

"Yeah, I met him awhile ago, said his name was Manuel. He's the hardest working young fellow I've seen in awhile."

"That's the one," the lawman said, "him and Marie have been working their heads off trying to save enough so they can get hitched and buy that little café from Henry Bragg. Only trouble is, every time they come up with the price, he ups it on them. I feel sorry for them but there ain't nothing I can do about it. She shore sets a good supper though."

"Tell you what, Marshal, how about me buying your supper tonight? Never did get use to eating alone, besides, it ain't every day a man gets to eat with the marshal unless he's on the wrong side of the bars."

"Don't see why not, all in the name of my civic duty, of course."

"Of course. Why don't I meet you there in an hour or so? I spotted a barbershop awhile ago. I think I'll go get my ears lowered and have a week's worth of whiskers shaved off."

"Might improve both our appetites," the lawman said, actually letting out what might be called a chuckle, as he called out to Matt's retreating backside.

The café wasn't as small as Matt had pictured it would be and it was as neat as a pin. Red and white checkered oilcloth covered each of the near dozen tables, all crowded with folks, both Mexican and American. Checking the food out as he made his way to the marshal's table, Matt was pleased with what he saw. It looked delicious. Marshal Tolleson sat at a table near the back, blowing on a saucer full of coffee.

"Sorry I'm late," Matt said, scraping a chair out and settling into it. "Took longer than I expected."

"Hope old Fred didn't charge you by the hour, you'd be too broke to buy my supper. Shore helped your looks considerable though," the marshal joked, trying to sip the steaming coffee from the saucer without burning his lips.

"Buenas noches, señor," a sweet sounding voice behind him greeted.

Matt quickly cut a glance around to see a pretty little señorita standing beside his chair. She was no bigger than a hiccup. Her long, coal black hair hung straight and long to near her knees. She had flawless, olive toned skin and flashing dark eyes that seemed to smile when she looked at you. She was a picture any man would have a hard time forgetting on a lonely night on the trail. In her hand she held an empty coffee cup.

"Don't reckon I ever seen anything prettier than a señorita holding a coffee cup," Matt told the marshal. "Buenas noches, señorita," Matt said, trying out what little of the language he knew. "Ud. Es muy hermosa.,"

"Gracias, señor, Ud. Es muy inteligente," she said, smiling sweetly, then added in perfect English, "Now, what would you two gentlemen like to order, or do you prefer we continue complimenting each other?"

Unfortunately, Matt had just taken a big swig of hot coffee, which he promptly choked upon, spewing some of it out. Meanwhile, both the marshal and the señorita were having a big laugh at Matt's expense.

"Why didn't you tell me she spoke perfect English?" Matt protested to the marshal.

"You didn't ask. Besides, you was having so much fun telling her how beautiful she is, I didn't want to spoil your fun."

"I was raised in San Antonio, señor," the beautiful señorita explained. "You'd be surprised what all I hear from people that don't know I understand English."

"Yeah, I can imagine," Matt said. "Just bring us a couple of the best suppers you got back there and all the trimmings to fill up a couple of hungry men, including one that just got through eating a lot of crow."

"I can sure do that," she said, still laughing. "Please don't be embarrassed, I was rather enjoying hearing how beautiful you said I was."

"Yeah, then you told me how intelligent I was for saying it."

The pretty señorita hurried off toward the kitchen while Earl Tolleson was still laughing.

"Tell me about this Henry Bragg fellow," Matt asked.

"Henry use to be a good man, lived right here in Laredo. Then he took a notion he could make lots of money on the other side of the river. He still owns several businesses here in town, including the one we're sitting in right now and the hotel you're staying in.

"He owns a big spread west of town, got a good wife and a boy about seven or eight and a girl that's about ten I reckon. Sorry as he is, he thinks the world of his family.

"He's smart, careful too. Far as I know he ain't broke no laws on this side of the river. He don't do his own dirty work, he's got shooters that do it for him. Two of them sit on elevated platforms in that big cantina of his. Both of them are crack shots, at least that's what I hear. Bad as his customers are, they don't dare start trouble in Boys Town.

"Besides the Rio Grande Cantina and gambling hall, he's got two big whore houses selling any size, shape, or color a man might have a hankering for. His higher priced girls—and I do mean girls—live in small, individual houses, provided by Henry Bragg, of course.

"Yeah, it's frustrating. If I had my druthers, I'd like to ride over there and clean out the whole kit and caboodle, but once I crossed that river I wouldn't last long enough to get down off my horse. Like I said, my jurisdiction stops at the middle of the river."

"Like I said," Matt said, "mine don't."

At that moment Marie glided up carrying two platters of delicious looking Mexican food. Matt thought he had died and gone to heaven. He was still admiring the plateful of food when she returned with a heaping bowl of fried potatoes mixed with peppers and onions and a bowl of Mexican style beans. On the third trip she set a pan of sopaipillas and a jar of sweet honey.

"Would there be anything else for you gentlemen?" she asked sweetly.

"What more could a man possibly want?" Matt asked. "I'm coming to understand why Manuel works so hard. Not only is he getting a beautiful señorita, but one that can cook too. Now that's a rare combination."

"Gracias, señor, you are most generous with your words. So, you have met my Manuel then?"

"Yes, I met him at the hotel. He's one of the hardest working young men I've seen in a long time. You two will make quite a couple."

"Enjoy your meals, señors," she told them before hurrying off to wait on other customers.

For the next hour or so the two men visited and enjoyed their delicious meals. Matt left five dollars on the table, enough to cover their meals plus an extra generous tip.

As they stepped out into the street, Matt turned to peer for a long minute at the lights across the river.

"I hope you ain't thinking what I think you're thinking," the marshal said.

"Reckon I might just mosey across the river and take a look around. Never can tell, I might pick up some information about Trotter."

"Hate to see you do that, Matt. Folks have a way of turning up dead over there real regular."

"Maybe we could have a cup of coffee in the morning and I'll tell you what I find out."

"You be careful," the marshal said as Matt headed for the livery.

Urging his big stallion down the bank into the belly-deep water of the Rio Grande River, Matt felt a twinge of uneasiness on the back of his neck. He had never been in Mexico before. He had heard all the horror stories and it made him wonder what kind of trouble he might be riding into—nevertheless, he urged his horse forward, determined to follow every lead that might help him find Trotter and his men no matter where it took him.

The river was only a hundred yards or so wide at that point. It got deeper as they went and Midnight had to swim part of the way. Still, it didn't seem like much to separate two countries. Matt's big stallion climbed the bank from the water and onto foreign soil.

A jumbled accumulation of flat-roofed adobe structures were scattered haphazardly along a dusty street that seemed to empty into a town square. Coming to it, he reined up and sat his horse as he swept a slow gaze over the area.

The square was crowded. Mexican pistolares, with their crossed bandoleers and tied down guns, drunken vaqueros with wide legged, ornamented britches, and tough looking American saddle tramps, all loitered against buildings or around the water trough in the middle of the square.

Most stood, clutching bottles and watching the endless parade of girls and women who strolled around the square. Matt saw most every state of dress and undress as they used every means they could to entice the men of their choice to accompany them to their rooms.

Four large buildings faced each other and formed the town square. Three were two story adobe structures that resembled hotels. Judging from the traffic going in and out, it was obvious they were all bordellos. The fourth building was, by far, the largest and sat directly across the square from where Matt sat. Rio Grande Cantina it said in large, faded brown letters splashed across the flat front of the building. He headed there.

Hitch rails in front of the Cantina were lined hip to hip with horses. Many stood three legged, a sure sign they had been there for hours. Matt found an opening at a small rail off to one side of the building, wrapped his reins around the rail and did a quick half-hitch.

He pressed through the milling maze of men that stood around the open double doors of the cantina. Most of these men weren't just vaqueros or cowboys out for a good time on Saturday night. These were hard men. Their faces were weather cooked and hard set by a lifetime in the hot sun. These were bone lean and leather tough men, their eyes shifty and constantly searching. These were men who knew how to survive by being tougher and more ruthless than those they encountered. These were the kind of men Matt had spent five years hard labor in Yuma Territorial Prison with. Men who, at the present time, were more interested in the bottles in their hands and the women hanging onto their arms, than they were the newcomer that squeezed past them.

At the door he encountered two exceptions. Both had a mean look on their faces and Henry rifles in the crooks of their arms. They stood guard on either side of the Cantina doors. Their gaze searched every man that entered. Matt drew their prolonged attention with more than a passing interest.

It might be easier to get into this place than to get out, Matt thought as he shouldered past those standing in the entrance. To say the Cantina was crowded would be an understatement. It was packed. A veil of thick smoke hung heavy in the air. The stench of stale whiskey, tobacco smoke and unwashed bodies filled the room and stung Matt's nostrils.

A three-piece Mexican band that seemed to be trying hard, but failing badly, to play louder than the laughter, cursing and yelling of the hundred or more that jammed the room.

A sturdy-looking bar lined the entire wall on Matt's left. Five bartenders worked frantically to serve the men who stood shoulder to shoulder along its length. Gaming tables lined the three remaining walls of the large room that looked to be at least eighty feet by eighty feet. Roulette, crap tables, blackjack and poker tables were all crowded with players and spectators who stood three deep in most places. Looked like Henry Bragg had himself a gold mine.

The center of the room held twenty or so tables, all of which were occupied with men busy emptying their glasses. At least twenty girls with too much paint on their faces and more out of their dresses than in, worked the room, hustling drinks and otherwise.

Looking around, Matt allowed there were likely more killers, robbers and just plain no-goods in this room than there had been in Yuma Prison.

He slowly scanned the room, examining each face. Not really knowing what he was searching for, but confident he would know if he saw it. Four men drew his special interest.

The first was a huge man in a black broadcloth suit who liked some covering on his considerable belly. His mostly baldhead glistened from the light of the lanterns that lined the walls. The man's slack mouth worked constantly at the cigar that hung from his lips. He moved among the customers, working the room. A slap on the back here, a handshake there, the wave of an arm as he motioned for one of the girls to refill and empty glass or bring another bottle. This was Henry Bragg.

Two men who drew Matt's interest were the two that sat on elevated platforms in straight-backed chairs. These were the shooters the marshal had told Matt about. He watched them for several minutes. Their gaze constantly swept the room back and forth, alert for any hint of trouble. These were professionals sure enough. Their alertness and the rifles lying across their knees told Matt these men were all business.

The fourth man that caught Matt's eye was a young fellow, most likely several years younger than himself. His black hat hung down his back on a leather neck cord, revealing blonde, curly hair that hung to his shoulders. Something about his cockiness and boisterous voice set him apart from all the others in the room. The man had gunfighter written all over him.

Matt found a table near the gunfighter that only had two Mexicans sitting at it. Without waiting for an invitation, he strode over, jerked out a chair and slouched into it. He conjured up his hardest stare and fixing it squarely on the two men, and it didn't them long to decide they had someplace else to go.

His two ex-table companions had no sooner left when a young, surprisingly pretty saloon girl sashayed up, draped an arm around his neck, leaned over, and whispered what she thought would be an irresistible invitation in his ear.

"Not tonight, I'm waiting on someone," he told her, shrugging off her arm.

"Maybe I'm the one you're waiting on and you just don't know it yet," she purred in what must have been, her most seductive voice. Leaning far over, she flashed him more than a devilish smile.

"Ma'am, I said, not tonight," he told her firmly.

Shrugging her bare shoulders, she stuck out her tongue at him in a childish gesture and moved on to find more receptive prey. The one she chose happened to be the blonde-haired gunfighter. She moved up behind him, slipped both arms around his neck and down the front of his shirt, then whispered something in his ear, biting playfully on his ear as she did. Whatever she said, he must have liked. He reared back in his chair, laughed loudly and shouted in a loud and boastful voice.

"Hey, bartender! Send us a bottle over here. Never let it be said that Reno ever turned down an offer like that."

Matt stiffened at the sound of the name. A flush washed over him and he felt that familiar burning on the back of his neck. A bitter taste of anger surged from the pit of his stomach and filled his throat. His mind instantly flashed back to that scene in their little farmhouse back in Arkansas. To the memory of his beautiful Amelia, lying naked on the floor, five ugly bullet holes leaving blackish holes where they invaded her body. This man was there— at the very least he allowed it—more likely did it himself. This was the famous Reno, a killer of women.

As quickly as the surge of anger had flooded over him, it washed away, leaving only a calm determination. He knew all too well this wasn't the time or the place for a showdown, but he also knew he had a job to do. Reaching down, he flipped away the traveling loops, thumbed back the hammers on both of his weapons and stood.

When he spoke he shouted the words out like rapid shots from a pistol, loud and clear and strong—words that somehow rang out above the noise of the room.

"You! The one called Reno. Stand up and step away from the table."

All noise suddenly stopped. The band stopped playing in mid-tune and fell silent. Gamblers stopped what they were doing and turned toward the voice. A strange hush fell over the room. Even the click-a-de-click of the roulette wheel sounded unusually loud as it wound to a stop.

Matt saw the gunfighter's body stiffen. His hands continued to hold his poker cards, his head didn't move, his eyes fixed straight ahead in a blank stare. The saloon girl jerked her hands away from the man's body as if it were suddenly red hot. She quickly straightened and backed away.

From the corner of Matt's eyes he saw the two platform shooters spring to their feet, heard shells levered into firing chambers and felt his body stiffen as rifles were lifted to their shoulders and trained squarely on him.

Matt saw the movement of people as they melted aside noiselessly, clearing a wide corridor from the line of fire around both Matt and the blonde-haired gunman.

"My name's Henry, Matt Henry, from up Arkansas way. I had a little farm and a wife I loved more than life. I had a six-year-old boy with hair about the color of yours.

"One day awhile back while I was out in the field plowing you and your gang of killers rode by. You raped my wife. When you finished with her you shot her five times just for sport. Then you cut my little boy's throat from ear to ear. For all that, Reno, you're gonna die. Right here! Right now!"

Again, Matt flicked a quick glance up at the platform shooters and stared directly into the nose of two rifles. Their fingers were on the triggers. He knew that at any second bullets might cut him down. If it had to be, so be it.

He saw the shooters' eyes cut down to their boss. Matt swung his gaze to Henry Bragg. The Cantina owner stood motionless, his stare fixed on Matt. Their eyes met and locked for a long moment. For a fleeting second, that seemed more like an eternity, the big gambler paused, as if contemplating the decision that would mean life or death for Matt Henry.

What would he decide? One nod of his head would mean certain death. Matt remembered hearing about the ancient gladiators that fought for the entertainment of the royalty. A thumbs-up by the ruler meant the gladiator lived, a thumbs-down meant his instant death.

Without breaking eye contact, Henry Bragg, for whatever reason, gave the slightest shake of his head. Matt didn't bother to look at the shooters again—he knew their rifles would be lowered. He swept his gaze back to Reno.

Seemingly recovered from the initial shock of being openly challenged, the gunfighter threw his head back and forced a loud laugh. Spreading his hands far away from his body he stood, kicked the chair violently backwards and turned to face his challenger.

"Did everybody hear this? This nobody farmer's gonna shoot it out with Reno."

Reno's cold green eyes crawled up and down Matt's body, pausing for a long moment at the Widow Maker strapped to Matt's left hip. Then across to the blue steel pistol with the black coiled rattler carved into the pearl white handle. Matt saw those eyes squint, then open wide.

"You got any idea who you're facing, mister?" Reno asked. "Nobody's ever beat Reno, nobody."

But the gunfighter's voice betrayed him. He didn't sound quite as cocky and sure of himself as before. Matt detected a sudden uncertainty. He decided he need to push it a little farther, to sow some more seeds of doubt in the man's mind.

"I want you to know what's gonna happen," he told the gunfighter. "The little lady there's gonna count to seven. Draw anytime you're ready to die, but when you do, one of two things are gonna happen.

"I'm either gonna draw with my left hand and put two loads of double aught buckshot right in your face and blow your head plumb off. Or, I might draw with my right hand and put five .44 slugs, one for every time you shot my wife, right through that tobacco sack in your left shirt pocket. Either way, you're gonna die.

"Talking's over. Start counting, lady. Do it now!" Matt ordered.

Matt's eyes found and locked on those squinting green eyes. He held the stare, never blinking, never wavering, and piercing the man's eyes, boring right into his soul. For a long minute the two men stood, locked in a combat of wills. Everybody in the room remained silent. Death hovered in the air, its stench filled the room, its presence waiting to see who it would claim tonight. Finally, the gunfighter's eyes wavered and began blinking wildly.

"Lady!" Matt shouted, "I said, count!"

The young saloon girl cringed backwards, shaking and looking terrified. So scared nothing but a hoarse whisper escaped her lips when she mouthed the word.

"One."

Reno glared back at Matt with a look of disbelief overwhelming his face, like he just couldn't believe someone, anyone, would dare face him in a gunfight, let alone openly challenge him.

"Two," the girl got out with a slightly stronger voice.

Matt continued his death stare that he had practiced many hours on. His eyes stared right into the gunman's eyes, never once blinking. He remembered what the old lawman had told him back in Arkansas. "A good gunfighter can kill you in the time it takes to blink your eyes."

"Three."

Matt felt his boldness had shaken the gunfighter's confidence. As an added measure, Matt curled his lips in a cruel smile and flexed the fingers of both hands.

"Four," the girl said.

Drops of sweat appeared on Reno's forehead. He licked his lips. His eyes blinked wildly and swung from side to side, as if searching for a way out. Matt could sense every gunfighter's worst enemy, fear, taking control of the man's mind and body. The two men faced each other, both knowing that within mere seconds one of them would be dead. Who would live? Who would die?

The Rio Grande Cantina was as quiet as a graveyard at midnight. Nobody dared move, nobody hardly breathed. It seemed time had simply stopped and everyone in the room was frozen in place. The long silence was finally broken by the reluctant saloon girl's terrified voice that had now risen to a squeaky shout.

"Five."

Matt knew the gunfighter would make his play sometime before the girl reached the final count of seven. He also knew the man's eyes would tell him the exact instant his mind made the decision to draw. The Town Tamer had said the signal that shoots from the brain to the hand, telling it to draw, always shows up first in the eyes.

"Six," the girl said anxiously, as if she anticipated somebody would die because she said it.

Suddenly, Matt saw what he had been watching for. A slight compression of the eyes, a tightening of the lips, an uncontrollable quiver of the cheek muscles. Reno was about to draw.

The man was fast...very fast. Without a doubt the fastest Matt had ever faced. In one swift, smooth movement, the gunfighter's hand streaked upward, grasping the butt of his Colt as it streaked past. Matt saw the man's pistol clear leather.

But this was about more than being a fast gun. This was about more than a lifetime of endless practice, or natural ability, or reputation. This was about justice and making wrong things right. This was about Matt's wife and little boy.

In less than a heartbeat, faster than the human eye could follow, the hand that only a split second before, hung casually at Matt's side, magically held the pistol with the coiled rattler on its handle and it was spewing out hot nuggets of death from its fiery mouth.

One! Two! Three! Four! Five!

Five times it belched fire, lead and smoke. Five times an ugly hole punched through the tobacco sack in Reno's left shirt pocket. The thunderous roar of the five shots were so close together, it would have been near impossible to count them. The combined force of the shots drove the gunfighter staggering backwards. He was stone cold dead before his body hit the floor.

Matt's sweeping glance, first at the platform shooters, then around the room, revealed nothing but stunned men with their mouths open. Disbelief was mirrored on their hard faces, stunned at what they had just witnessed. Not one seemed the least interested in buying a ticket to the dance.

Matt quickly snapped open his pistol, ejected the spent cartridges and thumbed fresh shells into place without once glancing down, his stare still sweeping the room. He slammed the pistol shut and dropped it into his holster. Striding over to the body he snatched the unfired Colt from Reno's lifeless grasp and shoved it down into his own waistband.

"I'm taking this man out of here," Matt said firmly, fixing his cold stare on Henry Bragg. "Anybody got any objections, now is the time to speak up."

The heavyset saloon owner dropped his eyes, slowly shook his head and turned away. Matt lifted the lifeless body to his left shoulder and strode for the front door. The crowd that had jammed the front doors to watch the fight, now melted aside at Matt's approach.

"Which horse did this man ride in on?" Matt demanded of a rifle-toting guard.

The tough Mexican pasted a cruel-looking half-smile on his lips and pointed to a sorrel gelding with a white blaze face. Matt hefted the body across the saddle and drawing his Bowie, cut a length of rope from the man's own lariat rope and used it to tie his feet, then ran the rope under the horse's belly and tied it to his hands on the other side.

Matt strode to his own mount, stepped aboard and walked his horse back to the sorrel. Reaching down, he gathered the horse's reins. Amid whispered conversations, he felt a hundred eyes follow him as he rode slowly across the town square, leading the sorrel.

"He beat Reno slicker'n-a-whistle," Matt overheard someone say, "that hombre, whoever he is, is so quick you couldn't even see him draw."

"Put five bullets right where he said he was going to," another said loud enough to hear, "and he done it faster than a man could count. Never seen anything like it."

"He's the fastest I ever saw," yet another agreed.

The dim light from the town square gave way to pitch darkness as Matt rode cautiously down the narrow street toward the river. An occasional light from a window cast a shaft of light onto the dusty street. A thin sliver of moon cast eerie shadows from every direction. Matt peered through the darkness into every shadow, knowing death could be lurking there.

He had passed several adobe shanties when he caught a movement out of the corner of his eye. He palmed the Rattler and thumbed back the hammer before he recognized the prodigal daughter from the Cantina as she emerged from the shadows.

"I, I'm sorry," she stammered, "I didn't mean to startle you. Mr. Bragg wants to see you."

Without waiting for a reply she half-spun on her feet and retreated into the darkness between two shacks. Though he was at a loss to understand why, he followed. She led him to the back of the Cantina, through a door into a small hallway. Coming to a door on the right, she tapped lightly and stepped aside for Matt to enter.

"Uhh-uh," Matt said, "you first."

Stepping to one side of the door, he pushed it open and shoved the girl through ahead of him.

Henry Bragg stood behind a large desk in a gaudily furnished office. He chewed on an unlit cigar, continually shifting it from one side of his mouth to the other. His red face was sweaty. His balding head shined in the lamplight.

"That will be all, Pearl," he told the girl, dismissing her abruptly. She slipped out quickly, apparently happy to do so.

"Thank you for coming, Mr. Henry. I wasn't sure you would. I'm Henry Bragg. I own this town and everything in it. That was quite a show you put on out there."

"It wasn't a show, Mr. Bragg. I killed a man that needed killing like I would kill a rattlesnake. No more—no less. I'm beholden to you for calling off your shooters, I didn't want to have to kill them, too."

"I don't believe I've ever encountered a man so sure of himself," Bragg said, opening a wooden box full of cigars and offering Matt one.

"No thanks," Matt said. "Somebody once told me when a man believes he can't do something, he's probably right. What was it you wanted to see me about?"

"I'm a businessman, Mr. Henry. Oh, to be sure, it's not the kind of business most folks would approve of and I can understand that. My wife and I were married twenty years before we were able to have children. Now we have a beautiful little boy and girl. I love them, Mr. Henry, just like you loved your wife and little boy. When I heard you tell what Jack Trotter and his gang did to your wife and son, well, nobody ought to do that to a man's family, nobody. That's where I draw the line, business or no business. That's why I called off my men.

"Trotter and his men were here, at least what was left of them. I'm assuming you had something to do with the rest of them not being along like they usually are. Jack left the day before yesterday. Two of his bunch stayed behind, Reno and one of Jack's boys, the one they call Luther.

"He's sweet on one of my girls named Rose. She's got her own place. Go out back, turn left, third house on the left. Like I said, killing a man is one thing, killing women and children like that is another."

"Thanks, Mr. Bragg, like I said, I'm beholden to you. By the way, beings we're talking, I understand you own that little café over across the river. Is it for sale?"

"Most everything's for sale, Mr. Henry, it's only a matter of price, but somehow, I can't imagine a man like you being interested in a small café in Laredo, Texas."

"Is it or ain't it for sale?"

"I guess I could let it go for a thousand dollars," the man said, finally lighting the cigar he'd been chewing on.

"I reckon I'd be willing to give you five hundred for it," Matt said, peeling the money from his pocket and tossing it on the desk. "Write me out a bill of sale."

The man hesitated only long enough to look Matt in the eyes. What he saw made him pull a paper from a desk drawer and write out a legal document, sign it and hand it to Matt.

"You know, Mr. Henry, A man like you could make a great deal of money hereabouts."

"Doing what?" Matt asked, shoving the paper into his pocket.

"There's a certain town marshal over in Laredo that's like a cockle-burr under my saddle. It would be worth two thousand dollars to me if he should—shall we say—have a fatal accident."

Matt felt a flash of sudden anger burn white-hot in his belly, rise warm on his neck and wash over his face. A hand snapped out and reached across the desk, grasping a fistful of the man's frilly shirt and jerked him halfway across the desk. Leaning over until his nose was only inches from Bragg's face, Matt spat out the words through clenched teeth.

"Now you listen to me cause I ain't gonna say this but once. You're talking about a friend of mine. You ain't nothing but a pompous little man with a belly full of self importance. The only reason I ain't gonna kill you right now for the offer you just made is because I owe you a couple of favors. You just used up one of them. If something, if anything, except old age, happens to Earl Tolleson, I promise you, Bragg, I'll be back. Do you understand what I'm telling you?"

You could have lit a cigar on the man's red face as he violently nodded his head. Matt turned him loose, wheeled and strode for the door. Outside, he left his horses tied where they were and made his way on foot past two small shanties, neither much bigger than a good-sized chicken coop, and peered through the darkness at the third house.

A dim light showed through the single small window. An Appaloosa with good markings stood three legged, tied to a bush beside the house. Judging by the number of horse droppings, the horse had stood there several hours.

Hammering back both guns, he put a foot to the flimsy door, kicking it completely off its leather hinges. An exceptionally pretty Mexican girl sprang from a small cot wearing nothing but a scared look.

Luther Trotter made a lunge for the pistol hanging in its holster on the back of a chair. He didn't make it. Matt's pistol barrel struck him just behind the left ear, sounding like a muffled pistol shot. The man dropped to the dirt floor like a sack of potatoes.

The girl didn't cry out or make a sound, or even act embarrassed. She just stood there in her birthday suit like it was an everyday occurrence. Come to think of it, maybe it was.

Jerking a blanket from the cot, he tossed it to the girl so she could cover herself while he emptied Luther's pockets. Matt pitched the wad of money he found onto the table, hefted the outlaw onto his shoulder and stalked out the door without a word.

A light still shone through the window of the marshal's office as Matt reined up, tied all three horses to the hitching rail and pushed through the door.

"Got a couple of customers for you Marshal," Matt said, as the lawman rose from a small bunk in the corner of the office and stomped on his boots.

"One needs a bed and the other needs burying."

Wiping the sleep from his eyes and ruffling his hair, the marshal followed Matt outside. Walking over to one of the bodies draped across their saddles he grabbed a handful of blond hair and lifted the man's head, staring at the face.

"Who is he?"

"That one goes by the name of Reno," Matt told the marshal. "He's supposed to have quite a reputation as a gunfighter, I think."

"Reputation didn't do him much good, did it?" the lawman commented, walking over to the other one.

"That one with the pump knot is one of Jack Trotter's boys, named Luther. He's likely to have a king sized headache when he comes around," Matt said. "Well, it's late and I'm tired. I'll tell you all about it over breakfast."

"What am I supposed to do with these fellows this time of night?" the marshal hollered at Matt's back as he took up his horse's reins and headed for the livery.

"Not my problem, Marshal. That's what they pay you all that money for," he called over his shoulder, lifting a hand to his new friend.

After seeing to his horse and returning to his hotel room, he propped a chair under the doorknob and started to undress. He had forgotten about the gunfighter's pistol he had shoved into his waistband. Withdrawing it, he started to lay it on the little table beside the bed when he noticed the notches.

Cut into the pistol's yellow bone handle were several of them. For long moments he stared absently at the gun. He had heard tell of men who notched their guns, mostly bullies and braggarts, he'd always figured. Sinking to sit on the side of the bed he let his finger drift slowly across each one, feeling it, counting as he went, wondering about the life each one represented.

Twelve. Twelve notches on a gun. Not much to testify of a life. Matt might well have been number thirteen. He had heard somewhere that thirteen was supposed to be an unlucky number. It sure had been for Reno.

Then it hit him. Wonder if one of those was for Amelia? Wonder if helpless women counted on the gunman's scorecard?

Matt nursed his third cup of coffee and visited with Marie when she wasn't busy waiting on other customers. He made arrangements with her for a special supper that night, explaining only that he had a special surprise for her and Manuel.

"Morning, Earl," Matt greeted the marshal cheerfully as the tall lawman strode in and pulled out a chair. "How's our prisoner this morning?"

"He's got a headache and a sore throat from cussing you all night. Thanks to you, I didn't get a wink of sleep all night. What did you hit him with? His head is as big as a pumpkin this morning."

"He run into the barrel of my pistol with his head," Matt kidded. "Did he tell you anything about the rest of the gang?"

"Nope, the only thing he told me was what his papa was gonna do to me after he tore down my jail. I'm thinking about taking him up to San Antonio tomorrow, just to be on the safe side."

"Might be a good idea," Matt said. "Trotter and the rest of his bunch rode out of Boys Town three days ago. I figure they're headed for a place down in Mexico called Anahuac, ever hear of it?"

"I reckon I have," the marshal said, "and it's all been bad. It's about two days' ride due south, but it sure ain't a place you'd be wanting to go. Say, now that I think on it, there's a Mex that walked in from there just a few days ago. Said his wife was sick and needed money to buy some medicine. He's working up at Peterson's store to earn enough for the medicine. He might be able to tell you something about the place."

"Thanks, Earl, I'll mosey up and talk with him after breakfast."

"So...?" the marshal said. "Are you gonna tell me about it or not?"

Matt related the whole story, just as it happened, leaving nothing out except the part about Bragg's two thousand-dollar offer.

"Now let me see if I got this straight?" the marshal said, "you just waltzed into that den of rattlesnakes, blowed a hole you could stick an ax handle through in a gunfighter with a reputation as the fastest gun around, then you pistol whipped the son of the most wanted outlaw in the country, slung them both across their saddles like stuck hogs and that bunch just let you ride out of there as big as you please? Is that what you're telling me?"

"Something like that," Matt said, sipping his coffee.

"Well, if that don't beat all," the marshal said, shaking his head in amazement.

Marie brought their breakfast and they both dug into it like they were starved.

"Oh," Earl said between mouthfuls, "almost forgot. I looked through my posters this morning, that's why I was late, that Reno fellow had quite a reputation. Two thousand dollars, dead or alive, and he sure qualified on the first part. What did you shoot him with anyway?"

"Five slugs from my .44, why you asking?"

"That's what the undertaker said, too. I laid a double eagle over the holes and covered all five. Never seen shooting like that. Oh yeah, I was telling you about the reward. Luther had a thousand dollars on his head, too. What're you gonna do with all that money?"

"Buy your breakfast I guess, course, I didn't know you had a double eagle when I agreed to it. Marie's fixing up a special supper for tonight. I've got a little surprise for her and Manuel. Hope you can make it."

"After all the extra work you've caused me, I figure it's a supper well deserved. I'll have to write you out a voucher for the reward money. We don't have a bank here in Laredo."

"Say you're taking Luther to San Antonio? How about leaving the voucher with Marshal McAllister? I'll pick it up later."

"Be glad to. You still dead set on following Trotter down into Mexico?"

"Yep,"

"Matt, for the life of me, I don't know how you done what you done last night and lived to tell about it. You can tell your grand kids you've been to hell and back."

"His name is Julio," the storekeeper told Matt. "He come walking in here, might near a week ago. He said his family was sick and needed to earn money for medicine. I didn't need anybody but I felt sorry for him and hired him anyway. He's leaving tomorrow and heading back home. Can you believe he walked four days to get here? He's a good worker, hate to lose him now."

"Mind if I talk to him?" Matt asked.

"Don't mind at all. He's out back loading a feed wagon."

Matt found the man just finishing up with the wagon. He was tall for a Mexican, real thin too, like he had missed too many meals, thin. He looked to be near thirty, maybe more. Matt found it hard to tell a Mexican's age. Right now he was dripping with sweat from loading the heavy feed sacks on the big wagon.

"Comprende Ud. Ingles?" Matt asked.

"Si, señor, I understand a little."

"Good," Matt said, "I hear you're from a place called Anahuac?"

"Si, señor. I am from that place."

"What can you tell me about it? I wish to go there."

"Oh, no, señor. You not go there. Very bad place for Americanos. Many bad soldados, many Comanchero. You not go there."

"Mr. Peterson tells me your wife is sick and needs medicine. I'd like to buy the medicine you need and have you guide me to Anahuac. Will you agree?"

"It is dangerous for you to go there, señor, but if you wish, I will guide you, si."

"Then it's settled. Let's go talk with Mr. Peterson, then we'll look up the doctor and get the medicine your wife needs. We'll leave at first light in the morning."

The storekeeper readily agreed and paid Julio the full week's wages. Matt and Julio went together to the doctor's office and got the medicine, then they walked to the marshal's office.

"Those two horses I brought in last night, what happens to them?" Matt asked.

"Depends," Earl told him, "I usually try to sell 'em to cover the burying. They're yours if you need 'em."

"Yeah, I reckon I do. Julio here walked all the way from Anahuac to get medicine for his wife. He's going to guide me there. He needs a horse."

"They're down at the livery. Tell old Luis they belong to you."

"Thanks, Earl, be seeing you at supper."

Matt traded one of the outlaw's saddles for a packsaddle and strapped it onto the sorrel. He threw his own pack on his pinto.

He and his new Mexican friend led the two packhorses up to Peterson's store to stock up on trail supplies. He bought four times the supplies they'd need, intending to give them to Julio when they got there.

He insisted that Mr. Peterson deck his friend out with new clothes from head to toe, then had Julio pick out a new dress for his wife, as well as new clothes for his three children. The Mexican was close to tears as they loaded their two packhorses with supplies.

After they returned the horses to the livery and removed the loaded packs, they walked to the hotel where Matt rented a room for his new friend and ordered up hot baths for both of them.

Julio looked like a new man when he and Matt walked into Marie's café that night. Matt was pleased to see that tables had been scooted together and even a vase of fresh flowers set on the table.

Marie's cousin was on hand to serve the other customers so both Manuel and Marie would be free to enjoy the special supper. Julio joined into the festivities and seemed to hit it off especially well with Manuel. Earl actually laughed on several occasions. It was a joyous time.

Over a cup of coffee after a wonderful meal, Matt stood to his feet. Everyone fell quiet, seemingly anxious to hear what their new friend had to say.

"Manuel, Marie, as Earl, here will tell you, I ain't much of a hand at wasting words, so I'll just get right to it. I came into town only a couple of days ago. You had never met me before, but in that short time, you all have made me feel a part of your life. I've never had much of that before and I don't mind telling you, it feels right good. Don't reckon I ever met two nicer, harder working folks than the two of you.

"There's been some times in my own life when I needed a hand. When I did, it seems like there's always been somebody there to reach out and give me the help I needed. I'd like to do the same for the two of you. I hear you've both been working your heads off trying to save enough to get married and maybe buy this little café.

"Julio and I will be pulling out first thing in the morning and I wanted to give you your wedding present tonight. This piece of paper I'm holding in my hand is a bill of sale. It says this building and everything in it now belongs to you, free and clear. When I ride back through here, I'm hoping I can look up on the front and see a sign that says, *Marie's.*"

It was one of those never to be forgotten nights.

CHAPTER VII

The Sojourner

"I am a stranger, and a sojourner
in a foreign land." (Psalms 39:12)

A bright, clear dawn gave birth to a velvety blue sky and drove the darkness away. The only sounds were the muffled crunch of hooves in the soft sand, the hypnotic rhythmic creak of saddle leather, or an occasional snort from one of their four horses. Matt and Julio rode in silence through the desert dawn, each lost in his own thought world.

As the two men rode, the country became increasingly more desolate. Windblown sand dunes, deep arroyos cut like great knife scars across the desert terrain mottled with blackened greasewood, octillo, cholla cactus, squaw bush and miles and miles of endless sand. Matt figured if somebody ever found a use for sand, he could be a wealthy man.

"It's gonna be a scorcher today," Matt said, squinting up at the blazing sun. The heat cooked into the white sand causing the distant horizon to shimmer with dancing heat waves. Not even noon and already a man could fry and egg on a flat rock."

They rode steady all day, stopping often to rest the horses. Twice Julio guided them up a canyon to a hidden water hole or rock tank he knew about. Matt knew that in the desert, water is life; one cannot survive long without it. The knowledge of where and how to find it is the most valuable information one can possess.

Since Matt had never been to Mexico, he asked a steady stream of questions about the land and the people. He figured knowing all he could about the country he was riding into could mean the difference between the success or failure of his mission.

Julio assured him that Mexico wasn't all sand. He spoke of the high mountain ranges like the Sierra Madre to the west. He told of lush green grassy river valleys. He talked of the people, of their hardships, their persecution by corrupt Mexican officials, of their daily struggle just to stay alive.

He told of his childhood as the son of a hacendados, one who owns land. He told how his father was a trainer of vaquero horses, known throughout all Mexico. He talked with sadness of the time, when he was only fifteen, when the local El Capitan and his men rode to their ranch and murdered his father and mother because the officer wanted his father's land. He explained that he was spared only because he was out riding his new pony.

Julio's voice took on a sound of hatred when he told of vowing to avenge his parents' death. How he practiced endless hours perfecting his skill with the throwing knife.

"It took me two years, señor," Julio explained. "When I was seventeen I was able to avenge the death of my parents."

"How did it happen?"

"I lay in hiding for many hours, señor, watching and waiting. I learned the evil man sometimes went riding alone on my father's ranch. I watched and saw that he rode the same trail to the river.

I waited for days. Finally, one morning he came. I stepped out from hiding and killed him with my throwing knife."

"Why don't you carry it now?" Matt asked.

"Si, señor, I always carry my knife."

In a move that was nothing but a blur of motion, Julio's hand swept up behind his neck, then swung forward in one continuing motion. The sunlight reflected off a sliver streak hurtling toward a nearby clump of sagebrush. The thin blade pinned a desert rattler's head firmly to the crusted desert sand.

"We will have rattlesnake for our supper," Julio announced proudly, sliding off his horse and deftly cutting the snake's head off.

"How did you do that?" Matt wanted to know, amazed at the Mexican's uncanny skill.

"My knife hangs down my back, señor, in a leather scabbard, suspended by this leather cord around my neck. The bottom of the sheath is held in place by another cord that is tied around my stomach."

"That's scary," Matt said. "Can you handle a gun, too?"

"My father taught me to shoot the rifle, señor, I am not good with the pistol."

Julio guided them into the mouth of a shallow canyon. For more than a mile they wound along the bottom of the twisted furrow in the desert. Finally they rounded a sharp cutback and came upon a fresh running little spring. It had formed a pool, maybe ten or twelve feet across of fresh, cool water.

They made camp beside the little pool. Matt watered and cared for their horses while Julio prepared what he called, pione bistec, or poor man's steak. Surprisingly, it was delicious. Julio explained that it was rattlesnake, cooked with potatoes, peppers and onions.

After supper they settled down with a cup of coffee and talked some more. Julio told Matt about his family. His face beamed with pride when he spoke of his wife, Marquitta.

"She is the most beautiful woman in all of Mexico, señor Matt. I would give my life for her this very minute. Rosetta, our daughter, is sixteen and looks just like her mother. Juan, our oldest son, is fifteen. Like his father and his father's father, He is a trainer of horses. Then there is Chico," Julio sighed and spread his hands. "There is no other like my Chico. He is ten years old, you will see."

Over the course of the next two cups, Matt shared about his own life. He told about his parents being massacred by the Chiricahua Apache when he was six years old and about spending the next eight years as a captive. He told his new friend how he learned the ways of The People, as the Apache call themselves, and spoke of his escape when he was fourteen.

He shared with Julio how he signed on with a cattle drive, of learning how to use a gun and of being forced into a fight and killing a man in self defense on his sixteenth birthday. He spoke of the five years hard labor in the Yuma Territorial Prison and of the beatings he endured.

He talked about his own family and their times of happiness and, with tears welling up inside him and a lump in his throat, he spoke sadly of the events of their death, of his recovery and his vow to bring their killers to justice.

"There's only five of them left now," Matt told his Mexican friend. "They are protected by a man called El Capitan. He's supposed to be the Mexican officer in charge at Anahuac. Do you know him?"

"Si, señor, I know him. He is a very bad man. Many bad men pay him much money to protect them. The Comanchero have a large camp not far from our village. They too, pay this man. My wife's sister works for him as a cook and housekeeper at his casa. She does not like to do so, but her husband disappeared three months ago and this is the only way she has to live. He has a very large hacienda on the banks of the Rio Salido River. Its walls are high and thick. There are many guards. He is a very dangerous man, señor."

"How many soldiers does he have in Anahuac?" Matt asked.

"Perhaps as many as one hundred. You must be very careful, señor, the El Capitan is very suspicious. He has many spies. He will know of your presence in Anahuac."

They talked far into the night but were up, had breakfast over and in the saddle well before the sun peeked over the horizon. By midmorning Matt saw what appeared to be an unbroken line of tall outcroppings up ahead and wondered how they would get through them with their horses.

"Is there a way through that line of hills," he asked, "or do we have to go around?"

"Si, señor, there is a way through. It is a narrow passage large enough for the horses to get through. It is very far if we must go around. It is very dangerous place, señor, the bandidos like to lie in wait for travelers and rob them. I myself had to climb over the mountains when I came."

"I sure don't like the looks of it," Matt said, concern coming onto his face.

Still some distance away, they reined up and sat their horses. Matt peered through squinted eyes at the surrounding area. Swiping the black, flat-brimmed Stetson from his head, he raked an arm across his sweaty forehead and turned to his Mexican friend.

"We can't afford the time to go around but I don't like the looks of it. I don't like it one bit. We best keep our eyes peeled and listen hard," he told Julio, pitching his friend the Henry rifle he had taken from Reno's saddle boot.

"Stay here. If you see or hear anything—anything at all— give me a holler. I'm gonna look around a bit."

He knew it was most likely a waste of time since tracks wouldn't last long with the stiff breeze blowing like it was and shifting the soft sand. Nevertheless, he rode a large circle searching for signs. Finding nothing, he rode back to where Julio waited. Matt loosened the traveling thongs and pulled back the hammers on both of his weapons to full cock.

"Go ahead and lever a shell into your rifle and let's ride real easy. If you see anything that don't look right, let me know right quick."

"Si, señor."

The pass looked long, maybe forty yards or so and very narrow, barely wide enough for a wagon to pass between the high rock walls. Cautiously, they approached the entrance. Matt swept his gaze back and forth, searching the sandy ground for any telltale sign, watching the far end of the opening, twisting to look behind them.

He was nervous. He felt that old familiar burning sensation on the back of his neck and he didn't like it. He listened intently for any sound that shouldn't be there. He watched his big stallion's ears for any hint of trouble.

Riding slowly, they moved toward the end of the pass, still no problem. Suddenly Midnight's ears twitched nervously and pointed forward. Something was wrong. Someone was there at the end of the pass.

They came from both sides of the opening, their horses streaming across the pass, completely blocking the way. Matt quickly counted nine of them, all tough looking Mexicans and well armed. Matt knew immediately they were Comanchero, the scavengers of the desert. The most ruthless, bloodthirsty excuse for a human to walk the face of the earth. A mixture of Mexicans, Indians and Americans, they were the rejects of every society.

Matt heard a noise behind them. He shot a quick glance around to see four more had somehow hidden until they passed, then moved into the pass at their back, blocking any hope of escape.

"Julio," Matt whispered as they sat their saddles, "Sit real easy and stay ready. When I say now, take out the one on the right with the shotgun, then belly down and ride like hell. Don't worry about me, I'll catch up if I can, understand?"

"Si, señor."

The obvious leader of the pack rode a dappled gray mare. The usual bandoleers filled with bullets crisscrossed his barrel chest. He wore two pistols, reversed, with the butts facing forward. His ragged sombrero sat on back of his dirty, shaggy hair. He had a chiseled, pockmarked face with a slash of angry mouth. Tobacco stains began at each corner and discolored his long unshaven beard. An overdone, faked smile revealed yellowed, tobacco-stained teeth, except for a gold tooth in front. His icy stare raked Matt from head to toe, pausing when he saw the sawed-off double barrel on Matt's hip.

"Aaah, gringo, ezz you lost? Maybeso you take a wrong turn at the river, no? You ezz in Mejecco now, gringo. Theeez ezz a bad place for gringo. Many bad hombres. You could get robbed or something."

Matt sat easy in his saddle, both hands on his saddle horn, not saying a word, just staring hard at the one doing the talking. It was a game. They both knew it would come down to a shootout, but first, he had to have his fun.

"Aaah, señor, madre de Dios, you find my black horse, sure enough what ezz stole from me. You bring it back to Tico Cruz, eh? Gracias, señor. Now eeef you climb off my horse, I take it and the packhorse too. Then you are free to go, eh? Tico Cruz is a fair man, eh?"

Times like this, a body does some mighty fast thinking. About the only story Matt could come up with on such short notice was pretty farfetched, but it would have to do. Maybe it would buy them some time. What the heck, he thought, we're likely gonna die right here anyway, what's one more little lie more or less?

"Looking for a friend of mine," Matt said with a straight face, "thought you fellas might have heard of him. I was kinda hoping maybe you might even know where I could find him."

"I -yi-yi," the Comanchero said, smiling broadly. "You look for a friend, uh? What ezz your friend's name? Maybeso we hear of him?

"He's called, Scar Face," Matt lied, remembering Julio had told him the leader of the Comanchero was a white man that had been raised by the Apache, just as Matt had been, and who used that name.

"Yes siree," Matt continued to pour it on thicker than molasses, "me and old Scar Face are blood brothers, we are. We both lived with the Apache, we're blood brothers, him and me. We got separated awhile back. I heard he was down in these parts and come to look him up. Scar Face and me are real thick. Why, I wouldn't be surprised if my blood brother done something real nice for the man that brought us back together."

The story was so ridiculous it almost sounded convincing. A sudden confused look came all over the bandit's ugly face. Clearly, he had intended simply to kill both Matt and the Mexican peon riding with him, take everything they had and ride away. Now, he was obviously doing some re-thinking.

"Ahh, thezz ezz your lucky day, gringo, I know of such a man. I will take you to him, but first, señor, I must ask that you remove your guns and drop them on zee ground."

Well, it had come down to it. Matt had no intention of surrendering their guns or going anywhere with this bunch. The time for playing ring around the rosy was over. It had come to shooting time.

Casually, he moved both hands toward his belt buckles, as if to do what the man asked. Suddenly his left hand darted to the butt of the Widow Maker, pushed down and as he swiveled his lower body in the saddle to the left, he pulled the trigger.

The twin loads of pellets exploded from the noses of the sawed-off and like a swarm of angry hornets, screamed forward, destroying everything in their path.

"Now!" Matt screamed above the roar of his shotgun.

From the corner of his eye Matt saw a sliver blade hurtle toward the fat Comanchero with the shotgun. Flicking a quick glance, Matt saw the knife bury itself deep into the bandit's chest, causing the man to drop his shotgun and grasp the knife with both hands, tugging frantically to pull it free.

Three of the outlaws were blown clear out of their saddles by the heavy pellets from Matt's Widow Maker. Horses screamed in agony and reared, unseating their riders. Even as the Comanchero leader clawed for his guns, Matt palmed his own pistol. Two rapid shots tore pieces of the man's shirt away from two holes in the man's chest, then blood came squirting from the holes. He toppled backwards from his saddle.

Matt heard Julio's rifle bark beside him. A puff of smoke reeled away on the wind and another bandit grabbed his stomach and slumped forward in his saddle.

A bearded man raised his rifle and Matt shot him. The bandit's face mirrored surprise, then sudden pain as his horse reared, spun and fell to its knees, the rider spinning from the saddle. The horse let out a pitiful scream.

Julio was charging straight through the mass of horses and men, riding full out, hugging the neck of his mount, slapping the Appaloosa on its rump with the barrel of his rifle. The sorrel packhorse was struggling to keep up.

Digging his heels deep into Midnight's flanks, Matt grabbed the saddle horn with one hand to keep from being unseated as the big stallion responded by setting his back hooves and shooting forward. Matt cast a glance over his shoulder to see if his little pinto packhorse was still with them. The lead rope was stretched taunt, but she was struggling hard and managing to stay on her feet. That same look revealed the four Mexicans that had entered the pass behind them were charging after them, firing as they came.

Twisting in his saddle, he threw two quick shots in their direction, hoping to slow their pursuit. It didn't. His gut tightened as a bullet glanced off the cantle of his saddle, only inches from his lowered face.

Up ahead, Julio's Appaloosa was running belly to the ground. His Mexican friend rode low, hugging the saddle, still slapping his horse with his rifle, urging it to greater speed. This amigo would do to ride with, Matt thought.

He knew they had been lucky. He also knew their luck wasn't likely to hold much longer unless he somehow got those bandits off their tail. Pulling up alongside Julio's packhorse and leaning far over, Matt cut the rawhide binding that held his big Sharps buffalo rifle in place and pulled it free.

"Keep riding," he shouted, "I'll catch up."

Veering to his left toward a jumbled pile of rocks he had spotted, he hauled back on Midnight's reins as he neared the rock pile. The big stallion skidded to a stop, even as Matt left the saddle and hit the ground running. He dropped to one knee beside a large boulder, dumped the .52 caliber cartridges from the small bag he kept tied to the handle and quickly fed the hungry chamber with four of the heavy bullets and slammed the gate shut.

The four bandits had split up, two riding hard after Julio and the other two coming straight toward Matt. They were most of two hundred yards away. He lifted the big long rifle to his shoulder and laid the sight on the middle of the lead rider's chest, took a deep breath, let it out and gently squeezed the trigger.

The explosion from the buffalo gun rocked Matt's shoulder. Like an unseen hand had suddenly swiped the bandit from the back of his horse, the rider spun crazily, twirling in midair, arms and legs askew. The man's body bounced like a child's rag doll along the ground, coming to stop in a plume of dust. Seeing his comrade fall, the other outlaw fought to turn his mount. Whipping the reins, he tried desperately to hurry his horse somewhere else.

Matt slammed another shell into the chamber and set the sights on the back of one of Julio's pursuers. The explosion was deafening. Blue-black smoke boiled from the muzzle as the heavy slug sped on its way towards its target. In the distance, the Comanchero arched his back and flew from his saddle.

Julio's remaining pursuer reined his mount in a wide turn and, laying flat in his saddle, headed back toward the opening as fast as his horse could carry him. Forced to aim low, the bullet hit the man's horse. Its churning legs buckled under him, sending the rider flying over the horse's head. Miraculously, the man scrambled to his feet and lit out afoot, running for the mouth of the pass.

Only one left and he was nearing the safety of the opening, his mount running full out. Matt rammed another shell in place and slammed the gate shut. He drew back the hammer. He laid the sight on the man's back. Just as the rider entered the shadows of the pass, Matt squeezed the trigger and knew satisfaction when he saw the fleeing horse swerve as the rider's weight shifted to one side, his rifle flying from his hands. Arms and legs flailed in a ball of dust.

Matt lowered the big rifle and watched as the only remaining Comanchero disappeared into the darkness of the pass, not even slowing down as he ran past his fallen comrades. Wherever he was headed, it would be a mighty long run.

Julio had turned around and was riding back toward Matt. Together, they made their way back to the scene of the slaughter. Dead and dying Comanchero were sprawled everywhere. Their blood made puddles of red in the white sand. Wounded horses squealed and snorted pitifully, the sound tugging at Matt's heart.

Matt turned away as Julio mercifully put them out of their misery.

While Julio gathered up the best of the weapons, along with the unwounded Comanchero horses, Matt went through the pockets of the outlaws. What little he found he handed to his Mexican friend.

"They most likely stole it from some of your people anyway," Matt told him, "You done real good awhile ago. I'm right proud to be riding with you."

Crimson sprays reached skyward from the setting sun and painted a cloudless horizon a bright red with its rays of light as Matt and Julio topped a line of low hills and gazed down at the winding Rio Salido River. Like a great snake it slithered its way across the desert countryside.

They crossed just after sundown, pausing to allow their horses, now numbering nine, to slake their thirst from the muddy stream. Pointing upriver, Julio showed Matt a large complex that, from that distance, looked like a fort.

"That is the El Capitan's hacienda, señor. It sits right on the bank of the river and is surrounded on three sides by high walls. Only the side facing the river is open. Armed guards patrol around the wall day and night."

"Sounds like a mighty nervous fellow," Matt said.

"It will be dark soon, señor, that is good. The eyes of many watch every movement from here on."

Another half hour brought them to a hill overlooking the small village of Anahuac. Matt peered through the settling darkness at a walled enclosure near the edge of the village.

"What's that?" he asked his friend.

"That is the soldaderas quarters," Julio said. "The stables for their horses are in the back. We must circle around the village, señor, my casa is four miles away on the far side of the village."

They made it without incident and rode toward the light from a single window. Julio quickly swung from the saddle and hurried into the house while Matt loosened cinch straps and pulled saddles from the tired horses. He turned all the horses, except his two, into a pole corral nearby.

A shaft of light streamed from an opened door as Julio appeared and motioned him inside. Matt strode through the door and came face to face with the most beautiful señorita he had ever laid eyes upon. The sight of her took Matt's breath away.

She looked to be about his own age. Her coal black hair cascaded over one shoulder and lay against the thin white blouse that stretched tight by the swell of her breasts. Matt's gaze dropped for a fleeting moment, then quickly looked away to seem proper. Her skin was without flaw, like creamed coffee in a china cup. Matt's throat ran dry and he swallowed.

"Buenas noches, señor," she said, tilting her head and offering a warm smile. "I am Avianna, Julio's sister-in-law."

"Si, señorita, Julio has spoken of you. How is your sister?"

"She is very ill, señor, but she will be better now that Julio has returned safely. We were very worried for him. It is so far and dangerous."

"Yes, it was," Matt said, not trusting his eyes to look at her. "We brought some supplies, I'll bring them in."

"I will help," she said, heading toward the door with him.

It took several trips, but they soon had everything inside. Matt drew back an empty chair and sat himself at the plank table. Avianna busied herself putting on a pot of coffee and preparing a meal from the supplies they had brought along with what little they had left.

"You arrived just in time," she told him. "We ran out of everything more than a week ago. I have been slipping a few things from the El Capitan's hacienda where I work, even so, it has not been enough. Perhaps a good meal and the medicine will help my sister feel better."

The coffee was boiling and the sweet aroma filled the small home. Matt glanced around the room of the small house. It was clean and neat but the poverty was apparent. Even for a hard worker like Julio, when there was no way to earn a living, to provide more than the bare necessities must be awfully tough.

"Julio told me of your husband's disappearance. Do you have any idea what might have happened to him?"

"No, señor, Benito walked to a small village looking for work, he has not been seen since. I am very fearful, señor. Many bad things happen in this part of Mexico. There are many bad men."

Julio parted the faded Mexican blanket that separated one of the two bedrooms from the only other room in the small home.

"Come, señor Matt, I want my wife to meet you," he said, holding the curtain aside.

Matt stepped through the door, followed by Avianna. He took one look at the beautiful lady lying in the bed and stopped dead in his tracks. She was the mirror image of Avianna.

"What is?" Matt stammered, looking back and forth between the two. He couldn't believe his eyes. It was as if he was seeing double. "You didn't tell me they were twins."

"Not just twins," Julio said proudly, with more than a little mischief in his face. "Identical twins. So close it is sometimes hard for even me to tell them apart."

"Well if that don't beat all," Matt said, amazed at what he was seeing. "I'd be afraid that might get me into trouble, if I was you."

"Si, señor," Julio's wife said, smiling. "It sometimes gets Julio in trouble, too."

Matt glanced at his Mexican friend and couldn't help cracking a grin when he saw Julio's face flush with embarrassment.

"Senor, Matt, this is my wife, Marquitta," Julio said quickly, seemingly anxious to change the subject.

"Welcome to our humble casa, señor. My husband has told me many things you have done for us. Gracias, señor. It is very good to meet you."

"It's good to meet you, too. It might take me awhile to get over the shock of seeing two such beautiful ladies all at once, especially two that look exactly alike. I have never seen identical twins before," Matt told her.

"Senor Matt is a very brave man. He has saved my life," Julio told them.

"Where are your children?" Matt asked. "I am anxious to meet them."

"They are staying at Avianna's casa until my wife recovers," Julio said.

"Well it's awfully nice to meet you, Mrs. Sanchez," Matt told her. "I hope the medicine helps you to recover quickly. I'll see if I can help Avianna in the kitchen, I'm sure the two of you have a lot to talk about."

Matt followed Avianna back into the kitchen. His eyes kept betraying him and lingered longer than they should on her swaying hips as she walked in front of him.

She insisted that he sit at the table as she took down a cup from a shelf and poured him a cup of steaming coffee. He purposely avoided looking up, afraid their eyes might meet, afraid his own eyes might reveal the forbidden thoughts that were in his mind.

"I'm looking for a man named Jack Trotter," Matt told her, anxious to change the direction of his thoughts. "He's a big man, red hair and beard. He wears a black patch over one eye. I don't suppose you might have seen him?"

"Si, señor," she said, stopping what she was doing and looking at him, "he and his woman are at the El Capitan's hacienda even now. They arrived a week ago."

"I see," Matt said, taking a long swig of coffee. "Tell me about the guards at this place. How many are there? Where do they sleep? How often do they change? That sort of thing, anything you can think of that might help me."

They talked for several minutes. She explained every detail of the large compound and about the guards. As they talked she finished up the meal and, drawing back an empty chair, joined Matt and Julio at the table.

Marquitta had eaten a few bites and after taking some of the medicine Julio had brought, finally drifted off to a restful sleep. They ate a delicious meal of spicy barbecued goat meat, beans swimming in juice speckled with cilantro and bits of cebolla onions, hot tortillas and lots of picante sauce.

It was getting on to midnight when Matt pushed back from the table and stood.

"It wouldn't be good for me to be here come morning. Someone might see me and cause trouble for your family. I'll be seeing you again real soon though. Thanks for your hospitality."

"Gracias, señor," Julio told him, extending a hand in farewell.

"Be careful, señor," Avianna said, her eyes lingering for a long moment on his. Matt felt his face flush and quickly tore his eyes away.

Slipping quickly out the door, he gathered the lead rope for his packhorse and booting a stirrup, swung onto his black stallion. Avianna stood in the doorway, the shaft of light from inside framing her beauty. Matt took one last look and reined his horse away and into the inky darkness of the night.

Out of the corner of his eye he caught a movement over near a grove of mesquite bushes. He swung a quick gaze, but saw nothing more. Maybe a dog or coyote, or even a stray goat, he figured.

Skirting the sleeping town, he watched his back trail closely, unable to shake the feeling he was being followed, though he saw nothing. Maybe I'm just nervous being in a strange country, he told himself.

He faced the wind and sniffed its fragrances, the acrid scent of sappy mesquite and a hint of dust. The desert was empty, bathed in soft starlight above the silent hills. Only a distant coyote's bark and a night owl asking its eternal question broke the quietness as Matt rode on through the night.

It took him most of an hour to get to the river, half that much to find what he was looking for. A dry wash, no more than a quarter of a mile from the El Capitan's walled hacienda. A thick grove of scrub willow hid the wash that ran down to the river. It ought to offer enough concealment for him to keep an eye on the comings and goings the following day while he formulated his plan. He figured to make his move the following night.

He let his horses drink their fill before picketing them in a small offshoot that offered good graze. He spread his bedroll on a flat place nearby, pried off his boots and settled down for some rest. He was dead tired.

By the time he heard his stallion's snorted warning and flicked open his eyes it was already too late. Through the light of a full moon, he stared up at twenty or more rifles in the hands of some mighty unhappy looking soldiers. He knew one wrong move would mean instant death in a hail of bullets.

A soldier in a uniform of the federales slid down the steep embankment and quickly removed Matt's weapons, jerked his hands behind him and tied them tightly. A long Mexican riata was tossed down to the soldier. He dropped a loop over Matt's head, down his body, and jerked it tight around his ankles. That gave him more than a hint of what they had planned for him and it sure wasn't welcome news. From his days with the Apache he had seen men dragged and it wasn't a pretty sight.

The free end of the woven leather lariat was tossed up to a giant of a monster that resembled a man. He was the biggest man Matt had ever seen. He had to be pushing seven feet and would easily weigh three hundred fifty pounds.

The giant caught the end of the reata deftly with his right hand. Matt's stomach did a flip-flop when he saw the monster do a half hitch around his Mexican saddle horn. In the big man's left hand he held what looked like a small tree. It was a pole nearly six feet long and as big around as the calf of Matt's leg. The bark had been stripped off and both ends were rounded. The giant wore a pistol but Matt suspected the big stick was his weapon of choice.

Sitting on a beautiful white horse beside the big Mexican was an army officer who, Matt reckoned, was none other than the notorious El Capitan. He appeared to be tall for a Mexican, very thin and wore a neatly trimmed mustache. He was almost handsome, at least until he spoke.

"Ah, hombre, you going to sleep your life away?" the man said in a faked friendly tone. It was a voice that could sound friendly while his hand slit your throat. "When I hear there is a gringo in our country, I come to offer my welcome and I find you sleeping."

The man wore a full Officer's uniform with the gold buttons of his jacket buttoned all the way to his neck. Gold braid adorned both shoulder boards and cap. He sat straight and tall in his silver trimmed saddle, one leg crooked around the large Mexican saddle horn and smoking a long thin cigar.

Matt saw the answer as to how they had known he was here before he asked the question of himself. He saw the El Capitan hand a coin to a fat little Mexican in a tattered serape standing beside him. That had to be one of the spies Julio had warned about and most likely what he had seen earlier near Julio's casa.

"Allow me to show you how we welcome gringos to Mexico, señor," the officer said, nodding to the Mexican giant.

The big man eased his gray down the bank and turned its nose up the dry wash, kicking the horse into a gallop. Matt watched with horror as the slack went out of the fifty foot reata.

Just before the leather rope played out, he leaped into the air and stretched his legs far out, hoping to prevent it from breaking both ankles when it snapped taunt and jerked him off his feet. The reata popped like a bullwhip when the slack went from it.

He landed flat on his back, knocking the breath out of him for a moment. The galloping horse dragged him along the bottom of the crusted sand wash. His body bounced like a rag doll as the left the crevice and headed out across the desert.

Speeding along on his back, the sand ground at his back like a whetstone sharpening an ax. Rocks and sticks embedded in the sand ripped at his clothes and skin, gouging out chunks of flesh from his buttocks, back and legs. The leaves of the yucca plant sliced and slashed him like sharp knives. Cactus and prickly pear pierced his body with a thousand needle-like spears.

The pain was unbearable. He clamped his jaws tightly shut to stifle the screams, determined to refuse them pleasure from his pain. How long the giant dragged him he didn't know. A black fog began to envelop him like a blanket. Finally, the welcome peace of total darkness brought an end to the pain. His last conscious thought was of Amelia.

A bucket of cold water shocked him into consciousness. He struggled to force his eyes open. He was lying inside a room on a tile floor stained red by his own blood. It was light. He couldn't believe he was still alive. Considering the way his body was hurting, he wasn't so sure being alive was such a good thing.

Glancing down, he was horrified at what he saw. He was completely naked. His body looked like a skinned jackrabbit. From his knees to his neck, he was nothing but a mass of cuts, bruises and sandy dried blood crusted over raw meat. A dozen open wounds were still oozing blood forming little puddles on the floor.

Sitting nearby watching, like a king on a throne in a large upholstered chair of red velvet and smoking another of those long, thin cigars, was the El Capitan.

Standing beside the chair was the man Matt had chased halfway across the country. The man he hated worse than a rattlesnake and had sworn to kill. Jack Trotter glared at Matt from a single eye, the other covered with a black eye patch.

On the other side of the Officer's chair stood an attractive woman with flaming red hair. Matt could only guess this was Lilly Sawyer, Trotter's woman.

"Ah, gringo, did you sleep well? Each time I see you it seems you are sleeping. How you like your visit to our country so far, gringo? Did you enjoy our little welcome for you, eh?"

If looks could kill, the smirking El Capitan would be as dead as a doornail. Matt was repaid for the look by a nod from the Mexican officer to the giant standing behind Matt. The brutal blow from the big stick brought the sickening sound of a bone snapping. At least one rib had just been broken, adding to the misery Matt's body was already in.

"Ah, gringo, you make yet another big mistake. In our country, when an officer asks a question, it is not a wise thing not to answer. Now we try again, eh? If I do not like the answer, El Toro will simply break something else. What is your name?"

Matt opened his mouth to speak, but the words wouldn't come out. On the third try he finally got sound to go with the words he mouthed.

"Henry, Matt Henry,"

"Ah, that is good, gringo, see how much easier it is when you answer my questions? Where do you come from, Matt Henry?"

"Wichita," Matt lied, knowing if he said Arkansas, Trotter would immediately put two and two together. "I'm from Wichita, Kansas."

"Why have you come to our country, gringo? What are you doing here?"

"I'm looking for work. A fellow I used to know said his boss might be looking for some men. He said I could find him down here," he lied, his side hurting with every word he spoke.

"Ah, you look for work, eh? What kind of work you do, gringo? Are you a herder of goats perhaps?"

"You saw the tools of my trade. Some say I'm a fair hand with a gun."

"Ah, then you are a—how shall I say it—a pistolero? Are you a pistolero, gringo?"

"It's a living," Matt replied.

Matt flicked a quick glance at Trotter to see if there was any sigh of recognition in his face. He knew the moment the outlaw figured out who he really was, there would be a permanent end to his suffering. Matt saw the outlaw lean over and whisper something to the Mexican officer.

"My friend wants to know the man's name that told you his boss might be looking for men."

"Calls himself Reno. I ran into him up at Boys Town a few days ago. He said to ask for a man named Trotter, I think it was, said he might be able to use me."

"Trotter?" the Mexican said, as if searching him memory for anyone by that name. "I never hear of a man by that name. Do you know such a man?" he asked, turning to the bearded outlaw beside him.

"My friend does not seem to know anyone by that name either. It seems you are out of luck, gringo. But do not feel badly, if you are still alive by tomorrow, I will find work for you."

The El Capitan pushed from the chair to his feet and headed for the door. Trotter followed. The woman with flaming red hair held back and spoke for the first time.

"He's bleeding all over your pretty floor, Captain. Let me clean and patch him up a little. He'll be worth more to you alive than dead."

"Alive or dead, what is that to me?" the Mexican officer said over his shoulder. "He is nothing but a piece of trash to be thrown to the dogs, nothing more."

"He looks very strong or he would be dead already," she argued. "He would make a good worker for your silver mine."

"Why are you wanting to mess with him?" Trotter asked, stopping to glare at her. "He'll be dead before dark anyway."

"Jack, you know how I hate to see anyone suffer. What would it hurt? Besides, it'll give me something to do, I'm getting bored hanging around this place."

Trotter didn't bother to reply he just shrugged, turned on his heels and followed the Mexican from the room leaving Matt and the woman alone.

"I'll get some rags and hot water and be right back," she said, hurrying from the room.

Matt laid his head back on the hard floor. He hurt all over. Every breath brought a sharp pain in his side where the giant had hit him. His body burned as if it were on fire from the raw skin and a thousand sharp needles. He tried to raise up and grimaced as a sharp pain shot through him.

The pretty redhead returned carrying a pan of warm water, several large rags and a tin of salve. She knelt beside him and bathed his face with a wet rag. Working gently, she plucked the cactus needles from his body until she could find no more, then carefully cleaned the open wounds and stuffed them full of the foul smelling salve. Even through the excruciating pain, the touch of her gentle hands felt good.

"Why are you doing this for me?" he asked, wishing he had something with which to cover his nakedness.

"You're the farmer from up in Arkansas aren't you? The one where the men all raped your wife and cut your little boy's throat?"

"Yes," he replied.

"I recognized you the minute I saw you. Jack still hasn't figured it out. If he had you'd be dead right now. I'm sorry about your family, there was nothing I could do. You're the one that's been following us, too, aren't you? Jack can't figure out what's happening to all his men. He's getting real worried about his boy, Luther. He's talking about going back to look for him and Reno."

"He'd be wasting his time. How come you didn't say anything when you recognized me?"

"I don't like what they did to you and your family. They didn't have to kill them. I don't like what they did to you last night, but there was nothing I could do. If I had said anything they would have killed me too."

"Why do you ride with them?"

"You think I have a choice? Good Lord, I'm as much a prisoner as you are. The only reason I'm still alive is because I do what Jack tells me to. I'm from a little town down in Louisiana called Ruston. One day Jack and his two boys rode through and happened to see me. That night they came back, murdered my husband, threw me across his saddle and rode off leaving my little seven-year-old daughter standing there screaming. I've tried to escape many times, but Jack always finds me, beats me half to death and drags me back. Someday I'll get away and find my daughter."

"I'm sorry, Ma'am, I didn't know how things were. If I live, maybe someday I can repay you for doctoring me up. I heard you mention something about a silver mine. What's that all about?"

"The Captain has a silver mine somewhere, I don't know where. He needs a steady supply of workers for it. Sometimes Jack brings him one or two as a present. From what I hear though, being sent there is the same as a death sentence. Jack says nobody ever leaves there alive."

"Do you think that's what they'll do with me?"

"Probably. If you live that is, or unless Jack figures out who you really are."

"I don't suppose you could find me some clothes, maybe a gun?"

"Clothes, yes, I think I can. A gun, I'm afraid not. They'd know it came from me and, like I said, Mr. Henry, getting back to my little girl is the most important thing in my life, even more important than helping you."

"I understand. Thanks, Miss Sawyer."

"Call me Lilly. I'm really sorry, Mr. Henry. I wish I could do more to help you. I'll go see what I can do about some clothes, I'll be right back."

While the woman was gone Matt tried to get up but found he was too weak to even rise. He lay back and thought about his situation. He was in a heap of trouble. Somehow, thought the prospects didn't look good, he had to find a way to survive but right now, it sure looked like his fat was in the fire.

Miss Lilly returned quickly. She had a pair of pants and a shirt. They were a little small, but would have to do. She also brought a double handful of beef jerky strips. Before she helped him slip on his pants, she used a strip of cloth to tie the jerky around his leg just below the knee.

"I thought that might come in handy if they do send you to the mine," she said. "I wish I could do more."

"You've done more than I have a right to ask. I hope I get a chance to make it up to you."

"Jack and the Captain rode into town. The Bull is sitting right outside the door eyeing me every time I come and go. You need some food. I'm going to see what I can find in the kitchen. I'll be right back."

"See if the cook named Avianna is there. If she is, tell her what's happened."

"Yes, she's here, I saw her just a minute ago. How do you know her?"

"It's a long story. Just tell her what happened to me. She'll know what to do."

Lilly returned with a big plate of food. With her help, he cleaned the plate. It helped. He felt somewhat better after eating.

"From the look on that Mexican girl's face when I told her what had happened, I'd say she's more than a passing acquaintance."

"She's just a friend," Matt said.

"Right now, you better get some rest. Good luck, Mr. Henry."

"It's Matt. Call me Matt. Thanks again for all your help."

CHAPTER VIII

The Groaning of the Prisoners

> "To hear the groaning of the prisoners;
> To loose those that are
> appointed to death." (Psalms 102:20)

It couldn't have been more than a couple of hours until the door burst open and the big Mexican waddled in. He prodded Matt with his pole and motioned toward the door. It took every ounce of strength Matt had in him to pull himself to his feet and stagger forward.

The giant shoved him toward two waiting horses. Matt knew there was no way he had the strength to climb up into the saddle; it looked ten feet high. The giant must have realized that too. He literally lifted Matt into the saddle.

As they rode, Matt tried hard to pay attention where they were going, but kept drifting in and out of consciousness, more out than in. It seemed he drifted endlessly, the world around him kept spinning like a child's top. At times he felt himself floating, as if his soul was soaring high above like a vulture in the sky, peering down, waiting to claim his own body that kept reeling in his saddle.

Surely this was death.

His mother was there. At times he could see her, standing in a white fog, her arms outstretched toward him, calling his name. Then she would disappear. Where did she go? He wanted to go with her.

The scorching heat bore down upon them. His lips were cracked and bleeding. His parched throat gritted each time he tried in vain to swallow. There was nothing to swallow. Each time he regained some degree of consciousness he would glance up at the sun through squinted eyes. He knew only that they had been riding for hours.

Near sunset they swung into the mouth of a deep canyon where the shadows swallowed up the fading sunlight. The heat was stifling as they rode along the boulder-strewn canyon. They rode for at least two miles before rounding a cutback and coming into a camp of some kind. Matt smelled the camp before he saw it.

He saw a dark hole dug into the face of a box canyon. Just outside the hole were two big piles of rocks. One, he figured, were scrap rocks from the mine, the other smaller mound, most likely the rocks containing traces of silver ore.

Three adobe buildings sat along one side of the canyon wall. A pole lean-to shed with a small corral fashioned from broken mesquite branches stood against the other wall. Matt saw four guards pull themselves out from under the shade of a small, thatched roof covering, their sanctuary from the boiling sun. Two rope hammocks were strung between the four posts.

The guards all walked toward the corral to meet them. All four were tough looking Mexicans who likely couldn't even remember the last time they had bathed. They were filthy. Three carried shotguns. The fourth wore a pistol and carried a long, blacksnake whip, rolled into a tight coil and hanging over the butt of his gun.

The guard with the whip dragged Matt from the saddle. Two of the other guards grabbed him under his arms and half carried him toward one of the large buildings. Beside the structure sat a large anvil. They clamped a pair of leg irons around both ankles and used a sledgehammer to crimp the linchpin in place, permanently. A short chain, forcing one to shuffle along, rather than walk normally connected the ankle clamps.

Apparently none of the guards spoke English, but with threatening gestures and a shove that sent Matt to the ground, they managed to get across they wanted him to go back to the corral.

El Toro was engaged in deep conversation with the guard with the whip. One of the other guards pointed to a heavy looking gunnysack tied behind the giant's saddle. Matt untied the sack and pulled it off onto his cut and bruised shoulder. A sharp pain from his broken rib coursed through his side buckling him to his knees, dropping the sack.

A loud swish was the only warning he heard before the whip cut into his already shredded back. Again he heard the whip cutting through the air and felt its impact as it laid open another cut from his shoulder to his waist. The cold sweat of anger stood thickly on his face. Teeth clamped, fists knotted, he cringed on the ground each time he heard the cruel hiss of the lash.

"Estupido gringo pig!" the head guard snarled, hawking and spitting a mouthful of foul smelling phlegm into Matt's face, then pointing toward the sack and toward the building.

Struggling mightily, Matt barely managed to pull himself to his feet. He gritted his teeth and from somewhere, found the strength to get the sack back onto his shoulder. One of the guards accompanied him to one of the large buildings. It proved to be the guards' quarters.

Four bunks lined one wall. Along the back sat a dilapidated looking wood cookstove. Nearby, wooden shelves held a few food supplies. The guard motioned for Matt to unload the sack. It contained a large sack of rice, a sack of black beans, a large container of tortillas and a string of peppers.

As they left the building Matt took note of a makeshift gun rack near the front door. It held a rifle, another shotgun and several boxes of ammunition.

Outside, the guard motioned for Matt to sit on the ground against the front of the guard quarters. He gladly complied. He leaned his head back against the wall and closed his eyes, considering his predicament. It sure didn't look good. It was abundantly obvious he wouldn't last long under the conditions he saw around him. He needed time to heal. He doubted they would allow him that time.

Forcing his eyes open, he scanned the camp, searching desperately for something, anything, that would offer a way of escape. He figured the two remaining buildings had to be where the workers stayed. Peering through squinted eyes in the growing dimness of twilight, he saw two Mexicans, who appeared to be nothing but skin and bone, emerge from the mine. Each had on his back a large leather pouch, suspended by a wide strap that fit over his forehead. Moving like zombies, their chained feet shuffled slowly toward the smaller of the two rock piles where they dumped their load of racks. Was this how it would all end? Matt wondered. Would he too, be reduced to a walking skeleton like those two prisoners?

The sun had long since disappeared and darkness was creeping over the canyon. The air was so hot and thick you could hardly breathe. One of the guards used a piece of metal to beat on an iron triangle, sending out a loud ringing sound. Matt watched as men began emerging from the hole in the wall of the canyon like a bunch of rats. He counted as they came.

Eighteen men shuffled and staggered out of the mine, only one of which appeared to be an American. Matt was horrified at their condition. Their skin was stretched tightly over their bones leaving a skeletal face. They stared straight ahead through glazed, empty eyes—eyes having the look of death.

Two guards brought a large metal pot from inside the guards' quarters and set it on a wooden bench. Another guard carried a stack of dirty looking tin bowls and cups, setting them on the bench.

As the prisoners shuffled towards the building, the head guard collected and accounted for every tool. Picks, shovels, drills and double jacks were carefully checked before the line was permitted to move on toward the bench.

Each prisoner was handed a bowl of whatever was in the pot and a cup of water dipped from a wooden barrel. They moved carefully, obviously not wanting to spill a drop of the precious food and water. After everyone had been given their ration, one of the guards motioned for Matt.

The guard ladled out a bowl of something that resembled soup but sure didn't smell like soup. The aroma from the putrid liquid reached his nose and something awful happened in Matt's stomach. The violent protest sent bitter bile up into his throat. Swallowing several times, he finally kept from losing what little remained in his stomach. Holding the bowl as far away from his nose as possible, he made his way over to where the American looking fellow sat.

"My name is Matt Henry, mind if I sit down?"

The man raised only his eyes, staring at Matt for a long minute without saying a word. Matt did some looking of his own. At one time this had been a big man. At least as tall as Matt, the man's broad shoulders told of a man used to a life of hard work. The firmness of his jaw, the set of his mouth, the unwavering eyes, all spoke of a man of character.

"Name's Joe Doyle," the man said. "Have a seat. You're the

first American we've had in a while. The last one was a scrawny kid that didn't last more'n two weeks. Welcome to paradise."

"Yeah, it sure looks like it," Matt said, easing gingerly down beside the man.

"Looks like somebody done a job on you. Let me guess, I'd say you got crosswise with the big sack of lard over there, the one they call The Bull."

"More like his boss, a fellow called El Capitan. He had the giant drag me, said it was their way of welcoming gringos."

"Yeah, I met him when I arrived in the country too, he's a bad one."

Again Matt looked down at the liquid in the bowl, took a quick whiff and made an ugly face, turning his head quickly away.

"I should have warned you," Joe said, "It's an acquired taste. It takes a while but believe it or not, you'll get use to it."

"Sure hope not," Matt said, taking a slow sip of water from his cup.

"First day or two it's best to take a mouthful and wash it down real quick with some water. Better go easy on the water though, that's all you'll get till morning. If you ain't gonna eat your soup, I'll take it."

"Be my guest," Matt told him, handing him the bowl and taking a bite of the single tortilla they gave him. "What's in that stuff anyway?"

"Believe me, you don't want to know. Like I said, you'll get use to it cause that's all you get. What we don't eat for supper they give us the rest for breakfast. You get two meals—if you can call them that—and three cups of water a day. If you give them trouble, or if they take a disliking to you, or if we don't get our quota for the day, they just take away the water."

"How long you been here, Joe?"

"Can't say for shore. I tried to keep track for awhile, but finally decided it didn't matter. The only way a man leaves this place is flat on his back on that little one-horse cart over yonder."

"What's the routine around here?" Matt asked, "so at least I can stay out of trouble and know what's coming."

"I just told you what's coming, a ride to hell. They found a hole in the ground up the canyon a ways, we call it the door to hell. That's where they dump the bodies. It must be getting pretty nigh full by now. That's all any of us got to look forward to. Sometimes I get to thinking it would mostly be a relief.

"In a few minutes, those that's got the energy, will walk over to that canyon face over there and relieve ourselves. You won't get another chance till morning. Most don't even bother no more. They get to where they don't even care about going on themselves.

"There ain't no cots, we sleep on the dirt floor. They let us out at sunup and count the ones that come out. If somebody is missing they send some of us back in to drag out the body and throw them on the cart and that's the end of that.

"We get another bowl of soup, a tortilla and a cup of water and we go to work in the mine. We've got so many of sacks a day we have to bring out no matter how long it takes. That way, the guards don't have to even go down into the mine. We work till we get our count, then we do it all over again.

"The only change from the routine comes about every three or four weeks. That's when The Bull comes with four big freight wagons. We load up the ore rocks from that smaller pile over there and he hauls it off somewhere, I don't know where."

"You say none of the guards ever go into the mine?" Matt asked.

"Not on your life. They're scared to death of the place. It's gonna fall in one of these days. When it does we're all goners for sure. The timbers are all old and rotten and we don't have enough to shore up where we're digging. They don't have to go in, they just lay in their hammocks in the shade and count the loads we bring out. We better get to the wall, they'll be locking us up any minute," Joe said, climbing to his feet.

Matt struggled to his feet and followed Joe over to the wall. No telling how many men had been there before them over the years, doing the same thing they were doing. The smell was unbelievable. While standing there, Matt saw the giant and the head guard with their heads together.

Their conversation ended and they both headed toward a skinny little Mexican sitting off by himself. The man appeared to be so weak he could hardly sit upright and struggled just to raise his head when the giant approached him.

Without warning, the long club of wood arched high, then around, striking the Mexican across one arm. Even from where Matt was, he could hear the bone snap with a sickening sound. Again and again the giant swung, smashing the men's legs, breaking ribs, beating him unmercifully. It was clear the sadistic Mexican giant wasn't trying to kill the man quickly, he was torturing him, prolonging the inevitable to inflict as much pain as possible before the inevitable. Matt had never witnessed a more ruthless beating.

Finally, apparently tiring of the game, the giant raised the club high over his head and brought it down with a mighty force. It struck the poor Mexican across the back, shattering the man's back. The Mexican didn't move again.

At the head guard's orders, two Mexican prisoners grasped the chain between the man's feet and dragged him to the little cart and loaded his body onto the death cart.

"Who was he?" Matt asked through gritted teeth.

"Some poor guy named Benito. I think he said he was from Anahuac."

"Could his name have been Benito Esquilla?"

"Yeah, I reckon as how it was. Only reason I remember, he spoke pretty fair English. You know him?"

"He was a friend of mine's brother-in-law. Seems he just up and disappeared a few months ago, nobody's seen hide nor hair of him since. The El Capitan gave his wife a job cooking and keeping house at his hacienda right after her husband disappeared."

"Reckon that pretty well explains why he disappeared then, don't it? She must be a looker, his wife?"

"Yes...she is," Matt said, mulling it over in his mind. "I guess you're right."

One of the guards rang the bell again and the prisoners began struggling to their feet. Like dead men, they shuffled in a line toward the two barracks building.

"Line up right behind me," Joe whispered, "maybe they'll let you go in our building, the man he beat to death was in our barracks. Better take a good breath of air though, it's the last one you'll get till morning."

Boy, had he said a mouthful. Several half steps before he got to the door the smell greeted him. The unseen stench poured out of the building like thick smoke, stinging his nostrils and turning his stomach. He grabbed his nose and twisted his head away as they shuffled forward.

The door was made of heavy planks with a metal bracket set into the adobe wall on either side of the door. A sturdy beam stood against an outside wall, obviously the one they used to drop into the metal brackets to secure the door.

As he moved through the door he peered quickly around through the semi-darkness of the room. Not one thing was in the room. Four walls and a dirt floor, that's all there was.

"Here, Matt, over here," Joe said, pulling him aside. "Stay as close to the door as you can. There's a narrow crack at the bottom, it lets in a little air."

They both sat down on the hard packed, sandy floor beside the door. Matt took his hand from his nose and held his breath while he ripped a sleeve from his shirt and wrapped it around his head, covering his nose and mouth. He hoped to filter out some of the putrid smell. It stank of stale air, body odor from men that hadn't washed in months, maybe longer, human waste and many suppers that wouldn't stay down—and death.

"Believe it or not, Matt, you'll get use to the smell."

"Don't for the life of me see how," Matt mumbled through the double thickness of the sleeve.

Between the hurting of his body, the unbearable stench and the constant groaning of the prisoners, Matt slept little if any that night. Each breath was a struggle and felt like it was only a fraction of what his lungs required. His mind whirled, trying to think of some way out of this hellhole, but finding none.

At last he heard the wooden beam lifted and the door swung open. One by one the men shuffled from the dark room. It was just breaking day. Slipping the cloth from over his mouth, Matt took a long, deep breath of air. His lungs made a sucking sound as they filled with the life-sustaining substance. Never again would he take breathing for granted.

As hungry as he was, he still couldn't bring himself to try the leftover soup and again, gave his to Joe. He gladly accepted it and drank it down like it was good. Matt munched on the single corn tortilla and sipped his cup of precious water, savoring every drop. Air and water, he thought, two things one can't live without. It's funny how you take things for granted and think nothing about them until they aren't there.

Suddenly remembering the supply of beef jerky Lilly Sawyer had tied to his leg he dropped his hand and felt. It was there. He looked forward to being able to enjoy a piece of it when they got into the mine.

The signal sounded and the prisoners climbed to their feet, accepted tools from the head guard and shuffled toward the hole in the mountain. Matt was pleasantly surprised when he felt the blast of cool air coming from the mine. The shaft sloped downward for thirty of forty feet before leveling out. They shuffled along forty yards or so before reaching the face of the shaft.

"I've been doing some thinking, Matt," Joe said. "You're in no shape to work right now, you need some time to recuperate.

You need to just rest a few days until you get your strength back or you won't last long around here. Find yourself a comfortable spot over there out of the way and take it easy. I'll explain to the others, they'll understand."

It bothered Matt, letting the others carry his part of the load for even a day or two, but he knew Joe was right. There wasn't much he could do anyway. He could barely lift his arms, let alone swing a double-jack all day. Reluctantly, he agreed and shuffled over to the side, swiped aside a few rocks and sat down.

Three scattered lanterns offered little light for the whole shaft. Matt watched through dim light from a single lantern in the working area. Joe went to work on the face of the shaft with a double-jack, swinging the heavy pick expertly, pulling down rock after rock from the face of the mineshaft. When he had pulled down a pile of rocks he traded the pick for a heavy sledge and began making small rocks out of big ones.

One of the Mexicans began loading the ore-bearing rocks into the backpacks of the carriers. When loaded, they shuffled laboriously up the steep shaft to the outside, dumped their heavy burden and returned for another load. So it went, hour after hour until they met their quota of four hundred loads.

Long minutes crept into hours and still Joe swung the heavy pick or sledge. Striking the rock wall with such force that Matt could only guess he was driven by sheer determination or anger, maybe both. Ever now and then he would pause to insert a long drill bit into a crevice, then use the sledgehammer to drive it home, opening a crack so he could get at it with the pick. Matt had never seen a harder worker.

After a while they all stopped for a well deserved rest break. Every man collapsed where he stopped, many to lay prostate and totally exhausted. Joe dropped down beside Matt, leaning his tired back against the wall and closing his eyes.

Matt had retrieved two strips of jerky from his leg stash a

few minutes earlier and now passed a strip under Joe's nose. A puzzled look washed over his face and his eyes snapped open.

"Wh-what in the— Where in the Sam Hill did you get that?" Joe asked.

"Remember me telling you about the red-haired woman that patched me up? Miss Lilly? Trotter's woman? Well, she tied a handful of jerky to my leg with a white cloth while she was doctoring me."

You would have thought it was the best present he had ever received. He passed the strip of jerky back and forth under his nose, sniffing it, savoring the sweetish aroma, wanting to make it last as long as he could.

"That's the most wonderful thing I have ever smelled in my whole life," he said. "Never in all my born days did I ever think a piece of jerky could smell so good."

They both took their time, nibbling at it, allowing the sweet morsels to melt in their mouth before swallowing.

As they ate, they visited and shared their stories. Matt told his new friend his whole life's story, leaving nothing out.

"That's quite a story, Matt," his friend said leaning his head back against the wall. "Tell me again about Julio's sister-in-law. Tell me again what she looks like and how beautiful she is."

Matt took his time and used every good word he could think of to describe Avianna's beauty. When he had finished Joe just shook his head.

"Man, oh, man, she shore must be a rarely fine looking woman. I don't reckon I ever seen identical twins, least if I did I didn't know I was. Are you saying they look exactly alike?" Joe asked.

"Like two peas in a pod," Matt assured him. "Julio's wife says even Julio sometimes gets them mixed up. I wish you could see them."

"Yeah," Joe said softly, his head leaned against the wall, his eyes closed. "Me too. At least I can imagine in my mind. That'll give me something nice to think about."

Finally the signal for noon came. The prisoners all shuffled from the mine and were given a cup of water, allowed to rest a few minutes in the hot boiling sun, then ordered back into the mine.

The afternoon passed quickly. Matt spent considerable time cleaning the worst of his wounds and repacking them with the salve Miss Lilly had stuck in his pocket. He felt guilty lying around while others did all the work, but being able to rest in the coolness of the mine was helping. By the time the signal came ending their day, he felt much better.

He tried again to force down a mouthful of the foul-smelling liquid, but he just couldn't do it, especially since he had eaten the jerky earlier. He spat it out and handed the rest to Joe.

"How did you end up in this place?" Matt asked his friend after they had been locked in for the night.

"I was the foreman for a big ranch up near Amarillo," Joe told him. "You might have heard of it, nice spread called the Triple T. We had near twenty thousand acres and grazed over three thousand head. The boss sent me to Amarillo to pick up a prize bull he had bought. While I was gone the Comanchero hit the ranch. One of my men that survived long enough to tell me about it said there was over a hundred of 'em.

"They killed everybody on the ranch, women, children, it didn't matter, wiped them all out. Then they just took their time rounding up the whole herd and headed them north like a regular cattle drive.

"By the time I got back and buried everybody, they had several days' head start. It wasn't no trouble trailing them. I followed them all the way to Crooked Creek just outside Dodge City, Kansas. They held up there and I waited and watched for three days before a cattle buyer showed up with a crew. They trailed the herd right into town as big as you please. I found out later the buyer was supposed to be one of the town leaders and an upstanding citizen and all, course he wasn't nothing but a lowdown, dirty crook."

"What happened?" Matt asked.

"Well, I rode in and told the town marshal all about it but he just laughed at me and told me I was loco. Funny thing though," Joe said with a little chuckle, "a few days later this fellow just up and disappears. The talk was he lit out before he was found out."

"Did he?"

"Did he what?"

"Did he just up and light out?"

"Reckon so, least nobody ever heard of him again. Well, anyway, by the time I got back on the Comanchero trail it was stone cold. I finally trailed them down here. Don't ask me what I was gonna do if I caught up to them, but it seemed like to me I had to try. I never had to worry about that though, I ran into the El Capitan's men and here I am, end of story."

"No sir," Matt said emphatically, "No sir, Joe, it ain't the end of the story. I don't know how, but we ain't gonna die in this place. Somehow we're gonna get out of here. Let's go over the routine again, maybe we missed something."

Again and again they went over every minute of the day, every movement, every possibility. Still, they came up with nothing. It sure looked hopeless.

"Three of the guards carry shotguns, only Carlos, the head guard, carries a pistol. Is there a guard on duty at night?" Matt asked.

"Can't say for shore," Joe told him, "but I think so. If you press your ear to the crack under the door, sometimes you can hear somebody cough or clear his throat, but I've never heard talking."

"Then that means there's only one on guard," Matt said. "Has anybody ever escaped?"

"A bunch tried just before I got here. They somehow dug a hole under the wall of the barracks. They didn't make it though.

The ones they didn't shoot that night they beat to death the next day. They left one old Mexican alive so he could tell the next batch what happens to anyone that tries to escape."

Thanks to the rest Matt was getting in the cool mine and the daily ration of a strip of beef jerky, his strength had gradually returned. The tin of salve had helped his wounds to heal and they too, were healing well. After a week of inactivity he couldn't stand it any longer and began helping with the work.

Matt began keeping count of the days by making a scratch on the wall of the mineshaft. The beef jerky ran out on the ninth day. By then, he had forced himself to begin swallowing some of the soupy substance they were given at every meal. It took a few days before he could keep it down, but it was either that or starve.

On the thirteenth day the head guard, the one named Carlos, beat one of the prisoners to death. It happened at the end of the day's shift when they were all shuffling out of the mine. The poor man was so weak he could barely stand, let alone carry the heavy backpack full of rocks. A few yards short of the rock pile his legs simply gave out and he fell, spilling his load of rocks.

Unfortunately, the cruel guard was standing nearby and flew into a rage. He grabbed his whip and played it out. The eighteen foot blacksnake made a swishing sound as it sped through the air, cracking like a rifle shot when the tightly woven tip found its target, cutting deeply into the man's flesh. The Mexican prisoner cowed on the ground, his legs drawn up in the fetal position. Again and again the whip lashed out, cutting the man to shreds.

Matt felt sick to his stomach that he and the others were forced to stand helplessly and watch this barbarous act of inhumanity. They could do nothing. The other three guards stood around them with their shotguns leveled squarely at them.

Finally, the prisoner's body stopped jerking when the whip landed. Nobody doubted he was dead. Two of his fellow inmates were forced to drag the body to the death cart for the final ride to the doorway to hell.

"There will be a special place in hell for a man that would do another man like that," Matt whispered to Joe, "and I'm gonna do my best to send him there."

On the seventeenth day their barracks was one man short for the morning count as they shuffled out. The annoyed guard recounted, then ordered Matt and Joe to go back in and find him. They found him lying near the back wall. He was dead.

Another fell dead two days later. He was on his way out of the mine with his load when he simply fell over dead. They lost two more on the twentieth day. One died in his sleep, the other made a lunge at one of the guards and was blown in half by the guard's shotgun. Joe figured the man did it on purpose just to end the misery.

"I reckon that's a faster way to go than starving to death," Joe said.

"Don't give up, Joe," Matt told his friend, "our chance will come. We're not gonna die in this hell hole."

They were now down to thirteen workers and it took longer and longer to haul out the daily quota which hadn't been reduced. Matt and Joe began helping with the task of toting out the loads of rock as well as doing their own work. Still, it was now well after dark before the bell would sound, ending their day.

"Wonder what's going on?" Matt asked his friend when the bell sounded at mid morning.

"Don't know, but let's go find out," Joe said, dropping his pick. When they shuffled out of the shaft they saw four heavy freight wagons backing up to the rock pile. El Toro sat his saddle on his familiar steel gray, holding the long club in his hand and glaring at six Mexican prisoners lying in the back of one of the wagons with their hands and feet tied.

"Looks like we've got some new volunteers," Joe said, shuffling toward the wagons. "Maybe they'll help lighten the load some."

"I take it we're about to load the wagons?" Matt asked.

"That we are, Compadre," his friend told him.

"Well, at least it'll be a change from our regular routine," Matt said.

"Don't go getting all excited," Joe told him, "they'll still make us haul out our quota after we finish the wagons. Oh, and watch out for The Bull, when he comes with the wagons he's usually on the prod to use that big stick of his. Don't give him a reason to pick you, you're just now healing up from the last beating he gave you."

The guards motioned for them to load the wagons. All four were backed up to the head-high pile of ore bearing rocks. Matt and Joe climbed up into the wagons and began taking the rocks as they were handed to them by the other prisoners.

Two of the guards were busy putting leg irons on the new prisoners. Carlos and El Toro had walked over and were sitting in the hammocks in the shade, sipping on a bottle of tequila and talking. That left only one guard left to guard the rest of them.

"Keep a sharp eye, Joe, this might be our chance," Matt whispered. "If I get the chance, I'm gonna go for that shotgun."

"Don't do it Matt, you ain't got a chance."

Matt watched the guard out of the corner of his eye, waiting and hoping he would get close enough. The guard carried the shotgun in the crook of his arm. He was leaning against wagon wheel two wagons over. It was too far for Matt to reach him unless he got closer.

They finished the first two wagons. Two wagons remained to be loaded, one of which the guard still lounged against. Matt chose that one and climbed up. Mexican prisoners were handing the rocks up one by one. Matt took one about the size of a man's head, turned and started for the front of the wagon, thinking to bash the guard with the rock, jump down and grab the shotgun and shoot it out with the remaining guards. He knew it was a big gamble but he had gambled with death his whole life. If he failed, well, it was better than dying a slow death of starvation.

He shuffled forward. Another two steps and he would be close enough. As bad luck would have it, Carlos called to the guard and he stepped away from the wagon, making his way toward the thatched arbor where the head guard and the giant sat.

The boiling sun was halfway toward the horizon past noon when they finished loading the wagons. They were all sweat-soaked and exhausted. Matt swept the sweat from his face with the back of his arm as they shuffled towards the shade of the canyon wall with their midday cup of water.

"It's gonna be a long day," Joe said, leaning against the sandy wall.

When the bell finally sounded and they were permitted to drag themselves from the mine the Big Dipper told Matt it was past midnight. Two of the older workers had to be helped from the mine. Matt and Joe half dragged them along, knowing the guards would kill them if they fell.

All of them were starved for both food and water but they were mostly too tired to even eat. Matt forced himself to swallow the stinking soup, knowing he must if he was to survive. His stomach churned, threatening to reject the foul tasting slop. He swallowed again and again, trying to keep it down. Finally, he could hold it no longer and emptied his stomach.

As the door slammed and they heard the heavy bar dropped in place, they all wondered if they would live till morning. Matt collapsed to the hard packed sandy floor, lying where he fell, not even having the strength to straighten his body. He worried what would happen when morning came. With the few hours rest they would get, would any of them be able to drag themselves up? He knew he needed every minute of rest he could get but he was too tired to sleep.

It was maybe an hour later when it came. At first he thought he was dreaming, but there it was again. A light tapping on the door. He raised his head to listen. There it was again: tap-tap-tap...

Scooting himself around and placing his ear to the now familiar crack, he listened. Tap-tap-tap. He reached a hand and softly answered with his own triple tap.

"Senor, Matt Henry," a voice whispered from outside. "Is señor Matt Henry there, por favor?"

Matt knew that voice. It was Julio! Matt's heart skipped a couple of beats and climbed into his throat. Julio was outside the door! He could hardly believe it. He sure hoped he wasn't dreaming.

"It's me Julio, Matt. Can you lift the bar from the door?"

The answer came when he heard a scraping sound as the bar was quietly removed and the door slowly swung open. Julio stood there before him, the moonlight framing his smiling face. It was the most beautiful sight Matt had ever seen. In his friend's hand was his bloody throwing knife. In the other he held the guards shotgun. Matt threw his arms around his friend and hugged him, then turned to wake Joe. He was too late, Joe stood behind him in the doorway. Matt accepted the shotgun Julio pressed into his hands.

"Joe, you come with me. Julio, wake the others but keep them here and keep them quiet, comprende?"

"Si, señor."

Matt paused long enough to rip off what little was left of his shirt. He knelt and wrapped it around the chain between his feet.

He didn't want to chance the rattle waking the other guards. Joe saw what he was doing and did the same.

Moving without a sound, they crept to the guards' quarters, pausing just outside the door to listen. Inside, it sounded like three crosscut saws going. All three guards were snoring loudly. Matt and Joe stepped through the door and shifted to their left to the gun rack. Matt handed the shotgun to Joe and lifted a pistol from its holster hanging on a peg. He stepped to the nearest bunk.

Carlos was there, sleeping soundly. Bypassing him, he shuffled to the last of the occupied bunks. Using the pistol as a club, Matt laid it alongside the sleeper's head, knocking him out cold. Turning to the next bunk, he repeated the process. Finally, he stood beside the head guard.

His mouth was open wide, snoring loudly. Matt stuck the nose of the pistol into the man's mouth and viciously shoved it into his throat. The evil man's eyes snapped open and bugged as big as a coffee cup. Recognition flooded his cruel face. His eyes flicked to his companions' bunks, then took on a look of despair when he saw the situation.

"Rip that blanket into strips and let's tie them all three up," he told Joe.

Matt found a lantern and lit it while Joe tied the three guards tightly.

"Joe, how about going and get the others and get Julio to help you take everybody's leg irons off. When you're through, bring everybody over here."

As Joe hurried off, Matt shuffled over to the gun rack and lifted the long whip from its peg. The cruel guard took one look and started shaking and whimpering like a whipped puppy. He shook his head from side to side. A steady stream of Mexican language that sounded like cursing mingled with pleas for mercy spewed from his ugly mouth, dreading to receive what he was so quick to dish out.

Matt threw one end of the whip over a heavy wooden beam in the ceiling, tied a slip knot and pulled it tight, leaving the other end dangling. He walked to the back of the room and got one of the large pots and set it upside down under the dangling whip.

When Joe, Julio, and the other prisoners walked in they found the hated guard standing on his tiptoes on top of the upended pot. His hands and feet were tied securely. The whip, now fashioned into a noose, stretched his neck.

The Mexican prisoners spat in his face as they walked passed him on their way to a table of food Matt had spread out for them. They all spent the next hour eating until they could hold no more and for the first time in a long time, drinking all the water they wanted.

"Wonder how long he can stand still on top of that kettle?" Joe asked, dipping another tortilla into a bowl of sauce.

"Reckon that depends on how bad he wants to live," Matt replied.

While they were eating Julio explained that by the time Avianna had gotten word to him about Matt's capture, their trail had already gotten cold and he was unable to follow. He had been forced to wait and watch, finally trailing the four wagons to the mine.

"I brought an extra horse, señor," Julio said, "I should have brought more. What will we do with all these prisoners?"

"When we finish eating, take a couple of the stronger ones with you and saddle three of those in the corral. Hitch the other one to that little cart. It's about time it was used for something other than hauling dead men. We'll put the weaker ones on it, some of these fellows don't have the strength to walk."

Julio talked to the prisoners and found out some of them wanted to go to their homes in a place called Candela. Others wanted to return to their families in a town to the west named Monclova. Still others wanted to go south to their casas in Sabinas Hildalgo.

"Joe, how about me and you scrounging up every container we can find that will hold water? These men will need every drop they can get before they get where they're going. Let's bag up the food that's left and send with them, too."

They gathered all the weapons they could find and loaded those that couldn't walk onto the little cart. Matt, Joe, and Julio climbed into the saddles and reined their horses around.

"Hold up a minute," Matt said, twisting in his saddle to stare back at the gaping hole in the face of the canyon. "Come on Joe, let's ride up there and tie a couple of these ropes to those first two timbers in that mine and see what happens."

The two horses hardly strained at all on the two ropes wrapped around the saddle horns with the other end tied to the rotten timbers holding up the roof of the mine shaft. Matt and Joe heard the loud rumble and twisted in their saddles to watch. When the cloud of dust had settled the entrance to the mine was sealed forever with half a mountain.

As the first blush of crimson from a rising sun crept over the rim of the box canyon and swallowed up the shadows, the strange-looking little procession came to a brief halt. Every eye peered back at the place that had been the scene of so much suffering and death. Tears of thankfulness escaped squinting eyes and flowed freely down seventeen faces, leaving tiny trails in the dirt that had lived there so long.

Back there, in the dark, stinking prisoners quarters, with the door shut and barred, lay two of the hated guards, their hands and feet tied tightly. In the guards' quarters, a whimpering, sniveling Carlos, stood on tired tiptoes, trying desperately to still the shaking kettle under his feet.

"It's over," Joe Doyle whispered to no one, "thank the good Lord, it's over. We've all spent our time in hell and lived to tell about it."

Silently they moved slowly across the desert. They looked hardly human. Clinging dirt masked hopeless faces that stared vacantly toward a distant nothing. Most still hadn't accepted that they were really free.

By mid afternoon they split up, each small group peeling off toward their homes and families. Julio, Matt, and Joe headed north toward Anahuac.

Still several miles from town they found a deep arroyo, the bottom choked with windswept mesquite bushes that offered some semblance of shade from the scorching sun.

"Let's hold up here until dark," Matt suggested, "we've got some talking to do."

Julio told them how Avianna had discovered how the fat little spy had turned Matt in.

"His spying days are over," Julio said, patting his throwing knife.

"Julio, I've been doing some thinking," Matt told him. "It ain't gonna be safe around this country for you and your family after what you've done for me, no matter how all this turns out.

"I've got it in mind to start a cattle ranch up in Arkansas and I'm gonna need lots of help. You told me one time how you and your boy liked to work with horses. So here's what I'm asking you to think about. If you and your family would consider coming up and helping me you and your boy could be in charge of all the horses we'll need. Maybe Marquitta and Avianna would kind of look after the cooking and take care of the house and all. I'll furnish you a good place to live and pay top wages. Now, I ain't looking for an answer right now, just think about it and talk to your family and let me know when you decide."

"Joe, I'm gonna need a top foreman to run the ranch. Would you consider coming to work for me? You've most likely forgot more about ranching than I'll ever know."

"Boss," Joe said, sticking out his hand, "you just hired yourself a foreman."

"I will talk with my family as you suggest, señor Matt," Julio said, "but I know what the answer will be. We would be happy to work for you."

"Okay, then it's settled, let's shake on it," Matt said, taking both of their hands and doing a three-way shake.

All three men's faces cracked with a big smile, the first one in a very long time.

"How is your wife feeling?" Matt asked.

"She is completely well, señor, thanks to you."

"No," Matt corrected his friend, "thanks to you. It was a mighty long walk you made to get that medicine.

"Okay, here's what I'd like you to do. As soon as it gets dark, Julio, you and Joe head for your house. Gather up your stuff. Take only what you have to take and can load on a couple of packhorses. Load your family on those extra horses we brought in and hightail it for the border.

"Joe, I'm depending on you to get them through safe and sound. Julio knows where the water holes are. Hide out during the day and travel mostly at night. You'll be less likely to run into any roving bands of Comanchero or Indians.

"When you get to Laredo, look up the Marshal. His name is Earl Tolleson, he's a friend of mine. He'll take care of you until I get there. If I don't show up in a week, head for San Antonio. Ask for the United States Marshal, his name is Dan McAllister. He's holding some money for me. If I don't show up it's yours to split.

"He'll also help you get to a ranch called the Circle C. It's owned by one of the best friends I have in the world, his name is J.R. Cunningham. Tell him the whole story, he'll know what to do."

"What are you gonna do, Matt?" Joe asked.

"I've got to see a man about a dragging."

CHAPTER IX

From Rags to Riches

> "Though thy beginning was small, thy
> latter end shall greatly increase." (Job 8:7)

Matt lay motionless behind the bundle of sagebrush. It had been more than two hours. The eerie cries of the chichada locusts kept up their monotonous serenade and concealed any sound Matt might make as he inched forward on his belly. He now lay only twenty feet or so from the path the mounted Mexican soldier had ridden for the past two hours.

Riding slowly, the guard rode a path from the river, along the ten foot wall of the El Capitan's hacienda, rounded the front corner of the compound and as far as the double door front gate, then back again. Another mounted guard did the same thing on the other side of the enclosure.

Matt knew there must be a guard on foot inside the front gate. He had heard the three talking several times. Avianna had told him earlier there was a guard on the inside along the riverfront.

To attempt to enter the walled compound without first taking out the guards would be a quick way to die. He was left with only one alternative. He must deal with the guards first. He had Julio's throwing knife, but he didn't have his friend's skill at throwing it accurately. He decided he would just have to do it the Apache way.

Several times he had counted to see exactly how long it took from the time the guard rounded the corner, until he came back around the corner. He had no more than six minutes. If he worked fast and everything went perfectly, he might be able to do it but it was going to be close.

Lying perfectly still, he held his breath as the horseman rode within twenty feet of where he lay behind the clump of sagebrush. He watched the man as he made his way along the eighty yard trek to the riverbank. The guard paused to inspect a big limb floating past, then turned his horse and headed back along the wall toward the front of the compound.

Thank goodness there was only a quarter moon. The man rode slowly past Matt's hiding spot, his tired horse plodded along the familiar path with its head held low. The rider rounded the corner and turned out of sight.

Matt sprang up and raced toward the wall, counting as he ran. He slid to his knees and using Julio's knife, began frantically scooping out a trench in the soft, sandy soil large enough for his body.

He had counted to sixty four times before he finished the long hole. He had only two minutes left. Working feverishly, he lay down in the trench and began scooping sand over his feet and legs.

Again he reached the sixty count. He had only one more minute to go before the guard round the corner. He had to be completely covered or the alarm would sound. His count reached thirty and he was only half covered.

Twenty, nineteen, eighteen. He worked desperately. Seventeen, sixteen, fifteen. The sand was smooth up to his chest. Fourteen, thirteen, twelve. He was covered up to his chin. Eleven, ten, nine seconds to go. The crunching sound of the horse's hooves reached his hearing.

Ducking his head, he pulled the single piece of sagebrush over his face and right hand that held Julio's knife. He held his breath as the guard rounded the corner and headed straight for where Matt was buried.

His heart was in his throat as the crunching footfalls of the horse's hooves came closer. The sand pressed into his body as the horse stepped within inches of him. Just after the horse had passed, Matt rose from his sandy grave. He took three giant steps and leapfrogged up onto the horse's back behind the rider.

Reaching out his left hand to cover the soldier's mouth, his right hand swept the razor sharp knife from between his teeth and raked it across the man's throat, doing its bloody job. Grabbing the horse's reins, he quickly calmed the frightened animal.

Lowering the man to the ground, Matt dropped beside him, quickly removed the man's jacket to his uniform and sleeved into it. He scooped up the soldier's cap and rifle before leaping into the saddle. Reining the horse around, he headed back toward the corner, counting as he rode. He needed to round the corner exactly as he was supposed to. Noticing that he was a little early, he slowed the horse. As he rounded the corner and approached the oncoming mounted guard from the other side, Matt slouched in the saddle and drooped his head as if sleepy.

"Es usted dormido, Felipe?" the fellow guard asked.

Matt only nodded his head, stalling until he came abreast of the oncoming guard. Then, reaching out, he clamped a strong hand over the man's mouth. Two down, he thought, two more to go.

Riding slowly and leading the second dead guard's horse, he retraced the route to the river. Tying the two horses to a bush on the riverbank, he slipped silently into the river. Floating on his back, with the guard's cap over his face, he let the current carry him downstream within an arms reach of the bank.

From under the edge of the soldier's cap, Matt could see the sleepy guard squatting at the water's edge. The guard held his rifle in one hand with the butt against the ground. Would the sleepy guard even see the floating cap?

"Que pasa?" he heard the guard exclaim, as he reached out to retrieve the floating cap from the water.

Matt's hand shot out of the water and clamped onto a handful of throat as if it were a bear trap slamming shut. He squeezed with all his might and jerked, tearing loose the voice box and stifling the cry of alarm that tried and failed to burst from the soldier's throat. A quick swipe of Julio's knife silenced the guard forever.

Slipping quickly from the water, Matt eased the dead guard's body into the river and watched for a brief moment as the lifeless form floated downstream. Wheeling and quickly scanning his surroundings, he saw a large hacienda surrounded by a green, well-kept yard.

Creeping along silently, he made it to the back wall of the large house. Sliding carefully along the wall, he could make out the front gate. The sliver of moon offered enough light to make out the form of the guard, leaning comfortably against the wall beside the gate.

Two lines of azalea flowering bushes lined a buggy path that circled from the front gate to the front door of the house. If he could get to those bushes, they might offer enough concealment for him to get close to the guard without being detected.

Bellying down, he crawled along the ground until he was safely behind the bushes. Using the bushes, he crawled to within a few feet of the unsuspecting guard who was busy rolling himself a smoke. Matt decided the best opportunity to take the guard by surprise would be when he lit his cigarette. He knew the light of the match for an instant would blind the man—he waited.

Matt bunched his legs under him and crouched like a mountain cougar, ready to pounce. Every muscle was poised to respond. The guard pulled a match from his pocket, turned and used the rough surface of the wall to strike the match.

That's when Matt sprang. He stifled the man's scream with the cup of a hand and the knife did its work. He quietly lowered the man to a sitting position against the wall. Scooping up the guard's rifle, he ran toward the stable.

Avianna had said the extra guards slept in a room next to the stable. He found it and carefully peered through the darkness through the open door. He could make out several cots but couldn't tell how many were occupied with sleepers. He slipped silently inside.

He found four bunks had snoring soldiers in them. Matt crept quietly along the wooden floor toward the sleeping guards. Using the knife, he made short work of the first two. The third woke suddenly and started to raise up when the butt of the rifle hit him squarely between the eyes, putting him back to sleep.

Only one remained. The loud thud of the rifle butt striking the guard woke the man. He raised up quickly, saw what was happening and raised his hands high over his head. He was smarter than he looked.

Matt tore strips from the man's own blanket to tie him securely. The young guard seemed appreciative and offered no resistance. He stuffed one of the man's own socks into his mouth and secured it with another strip of blanket to keep him quiet for awhile.

So far, so good, he thought. But he still had to deal with three of the most dangerous men alive. The El Capitan, Trotter and of course El Toro. He had special plans for that one.

Avianna had said the giant slept in a room right next to the El Capitan's room. Matt made his way across a red tile patio to a pair of glass pane doors that faced the river and which he figured was the master bedroom. Gently turning the knob, he was somewhat surprised when it opened. He paused to listen before pushing the door open slowly and stepping inside.

By dim moonlight filtering in through the glass doors he saw a large bed with high posts on all four corners. In the bed, he could make two sleeping forms. One was a man. The other was the woman with flaming red hair, Miss Lilly.

The man beside her snored loudly, his back turned toward Matt. If Miss Lilly and Trotter were in this bedroom, where was the El Capitan? That could be a problem. He crept carefully to the bed and, using the rifle butt, struck Trotter behind the ear. He wouldn't be a threat for awhile.

The woman awoke with a start and sat upright, clutching a bed sheet to her naked body. Matt clamped a hand over her mouth in case she cried out. She didn't.

"It's me, Miss Lilly, Matt Henry," he whispered loudly. "Where's the El Capitan?"

"That was him you just cold-cocked," she whispered back.

"What...? What's he doing? Oh—I see. Well then, where's Trotter?"

"He's gone to find Luther. Pulled out two weeks ago. Left me here with his friend. Like I said, I'll do what I have to do to survive. I'm glad to see you, Matt."

"You don't have to explain to me, Miss Lilly. I understand. Who else is in the house?"

"Just that dummy with the big stick. He sleeps in the next room. Your guns are hanging right over there on a peg. The El Capitan took a liking to them. Your knife is there too."

"Thanks. Put a match to that lamp will you?" Matt said, striding over and taking down his gun rigs and Bowie. He laid them on a bedside table.

Miss Lilly had wrapped herself with the bed sheet while she

lit the lamp. Her clothes hung over the back of a nearby chair. Matt saw her cut a gaze to them.

"I'll turn my back while you get into your clothes," he told her.

"Thanks Matt. Here I am, lying naked in bed with somebody, but I would be embarrassed for you to see me."

Matt turned his back, using the opportunity to look around the room. It was the largest bedroom he could ever remember seeing. Bigger than their whole home back in the boot heel of Missouri when he was small. It was furnished lavishly. Red upholstered sofas and chairs, fancy chest of drawers, even a fancy white bathtub. He had never seen one before. A huge painting dominated one wall. It was of a Matador with his red cape and sword, eluding a charging black bull.

"I'm glad you're alive Matt. How did you manage to escape?" the woman asked, hurriedly dressing.

"It's a long story, I'll tell you later."

"You can turn around now." She stood awkwardly beside the bed where the captain lay, still out cold. Matt used strips of the bed sheet Miss Lilly had discarded to tie the Mexican's hands tightly.

Lifting the officer's head by the hair, Matt backhanded him across the face. It took several times but the man finally struggled his eyes open. Matt saw recognition wash over his face and all the blood seemed to drain from it, turning it suddenly pale.

"Well, El Capitan, we meet again," Matt said low and sarcastically. "Here's what I want you to do. I want you to scream for help. I want you to call that big bodyguard of yours in here. We've got some settling up to do. Go ahead. Call him now."

The man hesitated and seemed uncertain at first, then, apparently deciding El Toro could handle the situation, screamed loudly.

"Socorro...! El toro...! Venga rapido!"

"Again," Matt ordered. "Call him again, louder."

Matt moved quickly to stand with his back against the wall. When the door opened he would be behind it. He was unarmed except for his bare hands. The Mexican did as instructed, this time even louder.

Matt braced himself against the wall and waited. While he waited his mind slipped back to the Yuma Territorial Prison and to his friend, Duke Hatcher. Matt wouldn't have survived his five years there if it hadn't been for the lifer that befriended him. He was the toughest man Matt had ever seen. He had spent most of the five years they spent together, teaching Matt how to kill a man with your bare hands. Now was the time to use what he had learned.

Suddenly the door burst open like a charging bull ran through it. The giant filled the open doorway. His massive head swiveled on his wide shoulders, searching for his master's cause of alarm. He spotted the officer trussed up and lying on the bed and the woman with red hair with her back pressed against the wall. He wobbled forward a few steps, his big club out in front of him. Matt kicked the door shut.

The giant whirled around, surprisingly agile for a man so big. A deep, rumbling growl escaped his snarling lips as he shuffled towards his enemy. Matt stood perfectly still, watching the man's every move. He saw the big man stop and spread his legs, bracing for a swing with his weapon.

With every ounce of strength in his weakened body, Matt lashed out with his booted foot. The blow found its target and buried itself deeply between the giant's legs with a sickening crunch. Dropping the club, the giant grabbed himself with both hands and sank to his knees in agony.

Stepping quickly forward and to his left, Matt grabbed a fistful of hair with his left hand and jerked the giant's head back, exposing the massive but vulnerable neck. Matt's right hand snapped open and locked, forming a hatchet weapon.

Like the string on a drawn bow, the hand drew far back, then shot forward with all the force of work-hardened arm muscles. The edge of Matt's hand struck the tender throat where the Adam's apple should have been, driving deep into the thick throat, closing off the air passage.

The giant shifted his hands to his throat, clawing at it, trying desperately to find a way to breathe. His eyes walled white with pain and sudden fear. Matt slowly moved around behind the kneeling Mexican. Opening both hands flat and drawing them far out to the sides, he clapped them together, both landing flat against the man's ears, the pressure of the blows bursting both ear drums. The great El Toro, the sadistic giant who beat men to death for the sheer pleasure of it, now let out a blood curdling, pitiful scream.

Again, Matt grabbed a handful of hair and savagely jerked the man's head far back. His right hand balled into a tight fist, leaving the thumb extended straight out, producing a frightful spiked weapon. In a high arch the weapon lifted, then streaked downward. The protruding thumb speeding toward the most vulnerable part of the whole body, the eye.

Striking with a terrible force the extended thumb drove deep into the giant's eye socket taking everything with it, utterly destroying the man's eye forever. Blood gushed from the hole where the eye used to be, spilling his blood with each beat of his heart. Again the weapon raised and again it shot forward, destroying the other eye, rendering the giant helplessly blinded for the rest of his miserable life. Still fighting to breathe, the bodyguard toppled over onto the floor.

Reaching down and picking up the big club, Matt hefted it in his hands, sliding his hands down to one end. As a man would chop wood, the long pole rose high above Matt's head and came down with a mighty force shattering the right kneecap, crippling him. Never again would this bully inflict pain and suffering as he had to so many. Never again could he use his size and strength to kill like he had killed Avianna's husband.

Matt tossed the big club on the floor beside the giant. For a long moment he stared down at the blind and deaf, helpless cripple.

"Holy mother of God!" Lilly exclaimed. "I've never seen anything like it. You weren't a man a moment ago, Matt, you were a killing machine. Jack better be glad he wasn't here. If he had any idea what kind of man is after him he'd ride right off the face of the earth."

"The Mexican was a bad man," Matt said. "I should have killed him but that would have been too easy on him. Miss Lilly, would you mind throwing a saddle on some horses for the three of us, we're gonna take a little ride. I saw my black stallion and little pinto in the corral awhile ago. See if you can find my packsaddle too, it's most likely in the barn. Pick out a good one for yourself too, compliments of the El Capitan. Me and the *El Capitan,* here, we got us some unfinished business to talk about."

"Be happy to," the woman said, hurrying toward the door, "they'll be ready when you are."

After she had gone Matt strapped on his guns and Bowie. He strolled over to the Mexican officer and glared down at him for a minute, remembering their last meeting. From the expression on his face, the Captain remembered too. He had just witnessed what Matt had done to his bodyguard. Now he looked as if he expected it was his turn. Grabbing a fistful of hair, Matt dragged the cowering officer out of bed onto the tile floor.

"Now, Mr. El Capitan, we never got the chance to finish that little game you taught me. Let's take up where we left off. But you see, it's my turn to ask the questions. Don't forget now, bad things happen when I don't like your answer. Are you ready? Here's the first question.

"Where's Trotter headed?"

"He said he was going to find one of his boys, that's all I know," the officer spat out bitterly.

"Good, I believe you. See how easy that is? Next question, when you captured me I had eighteen hundred dollars in my saddlebags. I want it back. Where is it?"

"Oh, señor, I did not know," the man said, lying through his teeth and faking surprise. "Perhaps one of my soldaderas has taken it. I will find him and punish him severely."

"Bull," was Matt's only comment.

Without another word Matt flattened out the man's hand with the fingers extended. He separated the right index finger and stretched it out, placing his foot on the back of the hand to hold it flat. Whipping out his big Bowie, he placed the razor sharp blade across the finger just below the middle knuckle and shoved down. The blade sliced through the finger like it was hot butter, severing it completely. A pitiful scream pierced the night. The Mexican officer began moaning and begging as Matt stretched out the second finger.

"Wrong answer, El Capitan. Let's try again, where's my money?"

"Por favor, señor, por favor," the man pleaded, but still shook his head, refusing to answer.

Again, Matt shoved down, severing the second finger, this time at the juncture with the hand. The man screamed and begged, but shook his head. This time Matt placed his foot on the man's forearm, laying the edge of the blade on top of the wrist.

"That's a bad choice, El Capitan, choosing money instead of your fingers. How much is your hand worth?" The man looked down through fear filled eyes at the big blade poised on his wrist and burst into tears, crying like a baby.

"Behind the painting," he finally sobbed out.

Striding over to the painting on the wall, Matt jerked it down. Built into the wall behind it was a combination wall safe.

"What's the combination?" he asked.

Whimpering and sobbing, the Mexican still hesitated, shaking his head, seemingly willing to part with his hand rather than Matt's money.

"I can do this all night, Captain, can you? If you make me come back over there. . .El Capitan, you lose a hand."

He hesitated only a moment, then seemed to give up; his will was broken. He blurted out the combination. Matt twisted the dials in the order the man said, then turned the handle and pulled. The heavy safe door swung open.

Matt's mouth must have dropped open a foot. What he saw inside the safe took his breath away. A long, low whistle escaped his lips. He just stood and stared for a long minute. It was divided and tied into bundles—stacks and stacks of money.

Reaching a hand inside, he picked up bundle after bundle, turning them over. He stared unbelievingly at them. There was both American and Mexican money, in every denomination he had ever heard of, most he had never seen. There was even one bundle of one thousand dollar bills. Not in worthless Confederate money, but in Unites States Treasury bills. He didn't know there was that much money in the whole world.

He saw four large leather sacks. The tops were tied with rawhide strips. Opening one he looked inside. It was filled with gold double eagles, twenty dollar gold pieces. The other three bags held the same. No telling how much money the Captain had rat holed away in that safe. No wonder he hadn't wanted to tell Matt where it was. He had the whole cotton picking Mexican treasury right there in that safe.

Where had all that money come from?

For a long moment he stood there, staring at the fortune before him. It was every man's dream...and yet, what was he to do? Should he count out his eighteen hundred dollars the corrupt officer had taken from him, close the safe and walk away? If he did, some other corrupt Mexican officer would get it. The El Capitan sure wasn't going to need it where he was going.

No, this was ill gotten money. This was money he had gotten for giving protection to Comanchero and bandits and outlaws. This was money stolen from the poor peons he was supposed to protect. This was money derived from the slave labor of all those who had died in the silver mine.

A beautiful set of hand tooled saddlebags hung on a peg near where his guns had been. Matt swept them from the wall and began stuffing them full of the bundles of money. When he finished, it seemed he had hardly made a dent in removing the contents of the safe. He turned and headed for the stable.

Miss Lilly already had Matt's black stallion saddled and had just thrown the pack saddle on his little pinto.

"I'll finish this one up," he told her. "Have you picked out a horse for yourself yet?"

"Well, the one I really like is the Captains white gelding. Except for your stallion, I think that's the most beautiful animal I've ever seen."

"Then that's the one you ought to throw a saddle on. Pick out something for the El Capitan too, he's going with us. I'll take my two with me. Come on up to the house when you finish."

Matt went into the tack room and was pleased to find his Sharps long rifle there. He also found three more pairs of saddlebags. Throwing them across his arm, he led his horses to the house.

Darkness retreated stubbornly and staved off the waking world. Dawn grayed the sky slowly. A blush of pink over the western horizon announced the pending birth of a new day.

They sat their horses at the edge of the river, watched the birth of a new day and allowed their horses to drink their fill.

Before leaving the river, Matt filled the half-dozen canteens he had found in the tack room.

"Let's walk our horses downstream a ways before we leave the water," Matt told Miss Lilly. "Maybe that will buy us some time."

Matt watched anxiously over his shoulder all morning as they rode. By noon they had passed safely through the pass where he and Julio had the run-in with the Comanchero. He pushed them hard, stopping only a few minutes at a time to allow the horses to blow. He knew they would be followed. The only question was, could they make it to the border before the El Capitan's soldiers caught up.

As the sun was spending its last rays, they pulled up at the mouth of the little canyon with the fresh pool of water. Leaning far over, he examined the ground closely. Nine horses had entered the canyon, then had left sometime later. They were all shod horses so he could rule out Indians. It had to be either Joe and Julio and his family . . .or Comanchero. Matt was betting it was Joe and his party and felt relief to know they had made it this far safely. He led his little procession up the canyon to the little spring-fed pool and climbed down.

"We'll water and rest the horses for awhile," he told the red haired woman. "If you're up to it, I'd like to ride tonight. Our only chance is to get across the Rio Grande before the soldiers catch up to us."

"I've spent the last two years in the saddle," she said, "another few hours isn't going to kill me. The soldiers would."

"How about rummaging around in my pack and see if you can find some coffee? I haven't had a cup in over a month. One shore would taste mighty good right now. I'll scrounge up something to build a fire and see to the horses."

A fire was going and coffee boiling. Matt was refilling their canteens when it occurred to him how good a bath would feel, he hadn't had one in way too long.

"Hey," the woman called, "I found a slab of bacon and some potatoes in your pack. Have we got time?"

"You don't know how good that sounds, Miss Lilly," he told her. "I'm way past hungry. Uh. . .Miss Lilly, I'd sure like to slip into that little pool of water and take me a quick bath. Do you suppose you could look the other way for a bit?"

"I suppose so," she said, chuckling, "but I don't see why you're so worried, I bathed your whole body not long ago, remember?"

"Yes, ma'am, I remember, but somehow it don't seem quite the same."

"You go ahead and take your bath. I promise I won't peek."

The water felt absolutely wonderful. He used sand to scrub the dirt and grime from his body, rinsed off, then scrubbed all over again. Climbing out, he shrugged into some of his own clothes from his pack and slipped on his moccasins. He was shocked to find he had lost so much weight his clothes hung on him.

By the time he finished the smell of frying bacon and fresh coffee filled the small canyon and made his taste buds tingle with anticipation. How long had it been since he had a decent meal?— way too long.

He ate all he could hold and that was considerable. When he finished he took a plateful over and took his time feeding the Captain, holding a cup of coffee for him to sip.

"You're an amazing man, Matt Henry," Lilly said as she sipped a cup of coffee and watched him feed the Captain. "I don't understand you, you cut off two of the man's fingers, then spoon feed him and help him sip coffee. You're a hard man to figure out."

"Yeah, I reckon I am. Seems like my whole life I've had to be violent just to survive. But that don't change who I really am, deep down inside I mean."

"This is a violent time we live in," the woman said. "I've seen things the past two years no one would believe, even if I told them. I've seen things I can never erase from my memory."

"No, ma'am, all we can do is just go on and make the best of what life we have left."

For several minutes they sat in silence, sipping their coffee, thinking of both the past and the future and enjoying the peacefulness of the moment.

"What's going to happen to me Matt? I mean, I know there's a wanted poster out on me even though I didn't do any of those things the others did. I know you're going to turn me over to the law. What will they do to me? Will I have to go to prison? Do you think they'll believe I was a prisoner and not one of them?"

"I don't know, Miss Lilly. I've been doing some thinking on that. Don't worry about that just yet, we've got a long ways before we get across that border. I've got a notion it'll all work out. Right now, we better load up and hit the trail."

The pack was loaded and Miss Lilly was in the saddle aboard the snow white gelding. Matt helped the Captain into the saddle and held his reins.

"Miss Lilly, I'd like for you to ride on down to the mouth of the canyon and wait there for me. Me and the El Capitan's got some settling up to do."

The woman flicked a glance at the Mexican officer, reined the white gelding around and rode away without looking back. When she was out of sight Matt took a rope from his saddle and quickly fashioned it into a noose. He threw one end over a rock that protruded out from the canyon wall about fifteen feet up.

The Mexican watched in horror as Matt readied the noose and realized what was about to happen. He began to whimper as Matt led the El Capitan's horse over under the dangling noose and dropped it over his head.

Great drops of sweat appeared on the officer's forehead. Raw fear twisted and distorted the Captain's face. In a quivering voice the man pleaded for his life.

"Por favor, señor. Por favor. I beg of you in the name of Dios. Do not do this thing. I will give you anything you want, por favor, do not do this."

"Don't seem to me you got anything left to give, El Capitan. You've been enjoying the dance for a long time, Captain, it's time to pay the fiddler."

Matt walked around to the front of the Mexican's horse and removed its bridle and dropped it on the ground. Then he toed his own stirrup and swung up into his saddle.

"While your thirsty horse stands there eyeing that pool of water, I want you to think about all the men you've murdered over the years. Think about how many families you've destroyed. How many little kids had to grow up without a daddy. How many men died in that silver mine making you money that won't do you one bit of good where you're going. What was it you said when I was lying there on the floor? A piece of garbage to throw out, you said. Adios, El Capitan."

Far up the canyon he could still hear the Mexican shouting curses after him. Then it suddenly fell silent.

Miss Lilly was waiting for him at the mouth of the canyon. She didn't ask. Matt kneed his big stallion into a short lope and was pleased to see the white gelding match him stride for stride, something few horses could do. Alternating between the short lope and a fast walk, they made good time, stopping every now and then to give the horses a breather.

For the first time since they met, Matt took time to study the woman that rode beside him. She was an extremely attractive woman, no wonder Trotter was taken with her, Matt thought. He guessed her to be thirty-something. She wore black, men's pants, but filled them out in a way no man alive could hope to. The white blouse she wore was stuffed down in her pants and she filled that out good, too. Her long, fiery-red hair caught rays from the rising sun and set her hair ablaze. Matt liked the way her loose hair blew in the breeze as they rode. She was all woman, sure enough.

The horses were as tired as Matt and Lilly. They had ridden all night and all day the day before. Matt watched their heads droop lower and lower and knew they had to let them rest awhile. If they ended up afoot they were dead for sure.

"We've got to rest the horses," he told her. "We'll stop over there in the shade of that outcropping."

Matt stripped the saddles from the horses and rinsed their mouths out with water from a canteen. That would have to do until they reached the river. He and Lilly sat side by side in the shade. As early as it was, the heat was already stifling. Today was going to be a scorcher.

"It's the beginning of a brand new day, Miss Lilly, in more ways than one."

"You're a remarkable man, Matt. I've never seen a man that was such a contrast of character. One minute you're the most violent man I've ever seen, the next you're softhearted, considerate and watching sunrises. I hope someday I can find a man like that."

"You can, Miss Lilly. Any man would be proud to have a beautiful woman like you by his side."

"See, that's what I'm talking about, I can't remember the last time someone called me beautiful. That's the nicest compliment I've heard in a long, long time."

All of a sudden a bad feeling washed over him. Glancing quickly down their back trail he spotted a plume of dust. He knew immediately what it was.

"Let's go, Miss Lilly. Help me saddle up real quick. We're gonna have company in just a few minutes."

They jumped up and threw leather on their horses, cinched them down and swung into the saddles. Another glance told him they were no more than half a mile away and coming fast. Matt did an extra loop around his saddle horn with the lead rope to his packhorse and heeled the big stallion into a run. Miss Lilly was a few yards ahead.

"Ride hard for the river," he shouted above the pounding of hooves.

He twisted in his saddle in time to see a puff of smoke from a distant rifle. Waste of ammunition, he thought as he urged the stallion to greater speed. Half dragging the little pinto behind, he couldn't hope to stay up with the white gelding.

Miss Lilly bent low in the saddle, holding her reins in both hands, asking the white for more speed, the gelding giving it. Her horse's churning hooves sent plumes of dust into the air, swept away by a hot western wind. That was some kind of horse, Matt allowed—and some kind of woman. He hoped she made it.

"Don't stop!" he shouted. "Get across the river and wait for me!"

The woman nodded her head and rode on, the gelding running flat out and belly to the ground.

Matt flicked a glance over his shoulder again and a chill shot up his spine. They were federales, likely some of El Capitan's bunch. There was twenty or more of them and they were closing fast. He knew he'd have to make a stand, but where? How? This was open, desert country. He swept a gaze ahead and saw nothing but a small knoll. That would have to do.

The little knoll was coming up fast. He circled it and brought both horses to a skidding stop. Grabbing Midnight's right ankle and throwing his shoulder against the stallion's side, he threw the horse to the ground, quickly did a half-hitch around the stallion's legs with a yard of rope slashed from the lariat on his saddle. He did the same with his Pinto. Grabbing his Henry rifle from the saddle boot and using his Bowie, he cut the buffalo gun from the pack and ran to the top of the knoll. Working fast he dumped the big shells from the leather bag he kept tied to the handle and began feeding them into the tube, glancing up between each shell. They were only a quarter mile away now, well within range of his Sharps.

Laying his Henry rifle near his elbow, he brought the big Sharps to his shoulder and sighted down the barrel. He picked out the man in the lead and hoped it was their leader. Propping the man's chest on top of the front sight he adjusted for distance and the wind and squeezed the trigger.

The explosion jarred Matt's shoulder. He had already fed another cartridge into the chamber and slammed the gate shut when he saw the man's chest suddenly blossom crimson and do a somersault over the back of his charging horse. Matt found another target, laid the sights on him and squeezed. A uniformed rider spun crazily and rolled from his galloping horse, arms and legs askew.

Again and again he fired but they kept coming. The big gun was too hot to touch. He dropped it and scooped up the Henry, levered in a shell and emptied four more saddles as fast as he could work his rifle. Bullets were kicking up tiny puffs of sand all around him.

They were right on top of him now. He dropped the Henry and clawed his pistol from its holster. A galloping Appaloosa at the front of the charging soldiers stumbled, sending the soldier flying over the front of the horse as if he had suddenly sprouted wings. Matt swung his pistol toward a charging horse and found the chest of the soldier, triggered off a snap shot and saw it tear the man from his saddle, his rifle flying skyward. Riderless horses bounded past, trailing broken latigo.

Matt heard a shout from somewhere and saw the few remaining soldiers jerking their horses around and encouraging their mounts to hurry to somewhere else. As he reloaded both his pistol and the Henry, he counted the retreating and beaten soldiers. Five. Only five were left. The rest were scattered across the desert for a quarter of a mile. Those five didn't even slow down to check their dead and wounded compadres.

She was there, sitting on the sandy bank under the shade of a big sycamore on the far side of the river. She held the reins of the white, sweat soaked gelding. When she saw him she stood, lifted a hand and waved happily as Matt rode into view. He splashed Midnight into the river and swam both of his horses across.

The hot wind lifted her flaming hair and swirled it across her face. She brushed it aside with the back of her hand and aimed a happy smile in his direction. She was a sight to behold, sure enough, one that would linger in his memory for a long time to come. She was a beautiful woman, one most men would die for. She had saved his life and he was beholden to her. At that moment he knew for sure the decision he had already made was the right one.

She ran to meet him as his tired horses climbed the bank of the Rio Grande.

As he stepped down she was there. Her arms encircled him and held him in a warm embrace.

"Oh, Matt, I was so worried about you. I'm so glad you're safe. What happened back there?"

"It was some of the El Capitan's soldiers. I sort of convinced them to let us go. Let's water and rest the horses. We've got some things to talk about."

They sat side by side on the soft sand under the shade of the sycamore tree and watched as their three horses drank their fill. Matt struggled within himself how best to say what had to be said.

"Lilly, what you said back there earlier, about you being wanted by the law. I figure that's probably true. I'm afraid it would be a long and difficult process to get it all cleared up. Even then, some lawman somewhere that didn't get the word might cause you a lot of trouble.

"You and I are the only ones that know what happened back there. As far as I'm concerned, Lilly Sawyer, the one that rode with Jack Trotter's gang, was killed by the El Capitan in a shootout in Anahuac, Mexico. That's what I'm going to tell the Unites States Marshal in San Antonio.

"Since nobody will be around to say different, you would be free to go find your daughter and start a new life under a different name. I'm afraid if we tried to get your name cleared through the courts, it would take a long time and you'd still be running the risk of winding up in prison."

Matt rose and walked over to his packhorse. He untied the pair of saddlebags he had prepared back at the knoll and handed them to her.

"There's twenty thousand dollars and a loaded pistol in those bags. There's a town called Kingsville about two days' ride due east of here. Once you get there, you can catch a stage going anywhere you want to go. I'll ride with you as far as the King ranch, after that you should be safe."

Lilly sat in stunned silence.. She stared up at a little puffy white cloud floating slowly across the pale blue sky. A tear escaped her eyes and glistened wetly on her cheek, swiped away by the back of her hand. Soft green eyes lifted to meet his. They held there for a long moment.

"You've given me back my life, Matt. I'll never forget you for that."

"We'd best get started." he told her. "We got a ways to go before dark."

CHAPTER X

Neither do I condem thee

"Neither do I condemn thee, go and
sin no more." (John 8:11)

A red ball of fire approached the distant line of hazy-blue mountains slowly, timidly, like a lover about to say a final good-bye. It gently kissed the lofty peaks one last time before dying for the day and being buried somewhere in the depth of the western horizon. Streaks of white-hot light shot across the sky as if from a great unseen cannon, careening off the few puffy white clouds and framing them in shiny silver.

The big stallion's powerful hindquarter muscles bulged as he drove up the steep bank of the Rio Grande River. Matt twisted a look over his shoulder and felt both pity and admiration at the pinto packhorse's efforts to match the efforts of the larger, more powerful stallion. They were all tired. It had been two days since Matt left Miss Lilly at Kingsville.

Matt pointed Midnight's nose toward the livery as they neared Laredo and felt a new surge of energy under him as if his mount somehow knew that rest, grain and fresh hay waited just up the street.

After seeing to his horses, Matt slung the three remaining saddlebags containing the money over his shoulder and pulled himself one step at a time toward the hotel. Joe was just coming down the stairs as Matt walked in.

"Well glory be!" he shouted, as he recognized his friend. "We were worried sick about you, Matt. It's been near a week. What happened? You look a sight."

"Yeah, I feel it too. I'll tell you all about it over breakfast. Right now I need a hot bath and a bed. Do me a favor, Joe. Run up to the store and pick me up a change of clothes like the new ones you're wearing. These are about to fall off me. Is everybody okay?"

"Everybody's fine, except for being worried about you. We made the trip without any trouble. I'll be right back with those clothes. Boy, I can't wait to tell the others you're here."

Matt asked the desk clerk for a room and a hot bath, then dragged himself up the stairs and flopped down on the first real bed he had felt since he left Laredo.

What he needed right now was some rest, good food and some time to gain his strength back. In just one visit, he'd had his can full of foreign countries.

The tapping on the door came faintly to his hearing, or was he just dreaming? Was he still in the stinking prisoners quarters at the silver mine? There it was again. He struggled to focus his tired mind and force his eyes open but his eyelids weren't anxious to cooperate. A voice called his name. It sounded familiar. Who was it?

"Senor Matt, it me, Manuel. I have your bath, Senor."

"Come on in," a weak voice spoke.

Had that been him that spoke? He struggled to free himself from the world of unconscious sleep and return to reality. He was so tired. His eyes pulled open. Manuel was setting the wooden bathtub on the floor near the window.

"It is good to see you again, señor Matt. We were all very concerned for you."

"It's good to see you, too. How's Marie?"

"She is wonderful, señor. She is now my wife. We were married only a week after you left. We are very happy."

"Tell her we'll all be down for breakfast in the morning. Tell her I'll be looking for one of those big steaks of hers."

"She will be very happy that you have returned safely, señor."

As Manuel was leaving in his usual trot, Joe pushed through the open door with a bundle of new clothes.

"You look plumb wore out, boss," Joe told him, a concerned look on his face. "You want me to tote you up a bite to eat from Marie's Café?"

"No thanks. All I want is a bath and this bed. Thanks for the clothes, I'll see everybody for breakfast about six."

Matt slept fitfully, too tired to sleep, too sleepy to stay awake. At least he was cleaner. He had spent over an hour in the hot tub of water scrubbing away the month and a half of grime, soaking, sometimes even dozing. He hadn't recognized himself when he glanced in the mirror and had shaved off the two months' beard he saw there. No wonder Joe had said he looked a sight. The bed had felt heavenly and his body had rested. Maybe it was his mind that was so tired.

He had awakened early, way too early to go downstairs, so he drug out the moneybags from under his bed and set about the task of counting it. He counted one of the bags of gold double eagles first and found it contained two hundred fifty. Since they were all about the same size he did a four times two hundred fifty and came up with one thousand. There was twenty thousand dollars, just in twenty dollar gold pieces. Minus a couple handfuls he had put in Miss Lilly's saddlebags. He hadn't even counted that in the twenty thousand he had given her.

Since he didn't have a pen and paper, he had to just make piles. When he finally finished he had ten piles with about ten thousand dollars in each pile. That didn't count the double eagles, so if he was figuring right, it all came up to a hundred twenty thousand dollars. All that was just in American money. He had separated the Mexican currency and hadn't even counted it.

When he finished he just sat there staring at it. There was a fortune lying there on that bed. More money than a hundred men could spend in a lifetime. One thing was for sure, he had enough to build that ranch he had always dreamed about—and then some.

After he stuffed all the money back in the saddlebags and slid them under the bed, he strode downstairs. It was just breaking dawn when he leaned against the post in front of the hotel and watched the birthing of a new day. It's funny how life takes twists and turns, he thought. Just a few short months ago he was flat broke, his family and future destroyed. Now he had twenty thousand head of cattle and a fortune in money. If that don't beat all, he thought, if that don't beat all.

He glanced up when he stepped onto the boardwalk in front of little café. One word said it all . . .MARIE'S. Matt broke a half grin and was pleased.

"What does a fellow have to do to get a cup of coffee around here?" he said loudly to an empty room, knowing Marie would be in the kitchen.

She came running out, wiping her hands on a dishtowel. A big smile occupied her pretty face. She ran into his open arms and they hugged.

"Oh, señor, Matt. It is so good to see you. Manuel told me you were back. Sit down, let me bring you some coffee. You look starved. You have lost so much weight. I will fix that."

She hurried to the back and returned with a pot of coffee and two cups. She poured them both a cup and joined Matt at the table. She was still smiling.

"It's good to be back," Matt said, blowing on the steaming coffee that was too hot to drink. "I like your sign, how are things going?"

"Good," she replied, "no, things are very good. The business is doing very well. As you can see, I have done some fixing up. I guess you heard about the marshal though?"

"No," Matt said, a concerned look overcoming his face. "What about him?"

"I'm sorry to be the one to tell you, I know you were friends. The marshal was killed. Shot in the back from ambush. No one knows for sure who did it. Some are saying Henry Bragg hired it done, others say it was the one you are looking for, Jack Trotter."

The news hit Matt like a runaway wagon. His face dropped and he stared into his coffee cup. He swallowed back the bitter taste of anger that climbed up his throat. Memories of his friend flooded his mind. He vaguely heard Marie talking but his thoughts drowned out her words. Shot in the back by some lowdown rotten coward too yellow to face him straight up. No man ought to have to die like that.

Was it Trotter? Out to get revenge because Matt captured his son? Was it Henry Bragg or one of his cronies collecting on the two thousand dollar bounty? Either way, Earl Tolleson was a friend of his and it had to be set right.

Matt was lost deep in thought and sipping coffee when Joe and Julio walked in some time later. They scraped out chairs and joined him.

"You okay, boss?" Joe asked. "You look like you just lost your best...oh, I'm sorry, Matt. Me and my big mouth. I guess you heard about the marshal."

"Yeah, Marie told me awhile ago. He was a good man. Nobody ought to die like that."

"I'm sorry, Matt, I know you were friends."

"We'll deal with it," Matt said. "How are you, Julio? Is your family well?"

"Si, señor, they are well. They are excited to be in this country, it is the first time for them. It is an adventure."

"I'm anxious to see them. I've never met the children, remember."

"Si, that is true, I had forgotten. They will be down shortly."

"Boss, I hope you don't mind, I took the liberty of picking up some clothes at the store when we got in. It was getting downright embarrassing walking around with more showing than covered. The man at the store said you were good for it."

"I'm glad you did, Joe. I'll go by today and settle up with them and the hotel too. The three of us got some talking and planning to do after breakfast."

All three of them followed Marie's instructions and pushed tables together so they could all sit together. She set a vase with fresh picked flowers on the table and set the table in preparation for the others.

It was a joyous occasion, marred only by the lingering sadness about the death of the marshal. Julio took great pride in introducing his children to Matt. Rosetta, the sixteen year old daughter was anything but a child, she was a woman in ever sense of the word. She was a spitting image of her mother and one of the most beautiful young señoritas Matt had ever seen. Juan, the fifteen-year-old boy, was tall and thin like his father. He was a handsome boy. No wonder Julio was so proud of his family. Then there was Chico. Matt and the energetic boy hit it off right from the start.

Matt was pleased to notice that Joe sat next to Avianna. He didn't miss the lingering looks they exchanged either. It looked like some sparking going on to him. He hoped it worked out; they would be good for each other.

After breakfast was over and the others had left, Matt, Joe, and Julio visited over another cup of coffee.

"Reckon everybody is rested and up to another little ride?" Matt asked.

"My family is ready, señor," Julio said quickly, "where do we go and when?"

"After we get through here, I'd like for you boys to take the packhorses up to Peterson's store and stock up on trail supplies. Get whatever you need for a week. I'll stop by and settle up with him later today.

"I'd like for you to pull out this morning and head for San Antonio. Check in at the hotel and wait for me, I'll be along in a few days. Joe, here's two hundred dollars. Use it for whatever your bunch needs after you get there. Look up the United States Marshal, his name is Dan McAllister, he's a friend of mine."

"He was here just before we got in, he come down to look into your friend's murder. Where are you headed, boss?" Joe asked.

"I've got to pay a debt I owe a friend," he said. "After you get to San Antonio, keep an eye out for a good sturdy covered wagon we could buy. Julio, see if you can find a good four horse team to pull it. If you locate what you think is good, go ahead and make the deal and I'll settle up when I get there."

Matt lingered longer after Joe and Julio had left to start on their chores. Marie found the time to share another cup with him while they talked.

"I appreciate you feeding my bunch until I got here, Marie," Matt told her, laying two double eagles on the table. "If that ain't enough to cover it, let me know."

"Oh, no, señor Matt. You owe me nothing. You have done so much for Manuel and I, we could never repay you."

"Nothing doing," he told her.

"That is far too much, señor. I have never met a more generous man than you."

"My ma used to tell me the good book said, 'Give and it shall be given back to you many times over.' I've found that to be true."

"Your mother taught you well."

"Have you heard any talk about who killed the marshal?"

"There is much talk. The United States Marshal from San Antonio felt it was the outlaw, Trotter, taking revenge for the hanging of his son. Most folks around here believe it was someone collecting on the bounty Mr. Bragg put on the marshal. I am afraid of what will happen to our town now that Marshal Tolleson is gone."

"I hadn't heard they had already hung Luther Trotter. Yeah, I'd say the town needs to hurry up and find another Marshal before the riffraff moves in and takes over."

"It has already started," Marie told him. "Henry Bragg is going to build a saloon up the street."

"Now that ain't good news. Looks like the town council could put a stop to that. Who's the head of the council?"

"Mr. Peterson, the store keeper," Marie told him. "He's having a hard time finding someone to take the job. He says without a Marshal to back it up, any law they pass isn't worth anything."

"Well, he's most likely right about that. He'll never find another like Earl Tolleson."

The sun rose shortly past noon when the little procession rode out. Matt stood on the boardwalk in front of Peterson's store and watched them go.

"Take your time and keep a close eye," he hollered after them.

They all turned in their saddles to wave goodbye again. It seemed like he was always saying goodbye to somebody, Matt thought. Joe led the way, with a packhorse on a lead. Matt couldn't help noticing that Avianna rode beside him. Julio and Juan brought up the rear, each with a packhorse behind them. He watched until they disappeared from sight then walked into Peterson's store.

"Glad to see Julio's wife and family up and around. Nice family. Say they're working for you now?"

"Yes, sir. I got it in mind to start a cattle ranch up in Arkansas. They've agreed to work with me. And you're sure right, they're a right nice family."

"Guess you heard the news about the marshal?" Mr. Peterson asked. "Terrible thing, don't know what we're gonna do without him. We're looking for a man to replace him but we won't find another Earl Tolleson."

"You sure said a mouthful there. I'm gonna be riding to San Antonio in a day or two, I can ask the U.S. Marshal to keep an eye out for a good man."

"I appreciate that, Mr. Henry, but he's already looking. The marshal thinks it was that outlaw, Trotter, that done it."

"What do you think?"

"Well sir, there's a lot of folks that believe Henry Bragg had something to do with it. I ain't one of 'em myself. By now, most everybody has heard about your visit across the river, right after that, the talk was that Bragg had backed out of his bounty offer on the marshal, can't rightly figure out why. Nope, I don't think it was Bragg. I'm leaning toward it being the outlaw and his gang."

"I heard Bragg is talking about putting in a saloon here in town. Ain't there something the town can do to stop it?" Matt asked.

"Oh sure, we could pass an ordinance against it, but who's gonna make it stick? I tried to talk him out of it but he just laughed at me and said he'd do whatever he wanted to do. With Earl gone, I don't see what we can do."

"With the saloon will come more trouble than this town's ever seen. Bragg will run the whole town in six months, but it's your town, you folks are the only ones that can stop it. Tally up my bill, will you? I need to settle up what I owe. I'm beholden to you for letting my folks have what they needed."

"Glad to do it, Mr. Henry, like I say, they're nice folks. Yes, here it is. It all comes to forty-six dollars."

Matt paid him, then stopped by the barbershop for a shave and haircut. Afterward, he went to the livery and checked on his horses, then went to the hotel, practiced with his guns for an hour, then spent the rest of the day resting.

He ate a leisurely supper by himself at Marie's, then, after good dark, went to the livery and saddled Midnight. He pointed his nose back across the Rio Grande.

Nothing seemed to have changed in Boys Town while he was gone. The happy sound of music from a Mexican band drifted across the cool evening air and would give one a false impression of the place.

Matt didn't use the street, choosing instead to circle behind the buildings and come up to the Rio Grande Cantina from the back. Hiding his horse behind a deserted looking shack, he slipped past the back door to the cantina and headed for the small house where he had found Luther Trotter. He wanted to talk to the girl that lived there. Rose, if he remembered correctly.

There was a light showing through the window but Matt saw no horse. Nevertheless, he approached the house cautiously. He peeked through the window. No one was there. Stepping inside, he closed the door and straddled a chair. He would wait awhile.

It took maybe half an hour before he heard footsteps. A slurred, gruff, Mexican man's voice, followed by a soft, timid-sounding girl trying her best to sound like something else. She was telling the man this was her house. From the sound of it, the man was leading a horse.

Matt pressed his back against the wall behind the door and waited. The girl entered first and stepped to the table, turning the lamp up higher. A large bearded Mexican wearing two bandoleras and two pistols staggered through the door. He had too much belly hanging over his belt and too much tequila under it.

He never knew what hit him. Matt's pistol barrel struck him just above his right ear and just below the brim of his straw sombrero. Startled for a moment, the girl wheeled around, but as Matt placed a single finger across his lips urging her silence, she didn't make a sound.

Working quickly, he hogtied the unconscious man with a strip of rawhide from several he'd brought for just such an occasion. Removing the man's guns and emptying his pockets, Matt dropped what money he found on the table.

"Do you speak English?"

"Si, señor, I speak English."

"I'm the one that was here before."

"Si, I remember. It is two times you have done this and given me money. Who are you, señor? What do you want from me?"

"My name is Matt Henry," he told her, straddling the chair again. "You are called Rose?"

"Si, señor."

"You are very young to be in a place like this. How old are you? How long have you been here?"

"I have been here two years, señor. My father sold me to señor Bragg when I was fifteen."

"Your father sold you?" Matt was shocked at what she said. "Why would any father sell his own daughter?"

"It is often done in our country, señor. Mexico is a hard country, there is little money. With the thousand pesos he was paid for me he was able to provide for my mother and little brother. There was no other way. My father was killed a year ago. What little money I am able to keep for myself I send to care for them. Without it they would starve."

"Where are you from?" Matt asked, touched by her story. "How far from here does your family live?"

"Our casa is one day's ride east, señor," she told him, "near the river."

"The man I took with me the first time, Luther Trotter, has his father been here to see you since then?"

"Si, señor, the father come first, he is a very bad man I think. He was very angry. He want to know about the man that took his son. I tell him what I saw, nothing more, I tell him that a big Americano burst in, hit his son and take him out and that is all I know. The next night the other brother come to see me. He want to be with me. He brag much, he say they take care of the lawman in Laredo for what they do to his brother."

"I see," Matt said, believing her story. "Have you seen either of them since then?"

"No, señor."

"Rose, let me ask you a question. Suppose you could leave this place and go home and no one would ever bother you again, would you want to?"

"Si, señor, very much I would like that. I hate this place but señor Bragg would never let me go and how would we live without the money?"

"Get your things together quickly," he told her, making up his mind and standing to his feet. "I'm going to take you home and see that Bragg never bothers you again."

"Oh, señor, por favor, do not play the joke with me."

"It's no joke, Rose, get your things together and be ready to go when I get back. I'll take you home."

Matt squatted to make sure the Mexican was securely tied, stuffed a rag in his mouth and tied it in place with another rawhide cord, then stood and strode quickly out the door. The girl was already gathering up the few belongings she had.

Moving quickly, Matt reached the back door of the cantina, listened for a moment, then pushed inside. He cat-footed down the hall and stopped outside Bragg's office door. Pressing his ear to the door and hearing nothing, he drew his pistol and pushed open the door.

Henry Bragg sat behind his big desk, a drink in one hand and an unlit cigar in his mouth. Surprise distorted his red, puffy face.

The drink dropped from his hand and the big cigar fell from his open mouth. His eyes bugged open wide and he clawed for the Colt in a shoulder holster. It was a good thing he had hired guns to do his killing. He was almighty slow getting to his pistol.

Matt lifted the Rattler to eye level and arm's length in one smooth motion. The man's hand stopped midway to the holster and froze there. Matt strode toward the frightened man and stopped only when the nose of his pistol pressed against Henry Bragg's bulbous nose.

"Howdy again," Matt said, as he patted the man down for hidden weapons with his left hand and found a derringer hidden in a boot holster.

"Wh-what are you doing here?" Bragg demanded.

"Keeping my word," Matt told him. "I told you I'd be back if anything happened to Earl Tolleson and I always keep my word."

"I. . .I had nothing to do with that, I swear," the man blurted out, his voice breaking. "That wasn't my doing. I canceled the offer I made."

"Maybe you did and maybe you didn't, either way, my friend's dead, ain't he? I warned you what would happen if my friend met with an accident, didn't I?"

Matt backhanded the man across the mouth, splitting his lip and bringing blood. Shoving Bragg backwards into his upholstered chair he shoved the pistol barrel into the gambler's open mouth and slowly thumbed back the hammer. The metallic double click must have sounded like a cannon to the man biting on the barrel of the pistol.

Bragg's eyes got even wider. Sweat popped out on his forehead and slurred pleadings came from deep in the man's throat. He shook his head back and forth as far as the gun barrel in his mouth would allow.

Matt wanted to scare the man, to put the fear of God in him once and for all. He wanted to scare him so bad he would never forget it. He stared hard into the man's pleading eyes for a long minute before he spoke.

"Give me one good reason why I should believe you," Matt said. "My friend ain't dead two weeks and already I hear you're putting a saloon in his town. Sounds to me like you knew it was gonna happen."

Matt withdrew the pistol slightly so the man could reply.

"Please, Mr. Henry, I swear on my mother's grave. I had nothing to do with it. Please don't kill me, please, I just want to see my children grow up."

"Well, they're gonna grow up without a daddy unless you change your ways," Matt told him firmly.

Pausing for a long moment as if trying to decide whether to kill him or not, Matt let the man suffer, let the fear gnaw at him awhile.

"Okay, Bragg," Matt said, removing the pistol barrel from the man's mouth, "I'm gonna give you just one more chance to prove what you're saying is true. If you want to live, here's what you're gonna do.

"First off, you're gonna forget about opening a saloon in Laredo, Texas. Those are nice, law abiding folks and they don't need your kind stinking up their town.

"Second, you're gonna get shed of everything you own in that town. I don't care how you do it, just do it. You got just one week to show me you mean what you say.

"Third, I'm buying back the girl named Rose. You paid a thousand pesos for her. She's already made you more than that, but here's your money," Matt said, counting out a thousand pesos and throwing it in Bragg's face. "If I ever hear of anything happening to her or her family, I'll be back and this time there won't be no talking, understand?

The man cowed in front of Matt, completely destroyed, sobbing and shaking uncontrollably. Unable to speak, he nodded his head vigorously. Opening the wooden box on Bragg's desk

Matt withdrew one of those long cigars and stuck it in the man's mouth.

"Chew on that for awhile, then I suggest you light it and smoke it clear down to a nub before you get outta that chair. It shore would make me mad if somebody followed me and when I'm mad—I get mean—and you don't want to see me when I get mean, Mr. Bragg."

Turning on his heels, Matt strode from the room leaving a shaking, broken man.

Rose was ready and waiting at the front door of her little shanty when Matt walked up, leading his black stallion. He swung down, helped her aboard the Mexican's big buckskin and tied her little bundle of possessions behind her saddle. He dropped one of the guns he had taken from the Mexican into the saddlebags he also found there. The other he dropped into his own saddlebag along with the Mexican money.

Toeing a stirrup, he lifted into the saddle and reined his horse around. The girl heeled the buckskin's flanks and followed closely. Retracing his incoming route, they reached the river without incident and pointed their horses' noses down river, staying close to the riverbank.

From time to time Matt pulled them aside into a clump of willow trees to peer down their back trail, each time seeing nothing. They rode the rest of the night with no conversation passing between them. He wondered about her silence, but chalked it up to the shock of being able to leave that place.

Matt constantly twisted in his saddle, peering back behind them, He knew in this country, it was as important to watch where you've been as it is where you're headed.

Just after sunup, he asked the girl to wait in a dry wash while he rode up a steep hill. From the top he could see their back trail for miles. Slowly scanning the land, he could see no dust at all. No living thing could move about in this country without leaving dust signs above their travels. Satisfied, he rode back down the hill and they resumed their journey.

With the morning came the heat. The blistering sun beat down mercilessly, cooking the desert sand white hot. Shimmering waves of heat bounced off its surface and were caught up by growing gusts of wind that drove billowing clouds of sand before it. It grated at their faces with its hot breath and stinging particles of sand.

"I'm afraid we're in for a blow," he shouted above the wind.

The girl rode with her head down, trying unsuccessfully to avoid the cutting sand that drove into their faces. Matt pulled his bandanna up over his nose and mouth and drew another from his saddlebags and handed it to the girl, motioning for her to do the same. His burning eyes strained through the growing cloud of dust, searching for some kind of shelter and found it.

With an arm he waved the girl toward a narrow dry wash that angled away from the river. It helped somewhat, but they needed more. He spotted a deep, washout and headed for it. He swung from the saddle and helped the girl down.

Wrapping an arm around her shoulder as they bent into the wind, he urged her inside. Snatching the bandanna from her face, he returned to the horses.

Their horses stood with their rumps to the wind, their heads bowed low to the ground, their long tails tucked between their legs. Matt tied them securely to a mesquite bush and tied bandannas over their eyes and noses.

Hurrying back to the shelter through the blinding dust storm, he crawled inside beside the girl and wrapping his arms around her, pulled her to him. There was no conversation, only the howling wind outside searching for them and the comfortable feeling of Matt's protective arms around her.

How long they sat there neither knew, but with the passing of time and the growing awareness of her young body snuggled against him, he became increasingly uncomfortable.

What was he thinking? She was only a girl. . .just seventeen, nearly the same age as Julio's daughter, at least in years. He jerked his arms away as if he had touched a red hot stove and sat upright.

"I best go check on the horses," he said, crawling out of the cave. "Wait here."

The wind was laying. Its dying gasps rushed off to find easier victims. He gathered the reins and led them back to the opening.

"We can go now, the storm's moved on."

As quickly as the wind started, it died down, leaving only the boiling heat behind. It was Mexico hot. A large sycamore leaned low over a sandy little beach, offering an inviting shade, and Matt headed for it. The girl must be exhausted, he figured, even as he was.

"Let's take a break and rest up a bit, the horses need to water."

He swung from the saddle and reached to help her down. Their eyes met...and lingered for a long moment. Her gaze seemingly searched his eyes, looking for an answer to an unknown question. Turning quickly, he led the horses to the edge of the river and loosened cinch straps so they could slake their thirst.

The girl kicked off her sandals and padded across the sand. She dropped to her knees at the edge of the water, cupped her hands full of water and brought them to her mouth again and again. Matt found himself looking at her closely for the first time.

She wore a thin white blouse that gathered around her shoulders and a faded red skirt that touched her ankles. Her long, coal black hair hung to her waist and stood in contrast to the youthful, flawless skin marred only by a thin ugly blue knife scar along one cheek. Somebody had cut her.

A cupped handful of water lifted as she leaned far back. She spilled the handful over her throat and neck. Matt's eyes followed the silvery trickles coursing over her bare chest. Her soft olive skin sparkled as the crystal droplets dampened the blouse where the thin fabric covered her. The backward motion of her body drew the thin blouse tightly over the swell of her breasts belying her seventeen years. He commenced an argument with himself.

She must have sensed his gaze upon her, as one often can, for her head suddenly swung in his direction. Once again their gaze met and lingered. Embarrassed at having been caught staring at her like that, he tore his eyes away and aimed a look toward the sky.

"Who are you, señor?" she asked as they sat side by side on the soft sand in the shade of the sycamore tree. "I don't mean your name, but who are you? What do you want of me? You tell me you gave señor Bragg the thousand pesos he paid my father for me, does that mean I now belong to you? Do you expect the same from me as he did? I do not understand, señor."

The words came out cold and flat, like something foul in her mouth that needed to be spat out. Suddenly everything became clear. He understood why she had been reluctant to talk to him. She had been used by men her whole life, why would she think he was any different? What else could she think? In her world nobody did anything without expecting something in return.

He paused for a long minute before answering, wanting to make sure he didn't say anything to hurt her. She had already had enough hurt to last a lifetime.

"It's not what you think," he tried to assure her, "it just didn't seem right to me for somebody to be sold like they were something to be owned, especially into a life like that. I've never had a daughter, but if I did, I'd want someone to do the same for her. You can relax, Rose, all I want from you is a big smile and to be your friend, nothing more."

Glancing up after he said it, he saw an image change wash over her face. It was a look of relief, as if a great mask had been removed, exposing the real young girl that occupied the woman's body. A pretty smile broke across her face, the first one he had seen since they met. It looked good on her.

"Gracias, señor, muchas gracias. You are the first man I ever met that asked nothing of me. I have decided, you are a good man, señor Matt, the first I have ever known except for my father."

"Well I'm sure glad we got that settled," he said laughing. "Now let's both just relax and rest for a few minutes."

They lay back side by side on the soft sand and watched the puffy white clouds drift slowly across the soft blue sky.

"When I was a little boy I used to lay on my back sometimes and watch the clouds," Matt said, "I used to try to figure out something a cloud looked like, like a horse or a dragon or a bird."

"I used to do that, too," she said, excitedly. Then her voice dropped almost to a whisper. "I used to slip off during the day and go down by the river, sometimes I'd lay there for hours. I watched and waited, hoping I would see a cloud that looked like a rider on a white horse and he would swoop down and snatch me up and carry me far away and no one would ever hurt me again."

"That's a good dream, Rose, hold on to it."

"Rosa," she said, raising to one elbow to stare into his face. "My real name is Rosa Hernandez."

It was mid afternoon when they swung south away from the river and climbed a long, sloping hill. Since their conversation back at the river, Rosa had opened up and now talked a steady stream, even laughing easily.

When they topped the hill they reined up and sat their horses. Below them lay a beautiful little valley. A small stream wound its way across the valley transforming it into a green oasis, a sharp contrast to the desert around it.

Off in the distance on the far side of the valley along the stream sat a small adobe house. A barn with a pole coral sat nearby.

"That's where we live," Rosa said excitedly, pointing to the house.

As they rode down the hill and across the valley, twenty or more goats lifted their heads from their grazing to gaze critically at the intruders that had interrupted their meal.

Unable to contain her excitement any longer Rosa kneed the buckskin into a lope. Her long black hair streamed out behind her, lifted by the wind. Matt felt good about helping her.

A small, towheaded boy, looking to be about six or seven, climbed from the streambed and spotted them. He broke into a run and raced toward the house, shouting at the top of his voice. The sound of his young voice carried across the valley.

"Madre! Madre! venga rapidamente!"

By the time his mother burst from the house to see what all the screaming was about, Rosa was close enough that she recognized her daughter. The woman lifted both hands to her mouth in surprise, then shuffled to meet her daughter as fast as her legs would carry her, her arms open wide, screaming as she ran.

Rosa flew from the horse and hit the ground before the buckskin was fully stopped. Her sandaled feet flew across the grass and the two of them fell into each other's arms, both sobbing uncontrollably. The boy wasn't far behind and joined into the happy celebration, hugging his sister's legs. Just seeing that scene alone was well worth the bother, Matt thought.

Finally, Rosa led her mother and little brother over to Matt, who stood awkwardly, toying with Midnight's reins.

"Madre, "she said, "Le presento, mi amigo, señor Matt Henry."

He thought the custom in Mexico was that she would present her hand for him to bow and kiss. Instead he was completely taken aback when she stepped forward and gave him a warm hug, but it sure felt satisfying.

"Gracias, señor, yo soy mucho gusto."

"She says she is very happy to meet you," Rosa told him.

"Tell her I am very happy to meet her, too. What's your brother's name?"

"His name is Carlos Hernandez, he is seven years old."

"Buenas tardes, Carlos," Matt said.

"Buenas tardes, señor," the boy replied, a huge smile breaking his face.

They all headed toward the house. The two women were both talking at the same time. Matt reckoned women were all the same everywhere. The boy walked beside Matt, looking up at him about every other step. Matt threw an arm around the boy's shoulder. That brought a happy look to the boy's young face.

The two women visited nonstop while they busied themselves in the corner kitchen area. Matt and the boy sat at the little table watching them. In no time, it seemed like, the women set a simple but delicious looking meal before them. Matt dug into the black beans, pepper-laced chili and corn tortillas and washed it down with coffee strong enough to be cattle drive good.

"Tell the señora the meal is wonderful," Matt told Rosa. "Don't reckon I ever ate better."

Matt sipped another cup of coffee and glanced out the open doorway. The sun was still an hour from the horizon. He considered whether to go ahead and start back. He saw the boy whisper something to his sister and she laughed.

"Carlos wants to know if you would like to see his swimming hole," she told him.

"Only if he will let me go swimming with him," Matt replied.

She looked surprised and laughed, telling the boy what Matt had said. Carlos must have jumped two feet off the dirt floor and didn't stop until Matt reached a hand to take the little hand in his. The boy half pulled him all the way down to the creek.

The boy quickly shucked his clothes right down to nothing and flew from the bank, hitting the water in a perfect dive. To a steady stream of pleading that he hurry, Matt pried off his boots and undressed down to his pants before jumping in. The boy screamed happily and climbed back to the bank and jumped back in, doing a preacher's seat, landing nearly on top of Matt.

They swam and played in the water until dusky dark. Against Carlos's pleading for just one more dive, Matt sleeved into his shirt and headed back to the house carrying his boots, with the boy walking by his side trying to match his long steps.

Rosa and her mother were sitting on a split log bench in front of their house. Matt spun a nearby straw bottomed chair and straddled it. The boy sat cross-legged on the ground next to Matt's chair.

"Would you like another cup of coffee?" Rosa asked, coming to her feet.

"You talked me into it," Matt said, "all that swimming 'bout wore me out."

Rosa hurried inside and returned with three cups of coffee. They visited until well after dark. It kept Rosa busy telling everyone what everyone else was saying. It was a nice time, a peaceful time, a family time.

Would you like to walk down to the river with me?" Matt asked, extending a hand to Rosa.

Looking surprised, but pleased, she glanced quickly at her mother, then back at Matt. Smiling broadly, she took his outstretched hand. Carlos jumped to his feet, obviously intending to go with them but a quiet word from his mother dissuaded him. Matt and Rosa strolled slowly down to the river where they sat down side by side on the bank.

For a long minute or two they sat in silence, watching the moon's reflection off the water and listened to the croaking of a thousand frogs.

"You've got a wonderful family, Rosa, and this is a beautiful place you have here. I can sure see why your father chose this place to build his home. I haven't seen any other houses. Does anyone else live nearby?"

"Si, my uncle lives only a short distance up the creek. There is a small village with a store near his casa, that is where we get the few things we need, besides, we have no money for such things."

"Don't you folks ever have trouble way out here? This part of the country is crawling with all kinds of hombres up to no good. Seems to me the Indians, Comanchero, and just plain no-goods would love to find an isolated place like this."

"We live simply, señor, we have nothing and they know this. They do not bother us."

"That fellow back there in your room that I conked on the noggin, he's gonna be awfully mad when he wakes up and finds his girl and his horse both gone."

"I am not his . . .girl, as you put it. I am my own girl."

"I'm sorry, Rosa, I didn't mean it that way. It's just that I'm worried for you and your family that's all. He's liable to come looking."

There was a quiet moment when neither said anything. Matt tossed a pebble into the swimming hole and watched the ripples break the beams of light from the moon.

"Matt," she said it softly, timidly, causing him to raise his head and turn toward the sound. "Could you stay here with us? You could have a good life here. I. . .I know you want me. Back in the cave, I felt so safe with you holding me and when we were by the river, I felt your gaze upon me, I saw the desire in your eyes and the way that you looked at me. I could make you very happy."

Wind tossed her hair about her face and she slowly lifted a hand to brush aside a stray lock from her forehead.

"My heart wants you, Matt, and my body as well. Could . . . could you ever love me knowing . . .?

He reached out a hand and took hers, and held it. A lump welled up in his throat. He realized how hard it must have been for her to speak those words. How could he explain to her? How could he make her believe her past had nothing to do with what he must say?

"Rosa there's nothing I would like more, but I can't. You see, I was married. I had a wonderful wife and a stepson about Carlos's age. We had a small farm a long way from here in a place called Arkansas. One day while I was out in the field plowing, a gang of killers raided my farm. They raped and murdered my wife, shot her five times, then they cut my little boy's throat from ear to ear. The men that done it was Jack Trotter and his boys, Luke and Luther and fifteen others of his gang. I've been chasing them ever since. I've got all but three of them and I can't stop until I get the rest.

"Maybe if we had met another time, but I've got a lot of folks waiting on me in San Antonio and they're depending on me. You're a beautiful young lady, Rosa. Any man would count his lucky stars to have you. Can you understand?"

"Si, I understand, Matt. You have done so much for me, it's just that I've never met a man like you. I had to take the chance and tell you how I feel."

"You'll meet somebody that will love you and take care of you. Wait until you meet the right one. You're a very special young lady, Rosa. He ought to be a very special young man to deserve you, don't settle for less than you deserve. Wait for that man on the white horse you told me about, you'll find him."

"I already did." she said, staring off into the night, "I just couldn't keep him. Gracias, Matt Henry," she whispered. She lifted a hand to touch his cheek and, leaning over, parted her soft lips in a tender, gentle kiss.

"We'd better be getting back." He got to his feet and reached out a hand to help her rise.

Hand in hand they walked slowly back to the house. They shared another cup of coffee and visited, then decided it was time to call it a day.

"I'm gonna get my bedroll and sleep down by the river," Matt told them. "Goodnight everyone. Buenas noches, Carlos."

He slept heavily and woke just as dawn was creeping across the pretty little valley. The steady drone of croaking frogs had died down for the first time since he'd spread his bedroll the night before. Stretching and ruffling his hair, he climbed out of his bedroll and walked the few steps down the bank to the small creek. A quick dip would sure feel good, he thought and shucked his clothes. The water was cold but felt good after he got used to it. He had just climbed out and headed for his clothes when he heard the voice.

"Good morning."

He jerked his head up to see Rosa standing not twenty feet away holding two cups of coffee. He wheeled and dove back into the water and came up sputtering, with only his head sticking out of the water.

"I didn't think you'd be up yet." She laughed at his shyness. "I brought you some coffee. I'm sorry, Matt, but I've seen a few men before, you know."

"Yeah, well, I wasn't one of them, at least until now. Just put the coffee down there by my clothes and I'll come on up to the house when I'm dressed."

She giggled mischievously at his embarrassment and set the coffee down, then turned and strolled back to the house. After he had made sure she was gone he climbed out, quickly dried off and dressed. The sun was just peeking over the far side of the valley as he strode to the barn where his horse was. He picked up the saddlebag with the Mexican money and made his way to the house.

Matt enjoyed the delicious breakfast of eggs and fried tortillas, spread with some sort of sweet preserves and coffee. As he ate, Rosa often glanced up at him, mischief dancing in her dark eyes.

"I'll be riding out right after breakfast," he told them, "but I want you to have this."

He reached into the saddlebags and withdrew a large package of Mexican currency and laid it on the table in front of them. He hadn't counted it, but from the domination of the bills he could see, it would certainly be enough to take care of them the rest of their lives—and then some.

Both Rosa and her mother gasped at the bundle of money. It was obvious from their reactions they couldn't even grasp that much money. Both ladies lifted their hands to their open mouths, stared at the money and shook their heads in disbelief.

"Oh, Matt," Rosa said. "Is it. . .is it really for us? I cannot believe it. Never have I seen so much. What will we do with so much?"

"Be very careful who you let know about this," he cautioned her. "It should be enough to provide for you and your family for the rest of your lives. You might want to use some of it to see that Carlos gets a good education."

"Gracias, señor Matt," she said, "we shall never forget you."

At that moment Carlos came bursting through the door shouting something, obviously alarmed. In rapid Spanish he spoke to his sister.

"What is it?" Matt asked anxiously. "What's happening?"

"Carlos says there are three riders coming this way and riding fast."

Matt scooped up the saddlebag and reached inside. He drew out the pistol he had taken from the bearded Mexican in her room and handed it to Rosa.

"Stay in the house. If they get by me, use this."

Wheeling, he burst through the door and headed for the barn. As he ran he cast a glance toward the distant hill. Just as Carlos had said, three riders were barreling down the hill on the far side of the valley, riding hard. There was no question in his mind who they were—the bearded pistolero Matt conked on the head and two of his buddies.

He snatched his Henry rifle from the saddle boot, levered a shell and leaned it against the wall, near the barn door. Loosening the throngs from both his side guns, he thumbed back the hammers to full cock and pressed himself against the wall, just inside the door.

He heard the pounding hooves as the riders drew near and reined down in front of the house. Chancing a peek around the edge of the door, he saw the riders spread out in front of the house, pistols in hand, their backs to the barn. The bearded one was in the middle.

"Hola un casa," the leader shouted gruffly, "Ella afuera! Rapido!"

Matt didn't understand what the man said, but he didn't like the way he said it. Since it was obvious they hadn't come for coffee, he decided there was no easy way to settle this. He drew the Rattler from leather and stepped through the door.

"Don't bother to turn around," he said loudly, not knowing if they understood English or not.

Apparently they didn't. The hombre on the right twisted in his saddle, swinging his pistol toward the sound. He died in the saddle with two shots in his left side. The one on the left jerked his horse around, snapping a shot under his arm toward Matt as he did. Speeding lead screamed past his ear. Matt crouched and fired as the man's horse reared, causing his shots to hit the man low. The Mexican grabbed his abdomen and glanced down. Blood squirted between his clutching fingers and his eyes walled white as he toppled from his saddle.

Only the bearded leader sat motionless, a pistol in each hand, the hammers back and ready to fire. Long seconds clicked by. Still, the man didn't move. His new horse was a dappled gray that pranced nervously. Matt watched him through squinted eyes, ready for him to make his play.

"Ezz you going to shoot me in zee back, hombre?" a grating voice asked.

"That's up to you. Back or front, makes no difference to me. You can step down if you'll keep those hands where I can see 'em."

The pistolero slowly drew a leg across the saddle and touched the ground, his two pistols still in his hands, far out to his sides and pointed down. As the man slowly turned, Matt leathered his pistol, the hammer still in full cock position.

Surprise overtook the man's face and his lip curled in a cruel smile.

"Ezz you the hombre that hit my head?"

"Yep."

"And it was you that took my horse?"

"Yep."

The man fixed a stare at Matt for a long minute, seemingly puzzled why this Americano would have holstered his pistol in the face of one with two guns already drawn.

"You one bad hombre, gringo, but I am going to kill you," he stated confidently.

"You figure on talking me to death?"

Squint lines appeared along the edges of the man's eyes as they suddenly narrowed. The eyebrows lowered. He was no beginner, this one. His hands moved fast and as one in a lightning move to swing his guns up in line with their target.

The Rattler barked twice, exploding twin holes in the man's barrel chest, one on each side of the crisscrossed bandoleers. He staggered backwards under the force of the impact, His knees sagged briefly, then he straightened and parted his yellowed teeth in an angry snarl.

"Your pistola ezz empty, gringo." The words croaked from

deep in his throat, a bullfrog's sound. "Now I kill you." His pistols lifted slowly.

"Not today. Not ever." Matt said softly, pushing down on the handle of the Widow Maker and touching the trigger.

The explosion sounded like a great clap of thunder. The force of the twin loads of buckshot lifted the Mexican clear off the ground, depositing what little was left of him flat on his back several feet away.

The horses bolted, galloped off a ways, then milled about. Matt watched them as he reloaded both weapons, then turned and strode to the front door.

"Rosa, it's me, Matt. Don't shoot, but don't come out either. Hand me out some blankets or something to cover these fellows with," he called through the closed door.

After a brief pause the door opened and she handed him some blankets. She cut her eyes toward the three dead men sprawled in the yard and gasped.

"Wait in the house until I call you," he instructed.

He gathered their weapons and covered the bodies, then strode to the corral and saddled Midnight. Riding out to the frightened horses, he gathered their reins and led them back to the house.

After he had loaded the three across their own saddles, tied them in place and covered them with the three blankets, he went to the house. All three were sitting at the table, visibly upset. Rosa leaped up and ran to him and threw her arms around him.

"Oh, Matt, we were so worried. We heard all the shooting and didn't know what was happening. Are you okay? Were you hurt?"

"I'm fine," he told her. "It's time for me to go."

"Couldn't you stay just until tomorrow? You can stay until then."

"I'm sorry, Rosa, I really can't. I'll take them with me so no one can tie them to your place. Maybe it's all over now and you'll be safe."

Although the boy didn't understand the words, it was apparent he knew what was going on and dropped his head sadly. A tear escaped his eye and crept slowly down his cheek. Matt went to him and dropping to one knee, took him by both shoulders.

"Rosa, tell him he is the man of the house and I am depending on him to take care of both of you. Tell him I will come back this way again and I expect to find him all grown up."

She told the boy what Matt had said. Finally the boy raised his eyes and searched Matt's eyes for a moment, then threw his arms around Matt's neck and held on tight for a long minute. Matt ruffled the boy's hair and stood up.

"Goodbye, Matt Henry," Rosa said. "I will always remember you."

"Vaya con Dios," Rosa's mother said, as Matt spun and strode out the door, afraid to look back lest they see the tears in his own eyes.

CHAPTER XI

"Who is my Brother?"
(Luke 10:29)

Matt wearily climbed the stairs to his hotel room. It was coming daylight. He was tuckered out. He had ridden all the previous day and all night. All he wanted to do right now was flop down on a soft bed and sleep for a week.

Leaving Rosa and her family had been hard, but he felt sure they would be all right now that the threat of the bearded pistolero had been dealt with. He had circled far from the trail and buried the bodies of the dead bandidos and turned their horses loose. At least they would have enough money to make a new start and live comfortably.

He propped a chair under his knob, checked to make sure his other saddlebags had not been disturbed and undressed. He placed his pistol under his pillow, stretched out and promptly went to sleep.

Sometime later the bright sun crept through the window and flooded his face. His eyes popped open and he was wide awake.

He had no idea what time it was, only that the sun was up and he was still in bed, something his pa would have never allowed. He rose, washed, dressed and went downstairs. Manuel was behind the desk, which Matt thought unusual. He didn't remember him ever working the desk.

"Buenas tardes, señor Matt. Did you have a good rest?" the young Mexican asked, even more cheerful than usual.

"Yeah, but what time is it?"

"It is mid-afternoon, señor. It must have been late when you came in."

"Early would be more like it, it was coming daylight. You having to work the desk too, now?"

"You have not heard? Marie and I have purchased this hotel from señor Bragg. He came to the café the day before yesterday and offered to sell it to us for two thousand dollars. Everyone told me it was worth much more than that. He even let us pay it out. It was such a good offer we could not refuse."

"Well, what do you know about that?" Matt said, pleased at the news. "Wonder what got into him?"

"It is very strange, señor, he sold everything he owned in Laredo all in the same day."

"Well, I'm glad to hear it. Sounds like you and Marie are gonna be mighty busy. When you get a chance, tally up my bill will you? I'll be riding out again at first light tomorrow."

"Si, señor, I will be happy to. It will be ready for you at your convenience."

Matt stood for a moment, thinking, his mind toying with an idea that had just occurred to him. Making up his mind, he turned and strode out the door. As hard as they worked, that young couple would most likely own the whole town in a year or two.

He headed for the barbershop and got himself a relaxing shave while he caught up on all the latest news. He had long since learned if you want to know what's going on, either go to the livery stable or the barbershop.

"Guess you heard about the big sell off?" the barber asked.

"Yeah, I heard Bragg sold the hotel to the young Mexican couple."

"Well, you ain't heard the half of it, he sold everything he owned in this town. The livery, the freight outfit, everything. Some say he's gone plumb loco. On top of all that, he's decided now he ain't gonna build that saloon after all. I swear, I don't know what's got into him."

"No," Matt said, "I hadn't heard all that."

"And we got us a brand new town marshal too. Right nice young fellow, appears to be. He started yesterday."

"Sounds like things are happening pretty fast around here."

"Yep, no telling what's gonna happen next, can't wait to see."

By the time the barber had finished with the shave, he had about talked Matt's ears off. He strolled up to Peterson's store to restock his trail supplies.

"Afternoon, Mr. Henry," the storekeeper greeted cheerfully. "Guess you heard the news?"

"Seems that's about all I been hearing today," Matt told him. "What's yours?"

"Well, we hired us a new town marshal yesterday. The U.S.Marshal up in San Antonio sent him down to talk with us and we hired him on the spot. His name's Chester Clay. He's just a young fellow, but he's got a lot of good experience. He was a deputy up in Amarillo for a couple of years before he rode with the Texas Rangers for three years. Says he's ready to settle down and put down some roots."

"Sounds like a good man. I hear Bragg has changed his mind about putting in a saloon here in your town."

"Yeah, that's the weirdest thing. Don't know what's got into him but we're all tickled pink about it. I can't believe it, but I even hear rumors he's thinking about closing down his whole operation across the river. I'll believe that when I see it though.

Why, the way he's acting, you'd almost think he got religion or something."

"Maybeso," Matt said, lifting a corner of his mouth in a smile. "I hear religion makes some do strange things."

Matt picked himself out a new pair of pants, a shirt and some underwear. He made arrangements for the trail supplies he needed, paid his bill, then headed for the marshal's office.

Two workmen were patching up the outside of the building with a new covering of adobe and a new boardwalk had already been completed along the front. Matt opened the door and stepped inside and hardly recognized the place. Earl would never believe it. The old furniture had all been replaced with a new desk, chair and cabinet. A brand new Henry repeating rifle and Greener shotgun hung on a new gun rack on the wall. There was even a special board just for the wanted posters that were tacked to it.

A thin young man stood from behind the desk when Matt entered. He was a clean-cut young fellow, almost handsome. Square jaw, clean shaven, well dressed, with a bright shiny new town marshal's badge pinned to his leather vest.

"I beg your pardon," Matt said, looking around, "I must be in the wrong place, I was looking for the Marshal's office."

"Yeah, it does look different don't it, that was part of the deal to get me to take the job. I'm Chet Clay, and like everything else in here, I'm new. Something I can do for you?"

"Nice to meet you, Marshal," Matt said, reaching a hand. "I'm Matt Henry. Marshal Tolleson was a good friend of mine."

"Nope," the marshal said, shaking Matt's hand and his head, "you can't be the Matt Henry I've been hearing about. He's nine feet tall and uses horseshoe nails for toothpicks. It's good to meet you, Matt. I've been hearing stories about you all over Texas."

"My papa always told me if a man believes everything he hears, he's either a fool or a preacher. You don't look like neither."

"I didn't say I believed 'em, I just said I'd been hearing 'em. You just get into town?"

"Yeah, I rode in about daybreak this morning. I'll be riding on come first light."

Matt moseyed over to the poster board and scanned the wanted fliers. Reaching a hand, he grasped one between thumb and finger, jerked it down and pitched it on the marshal's desk.

"You can cross that one off," he told the marshal. "She was killed in a shoot out a couple of weeks ago down in Anahuac, Mexico. Shot by a fellow they call El Capitan, he was the officer in charge of the local federales."

"You said, was. What happened to him?"

"I heard he hung himself. All tore up about shooting the woman, or something like that I hear. Anyway, she's one less of the Trotter Gang the law has to worry about."

The young marshal looked at the poster, sat down at his desk and pulled an official looking paper from a drawer. He dipped an ink pen into a container and started writing.

"Lilly Sawyer, huh? What was a woman doing riding with a bunch like that? From what I hear, they're the worse of the worst. Say she bought it down in Mexico? You actually see it happen?"

"Well, not exactly. I saw her after the ruckus was over though. Best I could tell, she was Trotter's woman. Trotter was paying this Mexican officer for protection. They had a falling out, over the woman I reckon, anyway, like I say, you don't have to worry about her any more."

"It says here there's a five hundred dollar reward on her. Don't hardly see how I could recommend you're entitled to it though, seeing as how you didn't actually bring her in."

"I ain't looking to claim no reward, Marshal, just telling you what I know. How's my friend, Dan McAllister?"

"He's busier than a one-legged man in a butt kicking contest. He's kinda watching his back ever since Trotter's bunch bushwhacked Earl Tolleson. Every lawman and bounty hunter in the country's looking high and low for Trotter now."

"Yeah, about time too, I reckon." Matt said. "I see you've got a brand new poster on him. Ten thousand dollars, that's an awful lot of money."

"I reckon it is. That's more than they're offering for that train robber from Missouri, Jesse James. The word is that Trotter murdered the son of some wealthy fellow from Illinois, he's the one that's putting up the money."

"Well, it's just a matter of time then," Matt said. "That much money will bring every bounty hunter in the country out of the woodwork looking to cash in. I'll be seeing the marshal in a few days, anything you want me to tell him?"

"Yeah, tell him after meeting you, I ain't believing nothing else he tells me, you ain't near as ugly as he said you was."

"Thanks, I think." Matt chuckled and heading for the door.

Manuel was still behind the desk when Matt strode into the hotel lobby.

"Could a fellow still get a hot bath around here now that we've changed management?" he kidded.

"Si, señor Matt," the energetic young man said, breaking into a trot toward the back door, "I will bring it right up."

He did. Matt spent the next hour or so soaking in the steaming hot water and felt nearly human again when he finally got out. He took his time dressing, then sauntered down to Marie's café. He was too late for lunch and too early for supper. Not a soul was around. Then he heard Marie busying around in the kitchen preparing for the supper crowd. He poured himself a cup of coffee and walked to the kitchen door and leaned against the doorframe.

"Reckon a fellow could get something to eat around here?" he kidded.

"Senor Matt," Marie said, looking up from her chores. "It is good to see you. Manuel said you were back in town. Did you have a successful trip?"

"Seems so," Matt said. "Manuel tells me you bought the hotel."

"Si, can you believe it? So many good things have happened so quickly. But I am concerned, señor Matt. The paper we signed with señor Bragg says he can take the hotel back if we are even one day late paying him. Is that the way it should be?"

"Well, if that's what all of you agreed to, then I reckon he would have that right. Let me give it some thought."

"How long will you be staying?" Marie asked as she worked.

"I'll be riding out at first light. Might be a while before I'm back down this way again." He drained his cup and walked over to refill it.

He strolled over to a table, scraped out a chair and folded into it. For long minutes he sat, sipping his coffee and thinking. When Marie brought out his meal he was still sitting there, staring absently into his coffee cup, lost in a world of thought.

"Is something wrong, Matt?" She set his steak and all the trimmings in front of him.

"Oh, no, I guess I'm just tired," he told her, "and maybe a little lonesome."

"I've heard it said there's no worse feeling that being alone, but as many friends as you have, you should never be lonely."

"I reckon a man can be alone, even in a crowd," he said quietly.

"Matt, I want you to know how much Manuel and I appreciate all you have done for us. Without you, none of this would have happened to us. We probably would not even be married yet. We are so happy, I hope someday you can find someone that will make you happy again."

"Thanks, Marie, seems like I've been hearing that a lot lately. Marie, I've had this notion rolling around in my head all day, see what you think about it. I was wondering if you and Manuel might like to have a partner in the hotel?"

"What do you mean?" she asked.

"Well, you said you owe Bragg two thousand dollars on it and you have to make regular payments on it. The way I see it, there's all kind of things that could happen that might cause you to be late paying him sometime. According to the paper you signed, he could take the hotel back."

"Si, I, too, am concerned about that."

"Well, what if I give you the money? I would furnish the money so you could pay Bragg off, with some extra so you could fix the place up some. You know, buy some new mattresses and stuff, those corn shuck mattresses are better than nothing, but that's about all. You and Manuel would own it and operate it and we would be partners. We wouldn't sign anything, just your word is good enough for me."

It looked like a great weight had been lifted from her shoulders. A huge smile wrapped across her pretty face and her eyes lit up even more that usual.

"Senor, Matt, that would be wonderful! Could you do that? It is so much money."

"Tell you what, why don't you run and get Manuel and let's sit down and talk about it some. If the two of you agree, then we've got ourselves a bargain."

Matt twisted in the saddle and peered back through the darkness at the sleeping town of Laredo. So many memories had been born there and now found lodging in his mind. Some of them good memories—a few not so good. He would take them out from time to time, relive them and smile.

He had given Manuel and Marie thirty thousand pesos, enough to pay Bragg off and an extra ten thousand to fix the place up and for operating money. He felt good that part of the El Capitan's ill gotten money was being put to good use.

Turning, he shot a glance back at his pinto packhorse, wrapped the lead around his saddle horn and kneed the big stallion into a short lope. He had a long way to go. Figuring he could average fifty miles a day, he ought to make San Antonio in three or four days. Settling into the saddle, his body fell into the rhythm of the horse's movements, allowing his mind to drift.

His friends back in Arkansas came to mind. I need to send them a wire when I get back to San Antonio and let them know I'm still alive and kicking. I'll bet Molly is growing like a weed. Wonder if they still think about me from time to time? It sure would be good to see her and J. C., but Arkansas is a world away.

Reckon Joe and Julio and the family made it okay? He worried about them running into trouble, but they were good men, they could handle themselves. They should be waiting at the hotel when he got there.

He couldn't wait to see old J.R. and Juanita again. He found himself thinking of them real often. What little he could remember about his own father was reflected in J.R. Cunningham. Wonder if Jamie is back from school yet? For some reason, he was really looking forward to meeting her. She was likely as ugly as homemade soap and a spoiled tomboy to boot. Would she be kind of like his sister?

Gray gradually became pink and pink became a pale orange, chasing away the early dawn. Somewhere beyond his line of sight a fire erupted and grew, sending its glow upward, splashing the bluing sky with a panorama of color. Then it appeared, at first only a sliver of brilliant light that quickly became an inferno of fire. The fiery ball was born out of the horizon and grew larger and brighter until its presence burned Matt's eyes as he stared at the spectacle. He blinked and turned his head away. The sun had risen on another day.

All day he rode steadily, stopping occasionally to give his packhorse a breather. He made it to the big bend of the Nueces River just before dark. He found a sheer bluff reaching forty feet high with a flat shelf overlooking the river at its base. It had good graze for the horses. With the bluff at his back and the river close by, he set up camp.

His experience living with the Apache had taught him a campfire could be seen for miles in flat land like he was in, so he dug a fire pit about two feet deep and heaped the loose dirt around the edge before building his fire in the pit. From a distance, only the faint glow from it should be seen.

He warmed up some leftover steak and biscuits he had brought from Marie's. Frying some potatoes to go with it, he enjoyed a good meal. Leaning back against his saddle and sipping a second cup of coffee, he stared up at a sky full of stars and relaxed.

He had just set his empty cup down and scooted down against his saddle when he heard Midnight's warning snort. His eyes flicked to his stallion and saw his ears twitch and point, as the horse swung his head and stared into the darkness, an unmistakable announcement that they had company.

The sudden swish of incoming arrows told him who the company was. Only his early training as an Apache warrior saved his life. Instinctively, he rolled to his left when he heard the familiar sound a feathered arrow makes when it hurtles through the air. Two of them buried deep into the saddle where his back had just been only a split second before. Two more hit the sand beside the saddle, one on either side.

The Henry rifle that had lain beside him was in his hand and he levered a shell into the chamber as he scrambled behind his packsaddle. Laying the rifle across the top, he peered hard into the darkness.

He already knew three things. There were at least four of them. They were Apache. . .and he was in a heap of trouble. The arrows came in together, which meant four had shot at once. Two aimed at his chest. The other two had aimed one to his right and one to his left, just in case he had jumped to one side or the other. The distinctive three columns of arrows, all tapered backwards, told him these were Chiricahua Apache, the same tribe who raised him years before.

Knowing who they were also told him something else that he didn't really want to know. More than likely, there were at least eight of them. He knew a Chiricahua raiding party seldom traveled with less than eight, especially this far north, unless, of course, they had lost some in previous encounters.

That they also had rifles, he had little doubt. But ammunition, for the Apache, was hard to come by. Guns were used only when arrows didn't do their job. His thinking was confirmed only seconds later when two flashes of fire blossomed from the darkness.

He fired at the nearest flash and heard a satisfying smack and grunt as the bullet hit flesh. Even as he pulled the trigger he rolled to his left and heard a thud as a bullet dug into the pack behind which he lay. Again he fired at the muzzle flash, knowing the slight delay had allowed the shooter to move, even as he himself had moved after he fired. Levering another shell, he used the pause to thumb back the hammers on his side arms.

While he waited for the next shot, he tried to figure out their next move. What would he do if he were in their place? He would most likely send a couple of warriors out, circle along the bluff and try to get behind him. A shot from his left missed badly. He figured it was meant only to occupy him while others made their move. On nothing more than experience and a hunch, he fired a couple of feet to the right and was rewarded with a scream of agony.

He decided the best defense would be a good offense. Crawfishing quickly backwards on his belly, he reached the edge of the sloping shelf and slipped over the side. He slid halfway down, then worked his way along towards his right in the direction of his attackers.

Creeping along the steep incline, it took a few minutes to go the forty yards he figured he needed to get behind them. Climbing back up the bank, he cautiously raised his head above the edge of the shelf and peered through the darkness. In the grass, only a few feet from Matt, lay a prostrate form. The Indian's head swung back and forth, searching the darkness for any movement.

Slowly, silently, Matt pulled himself up over the edge. Moving as silently as a snake, he crawled through the grass toward the figure not ten feet from him. Gently laying his rifle aside, he withdrew his Bowie and placed it between his teeth to keep both hands free. He inched forward, fully aware that one mistake, one stone dislodged, one crack of a dried leaf, would spell his demise. He was now only a body length away. He drew his legs up under him, bunching them like a mountain cougar. Sweeping the Bowie from his mouth with his right hand he sprang. As the weight of his body landed on the Apache's back, Matt felt the wind go out of the man. His left hand shot out and clamped over the Indian's mouth. A quick swipe of the Bowie sent another Apache warrior to the happy hunting ground.

Matt lay motionless on top of the dead warrior, waiting to see if his actions had alerted the others. Neither seeing nor hearing movement, he rolled off the man and bellied backwards to the shelf rim, picking up his rifle on the way.

Slipping over the bank, he made his way along the sloping bank, angling toward the river. If he guessed right, they would most likely have left their horses in the small willow thicket he had noticed that afternoon when he rode in. Usually, one of the younger warriors was left to guard their mounts. When he neared the thicket he bellied down again, moving slowly forward. As cautiously as a deer would approach an open field, he got to within twenty yards before he heard the shuffling of horses' hooves.

Luckily, the horse holder had his back to Matt. Quickly counting, he discovered there were seven horses. That meant there were only six attackers, three of which he had already taken out of action. In the dim moonlight, he could see the man held no gun. Both hands were busy holding the single rein on each horse an Apache uses.

The Indian ponies became aware of Matt's presence before the holder did. They became nervous and shied back against the reins, pulling hard to break free. This diverted the Apache's attention. Matt used the distraction to leap forward, clamp a hand over the man's mouth and let the Bowie do its work.

The horses bolted and broke free from the dying man's hands. Matt managed to grab four, but the other three charged off at a gallop. Well, so much for secrecy. The three remaining warriors now knew where he was.

He quickly wrapped the reins of the four horses around a sturdy sapling and tied a half-hitch, then broke into a dead run toward the bluff, searching for cover. He found it behind a large rock, dislodged from the bluff and lying on a flat shelf.

They came spread out and crouched over. All three had rifles. Their shadowy forms were perfectly outlined by the moonlight's reflection on the river behind them. Matt shot the one in the lead, levered another round and laid it on the back of a fleeing form heading for the safety of the river. He didn't make it. Matt's bullet struck him in the middle of his back. The warrior threw one hand containing his rifle into the air, dropping it. The other Apache clutched his back where the bullet entered. He rose to his tiptoes as would a dancer, staggered forward a few steps, then toppled over face first into the river.

The last remaining warrior did the unexpected. He charged directly at Matt. By the time Matt saw him coming, he didn't have enough time to lever another round into his rifle and fire, nor did he have time to put his side arms into action. Dropping the rifle, he was barely able to sweep out his big Bowie before the Indian's headlong dive hit Matt and carried him backwards.

Matt was flat on his back with the Apache on top of him. A sudden flash of moonlight reflecting off the Indian's blade knotted Matt's stomach as the knife plunged downward toward his chest. Matt's left hand shot out and seized the man's wrist, halting the knife's deadly journey in midair. Matt's right hand clutching his own knife swept around, headed for the warrior's left side only to be stopped short of its target by a steel vice hand that clamped onto his own wrist.

Locked in an embrace of death, the two combatants rolled on the ground, each trying desperately to gain the advantage. The Apache ended up on top, his knees firmly planted, one on either side of Matt's prostrate body. He stared in horror as the shiny blade in the Indian's hand inched lower and lower, the sharp point only inches from Matt's throat.

Summoning every ounce of strength left in him, he still could not stop the advancing blade driven by a powerful arm. Unless he did something quick, he had only seconds to live.

Swinging a leg high into the air, he hooked it around the Indian's neck and pulled down with all his strength. The warrior was swept backwards off Matt. The Apache somersaulted backwards and landed on his feet even as Matt scrambled upright. The two men stood crouched, facing each other, not ten feet apart.

Both of Matt's side arms were fully cocked and ready to fire. He knew he could easily draw either weapon and end the struggle immediately. The Apache knew it too, for his dark eyes flicked down to the pistol, then back to lock upon Matt's eyes, searching, asking an unspoken question.

As much as he wanted to live, he wanted even more to be a man of honor.

To an Apache, his pride was more precious than life itself. He would rather die with honor than live with dishonor. His deep sense of fair play would not allow him to take the easy way. This wasn't just a fight to the death; this was a quest of honor. Matt's left hand dropped to his belt buckles, undid them and let his guns drop to the ground. A look of both surprise and respect overtook the warrior's dark face.

Both fighters dropped into the fighter's stance, feet wide apart, knees slightly bent, weapon out in front. Matt's big Bowie played back and forth between him and his opponent. They began the cat and mouse ritual of circling each other, searching for an opening, inching ever closer, sliding their feet along the ground, never diverting their eyes from their adversary.

The Apache tried a searching slash, feeling out his opponent. Matt slid backward a half step, allowing the blade to pass harmlessly by. Matt faked a thrust, pulled it back at the last second and watched his opponent's reaction. The Indian swung his knife sideways, a move that would have taken Matt's hand off at the wrist had he followed through with his thrust. Good move, Matt thought. This guy was better than good.

The Apache tried a double slash followed by a thrust. Matt slid to his right. His hand shot out and closed around the warrior's wrist as it flashed past him. His own right hand swept upward, intent on impaling the Indian on his big Bowie. Instead, it was as if his hand suddenly struck a rock wall when the man's strong hand locked onto his own wrist, stopping it in midair.

Once again they were locked in a dance of death. Each man strained mightily to break the other's grip, both failing. Their faces were only inches apart. The warrior's face contorted into an evil snarl. A deep growling sound came from deep in his throat.

Realizing that his adversary was too strong for him to overpower, he knew if he was to survive, he would have to use something other than strength to win this battle. In a desperate move Matt let his legs collapse, dropping into a sitting position. At the same instant, he jerked forward, using the Indian's own momentum to catapult him into the air and over Matt. As the man hurtled over him, Matt's right knee lashed out and up, finding its target between the Apache's legs. Matt grimaced when he heard the sickening crunch.

Matt rolled to his feet and kicked the knife from the agonizing man's hand and dropped astraddle of him, a knee on each arm and the sharp point of the Bowie pricking the soft spot just below the Indian's Adam's apple.

The Apache warrior stared hard into Matt's eyes for an eternal moment. Matt saw not a hint of fear in those eyes, only resignation. The Indian closed his eyes, ready for a quick and painful death.

"How are you called?" Matt asked in the tongue of the Chiricahua Apache.

The warrior's eyes snapped open. A look of puzzlement washed his face. Again he stared into Matt's eyes before speaking.

"I am called, Spotted Horse. How is it you speak the language of The People?"

"I was raised in the village of Chief Elkhorn. I was called White Hawk," Matt told the surprised warrior.

"It has been many winters, but I have heard stories of you around the fires. It is clear you learned the lessons of the Apache well."

"I count coup," Matt said, touching the blade of his Bowie to the top of the man's scalp, then stood and offered a hand, lifting the warrior to his feet. "You are free to go in peace, Spotted Horse."

The warrior stood motionless, facing his former enemy, apparently still unable to believe he would not be killed. Finally, he reached a hand to meet Matt's own, and they grasped each other's wrists in a brother-to-brother sign of respect.

"Should we meet again," Matt said, "let it be in peace."

"So shall it be."

Turning his back, the Indian scooped up his knife and strode to the willow thicket and their horses. He loaded his fallen brothers across their ponies and led them off into the night.

It took Matt a long time to fall asleep. He kept going over the battle, again and again. For the first time since his battle with Two Bears, he felt remorse for those he had killed in combat.

* * *

By noon of the third day Matt rode into San Antonio. The same old holster greeted Matt at the livery as he unlimbered his tired bottom from his saddle.

"See you're still toting that big buffalo gun around, young fellow," the old timer said, spitting a stream of tobacco juice at a horse dropping.

"Yep," Matt replied, "and still as tired as all get out."

"Well, the hotel ain't moved none since you was here last. I'll double grain 'em and stall 'em separate with fresh hay, just like before. Don't worry about your pack none either, I'll see to it."

"For an old codger, you got a good memory." Matt untied his saddlebags and throwing them across his shoulder.

"If you weren't so dad blamed tired, I'd show you what an old codger can do. You got a passel of folks waiting on you over at the hotel, young fella. That Mexican fella's been talking trade on a couple teams of horses. Stubbornest fella I ever seen in all my born days."

Matt just cut a grin and headed for the hotel. He was glad to hear they had made it in and was anxious to see them and get to know them better.

The first one he saw was Chico. He was playing with two other boys about his age. They were all chasing an iron wagon rim down the street, guiding it with a stick. The boy spotted him and ran to meet him, grinning from ear to ear.

"Senor, Matt," he shouted loud enough to wake up the dead.

"Hola, Chico," Matt hollered back, opening his arms to catch the young boy as he ran into them.

The boy grabbed Matt and hugged him around the waist. Matt rumpled his young friend's long hair and they walked together toward the hotel. Obviously wanting to be the first to tell of Matt's arrival, the boy raced ahead to spread the news.

The ladies were all waiting in the lobby when Matt strode in. After they had hugged and said their howdies, Marquitta told Matt that the men had gone to the freight yard to look at some wagons. The women gathered around him, all talking and asking questions at once. It was an exciting homecoming. It felt good, Matt thought.

Matt rented a room and asked the women if they could all have supper together at six. He made arrangements for a hot bath to be sent to his room, then asked the desk clerk to arrange for a table for eight at six.

The room he was assigned happened to be on the ground floor, which suited Matt just fine. He didn't know if he had the energy to climb the stairs. After checking the sheets on the bed and finding them clean, he counted out a thousand dollars American money and a handful of double eagles from the saddlebags, rebuckled the bags and strode back out the door and headed for the bank.

"I'm Matt Henry," he told the bald-headed little man that greeted him as he walked into the bank.

"Fred Martindale," the man said, extending a hand to Matt. "I'm the President of the bank. How can I help you, Mr. Henry?"

"I see you have a walk-in vault over there," Matt said. "Mind if I ask who's got access to it?"

"Don't mind at all," the man said. "I'm the only one that has the combination. My cashier isn't allowed in it."

"Then if I leave these saddlebags in it, they'll be there when I come back to get them?"

"Most certainly. Whatever is in them will be completely safe, I assure you."

"Fair enough." Matt swung the three bags full of money off his shoulder and dropped them onto the man's desk. "I'm holding you responsible if something happens to them, understand?"

"Yes, sir."

Matt was reasonably satisfied that his money would be safe. He strode from the bank and tromped up the street to the San

Antonio General Store, as the large sign on the front said. It was the largest store he had ever been in. It had aisle after aisle of most anything a fellow could want. He noticed a large selection of women's clothing. That gave him an idea. Marquitta, Avianna and Rosetta all needed some new clothes, he figured, especially some store bought dresses.

He picked out a new suit of clothes for himself, along with some socks and underwear. While paying his bill, he noticed jar after jar of bright colored candy.

"Sack me up a some of that candy, will you?" he told the lady that waited on him. "Just mix it up, give me a couple sticks of all of it."

His bath was ready and waiting when he got back to his room and he spent the next hour soaking. Afterward, he climbed into his new suit of clothes and went looking for Chico. He found him still playing with the two boys and gave him the big sack of candy.

"Can I give my friends a piece?" the boy asked.

"Why sure," Matt told him. "They're your friends, aren't they? Friends ought to share with friends."

The boy made a big deal of picking out the piece he wanted to give each boy, then he and Matt walked side by side up the street.

"Senor, Matt," the boy asked, "are we friends?"

"Shore we are, son."

"Here, I want you to have a piece of my candy, too."

"Why not?" Matt reached out to the offered sack and selected a piece. "Come on, me and you are gonna get us a store bought haircut."

Chico's face beamed when the barber finished cutting his hair. He stared at his own image in the big mirror on the wall.

"I've never had a real haircut before," he said, making a face at himself. "It don't look like me."

"It makes you look all growed up," Matt told him, taking his own place in the chair.

The boy sat and sucked on his candy and watched as Matt got his own ears lowered and a much needed shave.

Supper was a grand affair. Everybody seemed excited and had something special to tell about their trip. Matt was relieved to learn they hadn't encountered any problems on their trip. Maybe he ought to start traveling with them, he thought. Seemed like trouble always had a way of finding him.

Joe told Matt that they had found a whole freight yard full of wagons.

"The owner is a fellow named Russ Stevens," Joe said, "he bought a whole passel of wagons from the Army after the war. From talking to him, I get the idea he got stuck with them and is hankering to sell. They're special built, I've never seen anything like 'em."

"After breakfast in the morning, let's mosey out and have a look," Matt said. "Julio, the old holster down at the livery tells me you're a mighty tough horse trader."

"We find some good freight horses at the livery, the old man is selling them for the owner of the freight yard. The old man is very stubborn."

"That's kinda what he said about you," Matt told his Mexican friend. Marquitta overheard the comment and agreed.

Matt was quick to notice that Joe and Avianna sat next to each other. A man would have to be blind not to see they were sparking.

"Glad to hear you didn't have any trouble on the way up," Matt told them.

"Nope, we saw a lot of sign but didn't see no hair."

"I had a passel of Apache visit my camp a few nights ago."

"What did they want?" Joe asked.

"Oh, nothing much," Matt said, "just my horses, my guns and my scalp. But not necessarily in that order."

"What happened, señor?" Juan asked.

"I sort of read to them from the book," Matt said, not wanting to go into details with the women present.

"I can imagine," Joe said.

"Marquitta, I was up at the store today and noticed some mighty pretty dresses. I'd like for you ladies to go shopping tomorrow. I want each of you to pick out two dresses apiece and shoes and...well, whatever you need to go with them. Get a couple of outfits for everybody in the family.

"After you've done that, how about picking out whatever supplies we need to outfit a wagon for a long trip. You know, pots and pans, medicine, food, bedrolls, blankets, rain gear, the whole works. I've already made arrangements with the storeowner and told him you'd be in.

"Here's your first month's pay," he said, handing them forty dollars apiece. "Thought you might see something else that catches your eye while you're there."

From the looks on their faces, those two gold double-eagles were more cash money than either of them had ever seen in their whole lives. Those looks made Matt feel real good.

It was late when they finished visiting and they all headed to their rooms. It had been a good day, Matt thought as he shucked his clothes and crawled into bed. It had been a real good day.

Joe, Julio, and Juan were already sipping coffee when Matt strolled into the dining room the next morning. Drawing back an empty chair, Matt folded into it and motioned for a cup.

"Thought you was gonna sleep all day, boss," Joe razzed him.

"Takes more some days than others," Matt said. "This was one of 'em. How's everybody perking this morning?"

"Ready and rearing to go."

"Joe, you don't look half bad when you're fed and washed up. Seems I'm seeing a new sparkle in your eye, too," Matt kidded his friend.

"Wish I could say the same about you," Joe returned tit for tat.

They laughed and kidded all through breakfast. They were just finishing up when the marshal pushed through the door and strode to their table.

"Well, if you won't look what the cat drug in," the marshal boomed out. "Matt, it's good to see you. I heard you was back in town and all in one piece too."

"How you doing, Dan?" Matt stood to shake the marshal's outstretched hand. "Have you met my friends?"

"Sure have, morning fellows."

"Drag out a chair and have a seat. You had breakfast yet?"

"Long time ago, but thanks anyway. Seems like you owe me one though if I'm recalling correctly."

"See you ain't changed any," Matt told his friend. "What did you do while I was gone?"

"I've been off my feed, but I'm feeling good now."

"Yeah, I reckon." Matt lifted his lips in a mild smile.

"I've been keeping track of your travels though, course that ain't real hard, all I got to do is watch the death notices that come across my desk. Guess you heard we hung Luther Trotter?"

"Yeah, I heard. Shore hated it about Earl getting shot in the back."

"Earl Tolleson was one of the best lawmen I ever knew."

"The dirty cowards didn't have the guts to face him straight up," Matt said, "course that's their way. You still figure it was Trotter that done the shooting?"

"Either him or one of his," the marshal said. "If I was a betting man, I'd put my money on Trotter himself. Guess you heard about the price on his head now?"

"Yeah, I reckon that'll bring the bounty hunters our of the bushes."

"It already has. Ain't a week goes by that one or two don't ride through, most near as bad as Trotter himself. Ten thousand dollars is a heap of money. You got any idea where Trotter's headed?"

"Couldn't even venture a guess," Matt said, "he'll turn up like a bad penny though, trouble is, wherever he shows up, people get killed."

"Did you meet the new marshal down in Laredo?"

"Shore did, seems like a good man. He said to tell you thanks."

"Knowing him, I kinda doubt that's what he said," the marshal said, cracking a grin. "Oh yeah, before I forget it, I've got that envelope I've been holding for you. It's over at the bank. The banker's name is Martindale."

"I met him yesterday. I'll stop off and pick it up sometime this afternoon."

"You gonna be in town long?"

"Nope, we'll likely be pulling out tomorrow. We're all headed out to the Circle C. I want the folks to meet J.R. and Mrs. Cunningham, then we're heading up to Arkansas."

"Their daughter made it in from back east. J.R. and some of his riders came in to meet the stage a couple of weeks ago. You ever met her?"

"Nope, haven't had the pleasure yet."

"Well, you shore got a pleasure coming, she's a pretty thing. Hey, I ain't got time to sit around jawing with you all day, I got things to do. If I don't see you before you leave, it's shore been good knowing you, Matt. Hope our trails cross again. Men, if this fellow don't treat you right, you just get me word."

"We'll be seeing you again, Dan." Matt stood and shook the marshal's hand.

After another cup of coffee, Julio and Juan headed for the livery to check out the harness for the big freight horses while Matt and Joe went to the freight yard outside town to look at the wagons he had found.

There were two dozen or so wagons in the yard for sale. Like Joe had said, most of them were custom built surplus Army freight wagons. They were specially built with extra wide wheels, heavy duty axles and were eight feet wide and nineteen feet long. They would do just fine for what he had in mind later on.

Also on the yard and sitting over by themselves, Matt spotted three Conestoga Prairie Schooners, as folks often called them. They had heavy, white canvas tops and looked to be brand new. He knew hundreds of the big Conestoga wagons had carried thousands of folks clear across the country to settle the west.

"What's he asking for the Conestogas?" Matt asked.

"He's asking two hundred apiece for them," Joe told him. "Says he'll take a hundred and fifty for the freight wagons."

"See if he'll take five hundred for all three of the Conestogas," Matt said, counting out the money and handing it to Joe. "You can see him later, right now let's go see if Julio can buy us something to pull them with."

The old holster wasn't there when Matt and Joe walked up. Julio and Juan were in the corral walking among the horses, looking them over. They saw Matt and walked over to the fence. As they all leaned on the pole fence and discussed the horses, the old holster limped up.

"You ready to buy them horses this morning?" he asked, cutting off a chew of tobacco and plopping it into his mouth.

Julio cut a look at Matt, who just shrugged and climbed up to sit on top of the rail fence. Joe joined him.

The big corral was full of horses, both riding horses and the heavier ones generally used for hauling heavy loads. They all looked pretty good to Matt. He was anxious to see how much Julio knew about horses.

Without comment the Mexican lifted a lariat from a post and played out a loop as he walked slowly among the forty or so horses in the corral. He selected a big, strong looking black with a white blaze face and deftly tossed a loop over its head.

Matt watched his friend as he took up the slack slowly so as not to spook the big animal. Juan joined him and they closely examined the horse. They pulled back its lips and checked its age by its teeth. They ran their hands gently down each of its legs and ankles and lifted each hoof to check them closely. They went through the same process with several of the big horses before strolling back over to the fence.

"They are worth thirty dollars apiece," Julio stated flatly, "no more."

"Thirty dollars?" the old holster screamed like a horse had just stepped on his foot. "Why that's out and out robbery! You ought to be ashamed making a offer like that. Them horses are worth sixty apiece if they're worth a dollar."

"Maybeso to you," Julio said, "not to us. We find better horses for less."

"There ain't no better horses in Texas than these at twice the price," he said, spitting a stream of tobacco juice at a nearby cat and hitting it square between the eyes.

Julio turned his back and started to walk off. Matt had an idea the little game wasn't over by a long shot, but he went along with it and started to climb down off the fence.

"Now just hold on there a cotton picking minute," the old timer said, putting on his best hound dog look. "I kinda took a liking to you fellows and you drive a hard bargain. Tell you what I'll do. Say you're looking for twelve horses? I'm gonna let you have the twelve for fifty apiece.

"Only bargain we take is thirty dollars apiece," Julio said.

"Why are you trying to rob and old man like me? Fifty apiece is like giving 'em to you."

"You stubborn old man. Hard of hearing, too. Thirty is all we give."

"Me stubborn?" The old holster snatched his battered old hat from his head and threw it onto the ground. With his stiff leg he kicked it, sending it careening off across the barnyard. "Now that's the pot calling the kettle black. You're the stubbornness dad burned Mexican I ever run into. You outta at least meet me halfway. Give me forty-five a head and they're yours, but you outta be plumb ashamed of yourself."

"We give forty-five apiece if you throw in the harness," Julio said.

"No sir! No sir! See, now there you go again. That harness is worth ten dollars apiece all by itself."

"We give forty-five apiece for the horses and the harness or they die of old age right there in your corral. That's our final offer, take it or leave it," the Mexican said emphatically.

"I reckon you got a deal," the old holster said, dropping his head and shaking it like he had just lost his best friend. "But I outta sic the marshal on you for stealing from a helpless old man."

Then, spitting a huge stream of tobacco juice at a horsefly and smiling a toothless grin. "I'd a took forty."

"We'd a give fifty," Julio said, glancing at Matt and smiling.

Matt laughed and paid the man for twelve horses at forty-five a head. As they strode away Matt patted Julio on the back.

"I shore dread the day we start negotiating your pay," Matt told him.

Joe left them to go to the freight yard and see if he could buy the wagons. Matt, Julio and Juan headed back toward the hotel. On their way they passed a little carpenter shop with all kinds of woodwork items hanging out front. Matt was fascinated by the quality of the work and on an impulse, turned inside.

"Let's take a look," he told the others, "I've never seen anything like it."

They squeezed into the small shop. It was piled from floor to ceiling with all kinds of wooden items. They saw tables and chairs of all sizes, rocking chairs, stools and chests. There was even a high poster bed made from dark oak.

Matt stopped dead in his tracks when he spotted the chest. It was the most beautiful thing he had ever laid eyes upon. It looked to be about three feet by five feet. He could see his reflection in the highly polished finish. All of the handles, corner protectors and hasps were made of solid silver.

"What kind of chest is it?" he asked the friendly looking lady that appeared from somewhere.

"Yauh," she said with a broken German or Swedish accent, "it is a hope chest. It is my husband's pride and joy."

"What's it for?" Matt asked, having never heard of that.

"Young ladies use it to store up things they will need after they get married. Do you have a betrothed?"

"Don't reckon so, ma'am, what's a betrothed?"

"Do you have a fiancée? Are you engaged to be married?"

"Oh, no, ma'am," he said, embarrassed at being so dumb.

"I am surprised," she said, smiling, "a fine looking man like yourself should have a lady."

"Well, thank you, ma'am. If I had one, I'd shore be thinking hard about buying her that chest." Matt trailed his fingers lightly along the smooth surface. "Your husband shore does good work. I've never seen anything prettier."

"Thank you. He is a master carpenter. His real love is building homes. He has built some of the finest homes in all of Germany. We come to this country after your war. My husband believed there would be much building, but alas, it was not so. There is many problems in Germany."

"Well, he shore does a good job, ma'am. If I ever find one of those betrothed, I'm liable to be back trying to buy that chest from you."

Before they got to the hotel Joe hurried up all excited.

"Just like you said, boss, we bought all three of the Conestogas for five hundred and I talked him into throwing in three spare wheels and six water barrels," he said proudly.

"Good job, Joe. I'd like for you fellows to hitch up two, four-horse teams and make sure the harness all checks out. While you got 'em hitched up, how about pulling them over to the store and loading up the supplies the women have picked out? I'd like to be ready to pull out first thing in the morning."

"We'll have everything ready and waiting, boss."

After they left, heading back to the livery, Matt went by the bank and picked up his saddlebags as well as the envelope containing the three thousand dollar reward for the gunfighter Reno and Luther Trotter. He then went to the telegraph office and wired another ten thousand dollars back to his friend in Arkansas.

"Do you want to send a message with this?" the operator asked.

"Tell him I'm fine and I should be there in a few more weeks," Matt told him.

Leaving the bank, Matt walked over to the livery to watch the boys hitch up the teams. He leaned on the rail for a few minutes, watching his three friends going through the familiar routine of adjusting the harness on the eight horses.

"Joe, can you spare a minute? Can I ask you something?" he asked, when his friend and foreman came to lean on the fence beside him.

"You bet, what is it?"

"You've been a top hand on a large spread, mind telling me what they pay their foreman?"

"Don't know about other outfits, Matt, foreman's wages at the Triple T was seventy-five a month and keep. Hands drew 'forty and found'."

"That squares with what I thought," Matt told him. "We've never talked about pay, but you're riding for the Fourche Valley Ranch now and we pay our foremen a hundred and fifty a month and keep. Julio will draw the same. We'll start Juan out at seventy-five as a wrangler. That sound fair to you?"

"Boss, that's way more than fair. That's pure-dee fine. I never made that much in my whole life."

"It's about time you did, then."

Matt called Julio and Juan over and explained his decision, then counted out their first month's wages to each of them.

"Figured you boys might be wanting some jingle in your pockets before we left town," Matt told them.

"Thanks, boss," Joe said, "I'm getting to like this job more every day."

"Gracias, señor Matt," Julio said, breaking a smile from ear to ear.

The sixteen-year-old boy just stood there, staring down at the money in his hand. It was obviously more money than he had ever even seen, much less that he could call his very own. His dark eyes flicked from the money to his father, then back to the money, then at Matt. He fingered away a tear before choking out the words.

"Gracias, señor Matt. I will do you a good job."

"Julio, could I have a word with you in private?"

"Si, señor," his friend said, a concerned look coming on his face.

"I'm thinking every ten-year-old needs his own horse. I was wondering what you'd think about me giving my little pinto to Chico? I saw him petting her awhile ago. She's a good, gentle horse that's followed me a lot of miles. I think she'd fit him just right. I wanted to talk with you first."

"Oh, si, señor, that would make him very happy. I will look at the store to see if they have a saddle that would fit him. Gracias, señor, Matt. You are a very generous man."

Matt had something on his mind and needed to do some thinking. He strode back to the hotel and flopped down on the bed, his arms behind his head and his feet crossed. His mind was giving birth to an idea. He closed his eyes and let it happen. A picture of his lifelong dream began to form.

As the picture began to take shape, he experimented with various ideas, rejected some, adjusted others, carefully fitting each piece into place in his mind. There were many details that would have to be worked out to bring his dream to reality, but the more he thought about it, the more excited he became. He had to talk to his old friend and mentor, J.R. Cunningham.

Matt had no idea how long he had been lying there, but a light tap on the door jarred him out of the future and back to the present.

"Yes, who is it?" he called.

"It is Chico, señor. We are all waiting for you."

Surely it can't be six o'clock already, he thought, leaping from the bed.

Jamming his Stetson on his head he strode quickly to the door. The boy stood there in a brand new pair of pants, a bright blue shirt with a white neckerchief tied around his neck and a new pair of cowboy boots.

"Well, don't you look snappy," Matt told him. "Don't reckon I ever seen a better looking cowboy."

A grin wrinkled his youthful face and brought a warm feeling in Matt's stomach. He reached and held the boy's small hand as they made their way to the dining room.

They were all there, sipping coffee and punch and talking excitedly. Matt took one look and felt pleasure. Marquitta sat by her husband. The dozen or more lamps that lined the walls reflected light off the beautiful woman's coal black hair, creating an aura that surrounded her head like a halo. Her beautiful wine-colored dress reminded Matt of a picture he had seen once of the Queen of England.

Across the table sat her mirror image. Except that she wore a different colored dress, one would have thought he was seeing double. Avianna sat next to Joe. From the look on his foreman's face, he was one proud fellow.

Rosetta was just as beautiful. Some day soon some lucky young man would be trying his best to put a rope around her.

Matt noticed other women in the dining room staring at their table. They had to be envious and most likely speculating what famous people these ladies were.

By sunup they were on their way. Matt led the procession as they headed east out of San Antonio. Little puffs of dust lifted from the black stallion's hooves as he high stepped sideways, slinging his big head. Matt held a tight rein, knowing Midnight wanted to stretch his long legs.

Matt swung a glance over his shoulder. Juan sat on the springboard seat and handled the double team hitch pulling the first big Conestoga. The boy had a handful of reins laced between his fingers, from time to time popping them to urge the big freight horses on. This boy was a chip off the old block, Matt thought. He would do. His mother and sister sat beside him.

Joe drove the other wagon. Avianna was by his side, sitting tall and looking proud. Julio rode the sorrel gelding, bringing up the rear and keeping an eye on their back trail. Six horses followed the wagons on lead ropes, three behind each wagon.

Chico was all over the place, but mostly riding stirrup to stirrup with Matt. Matt had given him the pinto that morning and Julio had bought him a brand new saddle. The boy cried when Julio led the pinto up and told him it was his.

They made good time. By noon they reined up and gathered to stare down at the San Antonio River.

"We'll water and rest the horses awhile," Matt told them. "Once we cross that river we're on the Circle C Ranch. It's still another day's ride to the headquarters though.

"We should hit the split fork of the Guadalupe River before sundown. We'll make camp there tonight. Not likely we'll run into trouble from here on in, but keep your eyes peeled just the same. Never can tell in this country."

All afternoon they rode steady. Telltale swirls of dust lifted skyward from their passing, sure to attract the attention of J.R. 's security riders, which suited Matt just fine. The horses pulled hard against their harness. Their necks and withers dripped sweat and foamy lather. Matt's own face was drenched with beads of sweat. He twisted in the saddle and sleeved sweat from his brow. He wanted to have their camp set up before dark.

Matt doubled back and, passing the first wagon, he told Juan, "Let's hurry these horses some. We need to make the river before dark."

The sun was kissing the top of the line of mountains when they pulled up under a grove of cottonwoods beside the river. It was a good spot. There was good graze for the horses and the water was shallow and clear.

"We'll camp here," he hollered.

Joe and Chico rustled up some firewood, Matt strung a picket line for all their horses, Julio and Juan took them to water. The ladies were all busy preparing supper. That's when Matt spotted a cloud of dust lifting toward the sky off to the east.

"Joe . . .Julio . . .Juan. We're fixing to have company. Grab your rifles and take cover. Stay out of sight unless I need you. Ladies, hunker down in the wagon. There's loaded pistols in the weapons box, use them if you have to."

Matt slipped the thongs from his side arms and thumbed back the hammers to full cock. He watched the dust spiral move steadily toward them, hoping it was the Circle C security riders, but he couldn't take the chance in case it wasn't.

As the riders drew near, Matt recognized the steel gray mount of the cold eyed little mixed breed named Jose Cruz, J.R.'s head of security. The knot in his stomach relaxed and he breathed a sigh of relief. Raising his right hand in the universal sign of peace, Matt watched the breed plunge his gray across the shallow river and rein up only a few yards away.

"Hola, Jose," Matt said. "I am Matt Henry, a friend of J.R. Cunningham."

"Si, señor Henry, we met before. You and your party are welcome. Mr. Cunningham will be most happy to see you again, señor."

"We were just about to have supper, would you and your men join us?"

"No, señor, por favor. You are very kind to ask. We have another report of an intruder we must check out, we must go. Adios, señor."

With that, he wheeled his mount and plowed back across the river and they quickly disappeared in a cloud of dust.

"I'm shore glad them fellows were friendly," Joe said, pulling himself up from behind a downed tree root. "I don't know if I ever seen a saltier looking bunch. Shore pity the man that gets crosswise with them."

The ladies crawled out of the wagon and finished preparing a delicious meal. Everybody ate like they were half starved—especially Matt. After supper they all sat around sipping coffee, laughing and telling stories. After awhile, Matt noticed Joe and Avianna get up and stroll down beside the river, hand in hand.

Long after everybody else had gone to sleep, Matt lay on his bedroll gazing up at the starry sky and wondered who else in the world might be staring at that same exact star at that very moment. Soon he yawned, checked to make sure his rifle and pistol were within easy reach and drifted off to sleep.

All too soon Joe touched his toe to wake him for his turn at watch. He rose, shook out his boots and stomped into them, picked up his weapons and strolled down to a big cottonwood tree. From there he had a good view of the whole camp as well as the horses. If trouble came, it would most likely be from a roving band of Indians, intent on stealing their horses. He had heard it said that Indians don't fight at night. Those that said it just hadn't lived long enough to learn better and weren't likely to.

Matt's senses were attuned to his surroundings. The normal night sounds were as much a part of him as the sound of his own breathing. The crickets, night birds and frogs were all part of the night. It was the sound that shouldn't be there, or when the normal sounds stopped, that was what he listened for.

The night passed without incident and morning came all too quickly. Dawn broke bright and clear, not a cloud in the sky. It would be another scorcher. Matt rose and gathered wood for the fire and coaxed the coals under the gray ashes back to life. He took the new coffee pot and went down to the river and got water for coffee.

Both Marquitta and Avianna were up by the time he returned. They busied around the camp as naturally as if they had done it their whole lives. Soon coffee was boiling and bacon frying in the pan.

Matt was squatted beside the fire sipping coffee when Joe stumbled up wiping sleep from his eyes. Julio was close behind.

"Does it ever rain in this part of Texas?" Joe asked, shaking a desert scorpion out of his boot and squashing it with the other.

"Might near as often as it snows," Matt told his friend.

"Now that's encouraging." Joe stomped his boots on and poured himself a cup. "What time you figure we'll get to the ranch?"

"Sometime before sundown I reckon."

"Can't for the life of me imagine a ranch this big," Joe said.

"Yeah, it's shore something to behold, wait till you see it."

They enjoyed a delicious breakfast of sliced bacon and fried potatoes, which Matt learned was called papa fritas, huevos rancheros, that turned out to be fried eggs with chili sauce, raw onions and grated cheese and tortillas. After breakfast the men all sat around sipping coffee while the women walked around a curve in the river to bathe.

It was well on its way to another hot day when they finally mounted up and pointed their horses' noses toward the sun. Near noon they spotted the first herd of cattle wearing the Circle C brand. Joe estimated there to be about five hundred head in the herd. Two vaqueros sat their horses nearby watching the herd.

"How many head you reckon your friend runs, Matt?" Joe asked as they rode along together.

"Something over two hundred thousand head right now," Matt told him. "That don't count my twenty two thousand head."

"Your what?" Joe twisted in the saddle and fixed his boss with a stare. "You never told me you had twenty two thousand head of cattle."

"Never saw a need to. I was afraid you might turn down the job."

"Well if that don't beat all," Joe said, swiping his hat off his head and sleeving sweat from his face. "I knew you wanted to start a cattle ranch but I didn't know you already had one."

"I ain't, all I got is a bunch of cattle and a dream, but I'm thinking on the other part. I'll let you know when I get it worked out in a few days. I want to talk to J.R. before I go spouting off."

"Twenty thousand head. Boss, I can't wait to see what else you got up your sleeve you forgot to tell us about."

"Appears to me you been doing some planning of your own."

"You mean me and Avianna?" Joe asked. "Shucks, if I thought she'd have a broken down cowboy like me, my boots wouldn't touch the ground for a month of Sundays."

"Never know till you ask," Matt told him. "She's shore a rarely fine looking woman sure enough and a good woman to boot, if I'm any kind of judge."

"But what if she says no? What if she don't think of me the way I think of her? What if it's too soon after her husband's death?"

"Joe, out here life don't allow much time for what-ifs, nor mourning either, for that matter. If you're gonna play the what-if game...what if she said yes?"

CHAPTER XII

A Suitable Help Mate

> "It is not good for man to live alone, I will make
> him a suitable help mate."
> (Gen. 2:18)

The big rance loomed large and impressive. It set on top of a hill—like a picture he had seen once of a castle in a far away land. The ladies stood up in the wagons and stared and pointed, holding one hand to their mouths in wonderment. How could one not be impressed? Matt wondered, it was shore something to see.

The sun was still an hour high when the little procession rolled to a stop near the pole log fence that surrounded the Big House, as the ranch hands called it.

J.R. and Juanita rushed from the house to meet them as Matt drew a leg over the saddle and swung to the ground. Joe gave the ladies a hand down off the wagon, then Julio and Juan pulled the wagons on down to the barn. Chico still sat in his saddle, staring around wide-eyed.

Matt strode toward the house and was met halfway and greeted with a big bear hug from both the big rancher and Mrs. Cunningham.

"It's good to see you, Matt." J.R. released his hug and held Matt at arm's length to stare at him, then hugged him again. "It's real good to see you, son. You just don't know how happy we are to have you back home."

"It's good to be back," Matt told them honestly.

"Welcome, everyone," J.R. said, turning to the others.

"Welcome to our casa," Senora Cunningham said, reaching to take the hand of both Marquetta and Avianna as Matt stumbled through the introductions.

"It's amazing," the rancher said, staring at the twin sisters and shaking his head. "I hope you'll excuse me for gawking, but I've never seen identical twins before and lovely ones at that."

"Gracias, señor," the sisters said, almost in unison.

"This is Chico," Matt said, as the boy finally worked his way up to stand beside Matt. "He's the boss hoss of our outfit. Son, this man is the best friend I've ever had and like my own father. He hired me when I wasn't much bigger than you."

"Buenas noches, señor," the boy said, exaggerating a bow from the waist and reaching out a hand in a grown-up greeting.

The rancher took the offered hand and shook it vigorously.

"Well, it's good to meet the boss, I always like to deal with the top man."

Matt's eye caught a movement at the house. He flicked a gaze and froze. An angel stepped from the house onto the front porch. His breath caught and held and forgot to breathe again. His heart skipped three or four beats and he stood in stunned amazement.

She was tall for a woman, not many inches shorter than Matt himself. But her height only added to the way she filled out her clothes. She wore black riding pants fitted tight around her legs.

The white shirt type blouse, buttoned down the front and open at the throat, was tucked into the pants and bulged in just the right places.

Her long, coal black hair was pulled back and tied with a long white ribbon and framed an angelic face. The full lips turned up slightly at one corner, causing an observer to believe that beautiful smile was a permanent presence. The brightness of it hurried the sun's departure below the horizon in pure shame. His eyes followed her as she moved smoothly, erect and proud, yet her obvious self-confidence seemed natural, not contrived. One by one she greeted the visitors. Matt tried hard to swallow the huge lump in his throat and failed as she worked her way to him.

A far off voice sounded like the big rancher's voice was speaking but Matt could barely hear what he was saying. Then J.R. was touching his shoulder to get Matt's attention.

"Son, I want you to meet our daughter. This is Jamie. Honey, this is Matt Henry."

Those dark, dancing eyes swung to him—and the world stopped turning. Their eyes met and locked upon each other— and held for the longest slice of eternity and Matt couldn't get his breath. She extended a hand without diverting her eyes. He reached for it and managed, somehow, to find it. The soft touch of it raced from her hand straight to his heart. He held it and never wanted to let it go.

"It's good to finally meet you, Matthew. I've heard of you most of my life," she said in a voice that sounded like an angel whisper. The birds must have stopped singing just to listen.

He was suddenly tongue-tied. He just stood there like a big dummy, unable to say or do anything but stare at the beautiful creature whose hand he was still holding. Finally, after what seemed like a lifetime, he came to himself enough to stammer out.

"Uh ...Uh...how do you do, Uh, Jamie. It's real, it's real nice, to meet you."

Still unwilling to let go of her hand, he bowed at the waist and gently brushed the back of it with his lips and lingered there for a moment. Was he dreaming, or did he feel a slight squeezing of her fingers as he kissed her hand?

"Take my word for it, honey," Matt's rancher friend was saying, "I've known him a long time and he ain't usually at a loss for words like that. Don't feel bad though, Matt. I've known her all her life and she still affects me that way too."

Matt reluctantly let go of the soft hand and looked quickly away, embarrassed at having made such a fool of himself. Now she would likely never speak to him again.

"Let's all go into the living room," Mrs. Cunningham suggested, "where we can be more comfortable."

The living room was spacious and grand. Four large, overstuffed sofas faced each other and formed a square conversation area. A highly polished square coffee table sat in the center on a thick, brightly-colored rug. A large bouquet of fresh flowers sat in the center. Walls covered with something that looked like a wine-colored fabric with designs held beautiful paintings in ornamented frames.

Joe and Julio joined them and they had barely sat down when a young Mexican house girl brought coffee in a shiny silver pot and served it in flowered china cups. Marquitta and Avianna seemed as awed by the impressive house as Matt was by Jamie. As hard as he tried to pay attention to what J.R. was saying, his eyes refused to obey and kept flicking back again and again to feast upon her for another fleeting second.

They were still visiting when a heavy-set woman Matt recognized as Ramona, their Mexican cook, came to the door and announced that dinner was served. The rancher led the way to the large dining room Matt remembered from his previous visit.

J.R. drew out a chair at one end of the table and held it for his wife, then took his place at the other end of the long table.

The big rancher motioned Matt to the chair to his left. Jamie moved to the chair next to his and stood. Matt slid the chair out for her and accepted the pretty smile she rewarded him with. He took his own seat and broke a half-smile when he noticed both Joe and Julio had followed his and J.R.'s example.

Ramona and her two helpers began serving large platters of delicious-looking steaks. The aroma of mesquite wafted up from the thick, juicy pieces of meat. A large bowl of baked beans, another of Mexican style fried corn on the cob and two baskets of fresh-smelling oven-baked bread were set before them. A jar of fresh honey with the comb made Matt's mouth water in anticipation. For the next hour, what conversation there was, was squeezed in between bites.

Supper being over, the men all retired to the back verandah to enjoy another cup of coffee and a big cigar. Mrs. Cunningham and Jamie took the ladies to get them situated in one of the three guest cabins situated on the hill overlooking the river.

"I'll say one thing for you, Mr. Cunningham," Joe said. "You folks sure know how to live."

"It wasn't always this comfortable," the rancher assured him, "the first few years we lived in a small shotgun shack."

"Don't get use to living like this just yet," Matt told his foreman, "It ain't like this where we're heading."

"Where are you heading, my boy?" J.R. asked.

"Well, sir," Matt said, taking a sip of coffee, "I'm needing to talk with you about that. Do you suppose we could spend some time together tomorrow? I've got these ideas rolling around in my head that I need to run by you and see if I've gone plumb loco."

"Certainly, we'll spend as much time as you want. But I doubt seriously that your ideas would fall into the loco class. Fill me in on all that's happened since I saw you last."

Matt took his time relating all the events, both good and bad, since he'd left the Circle C. He stressed Joe and Julio's role in saving his life. When he had finished, he asked Joe to relate his story.

Joe told how the Comanchero had raided the Triple T Ranch where he worked as foreman, how they had slaughtered everyone and drove the ranch's cattle to Kansas and sold them. He related how he had trailed them back down into Mexico before being captured and sent to the silver mine.

"I remember hearing about that," J.R. said. "The Comanchero are the scum of the earth. We still have trouble with them and have to be very watchful. Even as good as security force as we have, if they were to mount a full scale assault, we'd be hard pressed to fight them off."

"How many men do you put in the saddle?" Joe asked.

"Oh, we've got lots of men, well over three hundred, but only about a hundred draw fighting wages. But I'd put them up against twice that many. Most of our men are family men, simple vaqueros. At what they do, they're as good as any man that ever forked a saddle, but not every man is a fighting man."

"Yeah, we met some of your riders when they came to check us out. I shore would hate to tangle with them, especially the leader that wears that Apache headband. Who is he?"

"His name is Jose Cruz. His Apache name is Quick Killer. He's half Mexican, half Apache and one hundred percent poison. His mother was Mexican, his papa was a full blooded Apache warrior named Two Knives.

"His mother raised him until she died when he was ten. His father took him to live with the Apache. He rode with them as a warrior until his father was killed, made quite a name for himself too, I hear. Don't exactly know why he left them, he just showed up one day and asked for a job. I asked him what he could do and he looked me straight in the eye and said, I can kill the bad men for you.

"He's been with me going on ten years now and he's done what he said he would do. He's in charge of our security forces. He's proved he's the best there is at what he does. I've never sent him after a man yet that he didn't bring back, one way or the other, either in the saddle or across it."

"Joe and I were wondering how they always seem to know when somebody comes onto Circle C property and right where to find 'em," Matt asked.

"We use what we call border riders. We assign a rider to a particular stretch along our border. Jose trained them in the art of tracking. All they do is ride their assigned stretch. When they find where somebody has crossed onto the ranch they use either smoke signals or a mirror to relay the information to headquarters. Jose and his men find them and deal with the situation."

"Well it shore seems to work," Joe said.

"Oh, we have some slip through from time to time, but they soon discover it's a lot easier getting in than getting out. Well, it's getting late and I'm sure your folks are worn out. What do you say we call it a day? Breakfast is at sunup. Slim O'Dell, my ranch manager, will be joining us. You remember him, don't you, Matt?"

"Yes, sir, I met him last time I was here."

"Julio, I believe they have your family in the first cabin. Your sister-in-law will be in the second and Joe, I think you'll be staying in the last cabin. Matt, you'll be staying here in the house, first room on the left, top of the stairs. I believe they've already taken your things up to your room. Well, goodnight, gentlemen, it's good to have you here."

Matt lay there in the softest bed he had ever felt but couldn't sleep. Over and over he replayed the scene on the front porch. He went over every detail, reliving that first sight of her, the thrill of her touch, the crocked little lift of her lips when she smiled. What was happening to him? No one had ever affected him like she had. Finally, sleep came and with it came dreams of Jamie Cunningham.

A loud ringing of a dinner bell woke Matt from the soundest sleep since he couldn't remember when. He was instantly awake and sprang out of bed. Bright sunshine creeping through the curtained window told him he had overslept.

Pouring water from the blue speckled water pitcher into the matching wash pan, he quickly washed, shaved, and shaking out a clean shirt from his saddlebags, sleeved into it. The sweet smell of coffee and happy laughter guided him back to the dining room.

He strode into the room where the men folk were sipping a cup of coffee and engaged in deep conversation. Slim, J.R.'s ranch manager was there. Tall, thin waisted, with shoulders Texas wide.

"Sorry I'm late," Matt said, drawing out a chair and folding into it. "I figured I'd give you fellows a head start. I catch up right quick when it comes to eating."

"He ain't lying about that," Joe said.

"Matt, you'll remember Slim O'Dell, my ranch manager. I've already introduced him to Joe and Julio."

Matt reached across the table and took the leather tough hand that was offered and felt the strength of the man through a firm handshake.

"Sure do," Matt said. "How are you, Slim?"

"Doing well," the man replied.

"I was just explaining to Joe how we operate here on the Circle C," J.R. said.

"The ranch is divided up into eight districts," the rancher said. "Each district is pretty much self-sufficient with its own foreman, vaqueros, and its own responsibilities. Slim here oversees the whole operation. Once a month he meets with all his district foremen, then, we have a general meeting with everybody every three months.

Right now we're overstocked, we're running about two hundred-thirty thousand head on just under a half million acres. It stretches from the San Antonio River on the west to the Colorado River on the east. From near Austin in the north to the gulf of Mexico. The headquarters is smack-dab in the middle of it. Except for the King ranch, it's the biggest spread in the country."

All the men rose when Juanita arrived from the kitchen. Close on her heels, Ramona and one of her Mexican helpers carried platters filled with fried eggs, ham and fried potatoes. Another young girl brought plates stacked high with hot biscuits.

"If I ate like this all time I'd be big as a house," Joe commented. "I shore ain't complaining, mind you"

Matt was busy dishing out a plateful of food when Jamie swept into the room. She looked as fresh as a spring flower, Matt thought. He was the first on his feet and pulled out the chair next to his, not taking a chance she might choose another.

She wore beige riding pants with a leather area on the inside of her shapely thighs, highly polished brown high-topped boots and a chocolate-colored shirt, open at the neck. Her long black hair was again pulled back and tied with a chocolate brown scarf that hung down her back.

"Good morning everyone," she said happily. She walked past the chair he held and his heart sank. She went to her mother, bent and hugged her, then glided over to her father. She leaned down and kissed his cheek, hugged him, then returned to take the chair Matt still held for her.

"Good morning, Matthew," she said, lifting those dark flashing eyes to his and offering him a happy smile. "I trust you slept well?"

"Yes, ma'am, I did, thank you."

"Jamie, please call me Jamie," she said, allowing him to scoot her chair forward. "I trust you saved enough time from your meeting with father to go riding with me this morning? I'd like to show you the ranch."

Those dark, flashing eyes turned on him, found his and refused to let go, seemingly waiting for an answer to her question. It was a question, sure enough, but one to which there was only one answer. What fellow with a lick of sense about him would turn down a chance to go riding with an angel?

"Why, yes ma'am . . .I beg your pardon, yes, it so happens I did save time, just in case you should ask me."

She smiled broadly at his joke and turned her attention to the platter of eggs being passed to her. She hadn't been in the room two minutes and she already had him acting like a dumb schoolboy. He had to get ahold of himself.

"Miss Jamie, I understand you went to school back east somewhere?" Matt asked.

"Yes, I've been attending a finishing school in Philadelphia for the past two years."

"Did you enjoy traveling back east?"

"I suppose, but I'm a Texas girl. Have you ever been to Philadelphia?"

"Missouri is about as far east as I've ever been and that's more north than east."

"Father tells me you live in Arkansas, a place called Fourche Valley? It sounds like a beautiful place."

"It is," Matt said, "It's kind of like God was just practicing when he made Texas. After he got it all figured out, then he made the Fourche Valley in Arkansas."

"My, it sounds like a place I'd love to see some day. But don't be too hard on Texas until you've seen what I'll show you later today. Do you think you and father will be finished by ten?"

"We'll make it our business to be through by then."

After breakfast Matt and J.R. retired to the den to talk over another cup of coffee.

"What's on your mind, Matt?"

"I need your advice, J.R.," Matt said. "Well, ever since you hired me on when I was fourteen, I've had this dream that one day I'd own my own cattle ranch. I reckon most men have the same dream and I figured nothing would ever come of it so I settled down to being a sodbuster.

"But now, with the herd and all—and I've been able to lay

my hands on a little start up money—well, the fact is, I'd like to give it a try. I've got a little piece of land up in the Fourche Valley in Arkansas and I'm pretty sure I can get my hands on some more that joins mine. With some good luck and hard work, I believe I can put together a pretty good little spread.

"What do you think about me taking a herd up the trail to Kansas? I know it's already too late to try it this year. I'm thinking about putting a bunch together and heading them out as early as we can, right after the grass gets up good. That would give me time to get things started up in Arkansas and still get back here to put a crew together for the drive."

"You might have hit on something son, most of us have figured it was too big a gamble, what with the trail blockers taking the herds at the border. But if a man could get a herd through, he might do real good.

"Now that I think about it, there's a fellow you might want to talk with. His name is W.W. Suggs. He was a cattle buyer and took a herd up the trail earlier this year. He run into trouble at Baxter Springs and lost his whole herd. Now he's working for a young cattle buyer from Illinois named Joseph McCoy. From what I hear, this McCoy fellow's a lot like you."

"How's that?"

"Well, this fellow, Suggs, says his boss is a man that don't know the meaning of the word, can't. Kind of like you, I reckon. You see, Matt, we got more cattle in Texas than we know what to do with. The problem is we can't get them to market. The cattle growers in the neighboring states say our longhorns bring in what they call the Texas fever. Most folks say it's the ticks they carry. They don't hurt the longhorns, but they kill the shorthorn breed cattle.

"Several of the neighboring states have passed laws outlawing our longhorns. The jayhawkers and grangers have closed the borders and stop the herds before they can get to the railheads in Wichita or Dodge City. They're scared the ticks will kill their shorthorn cattle.

"It's not general knowledge, but I happen to know two big meat packers are building plants and starting up this year in Chicago. A company named Armour and another named Swift and Company. They're both gonna need lots of beef to keep those plants running. Them cows of yours standing out yonder are worth three-fifty, maybe four dollars where they stand. In Chicago, I'd say they're worth maybe forty a head in good Yankee dollars.

"So this young whippersnapper named McCoy comes up with this hair-brained idea of building a big stockyard way out in the middle of nowhere away from the regular railheads and all the trouble. He talks to the folks at Junction City, then Solomon City, then Salina, but nobody wants anything to do with it. He goes to St. Louis and tries to talk to the Missouri Pacific Railroad, but they think he's crazy and throw him out of the office. He goes to the Kansas Pacific Railroad and lays out his plan for them, they listen and finally agree that if he will build the stockyard, they will run a railhead to it, but they ain't willing to put any money for the project.

"I reckon most folks would have already give up and quit, but not this fellow. He just keeps on scratching and clawing and finally comes up with some financial backing, though nobody can figure out where he got it. Like I say, son, this fellow Joseph McCoy, sounds a lot like you. Kind of like a bulldog that gets ahold of something and won't let go.

"So anyway, he goes back to Kansas and buys some land out in a little mud hole called Abilene. There wasn't nothing there but a half dozen sod huts and a pretty valley, but that didn't stop him.

"He sets in building cattle pens strong enough to hold a bull buffalo and big enough to hold several thousand head of the wildest critters anybody could bring up the trail. Why, he even built a hotel with a hundred rooms and a livery big enough to hold a hundred wagon rigs and horses, all at the same time. Now keep in mind, there wasn't a dozen folks within a hundred miles of the place, not even a railroad.

"On top of all that, somehow he convinced the governor to lift the ban on Texas cattle along a mile-wide corridor from the state line and leading right to his place. He opened for business this past July but the cattle he expected to flood in to his place didn't come. With all the trouble and bad publicity about the Texas fever scare, the cattle buyers refused to come because they didn't believe the Texas drovers would and the Texas cattlemen wouldn't drive their herds there because they didn't believe the buyers would be there to buy their cattle.

"The long and short of it is, McCoy hasn't been able to convince either side his operation will work and the fact is, he's got to convince both sides it will work before it will."

"Sounds to me like McCoy's got himself a big problem," Matt said.

"Now, I got no idea if all this is gonna work. He can't seem to get any of the ranchers interested. Most of us don't cotton to the idea of driving a herd all the way to Kansas and then having it taken away from you at the border. Never can tell, might be worth your time to talk with him. Don't see how it could hurt."

"Where you reckon I could find this Suggs fellow?" Matt asked.

"He's going around talking to most of the big ranchers, but I'm afraid he's swimming upstream. Last I heard, he was staying at the hotel in San Antonio."

"Think I'll ride in and have a chat with him."

"He'll be at the big meeting we're having in San Antonio next week, too. Most of the larger ranches in Texas are getting together next week for a big pow-wow to talk about the problems we're facing in the cattle industry. Some of us think it's high time we form some kind of association so the politicians will listen to us.

"Say, how about coming to the meeting with me? Richard King will be there. I hear John Chisum of the Jingle Bob Ranch is coming. Charley Driskill and Colonel Ike Pryor will be there. It's gonna be quite a get together."

"But I don't even have a cattle ranch yet, all I got is a bunch of cattle and a dream," Matt protested.

"You likely got more cattle than most that will be there and besides, you're gonna build that ranch. Come with me as my guest. I want you to be there."

"If you're sure it will be okay, I don't see why not," Matt said. "One more thing, J.R., about me and Jamie going riding today, I mean, do I have your permission?"

"My boy, not only is it all right, I'm tickled pink about it. I'm happy the two of you have hit it off so well. Besides, it wouldn't matter if I approved or not, if that girl sets her mind to do something, wild horses couldn't stop her. Kinda like somebody else I know.

"She decided when she was a little girl she wanted to be a veterinarian. Her mother tried her best to talk her out of it. Told her that was a man's job, but Jamie had her mind made up and there wasn't no changing it.

"All during those two years in Philadelphia she worked with a German Veterinarian Doctor as well as attending the finishing school her mother insisted on. You'll find, my boy, that girl has a mind of her own. She decides what she wants and goes after it."

"I don't mind telling you, she shore makes me feel like a dummy when she's around. Never met a lady like her before."

"If you ask me, I don't reckon there's ever been a lady like her before, but that's a proud father talking. So you're riding into town tomorrow?"

"Yes, sir, I'm gonna try to hire a German carpenter I met the other day. I want him to convert some wagons into chuck wagons, then I'm gonna try to talk him into coming to Arkansas with us and build a ranch house."

"I can see all this ain't something you just cooked up last night. If I thought I could, I'd try to talk you into building your ranch right here on the Circle C. I'd gladly let you have all the land you'd need. But I know you wouldn't be happy till you've followed your own dream."

"Thanks for understanding, J.R., I really appreciate all you've done for me. My bunch will be pulling out right after the meeting next week. I want to go on ahead and take care of some things before the rest of my outfit gets there."

"If I'm any judge of men, you've got yourself a couple of top notch hands in Joe and Julio. My wife has fallen in love with Marquitta and Avianna. I've never seen two people who look more alike. I'll tell you straight, if I could, I'd keep Chico right here with us. He's quite a boy."

"Yeah he is," Matt said. "Listen, I appreciate the advice and I value your counsel. You've given me some pieces of the puzzle I've been trying to put together. I better go, I shore don't want that lady mad at me."

Matt ambled out to the corral. His big stallion trotted over to the fence and nuzzled him through the rails. He rubbed the black's nose and spoke to him in quiet tones as one would speak to a friend. The stable man, a friendly-looking old Mexican, came over leading a beautiful snow-white gelding, all saddled and ready to go. Most likely Jamie's horse, Matt thought.

"Buenos dias, señor," the old timer greeted, "would you like for me to saddle your horse for you, señor?"

"No thanks," Matt said.

Matt saddled Midnight and led both horses up to the Big House. Jamie saw him and hurried out carrying a wooden picnic basket in one hand and a colorful Mexican blanket over the other arm. Reaching out a hand, he took the items from her.

"I didn't know we were spending the night," he said, meaning it as a joke.

Her dark, dancing eyes cut a playful gaze in his direction. A thin grin creased the olive smoothness of her face.

"Never can tell," she said, toeing a stirrup and swinging easily into the saddle.

She reined her white gelding around expertly and held a tight rein as the long-legged mount high-stepped sideways and threw its beautiful head. It was obvious she was no novice at riding.

They rode stirrup to stirrup. The white gelding and the solid black stallion seemingly engaged in a contest to out prance the other. It must have been quite a sight for the vaqueros to watch as they sat their horses and watched the two as they rode by.

Herd after herd grazed contentedly on the thick bunch grass. Each herd numbered from five hundred to a thousand head. Each herd had at least two vaqueros watching them.

"Are all the herds about the same size?" Matt asked.

"Yes, except for those that graze the river bottoms where the grass is thick and high. Larger herds tend to eat the grass closer to the ground and trample what's left, slowing the re-growth. The bunch grass they are grazing on is perhaps the perfect cattle feed. It is one of the few grasses that contain all the nutrients needed for a healthy and prospering animal. It grows plentiful in this area, that is the main reason father chose this land for his ranch. Our cattle are the healthiest and fattest cattle in all of Texas.

"We keep vaqueros with every herd, not only to protect them, but also so they can get to know the cattle. We want them to recognize when one might be sick or need attention when she drops her calf. They also keep a close eye out for mavericks and don't allow them to mix with the herd."

"At the risk of sounding like a greenhorn, what's a maverick?" Matt asked.

"A maverick is a wild cow or bull without a brand. There are thousands of them scattered throughout Mexico and in the east Texas breaks. Some wander this far, they carry a disease called the Spanish fever, most call it the Texas fever.

"There's lots of differing opinions about what causes it. I believe it's caused by the tick they carry. Our vaqueros have standing orders to shoot any maverick on sight and burn the carcass. Once the disease gets started, it can infect the whole herd.

"You seem to know an awful lot about running a cattle ranch," Matt said.

"I've been raised in the saddle and tending cattle. I've worked with them all my life, I love it. I've ridden beside my father since I could walk, maybe before. My father always wanted a boy, but I'm the closest thing he got, so he tried to make one out of me."

"He didn't make it," Matt told her flatly.

"Well, thank you Matthew." She gave him one of those tantalizing smiles that drove him plumb crazy. "I'm going to take that as a compliment."

"That's how it was meant."

Their eyes met for a long moment before she touched heels to the gelding's flanks and was off like a shot. The white horse was fast, but Midnight accepted the challenge and easily pulled alongside.

When they reached a stream that meandered down from the high hills just ahead of them, they reined in, allowing their horses to wade into the cool, crystal clear water and drink their fill.

"Did you enjoy the finishing school?" Matt asked as they sat their saddles side by side.

"Actually, I attended two schools while I was back east. I attended a school for young ladies to please my mother and a school of Animal Husbandry to please myself. You'll probably laugh, but I'd like to be a Veterinarian. An animal doctor.

"I love animals, always have. That would let me carry my own weight around the ranch, either here at the Circle C, or the one my future husband will have. You aren't laughing."

"Why would I laugh? I think it's a wonderful goal. But what if your future husband ain't a cattle rancher like your father? What if he's a school teacher or something like that?" he teased her.

"He won't be," she stated confidently. "I've known since I was a little girl my husband would be a cattle rancher like my father. My father is the strongest, most wonderful man that ever lived. My husband will be like that too."

"Not many men like your father," Matt said.

"I agree, but one more is all I want," she told him, laughing. "Come on Matthew, I want to show you something special."

They rode toward the line of tall hills. One stood high above the rest, topped by a large, protruding rock formation. After a half-hour of climbing they topped out into a beautiful green valley dotted with scattered pine trees. A small, crystal clear lake lay in the very center of the little valley.

"This is absolutely beautiful," he told her as they sat their horses and admired the beauty of the place. "You were right, this is a special place."

Dismounting, they let their horses munch on the lush green grass. Side by side Matt and Jamie strolled toward the rock formation at the edge of the valley. A large rock, shaped something like a saddle, protruded out from the formation.

"I named this place Saddle Rock," she said. "Let's have our picnic here under this big pine tree."

She spread the blanket and they sat down. The fried chicken was delicious, the view breathtaking and the mountain top valley with its crystal lake was like something right out of a dream. But what made the place so special was sitting right beside him.

"I've been coming here since I was a young teenager," she told him, speaking barely above a whisper. "But even then, I knew that someday you would come and I would bring you here to see my special place. I've dreamed for years how it would be and now you're here and it's exactly as I dreamed it would be. Does that shock you, Matthew?"

"But how could you?" he asked, confused by her words. "You didn't even know me then, or for that matter, you really don't know me now, we only met for the first time yesterday."

"In a way, I feel I've known you all my life. My father has told me about you since I was a little girl. I used to sit around and try to picture what you would look like. Yes, Matthew, I know you.

"What I'm going to say will probably shock you, maybe even drive you away from me, but I'm going to marry you, Matthew Henry, I've known it for years.

"Father told me the tragic things that happened to your family. I'm very sorry. It must have hurt you deeply. I know it may be too soon for me to be saying these things, but I'm scared, Matthew. I'm afraid you'll go away again and I wanted you to know how I felt before you go. I wanted to see if maybe someday, you could feel the same way about me?"

Matt slowly reached a hand out to her. She placed her hand in his. Their eyes met. . .and locked there . . .and held. No further words were spoken. Nothing more needed to be said, for the promises seen in each other's eyes in those long moments were somehow more important than mere words, more meaningful than spoken promises, more lasting than any vows that could be said. Their lips slowly sought and found each other. . .and they kissed.

The setting sun was softly kissing the horizon when they rode up to the ranch house, handed the reins to the old Mexican stable man and they strolled up the steps together hand in hand.

Juanita happened to be coming down the stairs when they stepped through the door, still holding hands. She looked quizzically from one to the other, then somehow understood as Jamie rushed into her arms laughing and sobbing at the same time.

Together the three of them walked into the den where J.R. sat at his desk, working on a ledger book. He glanced up, saw something on their faces that brought him to his feet.

"What is it?" he asked quickly, a deep furrow plowing across his leathered face. "What's happening?"

Matt scraped a foot on the rug, bored a hole in the floor with his gaze, then looked up at the rancher who suddenly seemed ten feet tall. He tried to speak and discovered he had a severe case of lockjaw. Finally, clearing his throat to swallow down the huge lump that was stuck there, he took a deep breath and stammered it out.

"Well...uh, J.R...Sir, Jamie and I, well, we've been talking today and—"

"What is it, son?" the big rancher said, puzzled by Matt's uncharacteristic awkwardness. "Just spit it out, boy, what are you trying to say? Is something wrong?"

Matt cleared his dry throat once again, took a deep breath and just said it.

"Sir, Jamie and I would like to be married, I'm asking yours and Mrs. Cunningham's blessing."

The long moment of silence it took for it to sink in seemed to Matt like an eternity. Matt had never in his life been so scared. When it came, you could have heard the whoop all the way to San Antonio. J.R. leaped a good two feet off the floor. When he landed he rushed around the desk to grab both Matt and Jamie, one in each arm, in a hug that nearly squeezed the life out of them.

Juanita joined them, hugging, laughing and crying all at the same time. All the while the big rancher kept saying, "I knew it! I knew it! I knew all the time it was gonna happen."

Joe, Julio and his whole family were invited to join them for supper that night without being told the occasion. After a wonderful meal, the rancher rose to his feet. A hush fell over the room.

"I've got something to say I've been waiting a long, long time to say. I want everybody to know, I just couldn't be prouder than I am at this moment. I met Matt Henry when he was just a boy. Even then, I saw something in him that don't come along near enough in this old world.

"I saw a young fellow with sand in his backbone. One that, once he made up his mind about something, he was gonna get it done come hell or high water. I saw a young man who was as gentle as a house kitten, but when the need called for it, he could be as tough as Wang leather. That's the kind of man I always wanted for a son. Well, for some reason, the good Lord didn't see fit to give me that son—until now.

"I'm asking one and all to stand and lift your glasses in a toast."

J.R. paused to allow everyone at the table time to stand with him and lift their glasses.

"Here's to one of the finest men I ever met and to the most special girl that ever lived. I'm right proud to announce here and now that Mrs. Cunningham and I have given our blessings for our daughter, Jamie, and Matt Henry, to be man and wife. May they both find the happiness they so richly deserve in each other. A su salud y feliz!"

It took a good hour for the congratulations to die down. Jamie had set the wedding date for Saint Valentine's Day, February the fourteenth of the following year. The wedding would be there at the ranch and according to her, half of Texas would be invited.

The ladies, excited and all talking at once and already making wedding plans, moved their planning to the living room. The men took their coffee and retired to the verandah overlooking the river.

"You've got a lot on your plate, son," the big rancher said. "What with you starting a cattle ranch in Arkansas, putting together a cattle drive in the spring and now the wedding in February. That's an awful lot to get your hands around."

"Yes, sir, it is," Matt agreed, "but I've got a lot of good help and the best motivation a fellow could hope for. My pa always said, if a man ain't got something special to shoot at, he ain't likely to hit anything."

The men sipped their coffee and talked the most part of two hours. The others had left and only Mrs. Cunningham and Jamie were in the living room when J.R. and Matt came in. It seemed to Matt that Jamie's face had taken on a new glow.

"Well," the proud father asked, "did you ladies get the wedding plans all made?"

"Oh, father, it's going to be a wonderful wedding. It's going to be the biggest and most beautiful wedding Texas has ever seen. But it's already the middle of September, I'm not sure we can have everything ready by then."

"Yeah, that's only five months away," J.R. said, flicking a quick glance and smile at Matt. "Matt, reckon you ought to think about postponing this thing another year or so?"

"Not on your life, Matthew Henry," Jamie said, leaving no room for discussion, "we're getting married February the fourteenth, ready or not."

"That sounded to me like a no," Matt joked. "I think I'll take a stroll down by the river and count some stars, anybody want to join me?"

Jamie was the only volunteer. They strolled hand in hand down to the bank of the river and sat down on one of several log benches there. The light from a full moon bounced off the slow-moving water and sent rippling reflections into Jamie's sparkling eyes. Overhead, the stars winked at them and the songs the night birds sang seemed especially cheerful.

For a long time they sat in silence, basking in the beauty of the moment, the quietness of the night and the feeling of closeness they both shared.

"Jamie, there's something I need to say and it's important that you know what I'm feeling. From the moment I first saw you standing there on the front porch, something happened in my heart. I've always heard folks talk about love at first sight, but I never knew what it meant until I saw you.

"I loved my wife and stepson, Jamie. As strange as it might sound, I still do. Somehow though, in a different way than I did before I met you. I guess, well, I guess what I'm feeling is guilt. Not that loving you is wrong, but guilty that I've been given a chance for happiness that they weren't given. Can you understand what I'm saying?"

"Yes, Matthew. Yes, I understand and I respect you for those feelings. Matthew, I would never expect you to stop loving them. I know there will always be a place in your heart for the love that you shared and I will never feel threatened by it. She must have been a very special lady. But I believe she would expect you to rise above the ruins of the tragedy you all suffered and go on with the life you've been given. I believe she would wish happiness for you, just as you would for her."

"Thanks for understanding. Jamie, does it bother you that I've—?"

"Not at all." She looked him squarely in the eyes. "That has nothing to do with my love for you."

Matt swung a look up at the stars and stared transfixed at one particular star that seemed brighter than all the others.

"See that star over yonder in the east that I'm pointing at? That's the eastern star. I'm gonna have to be gone a lot for the next several months, but I promise you, no matter where I am or what I'm doing, every single night I'm gonna look up at that star. I'm gonna look at it and think of you and I'll know you are thinking of me. Somehow, that star will bring us together in our hearts and I'll take your memory out of my heart and love you all over again."

"Matthew, that's beautiful. I love you so very much."

She melted into his open arms. She turned, facing him, her head tilted back and her eyes closed. He pulled her close to him and at first barely brushed her lips with his. They tasted as sweet and pure as the morning dew. He pressed his mouth to hers, firmly, yet gently and lingered long. It was a kiss that sealed a love that would never die.

* * *

The sun was noon-high the second day after leaving the ranch
when Matt, Joe and Julio rode into San Antonio. The streets of
the normally bustling town were mostly deserted, driven inside
by a boiling September sun. Little plumes of dust lifted from the
hooves of their horses and were swept away by a hot eastern wind
as they made their way toward the livery.

The old holster looked up from his chore of forking fresh
hay into stalls and hobbled over to take their horses.

"Too blamed hot to be out," he allowed, spitting his familiar
stream of tobacco juice at a horsefly on a nearby railing. "You
fellows come back to buy the rest of them freight horses?"

"Not at your price, old man," Julio told him, swinging his
saddle over the railing of a stall. "You too high."

"See, now there you go again, you got to be the stubbornness
Mexican I ever laid eyes on."

"How many of those big horses you got left?" Matt asked.

"Well, now let me see," the old fella said, scratching his chin
in thought. "I still got the four you already paid for of course,
then, oh, I reckon I still got sixty or so left. You might just as well
buy 'em all, you won't find a better deal anywhere."

"He will still have sixty die of old age if he don't come down
to a fair price," Julio kidded.

"Don't know why you fellows even run around with this Mex,
the way he goes on."

"We'll see you later, old timer," Matt told him, swinging the
saddlebag filled with money over his shoulder. He had left the
other two at the ranch.

They hurried toward the hotel, bending their heads low and
holding tightly to their hats.

"Julio, while we're in town, I want you to check out all those
horses and the harnesses. See if they're sound, but don't make

any commitments just yet. Joe, check with the man at the freight company and make sure he's still got those freight wagons for sale. See what kind of deal you could make on ten of them, but again, we ain't ready to deal yet. If you boys have some other business you need to take care of, go ahead, I'll catch up with you later today."

"Is there a W.W. Suggs registered?" he asked the desk clerk as he was checking them in.

"Yes, sir," the man replied, "Mr. Suggs is one of our guests. I believe he's presently in the dining room if you wish to speak with him."

Mr. Suggs wasn't hard to locate since he was the only customer in the dining room. He looked to be a man in his mid-forties, average height and build. He wore his hair cut close and was losing some in front. A long handlebar mustache covered his top lip. He wore a black, three-piece broadcloth suit. Matt strode over to his table.

"You'd be Mr. Suggs, I reckon?" Matt asked.

The man looked up quickly from the newspaper he was reading, set down the coffee cup he had just taken a swig from and gave Matt a quick once over.

"That I would," he replied, laying down the paper. "I don't believe we've met."

"No, sir, my name's Matt Henry. I'm from the Fourche River country up in Arkansas. A friend of mine said you were in town, maybe looking to do some cattle business."

"Good to make your acquaintance, Mr. Henry. Have a seat. Are you a cattleman?"

"Well, I've got a few head, if that's what makes a fellow a cattleman I reckon I am," Matt said, scraping out a chair and folding into it.

"Henry? Matt Henry? Seems I've heard that name before. Sure, I remember, you're the one they call the Man Hunter, aren't you? Folks are talking about you all over Texas. How could I possibly be of help to you, Mr. Henry, considering your line of work?"

"Don't know about the talk and I ain't sure what line of work you're speaking of. Like I said, I understand you're looking for cattle."

"Matt Henry, you son of a gun!" Marshal McAllister hollered as he strode into the room, spotted Matt and headed for their table. "Somebody told me they saw you ride in. I knew if you was in town I could likely find you getting ready to feed your face."

"Afternoon, Dan." Matt stood and shook the marshal's outstretched hand. "I was planning on stopping by later on today. You know Mr. Suggs here?"

"Shore I do," the marshal said, reaching to shake the cattle buyer's hand. "We met a few days ago. What are you doing in town, Matt?"

"Rode in to get that steak you owe me, but I've got enough to buy you a cup of coffee," Matt said, motioning for the waiter to bring them both a cup.

"Hope I ain't interrupting some business you fellows got going," the lawman said.

"Naw, we was still in the getting acquainted stage," Matt told him. "J.R. said if I saw you to give you a howdy for him."

"How's that old scoundrel doing? Now come to think about it, that's an awfully dumb question to ask about one of the richest men in Texas ain't it?"

"You wouldn't be referring to Mr. J.R. Cunningham, would you?" Suggs asked, "the owner of the Circle C Ranch?"

"Yes sir, I shore would. Matt here, is like his own boy, least that's what J.R. says about him."

"Speaking of that," Matt said, "let me be the first to invite you to the wedding. Jamie and I are getting married on Valentine's Day out at the ranch. Hope you can make it."

"Are you joshing me boy? You and old J.R.'s daughter getting hitched, huh? Well I'll be a monkey's uncle. Can't believe a pretty lady like her is gonna marry an ugly fellow like you when she could have had me."

"I can't believe it either, Dan, but I'm shore one happy man."

"Lordy I reckon. You can write it down, Matt, I'll be there. Hey, I gotta be going. Stop by later on, I got some good things to tell you you'll want to know."

"I'll do it, marshal."

"Well, well, Mr. Henry," Suggs said. "I must apologize for misjudging you. From all the stories I've heard about you, naturally I just assumed . . ."

"My pa always told me, never judge a man till you've known him awhile. To be perfectly frank, Mr. Suggs, I don't care a flip what other folks are saying, I come here to talk cattle.

"Maybe we just got off on the wrong foot or something, suppose we just start all over again," Matt said, "Is it true you work for a fellow named Joseph McCoy and you're here looking for cattle?"

"Yes, sir, that's true."

"Is it true that your boss has built a stockyards in a place called Abilene, Kansas and that the governor has lifted the ban on Texas cattle along a mile wide corridor from the Kansas line to his yards?"

"Yes, sir, that's also true."

"I also hear your boss had a disappointing year because of all the bad publicity about the Texas fever scare. That you're having trouble convincing the Texas cattlemen to bring their cattle to Abilene because they're afraid there won't be any cattle buyers to buy their stock when, or even if, they are able to get them there, am I right so far?"

"You've summed it up pretty well, I must say."

"Well, Mr. Suggs, maybe we can help each other. I've got a proposal for you and your boss. What if your Mr. McCoy could convince the cattle buyers that he could provide all the cattle they needed? What if the Texas drovers became convinced they could get their cattle to market in Abilene and at the same time, get a lot of good publicity for his stock yards? Do you think he'd be interested?"

"Sure he'd be interested. But just how do you propose to do all that, Mr. Henry?"

"What do you reckon is the largest herd ever trailed from Texas to Kansas, Mr. Suggs?"

"Biggest herd I ever knew about was Jesse Driskill's drive last year when he took five thousand head to Wichita. It was in all the papers and everything. Folks are still talking about it. Most drives are three thousand or less. Why are you asking?"

"If Driskill's five thousand head made all the papers and caused such a stir, how much publicity do you reckon there would be if it got out that the first week of June next year, twenty thousand head of the finest beef in Texas would splash across the Smokey Hill River outside Abilene, fill up those pens and keep on coming until the whole Smokey Hill Valley was full?"

"That's impossible," the cattle buyer said, shaking his head, "nobody could make a trail drive of twenty thousand head, nobody."

"Begging your pardon, Mr. Suggs, but how do you know that? Nobody ever tried it before."

"I just know, that's all. I wasn't born yesterday, Mr. Henry," Suggs said, anger sounding in his voice and showing in his face. "You ain't talking to no greenhorn. I drove a herd up the trail earlier this year. I know what it takes to make a cattle drive."

"Yes, sir, and you lost the whole herd at Baxter Springs, to a bunch of two-bit rustlers and thieves. I don't mean to lose my herd," Matt said, pushing back his chair and standing to leave.

"Mr. Suggs," Matt said, glaring down at the man, "I somehow got the notion your boss was a man of vision, a man willing to take a chance in order to get ahead, a man that looked at things most folks called problems and instead, he saw possibilities. I reckon I was wrong. Good day to you sir."

Matt turned and headed for the door. He jammed his Stetson down hard on his head in disappointment and disgust. Why did some men insist on thinking so small? He wondered.

"Mr. Henry," Suggs called after him just before he got to the door. "Come back and sit down if you would, let's talk."

Matt stopped and stood motionless, staring down at the floor. Should he swallow his pride and go back? Should he walk out the door and forget the whole thing? What had he just got through saying about seeing the possibilities instead of the problems? He'd give it one more shot.

"You have my apology, Mr. Henry. I've misjudged you twice already, I hope you can forgive me. I'd like to hear your proposal."

"Okay," Matt said, turning on his heels and striding back and sitting down. "Here's what I'm willing to do. I'm willing to put twenty thousand dollars here in the San Antonio bank in an escrow account, saying I will deliver twenty thousand head of the fattest beef your Mr. McCoy has ever seen, to his stockyards in Abilene the first week of June. If I don't deliver for any reason whatsoever, the twenty thousand is his.

"In return, Mr. McCoy is to deposit twenty thousand dollars right here in the San Antonio bank, guaranteeing the purchase of my whole herd at a minimum price of twenty-five dollars a head. Anything short of that, he makes up out of the twenty thousand."

"But that's five dollars a head above the top price anybody paid for beef this year. What makes you think the buyers will pay twenty-five a head?"

"Oh, I'm willing to bet they'll pay more than twenty-five a head. First because the meat packers in Chicago will pay forty a head delivered. I figure it might cost two dollars a head to ship 'em there. That still leaves a nice profit for your boss.

"Second, I happen to know there are two big meat packers opening for business in Chicago this year. P.D. Armour and Swift and Company. They're both big operators and supply most of the beef for the whole east coast. They've got to have a lot of cattle to do that. Where else are they gonna get that many cattle but from Texas? I got me a feeling it's gonna be a sellers' market this year. I'm betting they're willing to pay top dollar to keep those packing houses humming.

"Thirdly, my herd will bring top dollar because they're the best cattle in Texas. These ain't walking skeletons with long horns and these ain't mavericks we've rounded up out of the bushes somewhere, these are range fattened cattle, the best there is. You're welcome to ride out to the Circle C and look 'em over."

The speechless cattle buyer sat in stunned silence, staring blankly at Matt for several long moments. It seemed to Matt that he was a man doing some mighty hard thinking.

"One more question, Mr. Henry. Supposing Mr. McCoy decides to go along with all this, what happens to all the money he's put in the bank?"

"If both of us keeps his end of the bargain, both will get our money back," Matt explained. "Look at it this way. All your boss has to do is get the word out about the twenty thousand head coming in the first week of June. If the newspapers hear about it, the cattle buyers will come. With all the free publicity he'll get about his stockyards, I figure he'll have that hotel of his as full as his cattle pens will be.

"The way I see it, I'm the one taking all the risk. If I ain't able to deliver, I lose my herd and my twenty thousand dollars."

"I'll have to say, Mr. Henry, that's the boldest scheme I've ever heard of. If you can pull it off, you're likely to go down in history. I don't have to tell you what a big gamble you're taking, but if you're willing to try it, I'm willing to take the plan to Mr. McCoy. When do you have to have an answer?"

"Well, the big meeting of all the ranchers is next week. I have to leave for Arkansas right after the meeting. If McCoy's money is in the bank before the meeting starts, we've got a deal, if it ain't, I'll just take the herd someplace else. I strongly suspect when I tell the Chicago packers which railhead my herd will be delivered to, that's where their buyers will be."

"But that won't give me enough time to go to Abilene and talk to Mr. McCoy. I can't possibly have an answer by next week."

"Ever hear of the telegraph?" Matt asked, pushing back from the table and clamping his hat on his head. "It's a wonderful invention."

From the hotel dining room, Matt headed for the carpenter shop. The nice German lady remembered him and greeted him warmly.

"Good afternoon, young man. Let me guess, you came back for the chest, no?"

"As a Matter of fact, you're half right. How much are you asking for it?"

"You know, of course, the hardware on it is all pure silver? It is truly a chest fit for a queen. The price is fifty dollars."

"It's a queen I'm buying it for, I'll take it," Matt told her. "Is your husband around? I'd like to have a word with him if I could."

"Yes, sir, he is in his vork shed out back. Please vait, I vill get him for you."

It only took a minute until she was back with her husband. He was a giant of a man. Taller than Matt by a good three inches, his wide shoulders and barrel chest strained the checkered shirt he wore. His rolled up sleeves exposed large, rock-hard arm muscles. He had a square set jaw and blonde hair.

"This is my husband, Joseph Von Strauss," the woman said proudly.

"I'm Matt Henry," he said, reaching out a hand.

Matt had always prided himself on the strength of his work-hardened hands and the firmness of his handshake, but for the first time in his life, he grimaced as the big man gripped his hand in a firm handshake.

"Mr. Von Strauss," Matt said, wanting badly to rub his hurting hand but his pride prevented it. "I'll get right to the point. I understand you build houses?"

"No, you have heard wrong," the big German corrected. "Most anyone can build a house, I build homes. I have built some of the finest homes in all Germany."

"I'm from the state of Arkansas, quite a piece from here. I'm starting a cattle ranch up there and I'm also getting married next February. I would like for you to build us a home. I want it to be something real special, like no other home you have ever built. I want it to be a surprise for my new wife.

"I was wondering if you and your wife would consider moving there with us and working for me. I will move you folks, provide a place for you to live and pay you a fair wage. Would you consider it?"

"Vhat vould you pay for me to do this?"

"How much do you usually get when you build homes?" Matt asked.

"I charge three dollars a day," the man told him.

"I'll pay you two hundred dollars a month if you will come to work for me. I have a Conestoga wagon over in the freight yard to move you and your stuff. What do you say?"

Matt could read in the man's face the excitement he was feeling inside. The big German swung a gaze to his wife who shot him a smile, squeezed her shoulders and began nodding her head excitedly. The big man joined the nodding contest and broke a huge smile over his face.

"Yuah, ve vill do this. Vhen do ve start?"

"You just did." Matt counted out ten, twenty-dollar gold pieces plus another fifty dollars for the chest.

"Here's your first month's wages in advance. I thought you folks might want to pick up some things before making the move.

If you could, I'd like for you to take a walk with me, there's something I'd like you to look at."

A long line of heavy freight wagons stretched along one whole side of the freight yard. They were large wagons, specially built for the Army. They had heavy-duty undercarriages and double thick beds that measured eight feet by nineteen feet. The iron-rimmed wheels had heavier than normal spokes and were ten inches wide to prevent the loaded wagons from sinking in soft sand or dirt.

"I'll be making a cattle drive come spring," Matt told the big carpenter, "I'll need five of these wagons converted into chuck wagons."

They strolled around the wagons, looking them over closely. Matt explained his ideas as to what the converted wagons should include, then asked for the carpenter's suggestions. The big man spent considerable time inspecting the construction of the wagons, stretching his long arms to measure here and there, then spent some time in deep thought. Matt waited patiently.

"Yuah," he finally said. "Ve can do vhat you vant."

"How long would it take to convert five of them?" Matt asked.

"I could complete them in two veeks."

"Good," Matt told him, "very good. I'll have my foreman come by in a bit and make arrangements for whatever supplies you need. His name is Joe Doyle. As soon as you finish the conversions, he'll get you folks loaded up and escort you out to the ranch. We'll all be leaving from there for Arkansas in about three weeks."

"Ve thank you, Mr. Henry. I vill build your home like no one has seen before, you vill see."

Matt headed for the hotel. He liked the big German and his wife, that is, as long as he didn't have to shake his hand again. Joe and Julio intercepted Matt with some exciting news.

"We just came from the livery, boss," Joe said. "We checked

the horses and we agree they all look sound. The harness is in pretty good shape too."

"Good," Matt said. "Joe, I want you to go back to the freight yard and buy us ten of those freight wagons. Then go look up the German carpenter, his name is Joseph Von Strauss, I just hired him. He's gonna convert five of those wagons into chuck wagons, see what kind of supplies he needs and see to it. They're gonna move to Arkansas with us too.

"Julio, make the best deal you can with the old holster and buy the whole lot of horses. Make sure we have enough harness for all of them. We'll need spare parts for the harness so we can make repairs along the way.

"I'll set up an account over at the bank in the name of the Fourche Valley Ranch. I'll fix it so either of you can draw on it for whatever you need. Pay for everything as we go, I don't want to owe anybody.

"Come on boys, let's mosey over to the hotel and have a cup, we've got a lot of planning to do."

They selected a table in the far corner and ordered coffee. Matt filled them in on his meeting with the cattle buyer and broke the news to them about his plans for a cattle drive in early spring.

"We've got a lot of work to do between now and then, boys," Matt told them. "I'm gonna be depending on the two of you to carry a big part of the load."

"How big a drive are we talking about here?" Joe asked.

"We're taking twenty thousand head up the trail to Abilene come late February," Matt told them.

Joe choked on a mouthful of coffee when he heard what Matt said. His eyes bugged as big as his coffee cup and his mouth dropped open in surprise.

"Did I hear you right? Did you say twenty thousand?"

"You heard right, Joe," Matt told him. "I'm talking about the biggest cattle drive this country's ever seen."

"Well, if that don't beat all," Joe exclaimed, slapping his leg. "Nobody's ever gonna believe it when they hear it. I'll say one thing for you, boss, they can't accuse you of small thinking. By crackies, if it can be done, you're just the man that can do it."

"No, Joe, we're the ones that can get it done. I can't do this without the two of you. Julio, after Joe gets the carpenter squared away, you fellows drive those freight horses out to the ranch. We'll let them graze there until we get ready for them in the spring. When you get there, tell J.R. I'll be staying in town until the meeting. Tell him I'll have a room waiting on him. I've got a lot of things to do between now and then. Who you reckon is the best trail cook in the business?"

"No question about it," Joe answered without even having to think of the answer. "Black man they call Moses. I don't reckon I ever heard him called anything else. He cooked for the Triple T when we trailed a herd all the way to Omaha, on the Platt River back in sixty-five. He's the best that ever went up the trail. All the big drives try to hire him."

"I never knew you trailed cattle," Matt said.

"You never asked me."

"Got any idea where I could find this fellow Moses?"

"He use to live in this neck of the woods somewhere, ain't shore exactly where," Joe told him.

"Thanks, I'll ask around," Matt said. "Well, you boys got any more questions?"

"Yeah," Joe said, cracking a grin, "but I'm scared to ask 'em."

They went their separate ways, each with plenty of work to do. Matt climbed the stairs to his room and counted out five thousand dollars from his saddlebag, then headed to the bank.

"Good to see you again, Mr. Henry," the banker greeted warmly. "How are things out at the ranch?"

"Things are going well, thank you, J.R. will be in next week for the big meeting. Sounds like it's gonna be quite a shindig."

"I'll say it is," Mr. Martindale said, offering Matt a cigar, which he politely waved off with a sweep of his hand. "I understand most every rancher in Texas will be there. Mr. King himself is organizing the whole thing. That meeting could very well alter the course of the entire cattle industry."

"Seems to me it could stand some altering," Matt suggested. "I'd like to open an account. I'm planning a cattle drive come spring and we're gonna be needing supplies and such. I won't be around much of the time so I'd like to fix it so either one of my two foremen can draw on it."

"That should be no problem. You must have a great deal of confidence in these men to trust them with access to the account. What are their names?" the banker asked, drawing a paper from his desk.

"One is Joe Doyle, the other is Julio Sanchez."

"I see. So this Mr. Sanchez, he is a Mexican then?"

"Do you have a problem with that?" Matt asked.

"Oh, no, sir, there's no problem as far as I'm concerned. I was just a little surprised, that's all. Not many ranchers in these parts have Mexican foremen. Especially one they would trust with their bank accounts."

"There's not many men like Julio Sanchez," Matt said. "I'd trust him with my life in a heartbeat."

"Very good then, how much would you like to deposit in your account?"

"We'll start with five thousand dollars, I'll add to it as we need to," Matt told him, handing the banker the money.

"Well then, is there anything else we can do for you today?"

"Not today," Matt said, pushing to his feet, "I'll be talking with you again in a few days on another matter though."

"I'll look forward to it," the banker said,

After leaving the bank Matt headed for the marshal's office. The lawman was bent over his desk doing paperwork when Matt strode in.

"Thought you'd got lost," Dan said, laying aside the papers.

"Had some business," Matt said, spinning the straight-chair and straddling it.

"What I needed to tell you," the Marshal said, "I heard some news about Trotter. Seems him and some of his bunch run into some U.S. Marshals out of the Van Buren, Arkansas District Court. There was a shoot-out at a place called Doan's store, up on the Red River.

"They killed Trotter's other boy, Luke by name, and a cousin from Illinois named Hank Trotter. Only ones that got away was Trotter himself and the Mex that runs with him. I reckon it was getting so hot for them everywhere else, they was hiding out in the badlands of Indian Territory."

"Glad to hear it," Matt said, "Too bad they didn't get Trotter and the Mex, they're the worst of the lot."

"None of my business, Matt, but seeing you talking with that Suggs fellow this morning. Well, its got my curiosity working overtime. You thinking about taking a herd up the trail for J.R.?"

"No, I'll be driving my own herd," Matt told him.

"Didn't know you had cattle, Matt. How many head you running?"

"Right now I've got something over twenty-two thousand head. We'll be taking the whole herd."

"You're joshing me."

"Nope."

"There ain't nobody looney enough to try driving that many critters all the way to Kansas, not even you."

"I've been called worse, but not lately," Matt told his friend. "Ever hear of a black trail cook called Moses? Somebody said he lived around here someplace."

"Shore have, most everybody that's got anything to do with cattle drives has heard of Moses. He lives about forty miles or so southwest of here, little place called Hallelujah."

"Kind of funny name for a town ain't it?"

"Ain't no town to it, ain't nothing there but a trading post. An old trapper and his young squaw runs it. He does some trading with Indians, Mexicans and a few passers-by that happens to stumble onto the place. Moses lives in a pretty little valley a few miles east."

"Think I'll ride out and have a talk with him in the morning," Matt said, rising and heading for the door. "Later."

CHAPTER XIII

Hallelujah!

> "Four living creatures fell down and
> cried, hallelujah!" (Rev. 19:4)

Matt reined Midnight to a halt. The big black stallion jerked his sweat-slick head, snorted to clear the sand from his nose and looked down, stepping sideways and swishing his damp tail at a pesky horsefly that suddenly appeared from nowhere. A hoof raised and pawed impatiently at the white-hot sand. The searing heat was merciless, unyielding, moving in hot blasts on a southwesterly wind. Sleeving sweat from his brow, he read the sign.

It was nailed to a scrub cedar hung wampee-jawed and contained just one word in hastily scrawled letters, Hallelujah. After peering through the shimmering noonday heat and surveying the single log and mud shack down the trail a piece, Matt reckoned as how the name expressed the total feeling of the fellow that tacked up the sign.

The dilapidated log shanty was built into the side of a sandy hill. Nearby, a makeshift pole corral contained a half-starved looking pony and a long eared donkey. Hallelujah!

As he neared, his searching gaze examined the four saddled horses that stood hipshot, layered with trail dust, their ribs standing out so clear a blind man could count 'em, their reins tethered to the top rail of the corral. Not liking the looks of the things, Matt thumbed back the hammers of his side arms.

A young-looking hombre in filthy clothes squatted near the single door and aimed an angry stare as Matt reined up.

"Don't bother to get off that hoss, Mister," the fellow snarled wickedly, "the place is closed."

Matt settled back down in his saddle and raked the man with a closer gaze. What he saw was a two-bit saddle tramp. Whipcord thin, his weathered face stretched tight over prominent cheekbones, mostly hid by unshaven stubble. The clothes he wore were filthy. His shirt was unbuttoned and his pants had more holes than a watering trough on Saturday night. The run-over boots were more off than on, but the Army .44 tied low on his right leg rested in a well-used holster.

"Looks open to me," Matt said in a voice barely more than a whisper. "Think I'll wet my whistle now I'm here."

Careful to keep his horse between him and the saddle tramp, Matt stepped from the saddle.

"Mister, the only thing you're liable to find here is trouble. Now, if I was you, I'd get back on that hoss and light out while you still can," the tramp hissed, pulling himself to his feet, his right hand hovering only inches from his pistol.

"Well, you ain't me, sonny, and if that hand makes a move closer to that hawg-leg, I'm gonna blow you to kingdom come, now that's just the way it is. You got a choice, you can either unbuckle that gun belt and let it drop, or you can die where you stand. Makes no difference to me either way."

Whoever the fellow was, his wagon was one brick shy of a full load. He clawed for the .44. The tramp's pistol slid clear of its holster and started its journey toward level, then stopped in mid-flight as two slugs from Matt's Rattler tore holes in his chest.

Shock overcame the tramp's face and his eyes walled white. His body lifted to tiptoes in a backward dance of death, ending with his back against the wall of the shanty, then slid lifelessly to a slumped sitting position.

Two more hombres burst through the doorway. The first fired wildly in Matt's general direction. The second clutched a pistol in one hand and his half-down britches in the other.

The blast from Matt's Widow Maker lifted the first off his feet, dropping him in a bloody mass three feet from his starting place. The one worrying about dying with his pants down dropped both his gun and his pants, both hands flying to what was left of his face, which wasn't much. He dropped to his knees as if kneeling, blood gushed between the fingers of both hands. Letting out a pitiful gurgling scream, he toppled onto his face in the hot sand. Dead.

Pasting his back against the log wall, Matt quickly reloaded his weapons.

"You! The one inside!" Matt shouted. "I know you're in there, throw out your guns and come out with your hands on your head unless you want to join these three gents in their trip to hell, makes no difference to me one way or the other."

"Don't shoot," a gravely voice called from inside. "I'm giving up, don't shoot."

"Throw your gun out the front door and walk out backwards with your hands high," Matt shouted, "I ain't gonna say it but once."

A pistol catapulted through the open door end over end, coming to a stop half buried in the soft sand. The back view of a burly, buffalo hunter type appeared just inside the doorway.

Shuffling his feet backwards a baby step at a time, he passed slowly through the open door and into the light.

He was bloody from his neck down to his booted feet, but it wasn't his blood. His long, dirty hair hung shaggily around his face and covered most of what the full, tobacco-stained beard didn't. Only the wide, evil-looking eyes showed through all that hair.

He wore no shirt. Only the top of dirty and bloody long johns covered the top half of his body. The blood-soaked pants were held up by one suspender over his left shoulder. The right one hung loose. The handle of a large skinning knife showed over the top of his right boot.

"In the dirt and on your face," Matt ordered. "If you even twitch, I'll blow you in half."

"You done killed my boys!" the man growled, his cruel eyes flicking to the bodies sprawled in the sand nearby.

The hulk dropped to his knees, then to his bulging belly, his right hand slightly under his body, inching close to the knife.

"Go ahead, Mister," Matt whispered through clenched teeth. "Go for the knife and give me half an excuse to kill you."

Without removing his gaze, Matt pulled a length of pigging string from his saddlebag and quickly tied the man's hands and feet securely, then drawing the two together, had him hog-tied in seconds. Reaching a hand, he removed the knife. Fresh blood stained the shiny blade of the long skinning knife. Something very bad had happened in this place. Somebody inside had died.

When he went in he wished he hadn't. Matt took one look and ran for the door. He didn't make it. His insides came up again and again as he staggered toward the watering trough and ducked his head in the slimy green liquid. He shook his head like a wet dog when he came up. His stomach churned and threatened to eject more. He swallowed repeatedly, trying to keep it down.

Growing up with the Apache, he had witnessed indescribable cruelty many times, but nothing he had ever seen prepared him for the scene inside the trading post.

It took a few minutes for his stomach to settle and longer for his nerves.

When they finally did he took a deep breath, gritted his teeth and headed back toward the door. As he strode past the hog-tied buffalo hunter, a fit of rage overcame Matt. His booted foot lashed out viciously and landed squarely in the man's mouth again and again, sending yellowed teeth and blood flying.

In blind rage he palmed the Rattler from its holster, thumbed back the hammer and pushed the nose of it within inches of the ugly face. He was only a hair-trigger's squeeze from blowing the man's brains out when he came to himself. No, he decided, that would be too quick, too easy, this animal needed to die real slow and real hard. Turning, he stalked back inside.

What was once a man hung from his heels, suspended by a rope thrown over a cross timber. He was naked—skinned alive.

Blood still dripped from the red carcass into a deep puddle on the earthen floor and the coppery scent of it threatened Matt's stomach again. Blowflies lifted and circled the bloody corpse, buzzing, then settling to feast again. Matt tore his eyes from the sight, knowing its gory memory would be etched in his mind forever.

Seeing coiled lariat ropes hanging on a peg, he strode over and pulled two down. Playing out a loop as he went, he stalked outside, cut the rawhide strip holding the man's feet and dropped the loop over the bloody boots and jerked it snug. Taking the loose end, he went back inside and tossed it over the rafter beside the rope that held the old trapper's body.

Hand over hand he dragged the buffalo hunter through the door and hoisted him into the air feet first beside the bloody corpse. A few quick slices from Matt's Bowie rendered the hunter as naked as the day he was born. A piece of the man's own blood-soaked long johns stuffed in his mouth and tied in place muffled the steady stream of curses. Using the second rope, he wound it around the two bodies, drawing them tightly together and tying off the rope.

It was then that he heard a soft moan from somewhere among the scattered supplies strewn about the trading post. In all the flurry of events he had completely forgotten about the young squaw the marshal said lived with the old trapper.

There was no light, only the dusty dimness that filtered from the open door. Squinting through near darkness, he cautiously picked his way through makeshift shelves and discarded trade articles.

In a darkened corner he found her. She lay naked on the sandy floor, her legs drawn up tight into a fetal ball, her bronze body smeared with blood. Matt's hands found a stack of Indian blankets and quickly covered the cowering girl. She looked to be still in the midst of her teens.

She was unconscious, yet her tear-reddened eyes were wide open, staring blankly, lost in a terror-filled memory. Her head rolled from side to side as if in perpetual denial. A low whimpering moan forced its way through tightly compressed lips.

Rising quickly, Matt wound his way back near the front to a wooden water bucket hanging by a leather cord from an overhead beam. Dipping the gourd dipper he found there, he also doused his neckerchief and squeezed it out on his way back to the girl.

Kneeling beside her, he gently bathed her face with the wet neckerchief. Countless tears had made trails down her cheeks through a mixture of dried blood and dirt from the earthen floor. Slipping a hand under her head, he let drops of water from the dipper drip onto her lips.

Finally, her lips parted, allowing a small amount into her mouth. She swallowed and her head ceased its rocking motion but the fixed stare remained.

Matt wrapped the blanket tightly around her small body, then rose, lifted her into his arms and carried her outside.

It was difficult climbing into the saddle with the girl still cradled in his arms, but urgency found a way. Wheeling his mount, he short-loped toward the east.

Topping a ridge, he found the valley the marshal had spoke of. It was a picture pretty little green valley with a winding stream halving it. A neat-looking log cabin sat beside the stream. Matt headed for it.

A herd of goats were scattered here and there and a few head of cattle grazed peacefully. A large, well-tended fall garden still held beans, greens and okra. A sturdy barn and a pole corral contained two well-fed looking mares. They trotted to the fence and expressed interest at the sight of Matt's big solid black stallion.

He waded his horse through the shallow stream and reined up in front of the cabin.

"Hello the house," he called out the widely held traditional request to approach.

The closed door was of heavy hewn boards and every window was covered with shutters of thick wood with a gun port in each. The cabin was a literal fortress.

"What you want?" came the shouted reply in a bullfrog voice.

"The girl from the trading post," Matt shouted back, "she's been hurt. She needs help."

The front door swung open. A tall, well-built black man holding a double barrel shotgun stepped onto the small front porch. Matt could also see the nose of a rifle stuck through one of the gun holes was still moving.

"What happened to the girl?" the black man asked.

"Four men killed the trapper and abused the girl. She's in a bad way and needs a woman's help. I didn't know where else to take her."

A heavy black woman in a flour-sack dress with a white apron tied around her large waist pushed past the man and hurried toward Matt and the girl.

"That poor child. What they gone and done to this sweet girl? Moses, you put down that gun and come get this poor child."

The big man leaned the shotgun against the wall and fleet-footed to do what his wife had commanded. Matt took a closer look at the man as he hurried toward them. He was completely bald headed and had large lips. He wore heavy buff-colored canvas britches held up by wide, red suspenders and no shirt. His wide shoulders and thick biceps rippled as he reached his arms for the girl.

"Be easy with her, Moses," the woman ordered, hovering within an arm's length every step of the way into the house. "Put her on our bed. Put her down easy now. Sammy, fetch me a pan of water and a rag!"

A tall, gangly boy in his late teens rose quickly from his window outpost still clutching a rifle. A quick glance from the woman brought a scowl to her face.

"Who you gonna shoot with that gun, boy? Put that thing down and do like I tells you," she told the boy in easy to understand terms.

He hurried to comply. There was no question who ruled the roost around this house. Matt left the doctoring in capable hands and walked out to the porch. Moses soon joined him and motioned Matt toward a cowhide bottom, straight-backed chair, then slouched his big frame into a weathered old rocker. He pulled, packed and put fire to a well-used corncob pipe before speaking.

"Who was they?"

"Don't know," Matt said honestly. "Looked like a buffalo hunter and three younger fellows, could have been his boys. Saddle tramps most likely."

"What'd they do to old Isaac?"

"They skinned him like you'd skin a rabbit," Matt told him, "looked like he was still alive when they done it."

"Oh, Lordy mercy," the man moaned, shaking his head. "Old Isaac was a good man. What happened to the ones that done it?" the black man asked, puffing on the pipe with those big lips and blowing puffs of sweet-smelling blue smoke into the air.

"The three younger ones are dead. The older one is most likely wishing he was right about now."

"Oh, Lordy, why they want'ta go and do a thing like that?"

"More'n likely they wanted the girl and he tried to stop them," Matt said, "that would be my guess."

"Yes, sir, old Isaac would shore-nuff try to do that all right. He thought a lot of that girl. He treated her good. Good thing you happened by. By the way, name's Moses Soloman."

"I'm Matt Henry. I rode out from San Antonio to talk with you."

"Why you want to talk to me?"

"I'm planning a cattle drive come early spring," Matt explained. "I heard you are the best biscuit roller that ever fed a trail crew. I came to see if you'd go with us. I hear you've been up the trail a time of two."

"Yes, sir, I reckon you could say that all right. Mister, I been up that trail so many times me and them water moccasins is on a first name basis. What brand your cattle be wearing?"

"The Double H brand from the Fourche Valley Ranch up in Arkansas. We'll be leaving from the Circle C ranch, that's where my cattle are."

"I thought I heard of every brand there is, but the Double H is a new one on me. I shore heard of the Circle C though. You a friend of Mr. Cunningham?"

"Yes, sir," Matt said, "we've been friends since before I was dry behind the ears. Me and his daughter are getting married come February."

"Well, sir, if Mr. Cunningham be letting you marry his daughter, that shore goes a long way in my books. There just ain't a better man walking this old earth than J.R. Cunningham."

"How much do you usually get for working a drive?"

"I gets fifty a month and all I can eat and that's considerable."

"I'll give you seventy-five and I don't care how much you eat as long as you feed us good. I pay a hundred-dollar bonus for every man that sticks with us to the railhead in Abilene. Only thing is, I need four more cooks just like you. You know anybody?"

"Four more? What you need four more cooks for? You don't

think I can feed a bunch of broken down drovers? I never heard of such a thing."

"I'll be splitting the herd up into five separate herds once we get started good. Each group will have about twenty-four drovers, so I figure I'll need five chuck wagons."

"Lordy, Lordy, Mr. Henry. How many critters you taking to need that many cowboys?"

"We'll be driving twenty thousand," Matt said.

"What you say?" the black man said, cutting his dark eyes at Matt. "Begging your pardon, Mr. Henry, but I never worked for no crazy man before. You joshing old Moses?"

"No, sir, we'll be trailing twenty thousand head all the way to Kansas."

"Lordy, Lordy, that shore would be some sight to behold," Moses said.

"Then you'll come with us?"

"Yes, sir, I'll shore nuff do that. It be worth the trip just so I can tell my grand kids about it, that's for shore. I reckon I can get you four more cooks too. They won't be as good as me, cause the good Lord didn't make no more of them, but they can keep them punchers full and happy."

"Don't reckon I ever seen a trail crew full and happy before," Matt said.

The big black man chuckled. "You shore right about that, yes, sir, you shore is."

"I done cleaned her up as best I can," Mrs. Soloman said, coming to the door and wiping her hands on her apron. "That poor child don't know if it's light or dark. It's gonna take some time to get her head straightened out. I done decided, she's gonna stay right here till she do and that settles that."

"Moses, them three fellows up there will need burying," Matt said. "Reckon you and the boy could take care of it? I'm taking the other one with me if he'll behave himself. If he don't, there'll be four to bury. I reckon the girl ought to have whatever is left, such as it is. That the way you see it?"

"That seems right. We'll see to the bodies."

"Will you stay for supper?" the woman asked. "We'll be having beans and greens and corn pone."

"Don't mind if I do if you got enough," Matt said. "Can't see no use traveling tonight."

Matt, Moses, and the boy saw them well before they reached the trading post. The big birds circled lazily on the lift of rising heat, then swooped down to join countless companions all competing for their share of the bodies that lay in the hot sand.

They sat atop the carcasses, their bloody curved beaks ripping chunks of flesh from holes in the stomachs. The corpse moved with eerie false life as the vultures tore at them.

"Hell of a sight ain't it," Matt said before drawing his pistol and firing to scare them off.

The boy leaped from his saddle and almost made it around the corner of the post before losing his breakfast and supper too. Matt felt sorry for the boy. His own stomach was queasy too. The smell of death hung over the place like a thick fog.

"I wouldn't advise letting the boy go inside," Matt told Moses.

"Yes, sir, Mr. Henry, I don't reckon you'll have to worry none about that."

While Moses buried what was left of the three by himself, Matt turned the horses into the small corral. He found some feed in a lean-to shed and primed the rusty old pump and filled the water trough. No reason they had to suffer, he figured.

"You might just as well take the horses with you," Matt said, "leave the donkey though."

When they were all finished with the burying, Moses and the boy mounted up.

"See you the first of January like we talked," Matt told the big black man.

"Yes, sir, Mr. Henry, sir. I'll shore nuff be there, Good Lord willing."

Matt watched them as they rode away leading the extra horses. He was glad neither of them had to see the sight inside. Bridling the donkey, he led it around to the front door of the shack. Only then did he go inside.

At first glance he thought the bearded killer was dead. Great swarms of black blowflies covered the two bodies that were tied together. They lifted reluctantly as Matt cut the ropes, but dropped back quickly to feast on the dried blood that covered the two bodies.

A grunt from the buffalo hunter when his body hit the floor told Matt the man was still alive. Taking two more blankets from the stack he had found the day before, he covered the trader's body with one. The other he carried outside. Tugging on the rope, Matt dragged the killer's naked body outside beside the waiting donkey. That's when the bearded one opened his eyes and mumbled around the gag in his filthy mouth.

"Mister..."

"Don't!"

Matt screamed at him, grabbing a handful of hair and jerking his head off the sand. The big Bowie was in Matt's hand and the needle-sharp point pricked the man's throat.

"The next word out of your filthy mouth will be the last you ever speak. I promise you, if you say one more word I'll cut your tongue out," Matt spat out the words like they tasted bad.

Rolling the man up in the blanket, Matt hoisted him across the donkey's back and tied the man's hands to his feet underneath the animal's belly. Then, he set about burying the trading post operator.

* * *

People stopped to stare and followed him down the street as Matt rode into San Antonio late that afternoon. It must have been a strange sight, sure enough. Matt reined up in front of the marshal's office and could hardly dismount for the crowd that had gathered. Hearing all the commotion, Marshal McAllister pushed through the door to see what was going on.

"Who you got there, Matt?" he asked, hiding a snicker and trying hard not to join the crowd in their laughter.

"A piece of filth," Matt said.

For the first time in quite awhile, Matt glanced at the donkey and its burden. What he saw explained what all the laughter was about. The blanket Matt had covered the man with had worked off.

"He was covered awhile ago," Matt commented, swinging out of the saddle.

"Couple of you boys get him inside and lock him in a cell for me," the marshal told some men standing nearby.

Matt soon sat in front of the Marshal's desk and told him the whole story. When he had finished, Dan walked over to the poster board, yanked down a flier, and handed it to Matt.

"The fellow you brought in is Jeremiah Perkins. The other three were likely his three boys. We've been after them a long time. They were bad ones, as you can see from the size of the rewards."

Matt glanced at the wanted poster that read, dead or alive.

"Three thousand for the old man and a thousand each for the boys, that's a pretty good day's work," Dan said.

"I want it to go to the young Indian girl when she gets well," Matt said, pushing to his feet.

"That's mighty decent of you, Matt, Mighty decent. I'll see it's done."

CHAPTER XIV

To him that believeth

"All things are possible to him
that believeth." (Mark 9:23)

Darkness still lingered just before the crack of dawn. A tinge of light gray hinted that daybreak wasn't far behind. Matt slouched a shoulder against a post in front of the hotel and sipped the steaming coffee he had mooched from the dining room.

He liked this time of morning. Everything seemed fresh and clean and rested from a long night's sleep. He watched and listened as San Antonio began to wake up. Here and there a lamp was lit and its golden beam cast an elongated square of light into the dusty street.

A rooster crowed on the north side of town, waking his friends to the south who set in with a steady chorus. Somewhere a dog barked. A blacksmith's hammer began its rhythmic beat. A three-team hitch pulling a heavy freight wagon rolled past. A wheel in need of grease gave off a steady squeak. One of the horses snorted and the driver wiped the last vestige of sleep from his eyes.

Draining the last sip from his cup, he strolled back to the dining room and joined a few early-bird coffee drinkers in their morning ritual. Finishing his second cup, he ordered breakfast. He had just finished the last bite when W.W. Suggs strode up to his table.

"May I join you, Mr. Henry?" he asked. "I've got some good news from Abilene."

"I always like to start the day with good news," Matt said, pointing his fork toward an empty chair.

"I just got word last night by telegram. Mr. McCoy has agreed to your proposal. His bank in Kansas City will be arranging to deposit twenty thousand dollars in the San Antonio Bank before the day is out. A signed agreement will be arriving in a week or so that you will need to sign, too."

"Then we've got ourselves a deal?" Matt asked, trying hard to mask the excitement he was feeling inside.

"We've definitely got a deal. He's already making plans for a big promotion to get the buyers to Abilene the first week of June. He's hired a circus to be there and he's throwing a big barbecue celebration. I've known him a long time and I've never known him to get this excited about anything before. I just hope you can deliver on your end of the agreement."

"The herd will be delivered in Abilene the first week of June come hell or high water," Matt told him.

"Mr. McCoy asked me to ride out and look your herd over. Maybe we could ride out together after the meeting?"

"That would suit me just fine."

After breakfast Matt strolled over to the blacksmith shop. The smithy was busy shoeing a line back dun that wasn't exactly cooperating. As he straddled the horse's back leg with his backside turned to the horse, the dun would kick viciously.

"Getting one like that kinda starts a man's day off wrong don't it?" Matt said.

"My papa tried to tell me I didn't want to be a blacksmith. That's just one of the things I should have listened to him about and didn't. What can I do for you this morning?"

"No hurry," Matt said, "I kind of like watching somebody else work for a change."

Matt stood and watched until the man finished with the dun and turned it into the corral out back.

"You're a might patient man," the smithy said. "Most folks expect me to just drop whatever I'm doing and take care of them. What you got on your mind this morning?"

"I'm Matt Henry. I need some branding irons. Wondering if you'd want the job?"

"Wish I had two bits for every iron I've cranked out in my life, I could sit on the front porch and watch the grass grow. What brand and how many?"

"The Double H," Matt told him, reaching for a piece of iron rod from a table and scratching three vertical lines in the dirt, then a single horizontal line across the middle, forming a double HH.

"Thought I'd seen 'em all," the blacksmith said, "but that's a new one on me. Where is your ranch, Mr. Henry?"

"The Fourche Valley Ranch, from up in Arkansas."

"If you don't mind me saying so, young fellow, you've come a mighty long way to buy your branding irons."

"My herd is grazing out on the Circle C," Matt told him. "I'll be starting a drive from there come early spring. We'll be cutting out the herd and trail branding before we go. What's it worth to make a iron like that?"

The smithy scratched his chin in thought, staring down at the picture in the dirt.

"That's a good brand," he said, still figuring in his head," it'll make up good. It ought to be worth two dollars apiece, I reckon. How many will you be wanting?"

"I'll need a hundred," Matt told him, pulling the money from his pocket and handing it to the man. "I'll have one of my foremen pick 'em up in a week. Will that suit you?"

"A hundred?" the man said, surprise and amazement overcoming his face. "You must be gonna do a heap of branding. How many head you got?"

"Twenty-two thousand," Matt said. "We'll likely need some horses shoed, too, but you'd have to come out to the ranch to do it. You want the job?"

"Might near scared to ask, but how many horses we talking about here?"

"Oh, three hundred or so."

"Mister Henry, for a job that size I'd might near go plumb to Arkansas. Just let me know when you're ready and I'll be there."

Matt went back to the hotel and made reservations for an extra room. He was afraid the hotel would be full for the big meeting and wanted to make sure J.R. had a room waiting.

He counted out twenty thousand dollars from his saddlebag full of money, put it into a bag by itself and headed for the bank. Mr. Martindale rushed to greet him when he pushed through the front door.

"I've been expecting you, Mr. Henry." the excited sounding banker told him. "Mr. Suggs just left a few minutes ago. He told me all about the agreement between you and Mr. Joseph McCoy. Most unusual, I must say. I've never been involved in a transaction like it."

"Well then, that makes two of us, Mr. Martindale. Did Mr. Suggs deposit the money?"

"I received a wire from Mr. McCoy's bank in Kansas City authorizing the deposit of twenty thousand dollars into an escrow account. I understand you will also be depositing the like amount into the same account and that both sums are to be held in escrow pending the outcome of your agreement."

Opening the saddlebag, Matt dumped the bundles of bills out onto the banker's desk. It made quite a pile. A quick glance at the banker's face showed a face full of surprise.

"If my tally is correct," Matt said, "there ought to be twenty thousand dollars there. I'd like for you to count it and I'll need a receipt."

Uh—yes. Yes, sir, Mr. Henry," the man stammered.

Matt watched as the banker carefully counted the money and wrote out a receipt.

"I understand from Mr. Suggs you will be attempting to take twenty thousand head of cattle all the way to Abilene, Kansas. Is that possible?"

"Well, if it ain't, I'm gonna be out an awful lot of money ain't I?" Matt said, shaking hands with the banker and striding out the door.

They began arriving two days later. At first only one or two at a time on horseback, then by wagon or buggy. People had heard, of course, about the big meeting. They turned out in droves to get a glimpse of men they had only heard about but never hoped to get to see. Men like Richard King, owner of the Running W of the Santa Gertrudis Ranch, the biggest spread in the country. Legendary names like John Chisum of the Jingle Bob Ranch, Charley Driskill, the man that drove five thousand head up the trail all at one time, Colonel Ike Pryor and of course, J.R. Cunningham of the Circle C Ranch.

You could hear the excited conversation begin to build and roll along the street like a big ocean wave. Long before anybody could see a thing, folks already knew Richard King was coming down the street. Matt leaned against a post in front of the hotel and watched the spectacle with amusement. The black buggy had red wheels and a black covering over the top. It was pulled by a matched team of sorrel geldings and flanked by a dozen heavily armed hombres who were anything in the world but cowboys. They all rode with rifles out and propped on one leg, pointed at the sky.

The man in the buggy was a big man in every way. Matt had heard he was a former ferryboat captain that made his money hauling contraband freight for the Confederacy. He was tall, wide-shouldered and a bit heavy around the middle, maybe, like one tends to get when he eats real good for a bunch of years back to back and somebody else does the heavy lifting for him.

His long black hair and mustache were well groomed and sprinkled liberally with gray. He climbed easily from the buggy and walked stiff-backed and square-shouldered, with his head held high. A perfect picture of a man used to having authority. Matt figured he put his britches on just like he did, one leg at a time.

J.R. rode in virtually unnoticed just before high noon. Matt stepped down from the boardwalk and greeted his friend as the old rancher looped his big chestnuts reins around a hitching rail.

"If I'd a knowed when you was coming I'd a hired a band," Matt kidded. "You should of seen all the commotion when Richard King arrived."

"Yeah," J.R. said, a grin lifting one corner of his mouth. "He kind of likes that sort of thing. He's a good man though."

"I already got you a room and paid for it," Matt told him as they stepped up on the boardwalk. "I was afraid they'd all be gone."

"I appreciate that, son. A right pretty young lady told me to give you a hug for her, but I'll just tell you howdy. Have you heard what time the meeting is?"

"Yeah, I heard Mr. King reserved the dining room for the rest of the day. I think the first meeting is at two o'clock. There's a big dinner at six."

"Gives us enough time for a cup then," J.R. said, as they headed for the dining room.

Over coffee and between interruptions when several ranchers stopped by to shake hands and say howdy to the well-known owner of the Circle C, Matt filled his future father-in-law in on his plans and the agreement with Joseph McCoy.

"I can't wait till King finds out about your drive," J.R. said, chuckling. "He'll be trying to figure out how he can make one with forty thousand in it.

"Son," the old rancher said, his face taking on a serious look. "I want you to know I'm behind you all the way. Now, don't take this some way it ain't intended, but I know all this is costing you a pretty penny, what with starting your ranch, the drive and the wedding. If you need any money, just say the word and you've got it."

"I appreciate that, J.R., but my papa use to tell me, son, a man ought to shuck his own corn. I reckon he was right."

The cattlemen began drifting into the dining room well before the scheduled starting time. They knotted up in little wads, engaging each other in deep conversation. Just before two, Richard King made his grand entrance and all heads turned in his direction.

King spotted J.R. and made a beeline in their direction, stopping several times to shake outstretched hands. The man had a voice to match his authoritative stature. The booming sound reverberated across the room.

"J.R., it's good to see you," the man said, a good fifteen feet before reaching them. "it's been way too long."

"Howdy, Richard," J.R. said, shaking the man's hand. "I want you to meet my future son-in-law, Matt Henry. Jamie's done got him roped, hog-tied and heating up the branding iron. Matt, say howdy to Richard King."

"Matt Henry, you say?" the rancher asked, reaching to exchange a firm handshake with Matt and rolling the name around on his tongue, like he was tasting it. "Seems I've heard that name before. Where you from, Matt?"

"I'm from the Fourche River Valley up in Arkansas, not far south of Fort Smith."

"Oh, yes, now I remember where I've heard that name. You're the one they're calling the Man Hunter. I've been hearing stories about you from my men. There's also some wild talk around town about a twenty thousand-head cattle drive? But they must have got it wrong. Everybody knows that's impossible."

"I'm begging your pardon, Mr. King, but how do we know it's impossible? Nobody's ever tried it before. I reckon there were folks that would have said it would be impossible to put together a ranch of half a million acres too—until you done it."

The big rancher stood in shock for a long minute, considering what Matt had said, then reached his hand out to Matt again.

"Allow me to shake your hand again, young man, this time out of respect. A man that would attempt something that daring has my admiration. J.R., looks to me like your daughter's got herself a fellow with lots of sand in his backbone. I'll be looking for an invitation to the wedding."

"I hope you can come, Mr. King," Matt told him.

The big rancher strode to the front of the room and raised his hands for silence.

"Friends and neighbors," he said in his booming voice. "I want to thank each of you for coming. I know we're all busy and you've come a long way so we ain't gonna waste your time talking about the weather.

"I expect most all of us know one another even if we don't have an occasion to get together much. Far as I can tell, there's only three men here that needs an introduction.

"The first fellow I want you to meet is a new neighbor. He's Major George Littlefield. He's put together a spread over east of here a ways. His cattle will be wearing the Lazy Z brand. Stand up George so everybody can see who to take your cattle back to when they stray.

"Likely some of you have already met the next man I want to introduce. He's been wearing out the seat of his pants making the rounds to most of our ranches. He works for a cattle buyer that's built a big stockyard up in Abilene. Now all he's got to do is convince you fellows to bring your herds over there. I'm sure he'll want to talk to you before you leave. His name is W.W. Suggs. Stand up and let the folks see you, Mr. Suggs.

"Now this last fellow I just met a few minutes ago. But he's a man you're gonna be hearing a lot more about. He's fixing to do something not a man in this room had the nerve to try before and that includes me. He's putting together a cattle drive that will be talked about from one end of this country to the other for years to come.

"Come spring, this young fellow is trailing twenty thousand head of longhorns all the way to Abilene, Kansas. He owns the Fourche Valley Ranch up in Arkansas and his cattle will carry the Double H brand. His herd is grazing out on the Circle C right now. I want you to meet Matt Henry, right back there. Stand up, Matt."

You would have thought somebody just throwed a fox in the chicken yard.

Bedlam was the only word to describe what happened next. Every man in the room rose to tiptoes and craned their necks to get a glimpse of the loco fellow who would try a crazy stunt like that. A buzz of conversation broke out as men asked one another if they heard right. It took several minutes before Mr. King could quiet everybody down.

"Gentlemen, if I could have your attention, please. Now, we all know why we've called this meeting. Makes no difference whether your spread is large or small, we're all faced with the same problems. Rustling is bad and getting worse. Between the

Comanchero, the Indians, the organized gangs of rustlers and every down-and-out saddle tramp this side of the Rockies, they're stealing us all blind.

"These are men that won't work, but they'll take what me and you have worked our whole lives for.

"Major Collins, from over at Fort Griffin, come by the ranch not long ago. He estimates the Texas ranchers are losing over two hundred thousand head a year to rustlers. The worse part is, there's mighty little the Army can do to stop it.

"Don't know about you, but I've got my craw full of it. I say it's time for the folks up in Austin to sit up and take notice. I say it's time they pass a law registering brands. It's way too easy for these fellows to take a running iron or a cinch ring and change our brands to something they just thought up around the camp fire the night before.

"I say, if the politicians got the notion, they could find enough money to hire more Texas Rangers and U.S. Marshals. But we all know they ain't gonna do nothing but talk until we put some pressure on them.

"Folks, we got enough beef right here in Texas to feed the whole country. Trouble is we can't get it to market. There's six states already that have passed laws banning Texas cattle from coming into their state. Kansas, Missouri, Illinois, Kentucky, Nebraska and Colorado have all outlawed our longhorns.

"Many of you have run into trouble firsthand. Mr. Suggs, the fellow I introduced just awhile ago, took a herd of his own north earlier this year. He got blockaded at Baxter Springs and the trail blockers took his whole herd.

"Between the jayhawkers and the grangers, they pretty well got us sealed off from all the markets and that's making our cattle worth next to nothing. Now, I can understand the legitimate shorthorn ranchers in Kansas and Missouri being scared of the Texas fever they claim some of our longhorns carry. But most of them fellows ain't nothing but pure-de old rustlers using that as an excuse to take our herds.

"Now, I've laid out our problems. We're not gonna spend our time rehashing all the problems we've got. We're here looking for answers. If you think you've got a good suggestion, stand up one at a time and have your say."

Over the course of the next three hours, one after another stood and said their piece. A few actually said something worthwhile, though most just worked their jaws with next to nothing coming out. Finally, J.R. pushed to his feet.

"Friends," the old rancher said quietly, so low most had to strain to hear. "I've been ranching here in this part of Texas for over thirty years. I've known some of you for most of that time. Them that know me know I ain't much on making speeches nor mincing words. So I'll just come right out and say what I've got to say.

"I've heard a lot of talk here today, but very little has been said. We've been pussyfooting around and we all know what's got to be done. Here's what I'm proposing. I say we need to form a Texas Cattle Growers Association.

"Standing alone, we ain't gonna get much of anything done. By banding together, by speaking with one strong voice, them folks up in Austin will sit up and take notice to what we got to say.

"We need a man that can take our requests and complaints right straight to the ones that can do something about them. We need a man they will listen to. We need a man that ain't afraid to stand up and speak his piece once he gets there.

"I'm making a motion right now that we form an Association of Texas Cattle Growers and I'm making another motion that we elect Mr. Richard King as our first President and spokesman."

* * *

As he thought back on it, there was no doubt in Matt's mind that September 22, 1867, the day the Texas Cattle Growers Association was formed, would go down as one of the most significant events in the history of Texas.

Now, near a month later, he settled against the cantle of his saddle and peered down the lonely road through the Ouachita Mountains. With any luck, he would be in Waldron before suppertime.

It was the middle of October and the maple, sweet gum and sumac were splashing their crimson red hue across the slopes and valleys of the beautiful Ouachitas. Suddenly an overwhelming feeling of loneliness swept over him. He thought of Jamie. He remembered her beautiful face and the crinkled corner of her easy smile and wished she was here to share the beauty with him. A grin creased his face as he lost himself in her memory.

It had been a busy month. After the big meeting in San Antonio, Suggs had accompanied him and J.R. back to the Circle C. The cattle buyer had been visibly impressed with Matt's herd and promised to relay his feelings to his boss.

Jamie loved the hope chest. They had spent every possible moment of the past three weeks together, taking long rides, picnics, long late night walks, making plans. They talked exhaustively about the ranch they would build together in Arkansas. They talked about her interest in crossbreeding and in doing research searching for the cause and cure of the dreaded Texas fever.

The three weeks passed way too quickly. It was a sad parting when Matt climbed into the saddle and headed his three Conestoga wagons northward. He, Joe and Julio would be back in less than three months to make preparations for the cattle drive, but it would be a long two and a half months for him and Jamie to be apart.

Matt traveled with the wagons until they reached the relative safety of Arkansas. He gave the others instructions how to reach the Fourche Valley, then rode on ahead to make preparations for their arrival.

It was mid-afternoon when he reined up in front of the Sheriff's office. He lifted in the saddle to stirrup down when the door burst open.

"Matt! I saw you ride up through the window and couldn't believe my eyes," Matt's old friend said, grabbing him in a bear hug. "It's so good to see you, son."

"It's good to be home," Matt said honestly, swallowing down a lump the size of a horse-apple. "How you been?"

"Tolerable," the sheriff told him. "I'm getting too old for this job."

"How's Molly? Growing like a weed I reckon."

"Getting prettier ever day," J.C. told him. "She shore misses you though. Ain't a day goes by she don't ask when I reckon you'll be back. Wait till she finds out you're home, she'll have a conniption fit. How about us walking over and surprising her?"

"I can't wait to see her."

They walked up the street together, their boots stirring up little puffs of dust that hung in the stillness behind them. A few people turned their necks and stared at the stranger with the Sheriff, then most likely deciding it was no one of matter, continued on their way.

Molly was standing on top of a wooden keg stacking canned goods on a top shelf when they entered the mercantile store.

"Anybody here know where a fellow could get a good apple pie?" he asked.

Molly froze. For a short moment she stood motionless, seemingly searching her memory to identify the voice behind her. Finding the answer, she screamed, her body twisted and she flew through the air into Matt's outstretched arms.

She clung to him. Sobs of happiness mingled with laughter wracked her young body. She relaxed her arms long enough to search his face, then hugged his neck again. Tears streamed down her soft cheeks.

Matt finally stood her down on the floor and held her at arm's length, sweeping her with an appraising look up and down.

"Let me look at you, girl," he said. "Why, you've grown mite near a foot since I've been gone. Didn't think it was possible but you got a sight prettier too."

"I've had a birthday too," she said proudly, "I'm thirteen now."

"Well, what do you know about that? I knew you looked different, you're a growed up teenager now. We'll have to have us a late birthday. How about tonight? I'll get the lady over at the café to cook up something special, just for your birthday."

"You don't have to do that," Molly told him. "Just having you home is the best birthday present I could ever get. We're not letting you out of our sight ever again, are we papa?" she said, hugging his neck again.

"Not if I can help it," J.C. said.

"I've got to stop by the bank and take care of some business," Matt told them. "How about we meet at the café about six? I've got some things to tell you about."

"Matt, all that money you sent back is over in the bank. I put it in an account in your name. That's a heap of reward money, you must have found them all."

"All but Trotter and the Mexican. Last I heard they was over in Indian Territory. They'll show up again one of these days."

"I'm anxious to hear all about it," the old sheriff said. "We'll see you at six."

Matt hurried by the café to talk with the nice lady. He told her what he wanted and she readily agreed.

"I'll fix up something special," she promised. "Might even have time to fix up a birthday cake."

"That would be good," Matt told her, hurrying out the door and toward the bank.

Mr. Wilkerson was at his desk when Matt pushed through the door. The banker recognized him and hurried to greet him.

"Welcome home, Mr. Henry. It's good to see you back."

"Thanks, it's sure good to be back. I'd like a word with you if I could."

"Certainly, have a seat. What can I do for you?" the banker asked.

"That thirteen thousand acres you was telling me about before I left," Matt said, "do you still have it?"

"Why, yes, as a matter of fact I do," Mr. Wilkerson said. "How much of it are you interested in?"

"Suppose a man wanted all of it. What's the least you would take?"

"All of it?" the banker asked, surprise overcoming his face. "Oh my, I'd have to give that some thought. Let me see...I suppose I could let you have it for six dollars an acre if you took it all. That's an awful lot of land, Mr. Henry."

"Does it all lie in the Fourche Valley, along the river?"

"Absolutely. You've undoubtedly ridden the river, you must know what prime land we're talking about."

"With the Government giving land away around here, looks to me like it might be hard to sell it for six dollars an acre. I was figuring if a man took it all off your hands he ought to get it for four dollars."

"Oh, I couldn't let it go for that I'm afraid," the banker said, shaking his head. "If I may ask, what did you have in mind to do with that much land?"

"Kind of had in mind to start a cattle ranch," Matt told him.

"That sure would make a nice ranch all right and most likely one of the largest in Arkansas. Tell you what I'll do, Mr. Henry. If you'll take it all, I'll let you have it for five dollars an acre and that's a dollar and a half under what it's worth."

"My pa always said anything is worth only what somebody else is willing to pay for it, Mr. Wilkerson. How much would that come to?"

"Well, let's see," the banker said, quickly doing some figuring. That would come to sixty-five thousand dollars, I'm afraid."

"Suppose I could give you thirty-five thousand now and the other thirty thousand a year from now? Would that be acceptable?"

"Why, yes, we'd have to draw up papers, of course, but that would be agreeable."

"Then I'll take it," Matt said. "Draw up the papers and I'll stop by tomorrow with the money."

"I'll have them ready. You realize there will be a small interest charge, of course."

"Of course," Matt said, pushing to his feet and sticking out his hand. "Make those papers out to the Fourche Valley Ranch with Matt Henry and J.C. Holderfield as full partners."

"J.C. is going in with you as a full partner?" the banker asked, his eyebrows lifting. "My, my, that is a surprise. Very well, Mr. Henry, I'll draw up the papers that way."

"If it's a fair question, how much does Jeb Hawkins and the Jenkins couple owe on their places? I'm gonna ride out tomorrow and try to buy their places, too."

"I hold a mortgage on Jed's place for a thousand dollars," the banker said. "The Jenkins place is paid for. They have a real pretty place, I sold them that land. I do understand they would like to sell it and move back to the Boston Mountains where they came from, though."

"Oh," Matt said, "that money J.C. put into an account for me? Change that account to the Fourche Valley Ranch and fix it so either me or J.C. can draw on it."

"I'll take care of it, Mr. Henry. Is there anything else I can do for you today?"

"Well, yeah there is," Matt told him. "If me and you are gonna be doing business together, how about just calling me Matt?"

"I must say, Matt, you've come a long way since that terrible tragedy. It's an extremely generous thing you're doing for J.C. I hope this doesn't mean he'll be giving up his job as sheriff."

"That will be up to him. Good day to you, Mr. Wilkerson."

"That's Byron," the banker said. "Please call me Byron."

Leaving the bank, Matt hurried by the Doc's house and invited him to Molly's birthday party at six, then headed for the general store. He invited Mr. and Mrs. Jamieson to the party and picked out a beautiful gold locket for Molly's birthday.

They were all waiting at the café when J.C. and Molly walked in. She looked like an angel in the pretty new dress Mrs. Jamieson had made for her. She was so excited she could hardly speak and for Molly Holderfield, that was a rare occasion.

After a nice supper, the lady at the café came out carrying a beautiful birthday cake with thirteen lit candles on it.

"Make a wish, then blow out all the candles and your wish will come true," Mrs. Jamieson told her.

"My wish has already come true," Molly said, looking at Matt with those big eyes.

She blew out the candles and everybody applauded and sang happy birthday to her. She squealed with delight when her father gave her a beautiful musical jewelry box. Uncle Doc gave her half a dozen hair ribbons and Mrs. Jamieson presented her with a beautiful shawl she had crocheted herself.

When Matt handed her the gold locket she cried. Mrs. Jamieson hooked it around her neck. Molly hugged everyone, thanked them for the gifts and cried some more.

"It's the first birthday party I ever had," she told them. "Thank you so much. I'll never forget tonight."

As everybody was leaving, Matt asked J.C. if he could stay for a cup of coffee. The nice lady that ran the café was in the kitchen cleaning up. Matt and his friend sat at a table sipping coffee for a minute before either said a word.

"J.C., do you recall me telling you about hiring on with that cattle drive back when I was fourteen years old? Well, ever since then I've had this dream of someday owning my own cattle ranch. I chalked it up to just being one of those childish dreams that nothing would ever come of. But over the years it just never would go away.

"Some things have happened lately that have given new life to that dream. A dream born such a long time ago on a Texas hillside in the mind of a fourteen-year-old boy. Now, I've made up my mind, J.C., I'm gonna follow that dream.

"Remember Mr. Wilkerson telling me and you about that thirteen thousand acres of land he had along the river in the Fourche Valley? Well, I went by the bank a while ago and bought us that land.

"I'm gonna build that cattle ranch, J.C., but I can't do it by myself. That's why I'm asking you to be my full partner. As of this afternoon me and you own thirteen thousand acres of the best land in this part of the country. I think I can buy us another two thousand that joins it.

"Together, I believe we can build the finest cattle ranch this part of the country's ever seen. I'd like to call it the Fourche Valley Ranch."

Matt pulled something wrapped in a rag from a nearby chair and laid it on the table in front of his dumbfounded friend. Peeling back the rag revealed a branding iron.

"That's the Double H brand, J.C.," Matt told him. "The Henry and Holderfield brand. I'm believing one of these days, thousands of head of stock are gonna be wearing that brand on their rumps.

"Well, what do you say?" Matt asked, looking into the suddenly teary eyes of his friend. "Will you do it with me? Will you be my partner?"

For a long couple of minutes you could have heard a pin drop. They sat facing one another, Matt staring at his friend, his friend staring down at his half-filled coffee cup. The old sheriff fingered a tear from both cheeks and slowly shook his head from side to side. His lips quivered and he lifted sad eyes to look at his young friend. Matt looked into those eyes and saw a broken heart.

"It's a good dream, Matt," he said, his whispered voice breaking. "I'd give might near anything if I could come in with you, but I can't.

"I've been nothing but a lawman most of my life, barely getting by. Fact is, son, though I'm ashamed to be saying it, I ain't got two double eagles to rub together.

"It might near breaks my heart the only thing I'm gonna leave that girl of mine is the memory of a broken down old lawman with worn out clothes and holes in his boots.

"I can't come in with you, Matt." his friend said sadly. "Don't you see? I ain't got nothing to come in with."

"Yes you do, J.C.," Matt said forcefully. "Yes you do. You've got wisdom and experience and backbone. You've got a wonderful little gal that worships the ground you walk on and you've got a friend that wants you to be his partner. Come in with me, J.C., let's build that dream together. What do you say?"

As Matt watched the face of his friend he witnessed a miracle. Right before his eyes he saw the face of a broken, hopeless, defeated man, suddenly transformed.

It started in the eyes. Hadn't the old lawman himself once told him that all emotions show up first in the eyes? Matt saw those aged, discouraged, saddened eyes give birth to a new hope and take on a youthful sparkle. He watched his friend's down-turned, quivering lips stop quivering. One corner of his mouth broke a crease in the closest thing to a grin he had ever seen on J.C.'s face before.

"Will it be hard work?" Matt asked a question not needing an answer, but giving it anyway. "You bet it will and there'll likely be times when law work might look pretty good. But if I'm any judge of a man, you're a man that's never been scared to tackle a job that's bigger than you. You're a man that's been a fighter, not a quitter. You're a man I want standing by my side. I believe in you, believe in yourself. Will you do it J.C.? Will you be my partner?"

Suddenly a full-blown smile plowed a furrow in his friend's leathered cheeks clear down to the edges of his mouth.

"If you'll have me," J.C. said, his voice full of newborn confidence, "I'll give it my best. . .partner."

Chairs scraped across the wooden floor as both men stood, reaching opened hands and clasping in a firm handshake and a back-patting hug, sealing a lifetime partnership.

The long hill seemed somehow longer as Matt finally topped out and looked down at the winding Fourche LaFave River. He pulled Midnight to a stop and leaned in his saddle, propping his crossed arms on top of his saddle horn and peered down into the beautiful valley he used to call home.

Across the river in a clearing sat their cabin—his and Amelia's. A cabin that held many good memories for Matt—and some that were not so good. It was those that he dreaded to face again.

The old place looked the same as he rode near. The grass had grown up in the yard. The splintered front door still hung in pieces. Otherwise, nothing had changed.

He deliberately avoided the cabin—choosing to spare himself the pain—and swung his stallion up the little hill in back. He slowly stepped down, ground hitched his horse and walked the few steps to stand before two small crosses that marked their graves.

His memory replayed the good times they had shared. The long walks, the picnics, the swimming hole, the time he pushed her so high in James's swing she screamed in fright and laughed at the same time. The quiet times together, the intimate times, the times they just sat quietly together on the front porch, sharing a warm cup of coffee on a crisp fall evening.

"Amelia, I loved you and James the best I knew how," he spoke softly, swallowing hard and blinking away moisture from his eyes. "The three years we had together were the best time of my life and I'll always have them in my memory. There'll always be a place in my heart for you and James.

"I never thought I could ever love again, but I've met someone that loves me and I love her, too. I hope somehow, you can understand. Sleep well, my love."

Touching two fingers to his lips, then placing them tenderly on top of Amelia's grave, a strange feeling of release and peace suddenly washed over him. He pulled himself to his feet, gathered Midnight's reins and swung into the saddle.

The Hawkins place looked deserted as he rode within sight. Maybe they had left, Matt thought as he rode closer. Then Jeb Hawkins stalked out of the house onto the front porch, still wagging that double barrel shotgun.

"Morning, Mr. Hawkins, Mrs. Hawkins ma'am," Matt noticed the woman standing just inside the front door. "Matt Henry, from up the river."

"I remember ye," Hawkins said, hawking and spitting into the yard.

"I rode out to see if your place is still for sale," Matt said, starting to wish he hadn't come.

"If'n it weren't, I wouldn't still be here."

"Supposing I wanted to buy it this morning, how much would you take for it?"

"Like I told you before, six-fifty an acre for the land, fifteen hundred for the house and barn," the man said, slouching against a post on the porch. "It ain't gone down none and ain't likely to."

"Tell you what I'll do," Matt said, looping a leg around his saddle horn and thumbing his hat to the back of his head, "I'll pay off your loan at the bank and give you two thousand dollars cash money, provided you can move out and be gone by this time day after tomorrow."

"Nope, can't do it. Ain't enough," the man said.

"We'll take it, Mr. Henry," the woman spoke up loudly, pushing through the door.

Then she lit in on her no good husband with a wagonload of words she'd most likely stored up for way too long.

"Jeb Hawkins, I've held my tongue and put up with your gambling away all our cattle and horses. I've put up with you putting on and playing like your back is hurt just to keep from having to turn a hand around here. I've even made excuses for you when you boxed me around when you had no call for it.

"But I swear, I ain't gonna keep quiet while you turn down the only offer we've had or likely to get on this run-down place. Don't know why anybody would even want it the way it looks.

"Mr. Henry, we'll have that wagon wheel fixed if I have to do it myself and we'll have what pitiful little we got loaded up and be gone by day after tomorrow and I'll be thanking you every step of the way. While I'm on it and while there's somebody to hear me say it, Jeb Hawkins, if you ever put another hand to me, I'll use that double barrel on you sure as God made green apples."

"Ma'am," Matt said, "if you folks will meet me at the Waldron bank day after tomorrow, we'll take care of the sale and have your money waiting on you. Good day to the both of you."

He couldn't hide the grin as he dropped his leg to the stirrup and wheeled his stallion, kneeing him into a short-lope. The verbal tongue lashing from Mrs. Hawkins seemed long overdue.

The Jenkins Ranch, as the burned-board sign on the overhead entrance read, was the exact opposite of the Hawkins place. Their place was neat and well kept.

The house was a log house looking to be maybe four rooms. It looked solid and well maintained. A split rail fence surrounded the house and small yard. Flower beds lined a path to the house.

There was a good-sized barn with a split rail corral. The red water pump seemed to be in good order and sat at one end of a long watering trough. Two wagons sat near the barn.

Matt only remembered meeting the young Jenkins couple once but they had seemed like a nice couple. The young and attractive Mrs. Jenkins stood on the front porch.

"Morning Mrs. Jenkins," Matt greeted, reining up near the yard fence. "Matt Henry, from upriver? We have the land right next to yours."

"Lands sake, Mr. Henry, I thought I recognized you. It seems like ages since we've seen you. I was real sorry to hear about what happened over at your place. Climb down and stay awhile. Johnny is out checking the stock, I'll ring for him."

She walked over to a bell hanging on the end of the porch and rang it. Matt took the chair she motioned him toward and she sat in the porch swing at the other end of the porch.

"You folks sure got a nice place here, ma'am. How many head of cattle do you graze?"

"We've only got a hundred and twenty, but ours are not just cows, they are a special breeding stock called Herefords. The breed was imported from England back in 1840. My father bought a breed bull and a dozen cows from a gentleman in Albany, New York named Erastus Corning several years ago. When we moved here to the valley, he gave his herd to us to develop. The Hereford breed is quite a remarkable animal. I'm afraid Johnny has lost interest in developing the breed though, he's more interested in developing a large herd, rather than the breed.

"Johnny loves to work with cattle, that's how we met. He worked at my father's Flying B Ranch up in the Boston Mountains. I love Johnny, but he's fiercely independent and wanted his own ranch. My father loaned us the money to buy this place and helped us get started.

"We love the Fourche Valley, but my folks are getting older and want us to move back home. My father wants Johnny to come back and run the ranch. We've got our place up for sale."

"Yes ma'am," Matt said, "Mr. Wilkerson at the bank was telling me you folks were thinking about selling. That's why I rode by. I'd like to talk with the two of you about it."

They passed the time of day until Johnny Jenkins rode up on a beautiful black and white pinto. He was a fellow most would call handsome. He was medium height and build with wide shoulders and black curly hair. His face wore a genuine-looking smile when he strode up with an outstretched hand.

"Matt Henry, ain't it? I'm real sorry about your family. Glad to see you up and around."

"Howdy, Johnny."

"Mr. Henry heard our place was for sale and wants to talk with us about it," Mrs. Jenkins told him.

"Oh," Johnny said. "You looking to expand your place Matt?"

"Thought I might. What are you asking for your spread?"

"Well, we've got a thousand acres of the best land in the valley. I hear land's bringing six-fifty an acre. The house and barn ought to be worth another two thousand I figure. Let's see, that would come to eighty-five hundred dollars I guess."

"Your wife tells me you've still got a hundred and twenty head of a new breed of cattle. How many horses you got?"

"We've just got twenty head," Johnny told him. "Pretty good stock, though."

"Are you interested in selling all your stock?"

"Well . . .sure, I reckon. I hadn't really give a lot of thought to that. Yeah, it would save me herding it all the way to the Boston Mountains. You interested?"

"Tell you what, Johnny," Matt said. "I'll give you twelve thousand for the whole shebang. Only thing is, I've got some folks coming in and I would need it by day after tomorrow. I know that's awfully quick. Why don't you folks talk it over and if you decide that's what you want to do, meet me at the Waldron bank the day after tomorrow and I'll have your money for you."

They said their good-byes, Matt booted a stirrup, waved again and swung away in an easy fox-trot. It was still early and he wanted to ride over to Abbot Mountain and check on young Billy McCraw.

All the way he worried about what he might find. Did the young fellow take Matt's advise and go home to care for his ma, or did he decide to ride the owl-hoot trail like his two brothers?

Matt finally found the small log cabin in a clearing beside a fresh running little mountain stream. It was built of peeled logs and looked sturdy and well kept. A lean to shed and a small pole corral held three well-fed horses. Several laying hens scratched and pecked nearby. It was a neat little place.

The steady ringing of an ax drew Matt's attention and he followed the sound. It led him across a cleared pasture where two milk cows grazing contentedly.

Young Billy was there. His shirtless, sweat-soaked back glistened in the afternoon sun. His shoulder and arm muscles rippled as he swung the double-bit ax expertly. Each stroke bit deeper and deeper into a large pine tree. It was apparent young Billy was no novice at felling trees.

Matt sat his horse at a distance and watched. Finally, a last mighty swing produced a cracking sound. Young Billy lowered his ax to the ground, armed sweat from his forehead and watched as the big tree crashed to the ground.

Matt kneed his horse closer. Only then did the boy become aware of another presence. His eyes flicked to the rifle leaning against a nearby tree.

"It's me, Billy," Matt said quickly. "Matt Henry."

Recognition filled his face and his body relaxed. The makings of a happy smile creased his lips. The boy had grown in the short time since they met, Matt thought.

"Oh yeah, howdy Mr. Henry," the boy said happily. "Glad you came by."

"Looks like you got your hands full there, Billy," Matt said. "That was a pretty big tree you just felled."

"Yes sir, they have to be a certain size or Mr. Bohannon won't buy 'em. He's got a sawmill down the mountain a ways. They bring mule teams and skid 'em to the mill. He pays me two bits for every one I cut for him."

"How many can you cut in a day?"

"On a good day I can bring down four, I did five one day, but I worked from daylight till dark to get it done."

"How's your Ma?" Matt asked.

"She died about a month after I buried my brothers. Their graves are over by the big oak tree yonder."

"So you're all alone now?" Matt asked, feeling sorry for the boy.

"Yes sir. It gets pretty lonesome sometimes, but I guess it could be worse."

They sat on the downed pine tree and talked for awhile. Matt told him about the cattle ranch they were starting and asked if he would be interested in coming to work for him.

"It'll be hard work, son," Matt told him, "but judging by what I just seen, it don't appear you're afraid of that. I'll pay you fifty a month and keep."

"Fifty a month?" young Billy asked, happily. "That's near twice what I can make chopping trees. Yes, sir, Mr. Henry. I'd shore like to work for you. When could I start?"

"You just did," Matt told him, fishing young Billy's first month's wages from his pocket. "You might want to ride down to the saw mill and let your boss know you're quitting."

Matt and Billy walked back to the cabin together, Matt leading his horse and Billy with his ax across his shoulder. They talked for an hour or more. Matt told Billy about his friends that were coming up the trail from Texas.

"They shouldn't be more than a day or two down the trail," he told the boy.

"You know where my cabin is down river. Take them there and wait for me. Think you can take care of that for me?"

"Yes, sir, Mr. Henry. I shore can. I appreciate the job, Mr. Henry. I'll do you a good job, sir."

"No doubt in my mind, Billy. You got a right nice place here, son. It would be a good place to raise a family some day."

"Yes, sir, I been thinking the same thing."

Matt camped that night beside the rushing mountain stream at Twin Forks, the pretty little spot where he had first met Billy McCraw. Since he hadn't brought his pack supplies, he had to make out on a couple pieces of beef jerky and a cold, hard biscuit. Settling down against his saddle he chewed on the tough jerky, listened to the sound of the of the water, wished for a cup of coffee and stared up at his and Jamie's star. He sure missed her, he thought as he pulled up his blanket against the crisp fall coolness.

He was up by daybreak, in the saddle and headed into the sprawling Fourche Valley before the sun peeked over the Ouachita Mountains. Mr. Martindale had told him what his land encompassed and how to find the approximate boundaries of it. He spent the whole day riding it, looking it over, making plans.

By nightfall he was dead tired and hungry as he rode into Waldron. He shore was glad the little café was still open and enjoyed a late supper and several cups of coffee before stabling his horse and curling up under his blanket in the hayloft of the livery. He didn't want to intrude on J.C. and Molly as late as it was and knowing they didn't have an extra bed.

Come morning, Matt washed up in the watering trough and made his way up the street to the café. J.C. was there and blowing on his coffee when Matt strode in.

"Morning partner," Matt greeted as he scraped out a chair, "you're up and at 'em mighty early."

"So are you," his friend said, eyeing him closely. "Where'd you spend the night to get here this early?"

"Slept at the Waldron Hotel, of course," Matt kidded. "Wasn't the first time I slept in a hayloft and likely won't be the last."

"You mean you was in town and didn't come and spend the night with us?" the sheriff asked, visibly put out.

"It was late when I got in and didn't want to bother you," Matt explained. "Hey, I got some good news to tell you about. I rode by and talked with both the Hawkins and the Jenkins couple day before yesterday. We won't know for shore till later today, but I think both of them are gonna sell us their places. I'm going over to the bank as soon as they open and have Mr. Wilkerson draw up the papers."

"None of my business, I reckon," J.C. said, "but I just don't understand where you're getting the money to do all this. You didn't rob a bank while you was gone did you son? I know you collected a heap of reward money, but it couldn't amount to that much."

Over several cups of coffee, Matt told his friend the whole story, leaving out nothing. He told about his encounters with the various members of Trotter's gang and how he followed them into Mexico. He told about his dragging and imprisonment at the silver mine work camp and of his escape. He related the story of his showdown with corrupt Mexican officer and his bodyguard and explained how he came by all the money.

Finally, he told about the herd of cattle his old friend had built for him and about the upcoming cattle drive. Then, he excitedly told his friend about Jamie and of their wedding in February.

When Matt finished the old lawman just sat, shaking his head in wonderment.

"Don't reckon I ever seen more bad things happen to just one fellow," J.C. told him. "It's about time some good things happened, too."

"Oh," Matt said, "I set us up an account over at the bank. It's in the name of the Fourche Valley Ranch. I fixed it so either me or you could draw on it. If it's okay with you, I'm gonna depend on you to see to it the bills and hands are all paid on time."

"I got some news, too," J.C. told him. "I resigned as Sheriff yesterday. I've been needing to do that for quite a while anyway. Figured if I was gonna do this thing, might as well go whole hog or nothing."

"J.C., I didn't say anything because I wanted it to be your decision, but I'm glad to hear it. Starting today, you're working full time for the ranch. What say we start partners out at three hundred a month? Does that sound fair? Then we'll split up whatever profit we make at the end of every year."

"Lordy, Matt, I never made more than eighty a month in my whole life. What do I need that much money for?"

"Don't worry," Matt told him, "Molly will use most of it keeping me supplied with apple pies."

When the bank opened Matt and J. C. was there. Matt explained to the banker about the offers he had made to the Hawkins and the Jenkins. He asked Mr. Wilkerson if he could go ahead and draw up all the papers they would need, not only for the purchase of the thirteen thousand acres, but also for purchase of the Hawkins and Jenkins properties.

Byron Wilkerson spent the whole morning preparing all the deeds, mortgage papers and abstracts involved. Near noon, Matt, J.C. and a young lawyer who had just opened his practice in Waldron walked into the bank.

"You know Mr. Raymond Poe, don't you, Mr. Wilkerson?"

Matt asked, introducing the attorney him and J.C. had just spent the last hour with.

"Well, not officially," the banker said, shaking hands with everyone. "I heard you just moved to town and was setting up your practice, but I hadn't had the pleasure of meeting you, yet."

"J.C. and I don't know a whole lot about all this legal stuff, so we figured we ought to get somebody that does," Matt explained. "We've hired Mr. Poe to represent us and the ranch."

"I'd say that was a wise decision," Byron Wilkerson said. "I'm sure Mr. Poe will find everything in order."

He did and by the time he was finished going over all the documents, Jeb Hawkins and his wife rolled up to the front of the bank in a wagon. The wheel was all fixed and their few belongings were piled haphazardly into the wagon.

After both Jeb and Mrs. Hawkins signed the papers, Matt paid off the thousand-dollar mortgage they had with the bank, counted out two thousand dollars and handed it to Mrs. Hawkins. Jeb never said a word during the whole thing.

"Mrs. Hawkins, I wish you the best of everything from here on out," Matt told her, "you deserve it."

"Well, Matt," the banker said, as they stood on the boardwalk and watched the Hawkins head east out of town. "Looks like you're well on your way to owning a fifteen thousand acre ranch."

"That sounds awfully good, don't it J.C.?"

"Shore does, partner."

"I spent all day yesterday riding it out. It's even prettier than I thought."

They looked down the street and, lo and behold two wagons, both loaded to the gills, were headed their way. Johnny led the way, his loaded wagon being pulled by a two-team hitch. He sat high, wide and handsome on the springboard seat. The black and white pinto that had caught Matt's eye was tied on a lead behind Johnny's wagon.

Johnny's pretty wife drove the second wagon, handling the horses like an experienced teamster. She had a smile occupying her face as big as all outdoors—she was going home.

"It shore don't take as long to get rid of it as it does to get it," Johnny Jenkins commented after both he and his wife had signed the papers.

Matt counted out twelve thousand dollars, handed it to the young fellow and reached to shake his hand.

"Wait a minute," Johnny said, "You need to take out for the eight horses and my pinto. When you asked me how many head of horses we had and I said twenty, I forgot we'd need some to pull our wagons."

"How much you figure those eight horses are worth?" Matt asked young Jenkins.

"Oh, I'd say they ought to be worth forty apiece, that sound about right?"

"Sounds fair," Matt said. "Would you trade the pinto and call it even?"

"You mean Thunder?" Jenkins seemed taken-aback by the suggestion. "That pinto's a good gelding, shore enough, but he ain't three hundred twenty dollars good. You got yourself a deal, Matt."

Matt and J.C. stood in the dusty street. They watched the Jenkins pull out of town and head north toward Fort Smith, heading for the Boston Mountains. Matt held the lead rope for the black and white pinto.

"That's shore a pretty piece of horseflesh," J.C. said, "kind of expensive, but pretty. What you got in mind doing with him?"

"Gonna give him to Molly if its all right with you."

Now and again there's a time in your life that you will never forget. Matt figured this was one of those times.

"Let's rein up a minute," he hollered to J.C. and Molly.

They had just topped a long hill looking down on the former Jenkins place. It set near the middle of a stretch of the Fourche Valley. Behind it lay the winding Fourche LaFave River. Scattered between where they sat their horses and the house grazed a herd of red and white Hereford cattle, their cattle.

A feeling of pride crept over Matt and he swallowed to clear his throat of the lump that appeared there.

"Them is our cows, J.C.," he said proudly, "yours and mine and Molly's."

"Are they really, papa?" Molly asked, proudly sitting tall on her new black and white pinto. "Are them really ours? They're so funny-looking, not like any cows I ever saw."

"Yep," her father replied, seeming to straighten taller in the saddle when he said it, "and that place yonder is our new home."

"Really? Is it really? I can't believe all this is really happening. I'm gonna ride on ahead and pick out my very own room. Is it okay, papa?"

"It's okay, honey," J.C. told her.

She touched her heels to the gelding's flanks and was off like a shot. Matt and J.C. sat and watched her as she rode down the hill and across the valley, scattering the cattle as she passed.

"I've never seen her so excited, Matt," the old lawman told him. "I want to thank you again for all you're doing for us. I can never repay what I owe you."

"J.C., I wouldn't be sitting here on this hill if it hadn't been for you and Molly. That little girl nursed me back to health and these guns you gave me saved my bacon more times than I like to think about. It's me that owes you."

The Hereford cattle looked strange to Matt, too. As they approached the herd he looked them over closely. He had grown used to the long, gangly, narrow-bodied longhorn. The Hereford were short, wide-bodied cows with much more fat. They wore short horns and distinctive white faces.

As Matt and J.C. rode near, the cattle raised their heads from the lush, belly-high grass only briefly, then returned to their contended grazing.

Matt counted three good-looking bulls in the herd. One stood out from the others. Jenkins had told him earlier that his herd bull was named Domino. He was a huge animal, looking to weigh well over fifteen hundred pounds. He left no question that he was the undisputed king of the herd.

The bull spotted the riders as they approached and lifted his massive head. He snorted and began to paw the ground, throwing dirt over his sleek red coat, contrasted by his white stocking feet and face. White bubbly foam dripped from his flaring nostrils. His dark, flashing eyes fixed a challenging stare.

Off by themselves, several Jersey milk cows grazed peacefully, their udders heavy with milk.

"I'll put them up in the corral at the house," J.C. suggested, "they ought to supply enough milk for our whole outfit."

"Good idea," Matt said.

They spent the next hour inspecting the house. It had a front room, a kitchen and two separate bedrooms. Molly had already laid claim to the smallest one near the back. Mrs. Jenkins had left the white curtains on the windows and there was a pole-log bed frame in each bedroom.

"Looks to me like all we got to do is move in," J.C. said happily. "It's a fine house. It'll be a good place to raise a little girl."

"I ain't no little girl," she informed him in no uncertain terms, "I'm thirteen."

"Begging your pardon, ma'am," her father said, bowing at the waist.

They saw the wagons the minute they topped the hill. The three white-topped covered wagons were nosed up under a giant oak tree only a stone's throw from the river and not much further from Matt's cabin. The white canvas tops of the Conestoga wagons stood out against the background of tall green grass and pine covered Ouachita Mountains. It was a beautiful sight.

"They've made it," Matt said excitedly, all three of them urging their mounts into a lope.

White smoke from a supper fire trailed lazily into the air. A gentle breeze interrupted its upward journey and carried little white whiffs off into the graying twilight. The sweet smell of fresh boiling coffee carried on the same breeze and joined all the smiling faces in a happy welcome.

Hugs, handshakes and howdies took awhile. A huge smile on Billy McCraw's face gave testimony that he was glad to be part of this happy group.

Marquitta was clearly in charge of supper preparation, passing out assignments to one and all. Avianna was frying venison from a deer brought by Billy and Juan after one of their hunting outings. Rosetta was peeling potatoes despite her constant glances at Billy. Chico and Molly had volunteered to go to the river for fresh water, even though none was needed.

Juan and Billy took charge of Matt, J.C. and Molly's horses, unsaddling, watering and hobbling them so they could graze.

"Mr. Von Strauss," Matt said, "you and the wife might want to stroll up to the cabin yonder before supper. It's shore nothing fancy, but it was my home for three years. If it suits you, we'll all pitch in and help move in your stuff first thing in the morning."

"Yah, vee vould like that. Vee vill be back quickly."

Matt and Joe watched the couple as they strolled hand in hand toward the small cabin. They seemed so happy, laughing, pointing toward the mountains and hugging as they walked.

"Boss, I wish you could have seen and heard them on the trip through the mountains. They were like two little kids coming back home. I think they're gonna work out just fine."

"How you and Avianna getting on?" Matt asked, feeling like he already the answer.

"Just between you and me, as soon as things settle down a mite and I get up the nerve, I'm giving thought to asking her to marry me."

"I figured that was coming. I just don't know why it took so long. Come on, let's get J.C. and Julio and walk down by the river till supper. We've got some planning to do."

They were still squatting on the riverbank talking when Marquitta called them to supper.

They ate a delicious supper. There was lots of laughing and joking all during and after the meal. Afterwards, they all gathered around the campfire against the cool autumn evening. The feeling of family shore feels good, Matt thought.

The next few weeks passed quickly. Everybody was as busy as a cranberry merchant. J.C. and Joseph went and looked at Billy's former employer's sawmill and not only bought it, but hired Mr. Bohannon to move it, set it back up and operate it. J.C. said that as much lumber as the carpenter was talking about needing, we would be better off owning our own sawmill.

Billy volunteered to work a timber crew and turned out to be an excellent timber man. He did such a good job, J.C. put him in charge of the timber operation. He had two men on bucking saws felling trees, two trimmers stayed busy with double-bitted axes and two skidders used mule teams to skid the logs to the mill. Not only were they getting all the lumber they needed, they were clearing much-needed pastureland.

In less than two weeks the German carpenter and his two helpers had the old Hawkins place looking like new. Three new bedrooms were added giving Julio and his family a beautiful four-bedroom house.

A long bunkhouse was built and cedar pole bunks were added inside, providing for up to twenty present and future workers. A new barn was built with a large, pole corral.

"Things are coming along pretty good," Matt told J.C. as they sat their horses watching all the work going on. "Let's take a little ride down river, I never have ridden all the way to our eastern boundary line."

As they rode they talked and planned. J.C. seemed to be more energetic. He somehow seemed younger. He sure was working hard.

"When Billy and his crew find the time," J.C. said, "I'm gonna have them lay in a good supply of wood for the winter. We might be in for a bad winter, I notice the squirrels shore are busy storing nuts away. It can get mighty cold in this valley."

"Might consider having Juan haul us some feed from town and store in the barn too," Matt suggested.

"When you figuring on leaving for Texas?" J.C. Asked.

"Another week or so. We need to start putting together our trail crew for the drive. We're gonna need close to a hundred men."

"I know Joe will be riding with you. Are you taking Julio and Juan too?"

"Yeah, I figure on leaving Billy here to help you. If you need to hire more men to take up the slack, go ahead."

"That Billy's turned out to be quite a worker. He ain't afraid to tackle anything you put him on and does a good job of it, too," J.C. said. "You never did tell me where you found him."

"Him and his two brothers tried to bushwhack me down at Twin Forks one night," Matt told him.

"Tried to bushwhack you? What happened?"

"His two brothers didn't make it," Matt said.

* * *

"I want everybody that ain't working timber or building to pitch in and help with the branding," Joe told the dozen hands at chow the next morning. "We want the Double H brand on everything that walks on four legs. Sonny, you and Ike are brand new around here so why don't you stoke the fire and keep the irons hot. Julio, how about you and Juan working the chute poles. Matt and I will do the branding. The rest of you boys will be catching and bring them in.

"You boys might want to ride right easy with them Hereford bulls, they can get mean, especially old Domino. Be real careful around him, he's a bad one. Any questions? Then let's get to it, the day's a wasting."

Matt had spent long hours with Von Strauss, going over in detail how he wanted the big ranch house built.

"I want it to be something real special," he told the carpenter. "I want something my new wife will be proud of."

"It vill be done," the man promised. "You vill see."

"I believe you," Matt told the big German, reaching a hand for a handshake before he remembered the man come near crushing his hand the last time they shook hands.

CHAPTER XV

Matt's Might Men

"You shall pass before your brethren armed, all the
mighty men of valor, and help them." (Joshua 1:14)

It was December 11, 1867. Two hard weeks riding since they
left Arkansas. Matt, Joe, Julio and Juan rode into Fort Worth,
Texas and checked into the Cattlemen's Hotel. After securing
rooms and enjoying a good hot bath, they found the eating
place recommended by the hotel manager and surrounded a
big steak apiece.

After lunch, Matt and Joe went to the local newspaper office
to have some handbills printed up. They ordered two hundred
fliers made advertising for experienced drovers. Matt had it in
mind to post them in every cow town from there to the border.

The newspaperman got curious and started asking questions
about the drive. When Matt mentioned they would be taking twenty
thousand head all the way to Kansas, the man got so excited he could
hardly contain himself and asked if he could do a story about it.

Come morning, the paper hit the street and the story spread like wildfire. Before their breakfast was good and settled, drovers started tramping into the hotel lobby in a steady stream, wanting to hire on. By noon the line was so long Matt decided they needed to split up. Matt hired the dining room. He, Joe and Julio all sat at different tables talking to man after man. Julio talked to the few Mexicans that applied.

"Let's be right choosy," Matt told them both. "If this turnout is typical, we're gonna be talking to an awful lot of cowboys. Pick only the best. If you got any questions about them at all, don't take a chance. We don't want no boozers or troublemakers.

"We pay fifty a month and keep, starting when you hire 'em. If they stick with us till the end of the drive, there'll be a hundred-dollar bonus for every man. They're to furnish their own horse, saddle and guns till the drive starts. From there on we'll furnish a string of mounts for them. Make shore they all understand they'll be expected to ride for the brand. In case of trouble, I don't want to have to wonder if they'll stick. We're looking for men with sand in their craw."

By dark, Matt had talked to over a dozen men and hired only four. Joe another three, and Julio found only two vaqueros to his liking. All nine we asked to hang around close. The remaining dozen or so still waiting to talk with them were asked to come back the next morning.

"Joe," Matt said. "I'll meet you and all the boys we hired over at the café. I'll arrange for their rooms and be along directly."

Matt rented a room for each of his new hands and headed for the café. They were all sitting around a large table jawing when Matt strode in and scraped out a chair.

"We were just shooting the breeze," Joe said, as Matt motioned for coffee. "Boys, this is Matt Henry. He owns the Fourche Valley Ranch, the outfit you'll be riding for. I'm sure he's got some things to say."

"Well, first off, I want us to get to know one another. For the next eight months or so, we're all gonna be closer than a newborn calf to its mama. We need to learn to trust and depend on each other. There'll most likely be times when your life will depend on the man sitting next to you.

"You'll be riding for the Double H brand. That stands for Henry and Holderfield, my partner. He runs our ranch up in the Fourche River Valley of Arkansas. I'll be handling the drive.

"Most likely you've already heard, we'll be trailing twenty thousand head up the trail come early spring. That'll be by far the biggest trail drive in history. We're looking to hire a hundred men but we're being right choosy. We ain't just looking for men, we're looking for the best cowboys that ever forked a saddle. Between us, we've talked to over fifty men today. You boys are the only ones that got picked and you ought to be proud about that.

"Now I'm telling you straight out, so there's no misunderstanding. There'll be no drinkers or troublemakers riding for the Double H brand. If that's your pleasure, you need to look somewhere else for your pay. What you do when you're on your own time is your business. What you do when you're drawing my pay is my business. Any man that sees it different best stand up and walk out right now and save us both a lot of trouble.

"These two fellows are Joe Doyle and Julio Sanchez. They're both foremen. You'll likely be seeing and hearing from them more than me, unless there's trouble. Anything these fellows say is the same as me saying it. Joe will be my range boss, Julio will be handling the vaqueros in our outfit and Juan Sanchez there, and he'll be in charge of our remuda.

"For the next month or so, we'll be cutting out the herd and trail branding. Somewhere near the end of February, depending on the grass, we'll be heading up the trail to Abilene, Kansas. Just so's you'll know, I've hired five of the best trail cooks that ever rolled a biscuit. I want you boys to be fat and sassy time we get to Kansas.

"Now, I'm gonna sit down and shut my flapper. I'd like for us to go around the table and one by one, tell us who you are and a little about yourself so we can get to know you."

At first, the men seemed a little shy and glanced back and forth apprehensively at one another. Finally, a tall drink of water unlimbered himself from his chair and the more he straightened out, the taller he got. He wore a handlebar mustache over a slash of a mouth. His face was weather tanned and his shoulders were too wide to walk through most doors without scrapping the sides. He had a look about him that would make most men walk around him.

"Guess I might just as well start. My ma always said I talk when I ought to be listening. My name's Ed Stovall, I've worked for the Rocking R ranch over east of here for the last ten years. I've been up the trail behind a herd more times than I care to remember. I got nothing bad to say about the Rocking R, they was good to me. I just felt like riding a different bronc for awhile. I'm looking forward to riding with you fellows."

When Ed sat back down, the man next to him stood. For a long minute he looked down at the floor, scraping a boot.

"I'm Sylvester Weber, most folks just call me Spud. Never been on a cattle drive before but I was raised on a cattle ranch. I've been punching cows since I could walk, maybe before. I fought with the south, proud I did. I've been looking for steady work ever since I got out. I ain't afraid of work and I'll fight if need be."

"My name's Herman Summers," the next man said. "I hail from Georgia. I was working for a small spread till it went busted. I been looking for work since. I'll do my share and then some and be there when the drive's over. Right proud to be with this outfit."

"Name's Rosco Haney," the next man said, standing quickly. "There ain't a horse I can't ride nor a steer I can't throw and I can rope a horsefly by its hind legs when it's chasing a she-fly."

Then, tipping his hat, he sat down to the chuckles of everyone around the table. There was no doubt about it, they had found the crew's jokester.

The room was quiet for a few moments before the next man raised his head slowly, then pushed to his feet. He was one of the ones Joe had hired. He looked more like a gunfighter than a drover. He shifted a matchstick from one side of his mouth to the other, then spoke in a low voice, barely above a whisper.

"I'm Chip Dawson. I've been a lot of things, I guess. Some I'd rather not talk about. Last three years I was town Marshal up in Wichita Falls. Wife died a few weeks back. Felt like doing something different."

"Calvin Lovett's my handle," the short, muscular fellow said as he rose. "I been a cowboy all my life I reckon. Don't know nothing else, shucks, I don't want to know nothing else. It's my life. I'm right proud to be riding with the Double H brand. I'll be there when the going gets tough . . . and it will."

The next man was one Matt had hired. From the moment he first laid eyes on the fellow he knew he was gonna hire him. He was Texas tall and leather tough. A thick patch of frosty gray hair crowned a weathered face burned bronze by a lifetime in the west Texas sun. His dark eyes barely showed through narrow eyelids. Deep turkey tracks creased his temples His jaw hung square and firm below a mouth that had a hard set to it.

"I'm Jess Tanner," he said, in a voice that caused one to listen. "I owned my own spread until the Comanchero burned me out and murdered my whole family. I joined up with the Texas Rangers under Captain Tackett after that. I've been riding with them for the last year. Ready to try my hand at ranching again. Reckon this is as good a place as any to start."

Matt decided right then and there that Jess Tanner had the makings of a foreman. He would keep an eye on this fellow.

Julio stood to introduce the two vaqueros he had hired, since they spoke little English.

"These vaqueros are named Jose and Pablo Valdez," Julio said. "They are brothers. They come from Mattamoros, Mexico.

They work on the Mendoza Ranch before signing on with a cattle drive in west Texas. The herd was lost to banditos at the Kansas line. They make it back this far before they must have work."

So far, Matt was well pleased with those they had hired. He figured if they could find a hundred more as good maybe, just maybe, they'd have a chance to get those ornery critters to Abilene on time.

All the next day they talked to men—good men—men who wanted and needed to work—but they hired only twelve. They were averaging hiring only about one out of every five. Many were inexperienced, some were obvious troublemakers, and some were just plain no-goods.

At daybreak the following morning they rode out. As they walked their horses down the street of Fort Worth, Matt twisted in his saddle to gaze proudly at the twenty-four good men. Men he figured would stick no matter how rough the going got.

Most every cow town they rode near, Matt dispatched a couple of riders to post fliers announcing the Fourche Valley Ranch would be hiring drovers in San Antonio until the first of the year.

Reaching Waco, they set up camp on the bank of a small, fresh running stream about two miles out of town.

"Some of the boys might want to mosey into town after awhile," Matt told Joe. "I'm gonna ride on in and tack up some fliers. I'll arrange for a place to set up shop and we'll work the town tomorrow and the next day for shore, maybe more. If you need me I'll be at the hotel."

Matt rode in and tied his horse in front of Sheriff Thompson's office. It had been way too long since he last seen his friend. Pushing through the door, he found Ben with his big feet propped on top of the same old dilapidated desk, his hat pulled down over his eyes, snoring loudly.

"If a man needed a sheriff, he'd be in a heap of trouble," Matt said.

Waking with a start, the sheriff shoved his hat back, took one look and jumped to his feet.

"Well, glory be," he shouted. "If you ain't a sight for sore eyes. Where you been boy? Ain't seen hide nor hair of you in a coon's age."

The big sheriff grabbed Matt's outstretched hand and came near shaking it off at the elbow.

"Howdy, Ben, it's been awhile. Looks like you're losing weight. Ain't nobody around to buy your grub since I left? You had supper yet?"

"On the pittance they pay me, I can't afford to eat but once a day and I had breakfast. Course, if you're buying, that's a horse of a different color."

"You haven't changed a bit," Matt told him. "Come on, I'll see if my credit's good over at Abby's place."

"She'll shore be glad to see you, Matt. We've missed you. What you been doing anyway?"

"I'm getting married, for one thing."

"Get outta here. You're joshing me."

"Nope. Come Valentine's Day. I'll be expecting you to be there, too."

"Who is she? Where'd you find her? Come on, boy, tell me all about it."

"I'll tell you and Abby about it over supper. Don't want to have to tell it twice."

Abby was pouring a cup of coffee for a customer when Matt and Ben walked in. Striding up behind her, Matt wrapped his arms around her waist in a bear hug. Whirling her head around, she let out a little scream, spun around and threw both arms around his neck.

"Matt Henry, I hate you for staying away so long," she told him, faking anger. "Where have you been? I've wondered about you so many times."

"It's a long story and one that will wait until things slow down around here. When you get the time, how about bringing me and this big lug they call the sheriff something to eat? We're both starved half to death."

They ate the wonderful dinner Miss Abby brought them, then lingered over a cup of coffee until the customers had all left. Abby brought a fresh pot and joined them. Yielding to their insistence, Matt related the events of his life since he left Waco.

"Go ahead," Ben egged him on, "tell her the most important part. I dare you."

"What?" she asked, looking from one to the other.

"Oh," Matt said, stalling deliberately, teasing her. "It ain't nothing much. I'm just getting married."

"You're what?" Abby shouted. "Matt, that's wonderful! Who is she? Come on, you've got to tell us all about it."

So he did.

"Shore wish you could come to the wedding," Matt told them, "Jamie says it's gonna be the biggest wedding Texas has ever seen."

"Sounds like you've come a long way since we've seen you last," Ben said. "You give up on finding the rest of Trotter's outfit?"

"Nope," Matt said, "last I heard they had a shoot-out with some marshals at a place called Doan's store up on the Red River. Seems Trotter's bunch come out on the short end of the stick. The way I hear it, the only ones left is Trotter himself and the Mexican. I'll get wind of them again one of these days."

"Yeah," Ben told him, "I heard the same news. How long you gonna be hanging around?"

"Day or two," Matt said. "I've got twenty-four of my men camped out of town a couple of miles. Some of them might be in after awhile to wet their whistle. They ain't the kind to cause trouble, though."

"Knew that without it being said," Ben told him. "They wouldn't be working for you if they was. Hey, I hate to run off and leave you two together. I know you'll be talking behind my back, but I gotta be running along. I'll catch up to you tomorrow, Matt. You watch out for him now, Abby."

"So long, Ben," Matt said, as his big friend strode out of the café.

"Matt, I'm so happy for you," Abby told him. "Remember, I told you when the time was right you'd find the right lady for you."

"Yeah, I remember. I shore do love her, Miss Abby. I hope I can make her as happy as she's already made me."

"She must be an awfully special lady. I still think she's getting the better end of the bargain, though."

"When you and Ben gonna quit playing ring around the rosy and get together? You know he loves you."

"I'd marry the big lug in a heartbeat if he'd ask me," she said, her voice growing soft. "We're such good friends, I'm afraid he thinks that's all I feel for him."

"You're wasting time and they ain't making no more of it," Matt told her.

They talked to thirty or more men over the next two days and hired seven.

Matt was well pleased. In his mind, two of the them stood out above the rest.

One was a man named Shorty Shepherd. The sheriff brought him around and introduced them as a fellow he'd known a long time. He was small in stature, standing barely over five feet but you didn't have to look hard to see there was a big man in that small body. His thick chest and wide shoulders told Matt here was a fellow that would fight a mama grizzly barehanded and not even work up a sweat.

The other man had worked for Joe on the Triple T for awhile. Joe said he had left to take a foreman's job up in Colorado. His name was Buck Wheeler. Matt liked the man immediately. Joe and Julio took the new hands on out to the camp while Matt went by to say his good-byes.

"Never can tell," Ben told him, "I might get down that way for the wedding."

"It's a long ride, but I shore would like it if you could," Matt told his friend.

Miss Abby cried, of course and hugged Matt tightly.

"You be happy, you hear?" she whispered as they hugged.

She tiptoed and kissed him on the cheek. Their eyes met for a long moment. He smiled at her and thumbed away a tear from her pretty cheek.

"You too," he said. Then spun on his heel and was gone.

He could smell the coffee a mile away. Juan took his horse and Matt poured himself a cup from the blackened pot over the fire and joined his men as they relaxed around the campfire. Around him, the men were laughing and joking and telling yarns, but Matt didn't hear a word they were saying. His mind was lost in a rush of emotions that tugged at his heart. He glanced up at the black canopy overhead and feasted his eyes on the eastern star and wondered.

The sky came dusky dark when Matt and thirty-two saddle-tired cowboys rode into San Antonio. They saw to their horses and headed in a straggling group toward the hotel. By doubling up, Matt arranged for them to know what it felt like to sleep in a bed for a change. He asked them to meet him in the dining room after they had stashed their gear and washed up. The last two customers were just leaving when Matt strode into the dining room.

"I've got thirty-two hungry cowboys that need feeding," he told the fellow that looked to be in charge. "Reckon you could rustle up a big steak and all the trimmings for that many?"

"Yes sir, Mr. Henry," the man said. "It might take a bit, but I think we can arrange that. It's good to have you back in town."

They went through several cups of coffee, but the meal was worth the wait. The men laughed and joked through the whole meal. If anybody even thought about the saloons down the street, they didn't let on. It's got the makings of a good crew, Matt thought.

Matt slept like a log and was up before good day. He mooched a cup from the early man in the dining room and strolled out onto the porch of the hotel. The deserted street lay still and dark. Here and there a lamp showed through a window. A rooster crowed. A dog barked. Matt leaned a shoulder against a post and soaked in the sights and sounds of a world waking up.

A tinge of light gray crept out of the east and swallowed up the darkness. He sipped his coffee and glued his eyes to the spectacle that always warmed his heart.

What was it his ma used to read to him and pa from her good book? "The heavens declare the glory of God and the firmament displays His handy-work." Well, He shore was doing a good job this morning.

Before his eyes the eastern sky became an artist's canvas, stretched from sky to sky and splashed with streaks of shimmering gold, radiant red and brilliant yellow, all mixed together. He dared not look away for fear he would miss a sight that would never be repeated in his lifetime. A shiver ran up and down his back. If only Jamie were here to share this moment with him.

It was December the twentieth. He had promised Jamie he would be home for Christmas. Taking one last look, he drained his cup and strode back inside and ordered breakfast. Jess Tanner and Buck Wheeler moseyed in, poured themselves a cup and scraped out a chair at Matt's table.

"Morning, boss," they both greeted, folding themselves into a chair.

"Morning fellows," Matt said. "You boys are up early."

"Never did learn to sleep past daylight," Jess said, blowing on his coffee.

"My papa said, dark was for sleeping, light was for getting things done," Buck agreed.

"He must have been kin to my pa," Matt laughed. "Glad you boys came down early, I've been wanting to talk. I've been watching you boys and I like what I see. I'm needing a couple more foremen. I was wondering if the two of you would be interested?

"My foremen will be in charge of a crew while we're cutting and branding. Then when we hit the trail, we'll be splitting up into five separate herds. I'll need a ramrod for each crew. Foreman's wages in my outfit is a hundred-fifty a month and keep. If you want the job it's yours."

Jess come near choking on a swig of coffee. Matt saw the look of shock that washed across both faces.

"Boss," Buck said, "that's more'n double what the job pays in most outfits. Is there something about this job you haven't told us about?"

"Nope," Matt assured them. "I just try to treat the other fellow the way I'd expect to be treated. Yeah, I know I pay more than most outfits, but I expect more, too. I expect my men to ride for the brand. To stick with me when the going gets rough and the good Lord knows we're gonna have some of them. This things we're doing ain't gonna be no Sunday school picnic. I'm gonna need some men with some backbone about 'em. From where I'm sitting, the two of you qualify."

"Can't speak for nobody but me, but if you're offering, I'm taking you up on it," Jess told him, sticking out his work-hardened hand.

"Same goes for me," Buck told him. "I'll ride stirrup to stirrup wherever you want to go."

Over the course of the next several minutes the rest of the crew straggled in two or three at a time. After they all had their coffee and were seated, Matt got their attention.

"Boys, I just got through hiring Jess Tanner and Buck Wheeler on as foremen.

"Starting now, whatever they say, is the same as me saying it. Anybody got a problem with that, see me after breakfast and pick up your time. I'll tell you now though, I'm still looking for two more good foremen. I'll be letting you know when I make up my mind.

"Later on this morning, Joe will be passing out a half month's pay for every man. I'm calling it a signing on bonus. You'll still get your full pay at the end of the month. It ain't but a few days till Christmas. Figured you might like to have a little jingle in your pockets.

"I've made arrangements with the hotel and dining room to take care of you boys for a few days. After Christmas, you'll be moving out to the Circle C Ranch to start work. You might want to enjoy this time off, likely it'll be the last you'll get for quite a spell."

After breakfast, Matt and Joe headed to the bank. Mr. Martindale saw them coming and rushed to meet them with outstretched hand.

"Good to see you, Matt. Joe. I heard you rode in last night with a whole crew of salty-looking fellows. Sounds like you're putting together quite an outfit."

"They're good boys," Matt said. "Still got a long way to go though. Somebody said you own that little building where the carpenter shop use to be. I'd like to rent it for a month or so,"

"Yes sir, I do own it, but I won't rent it to you. If you need it for a month of so, it's yours. May I ask what you're going to do with a small place like that?"

"We've been spreading posters all over saying we'll be hiring drovers till the end of the year. We need a place where we can headquarter and talk to the ones that come."

"It ought to be good for that," the banker said. "What else can I do for you this morning?"

"Joe needs to draw out some money to give the boys a little Christmas bonus," Matt told him. "Go ahead and be paying the boys," Matt told his foreman. "I'll catch up with you later."

Leaving the bank, Matt walked to the blacksmith shop.

"You wear out that hundred branding irons yet?" the smithy asked. "Be glad to make you up another hundred."

"Just fixing to start using 'em," Matt told him. "Gonna need some horses shoed before long though."

"You just tell me where and when."

"Right now I need you to burn me a sign in a board. I need it hung over the door of that little carpenter shop up the street before noon. Think you could take care of that for me?"

"Sure as sin," the fellow said. "What do you want it to say?"

"Just put Fourche Valley Ranch on it," Matt told him.

Juan took four of the boys with him and rode out for the ranch, aiming to pick up enough of the horses to pull the five converted chuck wagons and the five extra supply wagons they would be taking.

Julio and the two Valdez brothers, Jose and Pablo, mounted up and headed for Mattamoros with Mexican money and instructions to purchase as large a remuda of the famous Mendoza black vaquero horses and as he could bring back. Matt also asked Julio to hire a crew of twenty or so of the best vaqueros he could find.

It seemed like things were falling into place. If only Moses showed up on time with the other four cooks. Joe, Jess and Buck were busy carrying a couple of tables and chairs from the hotel dining room over to their new hiring headquarters. Matt strolled down to Jacob's Mercantile Store. He needed to pick up a Christmas present for Jamie.

"Good morning, Mr. Henry," Mrs. Jacobs greeted as he pushed through the door.

"Morning ma'am," he replied, letting his eyes stroll around the store, trying to get some kind of idea.

"I hear congratulations are in order? I think everyone in town is planning on attending the wedding."

"Yes, ma'am. It's gonna be something, I reckon."

"May I help you find something this morning?"

"Well, truth be known, I'm looking for something to get Jamie for Christmas and I'm plumb stumped. Hoping you might think of something."

"Jamie is a beautiful young lady and as nice as she is beautiful," Mrs. Jacobs said. "Have you picked out her rings yet?"

"Well, no ma'am, I haven't. To be honest with you, I hadn't even thought about it until just now."

"Let me show you what we've got," the lady said, moving quickly to a small glass case. "We've got some of the most exquisite wedding sets you'll find anywhere."

"What do you mean, sets?"

"Let me show you," she said, removing a pretty little box from the case and popping it open. "Take this set for instance. The one with the large diamond is the engagement ring. The gentleman gives it to his fiancée when he asks her to marry him. The matching gold band is the one you place on her finger when you are actually married."

"I never seen anything like that," Matt told her. "Do most married folk wear these?"

"Most that can afford them do. We keep a few sets for the larger ranchers that can afford to give their wives a set of rings like these. They are quite expensive."

"What would a set of rings like that cost?" Matt asked.

"As I said, this set is the finest we have in the store. It's a full carat, pear shaped diamond of the very best quality, set in a fourteen karat gold band. It sells for five hundred dollars."

"I'll take it," Matt said, unable to take his eyes off the sparkling diamond ring.

"It comes in the velvet covered box and I'll be happy to wrap it in some pretty paper for you, too."

While he was at it, he picked out a beautiful gold brooch for Mrs. Cunningham and a hand carved, imported pipe set in a polished wooden case for J.R.

"Is Mr. Jacobs around handy?" Matt asked.

"No," she said, "he's delivering a load of feed. I'm afraid he won't be back until late this afternoon. Is there something I can do?"

"Well, yes ma'am. My trail cooks will be coming in to load up on supplies for our crews. I wanted to make arrangements so they could pick up whatever they needed and I could settle up with you later."

"That will be no problem whatsoever," the nice lady told him. "I'll see they are taken care of."

"Thank you ma'am. If you'll tally up my bill, I'd like to settle up with you."

True to his word, the blacksmith had the sign over the door well before noon. Joe and the boys were already set up and talking to men from the long line out front when Matt crowded into the small building.

He watched and listened as his three foremen sat at a table. In front of the table sat a single chair. One at a time, the applicants came in, took the seat and answered the questions put to him by all three foremen. Most left disappointed. Every now and then one left with a big grin on his face and a job.

Matt was visiting with one of the lucky ones and happened to glance at the man in the chair facing his foremen. It was the bully named Bruno, the one that had forced the fight with Matt in front of the hotel.

Matt pinned him with a look. It took a minute before the bully looked up and another before recognition swept over his face.

"We can't use you, Bruno," Matt said evenly. "I don't need the likes of you riding for the Double H. Now take your friends with you and git."

The bully screwed up his face into an ugly scowl. His lips drew tight against tobacco-stained teeth, curling into a snarl. His dark eyes flashed hatred in Matt's direction. Lurching to his feet, he kicked the chair backwards, his right hand hovering a hair's breath from the Colt tied to his thigh.

As if on an unspoken signal, Matt's three foremen shot to their feet in front of their boss, their own hands hanging loosely near their own pistols. No words were spoken, there was no need. The message was clear.

Bruno got it. He whirled and stomped out the door.

"That fellow's attitude is liable to get him an early tombstone," Buck Wheeler said, easing back down in his chair.

"Yeah," Jess said, "he come mighty close just now, besides, we'd already voted."

"What do you mean, you'd already voted?" Matt asked.

"We've worked us out a system," Joe explained. "After we've all asked a man the questions we want, we take a vote under the table by sticking out one, two, or three fingers. If a man don't get a three finger vote from all three of us, he don't get hired."

"I'm shore glad I ain't applying," Matt told them, slapping them on the shoulders as he headed for the door, "I doubt I'd get hired."

As he walked outside, he noticed Bruno and four companions ride out of town in a cloud of dust.

It was still pitch dark when Matt stepped into leather, dallied the lead rope to his new packhorse around his saddle horn and pointed Midnight's nose east. He wanted to get an early start. He was anxious to get home for Christmas and see Jamie.

Holding his big stallion in a steady short lope, he made good time. By late morning he reached the pass leading through the line of Rocky Mountains to the San Antonio River on the other side. Even though he had been through the pass several times without incident, he eased Midnight back into a slow walk and thumbed back the hammers on both side guns. He hadn't lived these twenty-seven years by being careless.

The December sun was unusually warm and casting deep shadows inside the narrow pass. Reining his stallion to a stop near the entrance, Matt listened intently and sniffed the easterly breeze. He heard the desert sounds. The grating sound of the chichada crickets feeding on scrub mesquite bushes, clinging to windblown limbs. The soft scurrying of tiny feet in the sand as a desert rat ran for cover and the screech of a soaring hawk that had just spotted his next meal. All these sounds Matt heard and dismissed.

It was the sound that shouldn't be there, that he sought and found, carried by the gentle breeze. Midnight heard it too and let out a low rumbling snort from deep within his big body. He took one step backwards and pointed his eyes and ears straight into the pass.

Matt leaned to his left to rein the stallion around and the move likely saved his life. Two rifle shots shattered the stillness. Both from above, one from either side of the pass. One kicked up sand to Matt's left and sent it flying, the other didn't.

A white-hot pain ripped through his left side like a red-hot poker tearing him from the saddle. He saw the sandy earth rushing toward him. It slammed into him with a force that stole his breath away. Pain radiated from his side and numbed his whole body. A low groan escaped his lips. He fought to draw a breath but his mind told him not to move less the shooters finish the job they had started.

Lying sprawled on his back in the sand, his right arm stretched out above his head, his left arm partially covered by his body, the back of his hand touching the thick leather of the Widow Maker's holster.

Through narrowed, slitted eyes, he desperately searched his surroundings for some kind of cover, any kind of cover. There was nothing. Not a boulder, not a crevice, nothing. Even his horses had trotted on through the pass and out of sight.

Completely exposed like a sitting duck, he waited . . .His jaw muscles flexed as his teeth clamped shut, waiting for the expected next volley that would end his life.

The sky overhead was a brilliant blue-white. It burned his squinted eyes. He wanted to blink to clear the tears away, but knew his only chance was to convince the shooters he was already dead.

He had heard it said that just before one dies his whole life flashes before his eyes. His didn't. The only picture in his mind was a beautiful angel with long, shiny black hair, dark penetrating eyes and full, pouting lips with a cute little lift on one side, like the beginning of a smile. Come to think of it they were right. Jamie was his life.

The land lay still and deathly quiet. Only the heat seemed alive, tugging at his face, pushed there by the hot breeze.

The crunch of horses' hooves in soft sand reached his hearing. He listened. There were two men on foot—three on horseback. He heard the familiar metallic sound as someone levered a rifle. They would end it now.

"Well sir, he ain't so high and mighty now is he?" a familiar gruff voice bellowed. It was Bruno.

"Want me to pump a couple into him for good measure?" another voice queried.

"Naw," came the welcome reply. "Save your ammunition. He's buzzard bait. Can't you see all that blood? Besides, I hope he is still alive. I'd like him to be looking at me when I lift his scalp, then we'll see how tough he is."

The soft creak of saddle leather told Matt one of the riders was dismounting. Most likely Bruno coming to scalp him. He dared not open his eyes; his ears must be his eyes. Focusing all his senses into one, he strained to read the meaning of every sound. He heard the crunchy sound when the dismounting foot touched the sand. He heard the other two men as they approached nearer still. He waited.

A horse shifted a hoof, another snorted and swished a tail. These sounds told Matt the two remaining mounted killers were somewhere behind the three approaching on foot. The crunching footsteps drew closer. *Wait,* Matt forced himself...wait, another few steps.

Blocking out the excruciating pain in his left side, his fingers inched to touch the handle of the Widow Maker. Another step...summoning all the remaining strength in his body he half-rolled and pushed down on the handle of his sawed-off shotgun. His eyes flicked open. He adjusted the nose of the weapon.

And touched the trigger.

The deafening twin blasts sounded like two sticks of dynamite exploding at the same instant. The recoil jarred his body, sending stabs of pain shooting through him like lightning bolts. Despite the pain he forced his body to roll to his left.

Pistols barked. A bullet plowed a furrow in the sand only inches from his face, sending flying particles into his eyes. He clawed his own pistol from its holster and fired blindly in the general direction of his attackers. A horse wheeled and screamed pitifully. A body hit the ground. The sound of retreating hooves told Matt the final mounted killer had lit out. He swung his pistol toward the sound and fired until his gun was empty.

With the back of his hand he swiped at his eyes, trying desperately to rid them of the blinding sand. The particles grated and tore at his eyeballs. Fuzzy sight returned.

The Widow Maker had done its job on two of the men on foot. They were out of it and not moving. The third was Bruno.

He lay in the sand on one elbow, still clutching a pistol in his clammy hand. He struggled to his knees, toppled over onto his side, then struggled up again.

Matt's sight was coming clear. He saw the killer climb to his knees. He was badly wounded. The heavy pellets had torn great chunks of flesh from his massive chest. Blood spewed from gaping holes with every heartbeat. Yet, from some super-human source, he found the strength to climb to his feet.

Venomous hatred glared from the killer's eyes. His lips parted and curled in a snarling growl that sounded like a wounded grizzly. He stumbled forward toward Matt. The man's knees seemed to buckle, then straighten and stumble another step. Matt raised his pistol. At point-blank range he touched the trigger and heard the sickening sound as the hammer fell on spent cartridges. His weapons were both empty. . ..he was helpless.

The killer's pistol raised slowly in a clammy fist. Matt watched helplessly as the nose lifted level with his chest. Time was frozen for an instant when their eyes met.

Bruno's eyes widened, then glazed and walled white. He doubled over and fell face forward into the sand.

Like a white fog slowly lifting—his mind began to clear. That he had been unconscious, he had no doubt. How long he had been out, he had no idea. He squeezed his eyes hard shut, then opened them, hoping the scratchy milky screen would go away. It didn't.

It took all his strength just to move a hand to his wounded side. His hand came away wet and sticky. He lifted it close to his cloudy sight. The hand was covered and dripped blood. If he lay there he would die. He tried to raise his body but the strength wasn't there. He had to move, to get help. But how? Where?

Summoning all the strength in his being he managed to roll to his stomach. Arms struggled forward along the sand, fingers clawed deep. A booted foot dug into the sand and found a toehold. He pulled and pushed with all his strength. His pain-filled body moved forwards a few inches.

Seconds became minutes and minutes became who knows how long. Like a gut-shot animal he inched forward, a bloody trail marking his progress. He had no goal in mind. He only knew he must keep crawling. He refused to give up. The world around him spun crazily and still he crawled forward toward some unknown destination.

Again and again he reached. Clawed. Pulled himself forward, only to reach again. Then there was nothing. His hands clawed frantically at thin air.

He was falling, tumbling, rolling. His bloody hand touched something wet and cool. Water. His hand felt water. Was he dreaming? For long minutes he struggled between consciousness and the deep, dark blackness he remembered from other brushes with death.

Struggling his eyes open he saw the river. Somehow he was lying beside the river. He rolled over, his body half-in half- out of the cool, wonderful water. He plunged his head under and drank deep. The cool wetness soothed the scratching in his throat and shocked him back to near consciousness and slowed the spinning in his head. Reaching a hand he washed his eyes again and again. Finally his sight returned.

Pain radiated through his body and sat like a heavy weight upon him. He was weak. Drained of every ounce of strength. He knew he had lost a lot of blood and must somehow stop the bleeding or he would surely die. He felt his side and found the gaping hole.

Reaching a weakened hand he tore the bandanna from around his neck and dipped it in the cool water. He swiped the blood from his wounded side and stuffed the rag into the open hole. That simple action drained him of what little energy he had left. He lay back. The simple solution would be to just close his eyes and give up. To let the sweet peace of eternal sleep wrap its arms around him and carry him away. But how could he even think of giving up? He had too much to live for. He was suddenly ashamed for having thought it.

Think. He told himself. Think. His hand clawed at the edge of the water and came away with a handful of thick mud. He brought it to his side and held it there, stemming the flow of blood.

He heard a snort. Midnight was there. His warm nose nuzzling at him. He lifted a look. The saddle seemed to be an eternity away. He had to have help. If he could just... It was the only way.

Reaching a hand he grasped a stirrup. Pain shot through him as he pulled. His big body lifted. Using the stirrup he somehow managed to drag himself to his knees. Underneath the big stallion he saw the upward slope of the riverbank. If he could somehow crawl a few feet up the bank maybe . . .

"Stand easy big fellow," his voice rasped out.

Summoning all his remaining strength and ignoring the pain, he demanded his muscles obey. Somehow, from somewhere he found the strength to pull himself into the saddle. Beaded sweat stood heavy on his face and filled his eyes, the salty liquid adding to the burning already there. He couldn't lift a hand to wipe it off. He was getting dizzy.

"Old hoss," he said lovingly, "it's up to you now. You've got to get me back to town."

He remembered little after that. Fuzzy glimpses of sand, sun, bushes and sky. Everything spun crazily in a world that kept changing from dark to light then back again.. Nothing seemed real. Everything was an illusion. He clung desperately to the only thing familiar, his saddle horn.

At some point he felt hands pulling at him, trying to loose his hands from his anchor to reality. He felt himself falling. Hands snatched him out of the air. Everything was spinning, spinning. He saw fleeting visions of a stern-faced man bending close. Many people stared intently with solemn faces.

He floated in the air above a bed. Saw a dying man lying in the bed, then recognized the man as himself. How could that be? Then there was darkness. A black fog enveloped him like a blanket.

Light...and out of the light came her beautiful face. The face he kept locked away in a special place in his mind so he could bring back the memory and love her all over again. But where was the smile? The memory always wore a smile. Instead, tiny silver tears slipped from her dark, sparkling eyes and traced slowly down flushed cheeks. Gentle hands caressed his fevered brow.

She was there when he awoke, sitting by his bedside, holding his hand in hers. Her smile warmed him and soft lips gently brushed him as she pressed her face to his.

"Welcome back, darling," she whispered against his cheek.

He clamped his eyes shut, then opened them again to make sure it was real. His mouth went through the motions but no sound came out. She put a wet cloth to his dry, cracked lips, lifted a water glass to his mouth. He wanted to gulp it down but she allowed him only a few drops. He raked a swollen tongue across his lips.

"How long?" he managed a raspy whisper.

"Today is Christmas Day, Matthew, and I've just received the most wonderful present I could ever receive. You came back to me. You've been unconscious four days. You've lost a lot of blood but the doctor says with rest and lots of loving care you'll be fine. You do the first and I'll take care of the loving care."

"I let you down," he whispered. "I promised I'd be home for Christmas."

"Now you just hush that, Matthew Henry. We'll have our Christmas right here and it's going to be the best Christmas ever. Father was here. He refused to leave until this morning when your fever broke and the doctor said you were going to be all right."

Matt slept then. He didn't mean to. He didn't want to. It just came.

Sometime later a soft tapping on the door awoke him. A heavy-set Mexican woman pushed through the door with a towel across an arm and a big pan of water in her hands. Matt was later to learn her name was Estella. She worked for the doctor. He also learned she had bathed and cared for him while he was unconscious, a task she was about to do again.

To his utter embarrassment, she washed him thoroughly from head to toe and shaved off a week's stubble of whiskers. After she had applied medicine to his wounds, she wrapped fresh bandages around him tightly. But when she shook out a white flannel nightgown and held it for him to sleeve into, he balked like a Missouri mule. He wasn't about to wear a thing like that. But he did. A stern look might near as bad as his pa's convinced him to reconsider.

They had just finished when the door swung open and a pretty little cedar tree pushed through carried by Joe. Jess Tanner, Buck Wheeler and Shorty Shepherd followed close behind, also with their arms loaded with stuff.

"Welcome back, boss," Joe said cheerfully. "You look a sight better. The boys all figured if you was gonna spend Christmas in bed, you might as well have a Christmas tree. You can't celebrate Christmas without a tree."

"Thanks boys," Matt said. "I appreciate that."

"We can't stay, the doctor said you needed to rest more'n talk. We'll be back later," Joe told him as he and the others left.

After Matt had dozed for awhile, Jamie returned with an armload of Christmas decorations. Matt watched through loving eyes as she transformed the simple little cedar into the most beautiful Christmas tree he could ever remember.

"It's beautiful," he told her. "It's perfect," he said again and again. Still, she returned to it time after time, adjusting, then re-adjusting until she finally seemed satisfied with the results.

She seemed so excited. She was like a little girl, rushing in and out, finding new ways to change the little hotel room into one that reminded him of home. Her excitement must have been contagious too and Matt soon caught a good dose of it.

"Ask Joe to come up for a minute," he told her as she was leaving on one of her many trips.

"Jamie said you wanted to see me," his foreman and friend said as he came in. "How you doing?"

"I'm feeling a lot better," Matt said. "Tell me what happened. The last thing I remember was trying to climb on my horse and not being able to make it."

"Well, you made it somehow, though none of us can figure out how. You managed to hang on all the way back to town, too. That big stallion brought you all the way back. That's some kind of horse.

"It was one of our boys that spotted you. You come riding down the street all bent over, barely in the saddle and bleeding like a stuck hog. We had to pry your fingers loose from your saddle horn to get you off your horse. The doctor had us carry you up here. Him and his helper worked on you all night.

"We all rode with the marshal out to the pass where you was ambushed. I sent a couple of riders on out to the ranch to tell J.R. and Jamie. We trailed the other one to a cabin up river a few miles. He was scared to death and give up without a fight. The Marshal says he doubts he'll hang for it but he'll be bustin rocks a mighty long time."

"Looks like I'm gonna be laid up for a few days," Matt said, "you boys are gonna have to take up the slack for awhile. How's the hiring coming along?"

"Boss, you won't believe how the drovers are flocking in wanting to be part of the drive. You get the idea they think it might give them bragging rights or something. By my count, we've got seventy-six of the best punchers a man could find anywhere. They're all good, experience men. There's not a greenhorn in the bunch. Reckon we need to hold off till we see how many vaqueros Julio comes up with?"

"No," Matt told him. "I reckon I'd go ahead. I'd rather have a few too many than not enough. I believe I'd keep hiring up to a hundred or so. Do you know what happened to my packhorse?"

"Yeah, we found him at the pass. He was standing beside the river munching on bunch grass. We brought him back with us. He's down at the livery. If you're wondering about your saddlebags, I brought 'em up and scooted them under your bed. I figured that's where you'd want them."

"Good," Matt said, breathing a sigh of relief. "Real good. Get them out for me and lay 'em here beside me where I can reach them, will you?"

After Joe left, Matt took the little white package from the saddlebag and slipped it under his pillow.

Near dark, Shorty and Jess pushed through the door lugging a small table covered with a white cloth. Joe wagged in two cane-bottomed chairs and Buck came in toting two candles. As they all marched out Jamie came in carrying a tray holding two bowls of streaming, delicious-smelling soup. His stomach stopped its growling long enough to say thank you.

"What in the Sam Hill is all this?" Matt asked.

"This, my dear, is our Christmas dinner. Now, I don't want to hear any grumbling, because it's all the doctor will let you have."

"You won't hear any grumbling out of me, I'm starved half to death. Jamie, I appreciate all the fuss you're going to on my account."

"You're always telling me the things your pa told you, well, I remember something my father told me once, too. He said, 'Honey, always do the best you can with what you got.' So just close your eyes and pretend it's a big, juicy steak and act like it tastes good."

They ate their Christmas dinner by candlelight then enjoyed a cup of coffee afterward while they stared at the beautiful Christmas tree and talked in low, loving tones of the future.

Matt slipped a hand underneath the pillow and drew out the small package wrapped in white paper and tied with a pretty ribbon and bow. He was proud as a peacock when he handed it to her.

She spent half an eternity unwrapping the package. The small blue velvet box looked so small in her hands as her fingers slowly and carefully lifted the lid.

She took one look that didn't stop. Her eyes bugged wide. She gasped in a deep breath and didn't let it out. A hand flew to her open mouth. It seemed as if her gaze was frozen on the brilliantly sparkling diamond ring in the velvet resting place.

"Oh, Matthew! I've never seen such a beautiful ring!"

"I hope it fits," Matt said, feeling proud. "The lady at the store tried it on and her hand is about the same size as yours."

"May I try it on?" she asked.

"Sure you can," he said, "it's yours. She said the one with the diamond is the engagement ring. We're engaged, ain't we?"

"You bet we are," she said positively, as she slipped the ring on her finger. "It's perfect." Her face beamed. "Oh Matthew, I love you so much."

He lifted his face to give her a quick, gentle kiss.

"Not like that," she whispered, mischief sparkling in her dark eyes, "like this."

Her lips were warm and eager and open, as they sought and found his. It was a deep, searching kiss. A kiss that gave the briefest hint of a passion long held in check. A kiss of one ready to give herself without reservation to the one she had chosen as her life's companion.

Then, pulling a small package from the pocket of her floor-length dress, she handed it to him, excitement showing on her face.

"Merry Christmas, Matthew."

Matthew tore the wrapping paper aside, revealing a highly polished wooden case. He glanced questioningly at her. She nodded excitedly. He lifted the top. There, on a carpet of red velvet, lay a solid gold pocket watch. Its glistening mirror finish highlighted the engraved words, "To Matthew. The love of my life, Jamie."

Gently removing the beautiful timepiece from its resting-place, he cupped it lovingly in the palm of his hand. He moved the fingers of his other hand along the length of the attached gold chain.

"Jamie," his voice started to protest, "you shouldn't—"

"Shhh," she whispered, placing a single finger across his lips, holding back the words of protest. "Open it."

He did and thrilled to the soft musical sound of a song he recognized as 'Beautiful Dreamer.' Framed inside the cover, smiling back at him was a picture of Jamie.

Five days later, on December the thirtieth, just after sunup, a long line of wagons and horsemen rumbled up the main street of San Antonio and veered east. Ten wagons made up the long line, each pulled by a two-team hitch of strong freight horses. The wagons were all heavy Army freight wagons covered with gleaming white heavy canvas covers. Their eighteen foot beds were chocked full of an assortment of supplies and foodstuff. Saddles, ropes, blankets, bedrolls, weapons, seventy Army issue two-man tents and enough food supplies to feed a small army weighted the wagons and caused the six inch steel-rimmed wheels to cut deeply into the sandy soil.

Five of the wagons had been converted into chuck wagons. A large, drop down end-gate, now raised, covered a wagon-wide cabinet. The German carpenter had built drawers and cubbyholes that now were stuffed with cooking and eating utensils, medicine and a multitude of secret ingredients the five trail cooks would no doubt be sharing. A wide sideboard protruded from each side of the chuck wagons and would carry the bedrolls and rain gear for the drovers.

From a distance, the gleaming white tops must have looked like a large caterpillar inching its way across the barren countryside.

Much to his displeasure, Matt lay on a makeshift bed in one of the wagons. He would have much rather have been sitting beside Jamie on the seat in the front of the wagon.

In front of, on each side and trailing along behind the line of wagons, rode ninety-eight of the best cowboys ever assembled into one crew. The riders of the Double H. Matt was hoping Julio would ride in with another twenty or so when he came back with the Mendoza horses.

The work of cutting out and branding Matt's herd, that now totaled over twenty-three thousand head, was backbreaking work. Matt's crews quickly fell into a daily schedule of daylight to dark.

Two thousand head of the younger stock that Jamie had personally selected were separated out to eventually be taken to the ranch in Arkansas. She wanted to use them for crossbreeding.

The rest of the herds, once branded, were moved to a large valley along the Lavaca River where the entire trail herd would be assembled and trail broke.

Matt was about to go crazy being confined to bed. Every other day Joe came to his room and gave him a report on their progress. Even so, he became increasingly impatient with his recovery progress. Finally, after two weeks, he persuaded Jamie to let him ride in a buggy out to watch the branding operation. She reluctantly gave in, but only if she drove him.

It had been almost three weeks and still Julio had not returned. Matt began to worry. So many bad things could have happened. He began to question the wisdom of letting them go. He made up his mind, if Julio and the Valdez brothers weren't back in three more days, he would send a crew to find them.

Jamie was increasingly busy with the ten thousand details that had to be worked out for the upcoming wedding. It was now only a month away. Invitations had been dispatched and, according to her, if even half of those invited actually showed up, she didn't know how they were going to take care of everyone.

"We're a hard day's ride from anywhere," she complained. "I'm expecting two hundred people or more. What am I going to do, Matthew? Where will all those people sleep?"

"It might be a dumb suggestion," Matt said, "but what about setting up the two-man Army tents? I bought them for those miserable rainy nights on the trail, but it might be a good time to try them out. It might make a pretty good place to bed down some folks."

"Matthew, you're an absolute genius," Jamie exclaimed. "That's the answer. Why didn't I think of that?"

"Well, thank you ma'am, I'm glad I could contribute something to this wedding."

"Oh, don't worry, you're contributing the most important part of the wedding, you," she said, wrapping her arms around his neck and pulling him close in a warm embrace. "It's still four weeks until the wedding, Matthew. I don't think I can wait that long."

"Believe me, I know the feeling," he whispered.

They locked in a warm embrace for a long minute. Then Matt pushed her playfully to arm's length.

"Get away from me, devil woman. A fellow just has so much will power you know."

They laughed and strolled arm in arm down to the river and sat down on one of the split log benches. They spent long minutes talking of the wedding, of the drive and of their future together. They talked of love and home and family.

"How many children do you want Matthew?" she asked, laying her head on his shoulder.

"Aw, at least a half-dozen," he joked, for which he was rewarded by a punch in the ribs.

"Come on, be serious," she said.

"What makes you think I wasn't serious?"

Raising her head she saw the sheepish grin creasing his face and replaced her head on his shoulder. His arm was around her and he squeezed her tight.

"Seriously, I'd like at least a boy and a girl," he told her. "Maybe more. What about you?"

"I've already decided," she told him matter-of-factly. "We're going to have two boys and a girl. I'm willing to let you pick the order."

"Well now, whoop-t-do, that's mighty decent of you. At least I'll have something to do with that."

"You just better believe it," she told him, lifting her lips to plant a big kiss on him.

They were just sitting down for supper that night when they heard it, like a far off rolling thunder back in the south from the direction of the gulf. It was a steady rumbling sound that was drawing closer fast. Afraid it was one of those Texas storms that come up suddenly without warning, they all leaped to their feet and streamed out onto the front porch.

Matt and J.R. were first. They swung toward the sound. A giant cloud of dust rolled and boiled directly toward the house.

"What is it, Matthew?" Jamie screamed.

"It's Julio and the boys bringing in that herd of Mendoza horses," he assured her.

As the boiling cloud of dust drew nearer it gave birth to an emerging hoard of black horses flanked on all sides by at least twenty Mexican vaqueros. They seemed to materialize from within the dust cloud. As the charging herd galloped through the open gates of a large corral near the barn, the setting sun's rosy rays bounced off their sweat-slick coats, appearing to set them ablaze right before the onlooker's eyes.

"In all my born days," J.R. said, "I've never seen anything like that."

It was a sight none of them would ever forget.

A few days later Matt and J.R. rode out together to watch the branding operation. It so happened they come upon Julio's new crew of vaqueros. They reined up, sat their saddles and watched, fascinated by the efficiency and skill the Mexican cowboys demonstrated.

They worked in teams of two. One vaquero would select a cow or steer from a large herd, expertly throw his fifty-foot plaited rawhide reata over its large horns and draw it tight. His roping partner rode up from behind, catching both of the animal's hind feet in his loop and drawing it tight. With both riders pulling in opposite directions, the animal was soon stretched out on the ground. A third vaquero rushed up with a red-hot branding iron and touched it to the hair of the animal's rump, identifying the animal as belonging to the Double H brand.

The whole process took less that five minutes. Matt quickly counted the other teams doing the same thing. Five. That meant this crew alone was branding near sixty head an hour, or something over seven hundred head a day. The rest of the crew was kept busy stoking the fire, heating and running the irons to the branders and herding the branded cattle out to the holding valley.

According to Julio, one of the vaqueros he had hired had risen to the top like cream in a milk bucket. He was a handsome young vaquero whose only known name was Ramano. Matt curled a leg around his saddle horn and fixed a look on the young Mexican. He was one of those natural leaders that don't come along very often. He did his work and lent a hand to one of the others that might be having a harder time of it. He encouraged a younger vaquero whose hind leg loop snagged only one foot and helped another when a steer kicked loose.

"Good man," J.R. commented, obviously watching the same man as Matt.

"Yeah, he is," Matt said, still watching. "Julio tells me he's as good with a rifle as he is with that reata."

"Then he's hell on wheels," the old rancher said, stoking up his new pipe Matt gave him for Christmas.

"Shore like my pipe," J.R. said, putting fire to it and drawing in a deep puff. "Have I told you before?"

"Only about a dozen times," Matt told him.

"Well I'm telling you again," the rancher said, chuckling. "I shore got to give it to you, son, you've put together maybe the best trail crew I ever seen and I've been in the cattle business a long time. Seems to me you've put together a bunch of mighty men."

CHAPTER XVI

Until death shall part us

"Where thou diest, will I die. And there will
I be buried: the Lord do so to me, and more
also, if anything but death
shall part thee and me." (Ruth 1:12)

Time passed all too quickly. The branding phase was completed. The trail herd of twenty-one thousand head was separated into five smaller herds of about four thousand each. Now, the drover's day was spent constantly moving the smaller herds around the ranch, bedding them down come night, getting them up and strung out every morning, what the drovers called "trail breaking" the herd.

The blacksmith had arrived from San Antonio and was busy from first light until it was too dark to work. Every cowboy's dream was to one day own one of the famous Mendoza horses and Matt's riders waited anxiously for his foreman to assign him his string of mounts. Since the Mendoza blacks were already highly trained vaquero horses, that eliminated the usual process of every cowboy having to break and train his own mount. More importantly, the Mendozas were so superior to the standard mustang mounts a drover usually rode, that Matt figured they would need only three mounts in their string instead of the usual ten to twelve.

Every hand on the ranch had been pressed into double duty to help prepare for the rapidly approaching wedding. The high grass between the ranch house and the river had been cut and trimmed until it resembled a well-kept garden. Matt's seventy tents, minus one, had been set up in rows along the river and now resembled an army camp.

Both ladies and men's bathhouses were built along the river's edge. It was an ingenious idea thought up and suggested by the Cunninghams' cook.

It was a square building with no roof built near the water's edge. A wooden boardwalk ran from the bank to the door of the building. The sides were ten feet high and extended down into the water itself. Inside, there was only a half floor with steps leading down into the water. Benches lined the walls. Wooden buckets were provided for those that might be a little squeamish about actually going down into the water to bathe.

A dozen new outhouses were constructed and divided on two sides of the tent city. Long eating tables with attached benches were built and scattered around the yard. From the looks of things, they were actually expecting half of Texas like Jamie said. After all the preparation, he sure hoped she wasn't disappointed. Because like she said, the Circle C Ranch was a long ride from anywhere.

As the days slipped by and Valentine's Day drew closer, Matt could see everybody getting nervous, him most of all. The Mexican house girl had seen to it that his black broadcloth suit was clean and pressed. His only white shirt was pressed so stiff he doubted if his arms would bend, and he could shave in the reflection from his boots.

Matt's five trail cooks were doing double duty under the direction of Ramona, which didn't go over too well with Moses. Two large barbecue pits were dug and iron rotary bars were erected over them. By the following day, they would hold large shoulders of beef for the big barbecue celebration following the actual wedding.

It was February the thirteenth—only one more day. Long benches were built and set in rows looking enough to seat an army, but Jamie complained there was seating for only four hundred, not nearly for all she expected.

"Are you getting nervous?" Jamie asked as they strolled around watching all the preparation.

"Naw," Matt replied, "my hands just naturally shake like this. Ain't you?"

"Yes, but I'm more excited than I am nervous. Just think, out of all the women in the whole world, you chose me."

"The way I recall, it was mostly you that done the choosing, but you just beat me to it, that's all."

By noon they started arriving, a whole day before the wedding. At first only a buggy or wagon every now and then. Before long, a steady stream of people came. The tents began filling up. People excitedly staking their claim and setting up housekeeping.

To Ramona's credit, she had anticipated the early arrivals and had food prepared. Supper that night was a festive occasion with nearly a hundred guests sharing the evening meal.

J.R. and Juanita were the perfect hosts. They went about shaking hands, visiting, slapping backs and assuring everyone their coming early did not present a problem whatsoever.

Matt called Joe aside and they walked down to the barn together. After a brief conference, Joe recruited a couple of Double H riders and they all set out on a secret mission.

Not being able to sleep, Matt barefooted down the stairs near midnight and struck a fire under the leftover coffee in the kitchen.

He poured himself a cup and slipped out to the back verandah overlooking the river.

The moon was full, the sky was clear as a bell and a million stars winked at him as if they knew about the upcoming wedding. Tipping back his chair against the wall, he sipped on the steaming coffee and smiling, gave a thumbs-up to the eastern star.

Hearing a sound beside him he swung a look. His future father-in-law padded out, also barefooted and sipping on a cup of steaming coffee as he walked.

"Couldn't sleep," the old rancher said.

"Me neither," Matt replied.

"I couldn't get it off my mind, by this time tomorrow night I'll have that son I've always wanted. Matt, I just couldn't be prouder."

By Matt's new watch, it was near three in the morning before he and J.R. quit talking and called it a night.

Matt was up before good light and strolled down to try out the new bathhouse. The water was icy cold and it sure woke a fellow up right sudden. After a good bath, he went back up to his room and took his time shaving and dressing. He followed his nose to the kitchen where Ramona had a fresh pot going. He took a cup and returned to the back verandah.

The tent dwellers were beating a steady path to the new outhouses. By the time he drained his coffee cup, the waiting lines were a half-dozen deep.

By mid-morning the lines coming from San Antonio carried a steady stream of buggies, wagons and folks on horseback. J.R. had explained that people in these parts had little occasion to get together—when they did—they went all out.

He saw little of Jamie all morning. When he did, well wishers offering their secret advice on how to have a happy marriage usually surrounded her.

It seemed like the men didn't have any sort of advice along those lines for him. All they wanted to talk about was the cattle drive. He shook so many hands it felt like he was close to wearing blisters on his hand. He finally give up trying to explain how he was gonna take twenty thousand longhorns all the way to Kansas.

"I'm just gonna point 'em north and try to keep up," he felt like saying.

He was in the middle of doing it again when he heard a familiar voice behind him.

"You got time for a cup of coffee, cowboy?"

Whirling around, he couldn't believe his eyes. Miss Abby and Ben Thompson stood there side by side, all the way from Waco. He could have leaped ten feet.

"Wh— I don't believe it!" Matt shouted.

He grabbed Abby and hugged her tight, then shook Ben's hand like a well-pump handle.

"What in the world are you doing way down here? And together to boot?"

"It's a long story, pard," the big sheriff said. "We won't take the time to go into it right now. Looks like you're as busy as a one armed juggler. All you need to know right now is that Abby's done me the honor of becoming my wife. We were married two weeks ago."

"Yippee!" Matt let out a cowboy yell and caused a hundred heads to turn their way. "It's about time. I can't think of better news than that."

He grabbed Abby and hugged her again.

"Careful there partner, that lady you're hugging is my wife."

"I'm proud, Miss Abby," Matt said, "I'm real proud. Ben's the man you've been needing all along."

"I was wondering who the beautiful lady was my fiancée was hugging," Jamie said smiling, as she walked up.

"Honey," Matt said happily, "I want you to meet two of my very best friends. This is Abby."

"Thompson," the big sheriff interjected.

"Oh, yeah, this is Miss Abby Thompson. Her and Ben were just married two weeks ago. This is my—this is Jamie."

"It's good to meet you, Jamie. I can see why Matt gets tongue tied around you. You're even more beautiful than this scoundrel said you were." He shook her hand gently.

"Thank you, Ben," she said sweetly, doing a little curtsy, "and you're much bigger than he said you were."

Swinging her attention to Abby, Jamie swept her with an appraising look that quickly reflected approval.

"So you're the Miss Abby he's always talking about?" Jamie said. "If I had known you were so beautiful I would have been jealous."

"I've been telling Matt that you were a very lucky lady to get him, but after meeting you, I think he is the lucky one," Abby told her. "You're getting a good man."

"Abby," Jamie said, her face bursting with excitement, "I just had a wonderful idea. Would you consider being my maid of honor? I hadn't intended to have one, but I'd really like for you to. Would you?"

"Well, I don't know," Abby said, shooting a questioning look at Ben. "I suppose if you really want me to. I'd be honored."

"Then it's settled." Jamie took Abby's hand. "Come on, while you're helping me dress, you can tell me all the secrets about this man I'm about to marry."

"Well if that's the way it's gonna be," Matt said. "Ben is gonna be my best man, as long as he knows he really ain't."

Jamie and Abby hurried off in a little trot toward the house like two giddy little schoolgirls. Matt and Ben wove their way through the crowd toward the back, stopping often to shake an offered hand and accept a well-wisher's congratulations.

"How'd you two finally get together?" Matt asked his friend.

"Well, after you left this last time we got to talking about you getting married and all. One thing led to another and I finally got up the nerve to tell her how I felt about her. Come to find out, she felt the same way about me. We decided we'd wasted enough time so we got married the next day."

"Ben, there's just no way I could be happier about it. You two are made for each other. Listen, there's a big barbecue and shindig after the wedding. Let's get together then. Right now, I better go get dressed. I'd hate to be late for my own wedding and get myself in trouble the first rattle out of the box."

"You just hurry up and marry that girl before she wises up and backs out on you."

Matt slipped up the back way and climbed the stairs to his bedroom. He was so nervous he was all thumbs. He had trouble buttoning his shirt. He got his socks on wrong-side-out. He must have checked his reflection in the mirror a hundred times. Finally, he nervously took a deep breath and walked over to the window. He stared out, but saw nothing, as if in a trance.

His memory raced back to another time, another place. In his mind's eye he saw a little farmhouse back in Arkansas, a kid's swing in an oak tree, a flower bed beside the steps. He saw two little crosses at the head of two lonely graves. Brushing aside a tear, he stared off into the heavens and whispered.

"I loved you, Amelia. I still do. I reckon I always will. But I love Jamie, too. Wherever you are, if you can hear me, I hope you can understand."

Then suddenly another scene popped from his memory. It was another small farmhouse so long ago. There was pa, sitting in that creaky old rocking chair smoking his corncob pipe. A little cotton haired boy sat cross-legged on the floor in front of a pot-bellied stove, sticking a broom straw to the red glow on the stove's side and watching the smoke trail upward.

Ma was there too, sitting in her own rocking chair, holding her "Good Book" close so she could read by the dim light of a single lamp. He could still hear the words she read.

"Where thou goest, I will go. Where thou lodgest, I will lodge. Thy people shall be my people and thy God, my God. Nothing but death shall part me and thee."

Matt blinked his eyes and swiped tears away with the back of his hand. He checked his little vest pocket for the hundredth time to make sure the ring was still there. He slipped his new pocket watch from the other vest pocket and flipped it open, not to check the time, but to gaze at the beautiful face that smiled back at him. The strains of the music seemed to calm him some. The hands read one forty-five—fifteen more minutes to go. He strode to the mirror, straightened his black string tie one last time and hurried from the room.

Ben was waiting for him at the foot of the stairs. Matt led the way as far as the front door where he paused. The sound of a Mexican mariachi band added a festive atmosphere as Matt opened the door. All he could think of was, where did all these people come from?

Every head turned and a thousand eyes fixed on him as he and Ben made their way down the front steps and toward the throng of people. Matt's friend walked by his side as they made their way slowly down the narrow aisle. The long rows of plank benches were packed with faceless people all staring in his direction.

Wonder what they're thinking. Reckon they've guessed? Did they somehow know what he knew—that he didn't deserve to be here about to marry the most beautiful lady in the whole world?

They stopped in front of the old Padre from San Antonio. The Holy Man took one look at Matt and smiled. Is my tie crooked or something? Did I forget to slick down my hair? Why is he smiling? Matt forced a smile back at him. That was it, the Padre knew his secret.

Never in his life had he been so scared. He wiped his sweaty palms on his pants leg, slicked down his hair and felt his vest pocket again. Reckon folks can hear my knees knocking together?

"Is my tie straight?" he whispered to Ben anxiously.

"It's fine," Ben assured him.

The seven-piece mariachi band shifted into a tune Matt had never heard before and every eye swung toward the front door. It opened and out stepped Miss Abby. She was beautiful. The ankle-length, rose-colored dress she had worn earlier had been replaced by a breathtakingly beautiful floor-length soft blue dress. A long blue ribbon held her hair back and trailed down her bare shoulders. In her hands she carried a bouquet of white flowers.

Flicking a quick glance at Ben, a smile lifted the corner of Matt's lips as he saw the look on his friend's face and the new twinkle in his eyes. To the soft strains of the music, Abby made her way down the front steps, up the isle and took her place off to Matt's left a short ways.

The music changed again and broke into what Matt recognized as the wedding march. The old Padre motioned and everybody pushed to their feet. J.R. stepped through the door with Juanita by his side, her arm through the crook of his. They stopped, half turned and stood one on either side of the door.

Suddenly an angel appeared in the doorway and Matt's heart stopped beating. A long, muffled gasp swept through the five hundred or more guests as her beauty overwhelmed them. Seeing her standing there, he felt like God had granted him a glimpse of Heaven. She looked like the angel God would surely choose to welcome folks through the gates.

She paused for a long moment and time stood still. Reaching out her hands, she took the arms offered by those that had given her life. Walking between them, made their way across the porch and slowly down the steps.

The dress she wore was like nothing Matt had ever seen or even heard about for that matter. It was glistening snow-white. It started just below her bare shoulders and forgot to stop at the floor because it stretched out far behind her.

She wore a thin white veil that draped over her coal black hair and covered her face but failed to conceal the beauty of it. No veil could have hidden her soft olive skin, flashing dark eyes, or that cute little natural lift on one side of her full, perfectly shaped lips. He tried in vain to swallow the huge lump in his throat.

It was like a dream, or one of those visions he had heard about. Matt watched breathlessly as the angel floated closer and closer toward him.

"God, if I'm just dreaming, don't ever let me wake up," he whispered under his breath.

Pausing briefly at the front bench, Mrs. Cunningham stepped aside to stand with everyone else. J.R. and the angel continued forward and stopped beside Matt with the big rancher standing between the angel and the fellow that shouldn't be there.

The Padre motioned and the audience sat down. Again, the old Padre flashed Matt a knowing smile and began to speak.

"Dearly beloved, we are gathered here under the heavens to join this woman and this man in the bonds of holy matrimony. If there be anyone present who know just cause why this should not be done, let him now speak, or forever hold his peace."

The smiling old Padre paused for what seemed like an awfully long time. Matt held his breath and braced for the loud chorus of protests that were sure to come—but didn't.

"Hearing no objections," the Priest continued. "Who brings this woman as a candidate for this marriage?"

"I am her father," J.R. answered proudly. "Her mother and I present her for marriage to this man."

After speaking, the proud rancher stepped aside, assisting his daughter to move beside Matt. Afraid to even glance her way for fear she wasn't really there, Matt stared straight ahead.

"Very well then," the Padre said. "You Jamie, and you, Matthew, having come here willingly before God and these

witnesses, if you wish to make these marriage vows and assume
the obligations of the marriage covenant, please signify that mutual
desire by joining hands."

Matt reached out a hand, palm up. The beautiful angel's hand
lifted slowly and found refuge in his. The touch of her small, soft
hand sent chill-bumps up and down his spine. A surge of emotion
spilled over his whole being.

This was the essence of marriage, he thought. To him, placing
her hand in his represented the giving of herself, willingly,
completely. The joining of their hands in that instant was like the
waters of two mountain streams merging together. Never again
would they be two—but one—and nothing—nor nobody could
ever separate them again.

He swallowed another lump, swiped away a tear with
the back of his free hand and chanced a glance at the one
beside him. Those dark eyes were fixed on his face and
their eyes met—and locked.

He tried hard to listen to what the old Padre was saying but
all he could hear was the racing drumbeat of his own beating
heart. Then the speaker's words rang in his ears so loud he wanted
to cover them.

"Matthew, do you take this woman whose hand you hold, to
be your lawful wedded wife? Do you promise to love her, to
comfort her, to watch over and protect her? To provide for her
needs in sickness and in health from this moment until death shall
part you?"

What? What had the Padre said? Until death shall part you?
That's the same words ma had read from her Good Book. That's
the same words he had remembered just a while ago.

"Yes sir, I do," he heard himself promise.

"Jamie, do you take this man whose hand you hold, to be
your lawful wedded husband? Do you promise to love him, to
comfort him, to honor and obey him? To provide for his needs

both in sickness and in health from this moment until death shall part you?"

"I do so promise," she answered.

"Matthew, as a symbol of your love and as a testimony of the vows you have made here today. Today, would you place the wedding ring on the finger of your betrothed?"

Their eyes still lingered on each other's. Matt gently slipped the ring onto her finger. She smiled, even as tiny silver tears escaped her dark eyes and slowly trailed down her cheeks.

"Then, according to the laws of the great state of Texas and by the authority vested in me as a representative of God, I now pronounce that you are man and wife. You may kiss your wife, young man."

Gently lifting the veil, he did.

The five hundred guests applauded, but were quickly drown out by a loud chorus of whooping and yelling from a hundred and twenty something cowboys of the Double H brand, all standing together off to one side.

The afternoon was a blur of backslapping, good-natured joshing and offered congratulations. Even though he was no shake at dancing, Matt was the first, but certainly not the last, to swing his new bride around the circle to the lively music of the mariachi band. Seemed like every cowboy in Texas was lined up for the honor and Matt could have sworn some of them more'n once.

Matt and Jamie managed to spend some time visiting with Ben and Abby while they ate barbecue, Mexican baked beans and fried corn on the cob. It was late afternoon before they were able to slip into the house and change into their riding clothes. He hadn't told Jamie where they were going, only to dress for riding and take a change of clothes.

Leading her by the hand, they slipped excitedly out the back door. Joe was there, right on schedule, holding Jamie's saddled white gelding and Matt's black stallion. He handed them their reins and the lead rope to the loaded packhorse, then tipped his hat in farewell.

"Everything's ready, boss, just like you said. I'll do my best to hold the boys back to keep them from following and treating you to a shivery tonight, but you know how they are. Have a great honeymoon."

They were a good ways off before somebody spotted them and a yell went up, but Joe must have done his job, because nobody followed. It didn't take long for Jamie to figure out where they were headed and let out an unladylike cowboy yell.

The sun was kissing the horizon when they climbed the final slope and broke through the scattered pine trees into the clearing. Its fiery orange reflection skipped off the mirror surface of the little mountain lake and careened off into forever.

A gentle breeze whispered through the tall pines as Matt and Jamie dismounted and walked toward the giant pine under which they had first picnicked.

Now, its wide branches cast soft shadows over the snow-white tent that sat there.

The makings of a campfire waited patiently for the spark that would bring it to life. The boys had done good.

"Oh, Matthew, it's perfect. Only you would have thought of all this."

Ground hitching their horses, they strolled arm in arm out onto the saddle-shaped rock formation and watched their first sunset as man and wife.

Later, Matt put a match to the kindling, and unsaddled and hobbled the horses so they could graze. Jamie put on a pot of coffee and shook out the picnic blanket and spread the meal Ramona had packed for them. Both nibbled at the delicious food, too nervous to eat.

"Let's go for a swim before it gets too dark," Jamie suddenly burst out, leaping to her feet, laughing and running toward the lake.

Caught by surprise, Matt was far behind before he could set his coffee down and follow. He stopped dead in his tracks when he saw the first boot, then another. Next he came upon the beige blouse she had worn. Finally, a near the water's edge, he discovered her riding pants.

She was far out in the little lake, laughing and splashing around. Her bare, olive skin caught the last wink of the setting sun and framed her in masterpiece of beauty.

"Come on in," she shouted playfully, "or are you bashful?"

He hesitated for less than a heartbeat. Then, like he had done so many times as a small boy, he quickly shucked his clothes right down to his birthday suit and plunged into the icy-cold water.

Back then life was an adventure. Time stretched endlessly, and everything seemed possible, like now.

The warm morning sun peeked timidly between the tent flaps and crept to lie on their faces. Somewhere in a distant tree a mocking bird filled the morning stillness with its haunting melody and persuaded Matt from a contented sleep. He flicked his eyes open, then swung a slow gaze beside him. She was there, sleeping peacefully, her head resting in the crook of his arm, her long, coal black hair splayed over his chest.

Not moving for fear of waking her, he stared for long minutes at the beautiful face only inches from his. Her soft, even breathing was as quiet as a baby's sigh. The touch of her bare skin against his warmed him. He was the luckiest man alive.

No telling how long they lay there, an eternity wouldn't have been long enough. Finally her eyes opened. She lifted a hand to flick hair away from her face, then emitting a soft purring sound, snuggled her head closer against his chest.

"Good morning, Mrs. Henry."

"Ummm, good morning, Mr. Henry," she said.

Mischief sparkled in her dark eyes and the little curl of her lips marking the beginning of a smile. Reaching out a hand, she drew his lips to hers. The crush of her mouth was warm and wonderful.

After a long while, they arose and walked hand in hand to the lake. They swam and played in the chilly water, stopping often to mold their bodies in a lingering embrace.

Later, huddled beside the campfire, they sipped steaming coffee, listened to the birds chirping and talked awhile before she rose and began preparing breakfast like she had done it every day of her life.

"How long can we stay?" she asked hesitantly, afraid of the answer.

"Not near as long as I'd like to. We've got to start the drive day after tomorrow."

"Then why are we wasting our time eating?" Setting aside the skillet in her hand and sashaying toward him with that devilish little smile on her lips and a gleam in her eyes.

CHAPTER XVII

Pressing Toward the Prize

"Forgetting those things which are behind, and
reaching forth unto those things which are before, I press
toward the mark for the prize." (Phil. 3:13-14)

They sat their horses atop a rise overlooking the large river valley.
Matt, Jamie and J.R. swept their eyes back and forth. Far off to
their left, ten canvas-covered wagons poised motionless. Drivers
and cook's helpers stood on top of the seats with hands shielding
eyes pointed at the riders on the hilltop.

Not far from the wagons, a remuda of over two hundred coal
black Mendoza horses grazed peacefully on thick grass, seemingly
uncaring of the historic activities taking place around them.
Nearby, Juan sat erect in his saddle. He, too, peered at the hilltop.

Stretched across the vast valley, as far as the eye could see, a
sea of Texas longhorns grazed. Their mottled colors created a
rainbow of color against the high green grass of the river valley.
Scattered at regular intervals around the herd, over a hundred

cowboys sat easy in their saddles on black horses, coiled ropes in hand, peering at the three riders on the distant hillside, awaiting the command.

It was February 17, 1868. They had less than four months to trail twenty-one thousand head near a thousand miles, across a dozen rivers, through Indian territory and deliver them safe and fat to the railhead in Abilene, Kansas.

To most it would seem an impossible undertaking. No man in his right mind would attempt such a thing. These were some of the kinder things folks were saying. But like Matt had told his father-in-law, If you want something you've never had, you've got to do something you've never done.

Raising high on his tiptoes in the stirrups, Matt stretched his full six feet-three inches, swiped the black Stetson from his head and waved it in wide circles above his head.

"Head 'em up! Move 'em out!" he shouted at the top of his lungs.

A chorus of cowboy yells, yips and whoops echoed across the valley as a hundred twenty-four riders of the Double H took up the call. They moved into the vast herd, dusting rumps with their coiled ropes and reatas, encouraging the stubborn longhorns into a steady plodding walk northward.

"How far you figure to get today?" J.R. asked.

"Hope we can make twenty miles," Matt said. "I told the boys to push 'em hard the first few days. I figure if we can get 'em good and tired before we bed 'em down, we won't have near as much trouble from bunch-quitters wanting to turn back."

Matt and Jamie rode stirrup to stirrup most of the day. Both were fully aware that each step brought them closer to the time they would have to say goodbye. They had been married only three days, now they faced at least five months apart. It would be a long five months for both of them.

"Jamie, you do understand why you can't come along on the drive don't you?"

"I understand," she said, but not sounding like she completely accepted it. "I've wanted a thousand times to beg you to take me with you. But I was raised on a cattle ranch and I know a trail drive is no place for a woman. That doesn't stop me from wanting to be with you, though."

"I know," he told her. "I can't hardly stand the thought of being away from you, even for one day, much less five months. This is something that's got to be done. It will mean a lot to our future if I can pull this off."

"I understand, Matthew and I respect you for that. It will be difficult, but we'll make it."

"As soon as I get back we'll move to our ranch in Arkansas. The ranch house ought to be done by then. I'm anxious for you to meet my friends."

"I've written to my doctor friend in Philadelphia. I've asked him to ship me a supply of chemicals we were experimenting with before I left there. I want to do some research. Somebody is going to discover the cure to the Texas fever problem, it might as well be me."

"That's my girl. We'll move that two thousand head of young stock with us when we go. I know you're wanting to do some cross-breeding too. My pa always told me, son, if a man thinks he can, hard enough, he's more likely right than wrong."

"Wish I could have known your parents, they must have been special people."

"Yeah, they were. All they ever knew was working hard and doing without. They died trying to make a better life. Come to think on it, I reckon that's pretty much what we all do."

"I love you, Matthew," she told him, leaning far over and pulling his lips to hers.

Reaching out a strong arm, he lifted her from her saddle and set her across his lap in front of him and kissed her again.

"How come you call me Matthew?"

"Isn't that your name?"

"Well, yeah, but nobody ever called me that until I met you."

"To me, you're a Matthew. Of course, if you prefer, I could call you...let's see...I could call you sweetheart, or darling, or stallion." She nipped playfully at his ear.

"Matthew will do just fine," he said, embarrassed.

Near dusky dark they rode on ahead of the herd and found the wagons. They were arranged in a large circle with the front of the wagons pointed outward. Several supper fires were blazing and coffeepots were boiling. Five cooks and their helpers were busy preparing supper for tired and hungry drovers.

It was well after dark before they got the big herd circled and milling, ready to bed down. A few at a time, the tired punchers straggled in, saw to their horses and filed past the chuck wagon, more than ready for the plateful of grub and cup of coffee they were handed.

Each of the five cooks had prepared a different supper. The drovers were free to choose whichever suited his taster. Matt and Jamie chose to try what Moses had fixed. They enjoyed the beef stew, hot sourdough biscuits and fresh apple cobbler.

"If I eat like this the whole drive, I'm liable to weigh four hundred pounds by the time I get back," Matt said, sopping his plate with another biscuit.

"That would just be more for me to love," Jamie leaned over and whispered in his ear.

"This stuff you call coffee would float a horseshoe," a cowboy called out, joshing old Moses.

"Never did see one of you fellows but what you was a gripping about something or other," Moses called back and everybody laughed.

After supper, Joe and the other foremen got together around the fire and decided to put a double guard of night herders on two-hour shifts for the first few nights.

"I reckon even as tired as those critters are, we'll be plenty busy turning back bunch-quitters for a night or two," Joe told them. "But we can't afford to waste time tomorrow rounding up strays."

For drovers, the time after chow was the best part of the day. They liked sitting around the campfires, sipping coffee, joking to one another, or spinning some tall yarn that nobody believed but like to hear anyway.

Matt and Jamie listened with the rest when Roscoe Haney started telling about the time that they were swimming a herd across the Red River at flood tide.

"Yes, siree," he said with great fanfare. "A thousand pound longhorn lit out downstream swimming lickety-split. Well, sir, I knew right off my old mustang couldn't catch up to that critter cause he was already more'n thirty feet down the river. So I just shook out a loop and roped that steer by the tail and pulled that ornery critter right outta that river backwards."

"Roscoe," somebody yelled, "you know that's a big lie."

"Way I figure it," Roscoe said loudly, "It ain't a lie if everybody knows you're lying."

"I'll have to think about that one for a minute or two," Jamie laughed.

Over around the fire where the vaqueros were gathered, somebody broke out a Spanish guitar and struck up a lonesome cowboy tune. Few knew what the vaqueros were singing, but the sound of it was beautiful in any language.

Even as tuckered out as they all were, it seemed nobody wanted the night to end, least of all, Matt and Jamie. But they both knew that sometime tomorrow she would turn back to the ranch.

Finally, the drovers pulled their bedrolls from the outriggers along the sides of the wagons, rolled them out on a flat spot and turned in. They knew they faced another long and hard day tomorrow.

Dawn was still a ways off when eight men squatted around the roaring campfire, blowing on their steaming hot coffee, daring to sip now and then. Matt, J.R. and Matt's six foremen talked in low tones about the day's plans.

"Be light in an hour," J.R. offered, glancing up at the pitch-black sky. "One thing you can bank on, them critters will be on their feet and bawling at first light."

"Roll out!" Moses yelled, loud enough to wake the dead, running an iron around inside a metal triangle. "I ain't your mama to let you sleep all day."

Then, in a loud, sing-song voice that sounded like a bullfrog: "Bacon's in the pan, coffee's in the pot, crawl out and get it, while it's still hot."

The other four cooks took up the call and one by one, the cowboys rolled out. Before sunup, breakfast was over and the herd was plodding northward.

So far, water hadn't been a problem since Matt had decided to follow the Guadalupe River upstream as it meandered down from the northwest. His plan was to stay close to the stream to a point just north of San Antonio, allowing the cattle to drink their fill at least once each day. The herd seemed at ease, content to drift along, grabbing a mouthful of the belly-high river valley grass as they walked.

Matt, Jamie and J.R. had reined up on a hilltop and were watching the endless stream of longhorns. Off in the distance, they saw Joe riding hard toward them. Matt knew that meant trouble.

"Something's wrong. J.R., come with me. Jamie, you best stay here."

Kneeing Midnight into a gallop, J.R. and Matt hurried to intercept his foreman. When they met they conversed for a brief moment, then wheeling their horses, galloped off together. Joe led them to a point a few miles upstream. There, in a swag along the riverbank, lay ten dead cattle. Three young calves stood nearby, bawling for their dead mothers. The cattle had been skinned.

"Buck and Jess were riding point and found 'em," Joe told them. "They rounded up a few of the boys and lit out following the wagon tracks of the ones that done it."

"Hide peelers," J.R. said immediately.

"You mean they did that just for the hides?" Matt asked.

"Yep," the old rancher told him. "They're the scum of the earth. They slip in, catch some cattle unguarded and cripple them with a thing called a metaluna.

"It's kinda like a scythe, it's a curved knife attached to a long handle. They ride alongside a running cow, hamstring her with the thing crippling her. When they get several down, they skin them, leaving the carcass for the buzzards.

"If she's got a young calf, like those there, they'll die, too, without her milk.

"When they get a wagon load of hides they skedaddle, selling the hides for a good profit. Come on boys," J.R. said bitterly, "I want these butchers bad."

Along the trail, they came upon two more bunches of dead cattle. Like the others, they, too, had been skinned, leaving the rest of the carcasses lying where they fell. Another mile upstream near a grove of cottonwoods, they found them.

Buck Wheeler sat his horse, a leg hooked around his saddle horn, rolling a smoke. On the ground, Jess Tanner, Chip Dawson and Shorty stood around three shabbily clothed fellows with their hands tied behind their backs.

Matt and Joe reined up beside the huddle of men while J.R. walked his horse over to a nearby covered wagon. Lifting a tattered canvas top, he stared inside for a moment and sadly shook his head. Leaning over and reaching a hand into the wagon, he lifted out the long weapon that was still bloody, and flung it as far as he could throw it. Without a word, he reined around and walked his horse over to face the three captives.

For a long minute the old rancher sat his horse, staring intently down at the three. The hide peelers stood silently, gazing at the ground, refusing to look up at the big rancher on the horse.

"Throw some ropes over that big cottonwood over there," J.R. said, "and somebody loan these no-goods a horse for their last ride."

Three long ropes were quickly fashioned into nooses. The three were lifted up into saddles, then loops were dropped over their heads and drawn tight under their left ear.

Matt sat watching the tragic spectacle, amazed that none of the three had yet said a word. There were no excuses given, no protests made, no pleas for mercy. It was as if they knew the penalty for what they had done and had resigned themselves to their fate. They simply sat silently, staring straight ahead.

"I'd like your names for the book if you're of a mind?" J.R. asked sadly, yet firmly.

The first to speak up was a grizzled old buffalo hunter, the obvious leader of the three. His ragged old clothes were a bloody mess from the deeds he had done that day and likely many days before. A shaggy beard covered his face except for his cold, evil eyes. He chewed on a jaw full of tobacco and spat a stream of brown juice before speaking. His voice came out deep and gravely.

"Name's Jessup. Folks call me Blackie. Write it in your book if'n you're a mind."

A Mexican sat on the next horse in line. He was a middle aged looking hombre. He just sat there, shaking his head slowly, not saying a word.

The remaining fellow turned out not to be a man at all. He was only a boy, likely no more than fifteen. His young face reflected the fear he must be feeling inside. Lake blue eyes flicked nervously from side to side. J.R. fixed a look at the boy, seemingly searching the boy's eyes and face for something without knowing what.

"What's your name, son?" the old rancher asked, his voice no longer harsh.

The frightened boy swallowed hard. His lips quivered. Tears streamed down his dirt-crusted face leaving little trails where they had passed. He tried twice to mouth words, but nothing came out. Finally, he stammered the words.

"Jim, sir. Jim Bob Jessup."

"How old are you, son?" the sad old rancher asked the boy.

"I'm might near fifteen, sir," he said softly, flicking a glance at the older fellow with the same name, then back at the big man asking the questions.

"He your pa?" J.R. asked him.

"No sir, my pa and ma both passed on. He's my uncle. He took me after my folks were killed by the Comanche," the boy said, his voice breaking.

The old rancher sat silent for a long minute, as if deciding the boy's fate. Then his hand reached back and withdrew a knife from his hip and cut the rope from around the boy's hands and neck.

"I'm of a mind to give you a chance, boy. Maybe you're here of your own choosing and maybe you ain't. I'm hoping you ain't. They made their choice. Now they'll die for it. But I ain't ready to hang no fifteen year old boy if it costs me my whole herd."

J.R. nodded his head just once. Shorty swatted the two horses on the rump. The horses leapt forward, dragging the two men from their saddles. Their falling weight snapped their necks. Their feet jerked once. The only sounds were the hooves of the running horses in the soft sand and the soft squeaking of the ropes across the cottonwood limbs. The only movement was the gentle swinging of the bodies at the end of the short ropes.

"Leave 'em," the old rancher said, his voice taking on the coldness of before. "They don't deserve a burying. Unhitch them horses and set a fire under that wagon, too. I don't want anything around to remind me of men like that."

Walking his horse over next to J.R., Matt spoke with him in low tones for a minute. The old rancher nodded his head in agreement.

"Son," Matt said to the boy. "We've decided you'll go with us. We're driving some cattle up the trail apiece. We think it might be good if you'd tag along. I'll furnish you grub and a bedroll and start you out at thirty dollars a month if you'll help around the camp. That sound fair?"

"Yes, sir. I'd shore like that."

"Shorty, how about doubling him back to the chuck wagon. Tell Moses he's got another helper for awhile."

It was clear to Matt the incident had shaken the old rancher. There was sadness about his face that Matt had never seen before.

"We'll be hitting the northern boundary of the ranch soon," the rancher said. "I reckon me and Jamie better head back."

"I reckon," Matt said. "I'll ride back and let her know."

"Yeah," J.R. said, looking like a man that needed some time alone, "I'll be along directly."

Jamie was sitting on the riverbank. She held the white gelding's reins in her hand and stared at the running water as Matt rode up. Stepping down, he sat beside her and briefly told her part of what had happened, leaving out the hanging part. He figured if her father wanted her to know he could tell her.

"J.R. is on his way," he told her. "He thinks it's time for the two of you to head back."

"I was afraid you were going to say that," she said sadly, still staring at the water. She wept. Matt held her close as great sobs shook her body. He waited until the sobs quieted before touching her face and turning it toward his.

"Jamie, I'm leaving my heart here with you," he told her softly, looking deeply into those beautiful eyes, now sparkling from silver tears. "It will love you and be your constant companion while I'm gone. I love you more than my own life. I will be back and maybe we'll never have to be apart ever again. Keep your eye peeled on our star."

They kissed...and J.R. waited. Jamie turned her back and trailed a touching hand until their hands parted. She toed a stirrup and swung into the saddle, forcing herself not to look back. Matt watched until the sight of them disappeared over the crest of the distant hill. He mounted and pointed Midnight's nose north.

They followed the Guadalupe River two more days until they were twenty miles or so north of San Antonio. They struck due north, crossing the Colorado River two days later without incident.

Word somehow got out in nearby Austin about the largest cattle drive in history passing nearby. Folks drove and rode twenty miles in buggies, on horseback and by the wagonload to stand and gawk at the endless line of longhorns as they plodded past.

Another two days brought them to the Little Yegua River. They stayed close to it for a couple of days, then cut north again, hitting the Brazos River and following it to near Waco.

By allowing the cattle to drift, rather than driving them hard, they were traveling well. The constant availability of water, plus the thick grass in the river bottoms, allowed the longhorns to thrive. If anything, they were in better shape now than when they started. It took more time, but Matt figured the time was a good investment. It was March the tenth.

Nearing Waco, Matt asked Jess and Shorty to take two drivers and wagons into town to replenish their food supplies.

"Check with Sheriff Thompson and get the latest news and tell Miss Abby howdy for me," Matt told Jess. "While you're there, pick up a couple of changes of clothes for Jim Bob, I'm tired of seeing his bare bottom through the holes in his britches. We'll follow the Brazos all the way to Fort Worth so you won't have trouble catching up."

Even as large as the herd was, they had experienced little trouble crossing the rivers, at least so far. They simply were able to follow the river until they found the best crossing place.

They kept two point men scouting at least five miles ahead of the herd. Usually it was Buck and Shorty, but Ed Beaver had proved to be a fellow with a lot of sand too. Matt had recently hired him as his seventh foreman. The crew was working together real good and things seemed to be going smooth, maybe too smooth.

Jess and Shorty caught up in a couple of days and filled Matt in on the latest news. The bushwhacker that shot Matt had been tried in San Antonio, found guilty and sentenced to spend five years hard labor in the State Penitentiary. Ben and Abby were happy and sent their best wishes.

Jim Bob, the former hide peeler, had proved to be a good worker and seemed happy being part of the drive. After talking to Moses about the boy, Matt called him aside and gave him the new clothes and boots Jess had brought.

The boy looked at the new clothes and boots Matt held out to him with disbelief written all over his face. Those were likely the first new clothes the boy had been given in a long time, maybe ever. Matt had a feeling for the boy. He reminded him a lot of himself when he was about that age. He watched as the young fellow turned the new boots over and over in his hands, real gentle like—as if he were loving them.

"How you liking it?" Matt asked, pleased with the boy's reaction. "Being on the drive, I mean?"

"Mister Matt," the boy said, "I don't know how far we're taking these cows, but I hope we just keep on going. If you'll let me, sir, I want to do this the rest of my life."

"Moses tells me you're a hard worker. How'd you like to help Juan with the remuda?"

"Yes, sir!" the boy replied quickly, "I shore would. I been wishing I could do that someday. I'll do you a good job, Mister Matt."

"Moses!" Matt hollered to the big black man, "see the boy gets fitted out with a saddle and side arm. Let him catch him up a black horse and send word to Juan to show him the ropes."

"Yes, sir, boss," the black cook hollered. "I'll see that gets done."

"Then it's settled," Matt told the boy. "Starting today you'll be paid the same as the rest of the drovers, fifty a month and keep. Go with Moses and pick you out a saddle that fits your seat and throw it on one of them Mendozas. Draw you out a pistol rig and Henry rifle. I'm right proud of you son, you're gonna make a good drover. Oh, by the way, you're gonna look right smart in those new duds, too."

"Thanks, Mr. Henry, sir. First new clothes and boots I ever had."

They reached Fort Worth on March 25. For three straight days they slouched along in a driving rainstorm. The drovers' rode with the brims of their hats turned down to shed the rain. Their rain ponchos were pulled tight around them and they sat low and bent over in the saddles, leaning into the storm.

During those days, meals were mostly eaten standing, crowded under the canvas awning stretched over the cooks' working table. No matter what the cooks prepared, the rain made it into soup before they could gobble it down. At least the cowboys had a good dry place to sleep at night. Matt was sure glad he decided to bring the tents.

Heading straight north, they covered sixty miles in six days before reaching the Red River near a little trading post they called the Red River Station. The farther north they moved the colder the weather grew.

They reached the Red on March 31. The rusty Red River was running bank full from all the heavy rains. After a meeting with all his foremen, Matt decided they would sit it out for a couple of days rather than try a risky crossing that was sure to result in losses of cattle and maybe even men. They figured there was enough good graze to last the herd a couple of days, maybe more.

Spud Weber, the only man in the whole crew that had never been on a drive before, didn't take time to look around good before answering nature's call. A cottonmouth water moccasin took a bite out of his behind. Moses crosscut the bite and squeezed out the poison as best he could, doused it with whiskey and put a big chaw of chewing tobacco on it and tied it in place.

"You might have a tad of fever for a day or two," the cook told him, "but you'll live to tell your grand kids the story. If you're of a mind to tell it, that is."

All around the campfires that night, the boys had a bunch of fun wondering just how Moses got that snake poison out of Spud Weber's behind.

After waiting two days for the water to go down, it was still near bank full. Matt and his foremen had another meeting. Everyone agreed it was still too high for a safe crossing. Matt decided to send Jess Tanner and a four-man patrol upstream and another led by Buck Wheeler would head downstream.

"See what the river looks like," he told them. "Check out the grass, too. See if you can find good graze. Make sure you're back here by this time tomorrow or we'll be out of grass around here."

Matt watched anxiously the next day for the patrols to come in. Grass was gone within a three-mile radius. Time was running out. Jess and his patrol rode into sight first, their heads low. Jess sadly shook his head and Matt's heart sank.

What can we do? he wondered. If they tried to cross with the water as high as it was they would lose many cattle—worse, they could well also lose men. To turn back would be defeat and disaster. He was still weighing the few choices when Buck galloped in at full speed.

"We found it!" he yelled when he was still a good ways off.

Matt hurried out of camp on foot to meet him. His foreman had a big smile plowing a furrow across both cheeks.

"The river channel makes a sharp bend and flattens out about ten miles downstream," he told Matt excitedly. "There's lots of water, but it's spread out real wide and not near as deep. The sandbars ain't too bad, either. Me and my horse waded halfway across with no problem. The banks on both sides are sloped and the bottom is solid. It's a good crossing."

"All right then, that's it," he told his foremen, who had just ridden up. "Let's head 'em downstream. When we get to the crossing, hold 'em back a couple of miles from the river. We'll bed 'em down there tonight and bring 'em up a few hundred at a time in the morning. It'll take longer, but if we run into trouble we won't have so many to deal with.

"Shorty, take a few men and fell some trees to lash to the wagon wheels. Let's put some ropes on a chuck wagon and get it on across. It can take care of the crews working the far bank.

"Buck, pick you out a dozen men and work the far bank. Rig up some block and tackles to some sturdy trees and get some of those heavy ropes we brought along together. We can keep a tight line or two on the wagons coming across.

"Ed, get you a crew and do the same on this side. I don't want none of our wagons and supplies floating down the river."

Working hard from daylight till dark it still took four days to get the whole outfit across, but they lost less that a hundred head and no one was injured seriously. Everybody breathed a sigh of relief when the last longhorn crossed. They all agreed it was a job well done.

"You got yourself sixty miles of good graze before we hits the south fork of the Canadian," Moses told Matt the next morning as the two sipped a cup together before even the foremen showed up for their regular morning get-together.

"You got lots of creeks and such, too, so you got no worries about water. Like I tells you, Mr. Henry, I done been up this trail so many times I can might near follow my own tracks."

"Thanks, Moses, I'm obliged. By the way, I've been so busy I ain't had time to ask. How was that Indian girl when you left?"

"She doing right well when I left. Her and that boy of mine were making eyes at one another. That woman of mine aggin it on, too. Course, I reckon he could do a heap worse than that little gal."

"I made arrangements with the Marshal so the girl would get the reward for the men that done it," Matt told him. "The girl's got six thousand dollars coming when she gets up and around."

"Mister Henry, sir, that's the kindest thing I ever heard of anybody doing. That's a heap of money."

After the foremen arrived, Matt asked them what they thought about splitting up the herd.

"I figure if we drift 'em easy and spread 'em out, they'll do good. Moses tells me we got good graze and lots of water for the next sixty miles. My idea is to divide them up into five herds of about four thousand each. Keep 'em about two miles apart and spread 'em out. Let's drift 'em in a formation like a flock of geese flies. What do you think?"

"Never heard it done that way, boss," Jess Tanner spoke up, "but it sounds like a good idea to me."

"Don't know why nobody's had the gumption to try it before," Buck agreed.

"Sounds like a good plan to me," Joe said, glancing around at the others who were all nodding their heads.

"Where do you want the remuda, señor?" Julio asked.

"For now, let's keep 'em out in front of the point herd so

they can get some graze. If we smell any kind of trouble, drop them back into the middle of the formation.

"We'll be coming into Indian Territory pretty quick. There's Creeks, Chickasaws, Choctaws, Cherokee and Seminole up ahead. We don't know which is friendly and which ain't. Until we know, tell the boys to ride with their eyes open and their guns handy. Further up the trail I hear they're charging to let a herd pass through without trouble. I'm willing to pay a fair price to avoid trouble, but nobody's cutting my herd.

"I'm gonna ride on ahead and look things over. I'll be in and out from time to time. While I'm gone Joe will be in charge. Whatever he says is the same as me saying it. Any questions? All right then, let's get 'em out of those sacks and into the saddles."

Matt ate breakfast with them, then loaded his packhorse and tied his bedroll behind his saddle. He tied the big Sharps on top of his pack and swung into the saddle.

By mid-morning he was a good six or eight miles ahead of the point herd. All morning he had ridden in an ever-widening sweep, back and forth, keeping his eyes glued to the ground for any sign of trouble. The country was now heavily wooded with only sparse openings. It would slow the herds down.

He continued his sweeping pattern all day, still finding nothing. Just before dark he came upon a little stream that flowed fresh and clear. It crept through a stand of sweet gum trees that would make a good camping place.

He cooked himself a good supper, then sat back against his saddle to enjoy another cup. Smoke from the small campfire curled lazily upward and was scattered into nothing by the early growth of the sweet gum. He stared up through the branches and finally found their star. Wonder what Jamie's doing right about now? Matt thought.

* * *

He had been out three days before he struck a sign. Unshod ponies had come out of a streambed, climbed the bank and headed single file in the direction of the herd. Stepping down, he knelt to one knee and fingered the tracks. They were still damp. The tracks were no more than an hour old. Studying the tracks closely, he guessed there were twenty of them. Too big to be a hunting party, more likely a raiding band out looking for trouble. That meant he had to get back and warn his men.

Figuring he was a good twenty miles from the herds, he slanted to his right to put a couple of miles between him and the raiding party. That done, he struck out toward the herd at a short lope.

Buck was ramrod of the lead herd and already had them milling and ready to bed down for the night when Matt rode into his camp. He poured himself a cup and squatted by the fire beside Buck and Shorty.

"I cut sign about twenty miles north. Looked to be near twenty or so and headed this way. No more than that won't be a threat to the herd, but they shore might be to the remuda. Any Indian worth his salt, no matter what feathers they wear, would risk his scalp for one of those Mendozas.

"Shorty, take some boys and help Juan and Jim Bob move the remuda back inside the formation, they'll be safer there. Buck, I reckon we ought to double the nighthawks, too."

They slept with one eye open that night but there was no sign of the Indians. Matt knew you only saw an Indian when he wanted you to see him—it was those you couldn't see you needed to worry about—and he did.

"I figure they'll dog us for awhile," Matt told Buck, "waiting for a chance to get to the horses."

Another day passed and still no sign of trouble. They would be coming up on the south fork of the Canadian River by sometime the next day. Maybe the presence of so many armed riders had discouraged the Indians, but Matt doubted it. His hunch proved right.

It was early, not yet mid-morning when he spotted Julio and his ramrod, Ramono, riding toward them, hell bent for leather.

"Señor Matt," Julio called out, tugging his Mendoza to a skidding stop. "One of our vaqueros has been killed."

They rode together to a willow thicket not far from the herd Julio and his vaqueros were working. Apparently the young Mexican had gone in after a stray, which still stood nearby munching grass. He lay stripped naked. Everything had been taken—clothes, boots, weapons, his horse and saddle, everything. The final insult...he had been scalped.

"His name was Jesus Gonzales," Julio said. "He was only eighteen."

Matt could feel the color rising warm in his face. His eyes narrowed and fastened themselves on the awful sight before him. The coppery scent of blood hung in the air and caused his stomach to churn. His cheek muscles throbbed and his face tightened, then he looked away. White-hot anger flushed through him but he knew he had to control it. Rage was a luxury he couldn't afford just now—he had work to do.

Kneeling, he studied the tracks for a long minute, maybe two. He fingered each of the tracks, etching them in his mind, reading them as surely as if he had watched it happen. His searching gaze swept the area, seeing what could not be seen, discovering what no man should have been able to know.

"There were six of them," he said to no one in particular. "Four sat their horses while two did the deed. The scalper was a heavy man, left-handed. Somebody have a cook restock my pack supplies, I'm going after them. Joe, put a cross where you bury our man. Ramono, I'd like you to come with me."

All day they followed the tracks of seven horses, one without a rider. It was clear from the start the Indians knew they would be followed. They tried every trick in the book to hide their trail. At times Matt and Ramono had to ride a creek bank for a mile or more to find where they had left the water. They changed directions often, sometimes doubling back on their own tracks, then striking out in a different direction, using a bush to brush out their tracks.

"These hombres are mighty careful," Matt told his partner as they bent low, following sparse sign.

"They have split up," Ramono pointed at six different sets of prints splitting off in six directions. "Do we split up also? Which trail do we follow?"

"No," Matt told him, "we stay together and follow the one leading our Mendoza. I figure where that fellow goes, the others will meet up with."

They found them not long after good dark had set in. Not from sight, for the night had long since hidden their trail, but from smell. Obviously, the Indians had convinced themselves they had been so clever disguising their trail and that they had gotten away safely they did a foolish thing—they built a fire.

When one has learned the scents of the natural land, the unnatural is like a light in the darkness. Matt sniffed the air and knew the scent it carried and knew from where it came. The smell of burning wood traveled on the wind for long distances and could not be hidden.

They chose a deep gully with a thick stand of scrub willow lining either side. Tying their horses a good ways off, Matt and Ramono light-footed toward the gully. They bellied down and crawled the last twenty yards to the rim and peeked over the edge.

The light from their small campfire lit the small clearing beside a small stream. Six Indians sat cross-legged around the fire. They passed around a bottle of something, most likely celebrating their being able to outsmart the white-eyed drovers.

They wore long leggings, breechcloths and moccasins. Their hair was worn long and loose about their shoulders. Their faces were smeared with streaks of paint of all colors and gave an evil look to their ugliness.

One of the Indians, a big fellow, took a long swig from the bottle, mumbled something Matt could not hear and leaping up, did a little mock dance, dragging a hank of hide and hair from his belt and waving it in the faces of his companions.

Matt shivered as a cold chill of anger swept through him and cut him like the edge of a sharp knife. A cold sweat broke across his face and his eyes blazed with the fury he felt inside.

He tore his gaze from the scene and forced himself to sweep the area. Seven horses, including the Mendoza, stood not far away, their forms outlined by the three-quarter moon. They were tethered to a line stretched between two small trees.

"Stay here," Matt whispered, "Don't fire till I do. Make sure not one gets away." The Mexican nodded and eased his Henry rifle up in front of him.

Craw-fishing backwards a ways before rising to a crouch, he made his way parallel to the gully a good forty yards or so before sliding down the bank and into the thick bushes that choked the bottom of the gully. He moved in a low crouch toward the faint glow of the campfire with the weariness of a buck deer. He carefully placed each foot and felt what lay underneath before shifting weight to it. A snapped dry twig would send a sure alarm.

Removing the thongs and thumbing his side weapons to full readiness, he sank to his knees and moved like a shadow, inching his way ever closer to the unsuspecting Indians. Just outside the ragged circle of light he paused, bunched his legs under him, sucked in a deep breath then let it out—and sprang forward.

Landing on his feet well inside the light, he swung the snub-nosed twelve-gauge level and touched the trigger.

The intensity of the blast ricocheted off the walls of the gully with such force it shook the ground. Two of the warriors nearest

Matt leaped to their feet and whirled to face him. Their bodies absorbed most of the heavy double aught buckshot and the impact blew them completely off their feet. Their actions, however, somewhat shielded their companions.

The remaining four dove for their weapons, snatching them up between heartbeats. The Rattler in Matt's right hand blasted away, sending two slugs into one Indian while he was in the midst of his dive. Matt's eye caught the movement of one rolling to his right, clawing a pistol from his waistband and raising the weapon as he came to his knees. Two rapid shots to the man's chest toppled him over backwards.

Only two remained. One of those emitted a shrill, blood-curdling scream and charged directly at Matt. Light from the fire reflected off the shiny blade in the warrior's hand. He was so close Matt could see the snarl on the face of the savage.

Matt fired point blank, saw the Indian's chest explode, then fired again. The man's momentum carried him into Matt, toppling him over.

The last remaining warrior stood on the other side of the fire, his feet planted and well apart. Waist-high, he held a rifle—and it was pointed squarely at Matt. The black scalp dangled from the man's belt and an evil, knowing smile curled his lips as he slowly levered a shell into the rifle. Matt pulled the trigger of the Rattler.

A sickening feeling hit him in the pit of his stomach when he heard the pistol snap on a spent cartridge. Both of his guns were empty. That's the second time I've made that mistake, Matt thought, and most likely the last.

He braced for the rifle slug that would surely come. His body instinctively flinched as the crack of a rifle rang out, but the expected impact never came. Instead, the Indian's body suddenly flew sideways, half of his head blown away by a bullet from Ramono's rifle.

Matt raised his empty pistol, wagged it in the air saluting his compadre on the bank and for the first time since he leaped into the circle of light, took a deep breath. The whole encounter had taken only a few seconds.

After checking each warrior and gathering their weapons, he scooped up a blanket and wrapped the scalp in it before Ramono joined him.

"Gracias, amigo," Matt said, "That was one fine head shot. What if you'd missed?"

"I never miss, señor," the handsome Mexican replied. The way he said it didn't sound like bravado, just a plain fact.

They intercepted the herd before noon the next day. Ramono rode on to report to Julio while Matt stopped at the lead herd to give Joe and Butch a thumbnail sketch of their encounter, stressing Ramono's part in the fight.

"How are we doing?" Matt asked his foremen.

"We'll be coming to the Canadian by dark," Joe told him. "I was thinking we'd pull up pretty quick. The herds are well watered and I'd hate to have to beat them away from the river all night."

"That's good thinking," Matt told him. "That'll give the boys a short day and give us a chance to scout the river."

"I'll go tell the cooks what we're doing," Butch said.

"Think I'll ride on back and tell the other boys what we've decided. Joe, why don't you ride on up and look the river over."

Matt sat squatted by the fire talking with Julio and some of the boys when Joe rode up and stepped down. One glance told Matt what he didn't want to know.

"The news ain't good, boss," Joe said, pouring himself a cup from the blackened pot. "The river's wide and shallow, but boggy.

I rode out just a little ways and my horse sank below his knees. I rode the river for a couple of miles each direction before it got dark on me. Didn't find nothing better."

"We'll send out a couple of patrols at first light," Matt said, trying to sound positive, but feeling anything but. "There's grass here for a couple of days. We'll find a crossing. . .we've got to."

Matt slept fitfully that night. He tossed and turned, worrying about the news Joe had brought. What if they couldn't find a crossing? What would he do? Not being able to sleep he shook out his boots and pulled them on. He got up, stoked up the fire and swung the leftover coffee over the fresh flames. It was boiling when Moses crawled out from under the chuck wagon where he slept.

"What you doing staying up all night, Mr. Henry?"

"Seems we got ourselves a big problem, Moses," Matt told him. "The river's boggy up ahead. If we try to cross the herd we'll likely lose 'em all. We're gonna send out patrols come first light to see if we can find a crossing."

"Ain't no need to send out them folks, Mr. Henry. Like I been telling you, I done been up and down this trail more times than I can count on all my fingers. The crossing you be looking for lies about ten miles down yonder way."

"Are you sure?" Matt asked, wanting to believe his cook, but fearing the news was too good to be true.

"I'm telling you the gospel truth," the big man said.

"Moses, if what you say is true, there'll be an extra bonus in your pay when this drive's over."

When his foremen arrived for their pre-dawn meeting, Matt shared the problem up ahead, then told them what old Moses had said.

"Joe and I will ride on down and take a look-see," Matt told them. "but in the meantime, go ahead and head the herd that way. In the first place, I trust old Moses. In the second place, we already know we can't cross up ahead."

After a quick breakfast, Matt and Joe swung into the saddles and headed downstream. By mid-morning they found the crossing, just where Moses had said.

A solid rock shelf lined the bottom of the river and stretched near a mile wide. Banks on both sides of the river sloped gently into the swift running water. It was a near perfect crossing.

"We'll have to bottleneck the herd to keep 'em on the shelf," Matt said, "but we couldn't ask for a better crossing. It's too late to start anything today, let's hold 'em back and start 'em across at first light."

The hands all ate breakfast earlier than usual and had already caught their mounts and were in the saddle while it was still an hour before daylight. Matt toed a stirrup, swung a leg over the saddle and kneed Midnight toward the river. Coming up on the rise overlooking the crossing, he reined up and peered into the pre-dawn darkness. Moonlight bounced off the swift running water and caused it to shimmer as it hurried down the river on its way to somewhere.

It was April 16 and the weather was still a little nippy. He turned up the collar on his sheepskin jacket and hunkered down a mite as he watched the frosty little clouds his breath made. They had been on the trail two months. He missed Jamie something awful.

Above the bawling of twenty-one thousand longhorns, a fellow ain't likely to hear much of anything. Occasionally though, he could make out the yips and yells of his riders trying to convince the stubborn critters to move along. Funny how when you live with all that bawling sound every day, a fellow might near gets use to it after awhile.

At their early morning meeting, they decided to put cowboys every few feet in the river on both sides of the rocky shelf, creating a path for the cattle to stay in. One crew crossed to the other side to keep them bunched after they crossed. Another crew held the main herd back, allowing only a thin, steady line to come forward at a time.

The day broke bright and clear, not a cloud in the sky. As good light spread across the river, their mossy-horned old bell cow, Bossy, stepped into the swift water, dipped her nose to take a quick swig, then plodded straight across like she was taking a Sunday stroll. As they had done for the past two months, the others followed her lead.

All day long the line kept coming. A steady stream of longhorns of every color: Reds, blacks, whites and every combination in between. Their long horns sometimes stretched from five to seven feet from tip to tip.

Matt could see the long trails of smoke from supper fires on the north side of the river. It reminded him how hungry they all were, tired too. Finally, just after sundown, the drag riders pushed the last stubborn critter into the water. It had been a long day, but a good crossing.

After supper they sat around discussing the days crossing. Not one cow had been lost. Not one drover injured. It don't get no better than that, Matt figured.

"While we were crossing today," Joe told them, "Shorty and I scouted up ahead. We've got some heavy timber coming up. While we've already got the herd in one bunch, we might want to keep 'em together and string 'em out. If those critters get separated from the herd in those woods, it'll take us a month of Sundays to drag 'em out. There won't be no grazing, so I suggest we push 'em hard and lay down as many tracks as we can. Anything you want to say, boss?" Joe asked.

"Only that you boys are doing a good job. Pass my thanks on."

They made good time. The following day they crossed the North Fork of the Canadian with no problems. It wasn't nearly as big as the south fork. The Cimarron lay in their path and they crossed it three days later. Thirty head were swept down river, but no drovers were injured.

With only temporary breaks, they traveled through heavy timber for the next five days. It was May 2. Unless they ran into major problems, it looked like they would make Abilene on schedule by the first week in June.

A low rumbling woke Matt from a sound sleep. Off in the distance to the southwest a storm was brewing. A steady flashing of lightning lit the huge, angry-looking clouds. Glancing up at the still visible Big Dipper, he judged it to be near two in the morning. The wind was beginning to pick up and the smell of rain reached him on the stiff breeze. The absolute last thing they needed right now was a bad storm, but it sure looked like they were about to get it anyway.

Matt climbed out of his bedroll, quickly rolled and tied it, shook out his boots and stamped them on. All around him drovers were doing the same. They knew all too well how dangerous a storm could be to a trail herd.

The steady rumbling of thunder was growing closer and louder. A few big raindrops began falling and hit Matt's face as he swung into the saddle.

The herds had barely settled back down from their nightly midnight stand up and stretch routine. Now, some were beginning to stand again, lowing nervously. If lightning started, they were in big trouble, Matt thought.

"Shorty," Matt heard Joe shouting above the now howling wind, "Take some of the boys and help Juan move the remuda right quick. Move them upwind, if the herd runs, they'll likely head downwind."

"Everybody in the saddle!" Buck screamed, from one of the camps nearby.

The cooks and helpers were hastily loading pots and pans

and lashing down wagon covers. Matt shot a quick look at the clouds and didn't like what he saw. They were a rolling, boiling, mass of churning gray-black clouds.

The herds were all on their feet now, standing nervously with their tails to the storm, waiting, lowing pitifully. The lightning had grown increasingly intense and now lit the countryside nearly as bright as day. It was getting closer.

Matt kneed his stallion downwind, knowing that would likely be the direction the herd would run should they stampede. He saw—rather than heard—his experienced foremen waving directions for other riders to do the same.

It was no longer a question of if the herd was going to run, the only question was when. The answer came all too quick. A jagged, blue-white streak of brilliant light suddenly shot out from the boiling mass of clouds. A huge old sweet gum tree was its target and it made a direct hit, splitting the tree in half and exploding in a ball of fire. The whole countryside lit up in an instantaneous flash of light. A deafening clap of cracking thunder followed on its tail and literally shook the ground. As one, the whole herd burst into a run.

"Stampede!" the cry went up from every throat.

Matt put heels to Midnight's flanks and held on. The big stallion shot forward. Within two leaps he was running full out, belly to the ground. A look over his shoulder told him he was headed in the right direction. He was out in front of the herd. From the corner of his eye he saw a rider swinging in alongside him. It was Joe. He shouted, his booming voice nearly lost in the thunderous roar of a hundred thousand pounding hooves.

"Let 'em run, then we'll turn 'em!"

A dozen or more riders were there, slapping their black Mendozas on the rumps with coiled ropes, asking for more speed and getting it. Lesser horses might have gone down in front of the charging herd.

Time was lost. There was no time. There was only the reality of the moment.

Trees flashed by. Bushes and limbs materialized from nowhere and tore at his legs. Midnight swerved to avoid some obstacles, leaped over others, and Matt held on lest he be thrown from the saddle.

At last, the herd tired and began to slow. That was the signal the experienced cowboys had been waiting for. Needing no direction, they swiftly and efficiently brought their mounts into position on the right flank and swung coiled ropes, crowding the running longhorns farther and farther to the left. Slowly but surely they turned the leading cattle, forcing them back on themselves into a circle.

Gradually, the tired cattle began to mill, then stop, their heads hanging low to the ground. They had run out. All of a sudden it dawned on Matt for the first time, it was full day.

They buried two men that day just before sundown. One was named Lou Oliver, from a little town in east Texas called Nacogdoches. The other was Spud Weber, the tenderfoot first time drover that had been snake bit earlier.

A hundred thirty-two cowboys and cooks stood with hats in hand as the blanket wrapped remains, which weren't much, were lowered into open graves. The ropes used to lower them were pulled free as Matt stepped to the head of the graves. Swallowing down one of those lumps in his throat, he stared for long moments at the two graves.

"They were good men," he said. "They did the jobs they were hired to do and did them well and died doing it. Don't know how a man could do more than that.

"Before we left Texas, Mr. Cunningham called this crew, 'Matt's Mighty Men.' You're that and more. Now, it falls on us to bury two of our own.

"When we ride on, we'll be leaving behind two mighty men, Lou Oliver and Spud Weber. . .may they rest in peace."

* * *

It took the best part of three days' hard work to round up the strays. When the final count was tallied, the stampede had cost them two good men, two horses, three lost days and three hundred-eighteen head of cattle, many of which were yearlings and younger calves.

The cooks butchered those that weren't trampled too badly, so the drovers could enjoy steak for a change. They were enjoying one of those good meals when one of the outriders came galloping into camp. He dismounted even as his horse was sliding to a stop and hit the ground running.

"Indians!" he shouted breathlessly. "Don't know how many, but there's a whole passel!"

"Which way?" Matt asked quickly, throwing out the remains of his coffee.

"Coming in from the north. Riding slow and all bunched up."

"Mount up!" Matt shouted. "Buck, you and Julio take a few boys and go help Juan and Jim Bob with the remuda. Put some men with rifles around the horse herd. Tell them to shoot any man that so much as looks close at one of those horses. Jess, take thirty men and swing out a ways on the left flank and stay out of sight until I need you. Ramono, do the same on the right flank. Stay hid, I don't want 'em to know you're there until the right time."

With forty-something men riding behind him, rifles out, with the butts propped on their legs or hips and the noses pointed at the sky, Matt rode slow to intercept the Indians. He figured they wanted to parley rather than fight, else they wouldn't be coming in bunched up and riding slow like they were. Dawn was just breaking.

Matt reined up. As if by an unseen signal, his men slowly walked their horses into position, spreading out into a long line facing the oncoming Indians. A sweeping glance told Matt there were nearly sixty of the red men. Their horses wore designs of paint of every description. Hand prints in various colors, circles and wavy lines. The good news was, the Indians wore no paint on their faces. They, too, spread out in a line facing Matt's riders.

The Indian was tall and well muscled. He demonstrated his leadership by heeling his brown and white pinto forward. Matt did the same. While he was doing it he searched the man with an appraising gaze.

He was impressive, sure enough—most would likely call him handsome—for an Indian anyway. His shoulders were wide. He was thick chested. His long hair hung in plaids down his bare back. He wore only beaded moccasins and a breechcloth. A rifle lay across his thighs, held by his right hand. His face was hard looking, like it had been hacked from pure granite. His dark, cagey eyes were doing some appraising of their own.

"Me Running Wolf!" he said firmly, pounding a fisted hand on his chest. "Chief of the Kiowa."

Matt figured that was supposed to impress him, or scare him, or something. He waited.

"You pay Wohaw to cross Kiowa land."

"How much Wohaw?" Matt asked.

The man's gaze swept the line of Double H riders before he answered. Matt figured the man was deciding how much to ask depending on how easy it would be to just kill them, take what they wanted and be done with it.

"You have much cattle. You pay two hundred cow. You pay twenty black horses." The man palmed his hand and drifted it outward, meaning 'that settles it.'

"No." Matt shook his head for added emphasis. "I give you one hundred cows, no horses," Matt said, returning the same sign.

"You! Tejanos! No good!" The Indian spat out each word like it tasted bad. "You no pay, you all die, then we take all," the chief bluffed.

"Jess! Ramano!" Matt said loudly.

As he spoke, the forty men behind Matt lowered their rifles level with the Indian across from them. From the right and from the left, sixty more Double H riders swarmed out from the woods in a battle line, all with rifles ready to do business.

Swiveling his head quickly, first to the right, then to the left, the chief saw he was completely boxed in a cross-fire and facing a hundred rifles in the hands of the 'no good Tejanos.' His dark face took on a more agreeable look.

"I don't like threats, chief," Matt said clearly. "Like I said, I'll give you a hundred cows and you can go in peace, or you can all die where you sit. Your choice."

For a long, tense couple of minutes they sat facing each. One wrong move by either Matt or the chief in the next heartbeat and many men would die. Matt's eyes narrowed and fixed on the eyes of the chief. He saw no fear, no hatred, only indecision. He waited, then breathed a sigh of relief when the chief lowered the nose of the rifle toward the ground.

"We take cows. You go in peace." The chief wheeled his pinto and rode away.

A dozen Indians stayed behind, but their weapons were carried in a non-threatening manner.

"Joe," Matt hollered, "cut out a hundred head."

Beyond the Cimarron River, the land was pretty well open and flat. They separated the herds again to get better graze and drifted them along, covering about ten miles a day. Matt scouted on ahead and reached the salt fork of the Arkansas without further incident. He found a good campsite, made camp and waited out the herd. He used the time to search the river for the best crossing and to take a much-needed bath.

He located a good crossing just below where the Chilaskia River flowed into the Arkansas. The herd arrived three days later.

They spent two days crossing. It was May fifteen. He only had three weeks to reach Abilene and was beginning to get concerned.

They followed the Chilaskia northward and camped just shy of the Kansas line on May twentieth. Time was running out. Matt knew Abilene was still some hundred-eighty miles due north. Moving at ten miles a day they wouldn't make it.

"We've got to make better time," he told his foremen at their meeting the next morning." From here on out we've got to average at least fifteen miles a day. I've given my word this herd would be in Abilene the first week of June. Whatever it takes, I aim to have 'em there."

"We can do it, boss," Joe said, sweeping a glance at the other foremen for agreement. "Can't we, boys?"

"You betcha," Butch said.

"We can do it," Ed Stovall agreed.

Matt's glance around the fire revealed every head nodding.

"All right then," he said. "There's something else we need to talk about. The Kansas line ain't no more than a couple of miles over yonder. I hope I'm wrong, but unless I miss my guess, we're likely to have visitors any time now. I figure we'll run into some trail blockers in the next day or two. From what I hear, they usually prowl along the state line. We want to be ready for them when they come, so here's what I want us to do...."

All ten of the wagons of the Double H outfit had pulled well ahead of the herds and set up for the evening meal. They were arranged in a full circle with twenty yards or so between each wagon, much like the method used by wagons trains.

Supper fires were going, coffee pots boiling and cooks were busy doing what cooks do. Matt and a dozen of his men sat around a fire in the center of the enclosure sipping coffee when a single rider galloped in with a brief message.

"Here they come."

They swept in from the north, riding hard, bunched up and short-loping their fifty or so mounts. They rode straight for the Double H camp and any onlooker would judge them a tough-looking bunch. They split in half with military precision just before reaching the circle of wagons, riders pouring in through every opening, rifles in hand.

Matt and his dozen men stood to greet their visitors as they plowed into the circled camp, their horses scattering the supper fires, knocking over coffee pots and completely surrounding the Double H drovers.

A big man riding a solid white gelding stepped his horse forward from among the others. Matt had already judged him the leader. He looked the part.

He wore a suit and a white Stetson and could easily be mistaken for a rancher, were it not for the Colt in the well-greased holster tied low on his right hip. The long coattail was pulled back away from it.

Matt judged him to be in his early forties, clean cut, well built, most likely an officer in the Army from the way he sat his saddle. He twisted in the saddle, looking the entire camp over carefully, finally fixing his attention upon Matt. His searching gaze swept Matt from head to toe then back again, pausing momentarily at the guns on his hips.

The fellow's ice blue eyes stared long and hard at Matt, who stood, sipping coffee from the cup in his left hand. Matt peered through slitted eyes over the rim of his coffee cup at the intruder.

"My name's Ballinger," the man said in an authoritative voice, like he was giving an order to an underling. "Clay Ballinger."

He said it like it was supposed to mean something special to the man that heard it. It didn't.

"I'm the president of the Kansas Cattle Association. I'm sorry to have to tell you gents, but we're going to have to quarantine your herd. Your Texas longhorns carry the fever. It's killing off our Kansas shorthorn cattle.

"We'll take the herd and hold them in quarantine until we've had a chance to inspect them. If we find they don't have ticks, you'll get your herd back. If, however, we find they're carrying ticks, the herd will be destroyed. I know this sounds harsh, but it's the only way we can protect our own herds. The law is on our side. Do you have any questions?"

"Yeah," Matt said, "I've got a question. Just how you figure on taking my herd?"

"Well, Mr. . . .I didn't catch your name."

"Name's Henry, Matt Henry. I'm asking again. How you figure on taking my herd?"

"Well, Mr. Henry. I was hoping you were a reasonable man. We'd like to do this without violence, but as you can see, we're prepared to use force if necessary."

Matt took his time taking one last swig from his coffee cup, threw the remaining dregs out and bending, set the empty cup on a nearby log. When he did, his watching men saw the signal and the canvas tops of ten wagons were suddenly jerked up by ropes, revealing a hundred rifles trained squarely on the shocked riders. They saw what had happened, realized they were outgunned and caught in a crossfire, and raised their guns high in the air over their heads.

"Mr. Ballinger," Matt said evenly. "You might ought to take another look around you."

The surprised man jerked a look over his shoulder and saw the situation. Blood drained from his face and it took on a chalky-white look. Kinda like he got sick all of a sudden.

"You see, Mr. Ballinger. Here's how it is. We're willing to die to keep our herd. The question is, are you willing to die trying to take it?"

The man knew he was beaten. Only an out and out fool would make a wrong move when he was under the gun like they were and he was no fool.

"You've won this round, Mr. Henry," the man said bitterly, "but this ain't the end of it. We'll be back."

"Well, sir," Matt said, "I was kinda afraid you might take that kind of attitude. Mr. Ballinger, we just plain don't have time to go through all this again, so I reckon before you go, you and your boys ought to shuck them guns and drop 'em on the ground and I mean like right now!"

Rifles hit the dust first, then the gun rigs the riders quickly unbuckled and dropped at their horses' feet. Matt's cooks and helpers appeared from somewhere and quickly gathered up the weapons.

"Right easy like now," Matt ordered, "climb down off them horses."

Again the cooks appeared, gathered the reins and led the horses out from the circle into the darkness.

"Just one more thing and you boys can go," Matt said. "Shuck them clothes and boots, right down to your long johns."

At that command the men hesitated, glancing quickly at their companions, but only for a moment. The chilling sound of a hundred rifles being levered had a convincing ring about it. They peeled right down to their underwear— at least them that were wearing any.

Once more the cooks did their routine, moving among the men, gathering the pants, shirts and boots lying at the men's bare feet. They lugged the armloads over to the fire and threw them in. Ballinger's riders watched helplessly as the flames licked higher, consuming their boots and clothes.

"Now, Mr. Ballinger," Matt told the man standing there before him, barefooted and in his long johns. "I don't know how far it is to where you come from, but I figure it's quite a piece, so I reckon you better get started.

"Oh, just so's you'll know, my men have orders to shoot on sight any varmints we find poking around our camp or herd. I'd shore hate it if they mistook one of you. Just one more piece of advise for you boys. If I was you, I believe I'd find another line of work. Now git!"

The fifty humiliated men straggled from the camp off into the darkness mumbling all sorts of threats and unkind words. A hundred Double H cowboys filled the Kansas night with hollers, catcalls and uproarious laughter.

They posted a double guard around the camp that night and had twenty armed men on two-hour shifts around the remuda, but nobody saw hide nor hair of a Kansas trail blocker ever again. It was like the Kansas prairie had just swallowed them up.

For the next ten days the drive went well. The five herds were spread out with five miles separating them. They made the fifteen miles a day. Sometimes they had to drive until well after dark, but they didn't end the day's drive until they had reached their goal.

"Boys, you've done good," Matt told his seven foremen at the pre-dawn meeting. "I figure we can't be more'n twenty-five miles from Abilene. I'm gonna ride on in and see how things shake out. They tell me the Smoky Hill River is just a few miles shy of town. When you get to it, bunch the herd and wait word from me. Any questions? Okay then, I'll see you boys in Abilene."

Saddling Midnight and tying on his saddlebag that contained what was left of his money, but leaving his packhorse behind, Matt booted a stirrup and settled into leather as the big stallion slipped smoothly into an easy short-lope. Lifting a hand in a howdy to his night drovers as he rode past, he pointed his mount toward Abilene.

As he rode, he watched the first blush of gray that preceded dawn creep across the Kansas prairie. It broke bright and clear, revealing a table-flat land as far as the eye could see. A few puffy white clouds drifted lazily overhead, marring the otherwise soft blue canopy that stretched from here to yonder. The eastern horizon gradually gave birth to a collage of color belching mixtures of white, pink, yellow and orange, splashing them across the soft blue overhead canvas.

An overwhelming feeling of loneliness overtook him. He sure missed Jamie.

CHAPTER XVIII

Between Honorable Men

> "Wisdom and knowledge is granted unto
> you, and I will give you riches and wealth
> and honor." (I Chronicles 1:12)

The Kansas sun hung noon-high and blistering hot as Matt splashed across the shallow Smoky Hill River. Up ahead across the flat prairie he could see Abilene, Kansas. It was June 3, 1867. They had done the thing few thought possible. They had made it.

As he rode nearer, a wave of excitement swept over him. Chill-bumps danced up and down his spine at what he saw. The place was a beehive of activity. Giant multicolored tents stood stretched just outside town, their high poles protruding above the tops flying colorful pennants.

Wooden grandstands now sat empty, but Matt could picture them crowded with excited and cheering people, watching the circus below. He saw huge elephants, buffalo and beautiful horses. He saw families in wagons, fancy-dressed ladies in fringe topped buggies and men on horseback, all moving like an army of ants, hurrying somewhere.

One large building loomed above the others. It stood three stories high and spread out along one side of the wide street. It was the largest hotel he had ever seen. A hundred rooms, Mr. Suggs had said. Lord, a fellow could get lost in a place like that. He twisted in the saddle and craned his neck to gawk as he rode past on his way to the livery, identified by a thumb jerked over a fellow's shoulder when Matt inquired.

"Yes, sir," the black fellow said, as Matt reined up just inside the big double doors of the livery. "That's shore a fine-looking stallion you riding there, sir."

"Thanks," Matt said, handing the man the reins and a half-eagle. "Double grain him, stall him separate with plenty of fresh hay. When you get the time, curry and brush him, too. What's going on around here?"

"Why ain't you heard? They's supposed to be bringing in a big herd of cows all the way from Texas. They's saying there's gonna be twenty thousand in that bunch, though to tell the truth, I ain't gonna believe it till I sees it with my own two eyes."

"Is that so?" Matt quizzed the man. "Where'd all these folks come from? I didn't know there was this many people in Kansas."

"Mister, we got folks from places I ain't never heard of. Chicago even, they're saying. Beats all I ever seen. Don't you worry none about this black horse, mister, I's gonna give him special treatment, that's for shore."

The sign across the front of the hotel said, *The Drover's Cottage.* Matt stepped up onto the boardwalk and pushed through the door. The lobby was bigger than most hotels he'd ever seen. The little bald-headed fellow at the front desk had a red face and a sour look about him, like he had just bitten into a green persimmon. He glanced up, gave Matt a critical look and went back to whatever he was doing in the big black book he was scribbling in. Finally, he peered over the top of the tiny spectacles and raked Matt up and down with a disapproving glare, cocked one eyebrow and backed up a step.

"May I...help you?" he asked, squashing up his nose like he had just smelled something a long time dead.

Matt spun the register book and dipped the pen to sign his name. Maybe the fellow had a point, he allowed, his clothes were trail worn and the closest thing resembling a bath in the last three months was a quick dip in a muddy river.

"Do you have reservations...sir?" old persimmon face challenged.

"Don't reckon I do," Matt told him. "I just rode in. Big a place as this is, looks to me like you'd have rooms for the asking."

"I'm afraid not sir. We're completely full," the fellow said, looking as if it pleasured him greatly. "You might try the stable, I understand they're renting out space there."

"Matt Henry!" a familiar voice called out.

W.W. Suggs came striding up, a big smile on his face and a hand out.

"Did you just now arrive? I've been expecting you. Have you checked in yet? We reserved our finest room for you. Amos, give Mr. Henry the key to room number one please."

The man's eyes bugged and his face got so red a fellow could have lit a cigarette on it. He dropped his eyes when he handed Matt the key.

"Well, Matt, you actually made it," Suggs said, shaking Matt's hand. "Mr. McCoy will be very pleased. I have instructions to let him know the minute you arrive. To be perfectly honest with you, I had my doubts. When will the herd be arriving?"

"They'll be here in a couple of days," Matt told him. "I told my boys to hold 'em at the river."

"Very good. Well, is there anything you need? Is there anything I can do for you? Anything at all?"

"Well, since you asked. Seems like you got a heap of influence around here. Reckon you could rustle me up a hot bath? I could use a change of clothes, too, if you could manage it, these are about used up," Matt said, handing Suggs two double eagles.

"Keep your money, Matt. Mr. McCoy owns everything in town, including this hotel and the mercantile store. Your bath will be brought to your room right away and I'll be right back with your clothes. Your room is right down the hall, first door on the left. Room number one"

Matt strode to the first door, inserted the key and pushed open the door. He took one look and backed out a few steps to double check the number on the door.

Yep, that's what it said, number one. He stepped back inside.

He swept the room with a slow gaze, closed his mouth and retraced the route his eyes had just taken. He'd never even heard of a room like that. It was three times bigger than any hotel room he'd ever seen. Lord, half his trail crew could bed down in here, he thought.

The embossed cloth covering on the walls was a deep wine color. It looked so rich he couldn't resist reaching a finger to trace slowly along the silky surface.

A soft, flowered rug covered most of the floor and looked like it came from one of those far off countries. The bed was so big he could sleep crossways and still have room left over.

Curiosity got the best of him and he strode over to peek behind a folded wooden screen. What he saw was the fanciest bathtub he'd ever seen. It was big enough for most of a man to lie down in and it had a slick white surface. It set up high on four gold-colored legs. Right then and there he decided he had to get one of those for their new home. Jamie would like that. He was still shaking his head in wonderment when there was a knock on the door.

"Mr. Henry," the voice called, "I have your bath, sir."

Matt enjoyed the bath so much he lingered. He had scrubbed

off two layers of trail dirt and was working on the third when Suggs tapped on the door and called that he had Matt's new clothes.

"Come on in," Matt hollered out from the screened bathtub.

"I'll lay them on the bed," Suggs told him as he entered the room. "I told Mr. McCoy that you'd arrived. He was very pleased. When it's convenient, he'd like to see you. His office is in the bank."

"You mean he owns the bank, too?"

"Like I said, he owns everything in town. He built it."

"Tell him I'll be along directly," Matt said from behind the screen, scrubbing good behind his ears like his ma had always told him. "I don't suppose your boss owns the barber shop, too?"

"Matter of fact he does," Suggs told him, actually chuckling out loud, "I'll send the barber right over."

Matt heard the door close, relaxed a little longer in the warm water and finally climbed out reluctantly and dried off with the big fluffy towel hanging from a holder on the back of the screen. Maybe I misjudged that Suggs fellow, he thought, he's right handy to have around.

He had just finished admiring the new suit Suggs brought and stepping into the pants when the barber tapped on the door. Matt strode over, opened the door and let him in. He was a nice old fellow and they visited while Matt got relieved of nearly four months' worth of hair on both his face and head.

"Mr. Suggs tells me you're the one that's bringing in the big herd from Texas."

"Yes, sir."

"That must be exciting, bringing that many cattle all the way from Texas."

"It got that way from time to time," Matt said. "How long has this town been busy like this?"

"Better part of a month now, I guess it is," the old fellow replied. "Little over a year ago, this place wasn't nothing but a few little sod huts in the middle of the prairie. Mr. McCoy's built the whole kit and caboodle. They're still building too. Fast as they get a building up, he puts some kind of business in it. He's sure got big ideas, that fellow has, nice fellow too.

"Guess you seen the big circus tents when you rode in? It's really something, never seen nothing like that. I've been every day since it's been here, going again after awhile too if I ain't too busy. A fellow needs to relax every once in awhile, wouldn't you say?"

"Yeah," Matt said, "I reckon you're right."

When the old barber finished there was enough hair on the floor to stuff a good-sized pillow. He paid the man generously and turned his attention to his new clothes Suggs had brought.

He turned the black, hand-tooled boots over in his hands admiringly. They were so shiny he could see his reflection in them. He stomped them on and sleeved into the white shirt and tied the black string tie. The suit was a soft gray color made of rich-looking material. He clamped the black leather-banned Stetson on his near bare noggin as he strode over to the big stand-alone mirror.

Lord, that fellow looking back at him didn't look nothing like the Matt Henry he'd come to know. He was still getting acquainted with the hombre in the mirror when somebody knocked on the door.

"Who is it?" Matt called out.

"I'm Myron Sinclair, Mr. Henry," the voice said through the door. "I'm with Swift and Company out of Chicago. Could I speak with you a moment?"

Matt swiped his new hat from his head and pitched it on the bed. He opened the door and stepped aside to let the man in. A quick glance revealed a smallish fellow, most likely in his forties, kinda big around the middle like he hadn't missed many meals in awhile. His face was milky white with heavy jowls that hung down under his chin. He wore small, horn-rimmed glasses over nervous-looking eyes and a black suit that was a mite small.

Matt took the hand that was offered and felt a timid, clammy handshake. If you didn't see him standing there, you'd swear the man was stone cold dead.

"What can I do for you?" Matt asked, motioning toward one of the two upholstered chairs.

"I'll get right to the point, Mr. Henry." The man leaned forward in his chair and took on a serious look. "I understand you have a rather large herd of cattle you're bringing in from Texas?"

"Yes, sir, I reckon you could say that."

"Twenty thousand, I hear?"

"Nearer twenty-one," Matt corrected.

"I see," he said, pinching the jowls under his chin in contemplation. "As I said, I represent Swift and Company out of Chicago. We've just opened the largest, most modern meat processing plant in the country. Our plans are to supply beef for the entire eastern seaboard from that facility.

"Mr. Henry." The man leaned even closer and lowered his voice like he was about to reveal a secret or something. "I've been sent here with the authority, not only to purchase your entire herd, but to pay you a very generous price for your cattle."

"Beg your pardon, Mr. Sinclair, but you haven't even seen my cattle yet."

"Mr. Suggs tells me he saw your herd when he was in Texas and that they are acceptable. I'm willing to buy them sight unseen, providing, of course, we can close the deal right now."

"Seems to me this might be a mite sudden. Just out of curiosity, what kind of offer did you have in mind?"

"Well, you understand of course, any offer I make would have to be in the strictest confidence, might I assume that, Mr. Henry?"

"You might assume that, Mr. Sinclair."

Once more the fellow scooted forward to the very edge of the chair. Matt was worried he might fall right off into the floor.

The man shot a glance from side to side, like he was scared there was someone else in the room that would hear what he was about to say, then spoke barely above a whisper.

"Thirty-two dollars a head," he whispered, offering a generous smile. "But I feel I must warn you, Mr. Henry. That offer leaves with me when I leave this room. Are you ready to consummate the agreement, sir?"

The man didn't wait for an answer. He pulled a legal-looking paper from his inside coat pocket and held it out toward Matt.

Matt leaned back in his chair and pasted what he hoped would resemble a disappointed look on his face, even though inside, his heart was doing flip-flops.

"Thirty-two? Frankly, Mr. Sinclair, I have to tell you, I'm kinda disappointed with the offer. I was expecting more."

Twin furrows plowed across the man's forehead and his eyebrows dropped out of their way.

"More?" the man near shouted, looking like Matt had just slapped him across the face. "More than thirty-two? Why that's seven dollars a head above the highest price we paid anybody last year. I assure you, Mr. Henry, no one else can match such a generous offer."

"Well, like I said, Mr. Sinclair," Matt said, pushing to his feet. "This might be kinda sudden to make a deal, but it shore ain't last year. I reckon I'll take my chances and nose around a bit before I decide, but thanks for coming by."

The man looked like a whipped puppy. He started for the door, hesitated and turned half around, then jammed his hat on his head with gusto and tromped out the door, mad as a wet hen.

Matt curled a grin as he closed the door behind the presumptuous cattle buyer and strode to the bed to get his hat. Before he even got it on though, another soft tapping came at the door. This place was busier than flies on a cow patty, he thought, striding back and opening the door.

A tiny fellow, no bigger around than a fence post and about as tall stood there, nervously holding a bowler hat in both hands. His face was thin and gaunt-looking. He looked up at Matt through sad-looking eyes, like a homeless puppy dog.

"Are...are you Mr. Matt Henry?"

"Yes."

"Mr. Henry, my name is Sol Israel. I'm a reporter for the Kansas City Newspaper. Could, could I have a minute of your time?"

For some reason Matt felt sorry for the fellow. It was clear he was new on the job and nervous as a tomcat in a room full of rockers. Against his better judgment, he invited the man in.

"What can I do for you, Mr. Israel?" Matt asked after they both were seated.

"To be honest with you, Mr. Henry, this is my first assignment and I'm scared to death. My newspaper sent me to cover this story to...well, sort of try me out I guess.

"Mr. Underwood, our boss, said to just come and write down what I saw. But I was thinking on the train coming here, if I could actually talk to you and, you know, get the real story. Not just what the cows looked like when they came into town, but what it was like to drive all those cattle all the way from Texas, nearly a thousand miles. I could tell about the cowboys, how they live, what they're like, maybe about some of the problems you had along the way. You know, I don't want to just tell the story, I want to tell the story behind the story."

"Well, to tell you the truth, Mr. Israel, I was just headed out the door for an important meeting," Matt told the man honestly. But after he said it, he saw the disappointed look on the poor man's face and added. "But if you could meet me in the dining room at say, three o'clock, maybe we could talk then."

The man's face immediately brightened and a happy smile broke from ear to ear. He stood quickly to his feet and reached out a hand. Matt took it and was surprised at the firmness of the small man's handshake.

"Yes sir, Mr. Henry," the man said happily, still shaking Matt's hand and nearly shaking it off at the elbow. "Thank you, sir. I'll be back promptly at three this afternoon."

Now why did I go and agree to a thing like that? Matt asked himself as he closed the door behind the reporter. Then remembering the man's smile, he knew the answer ever as he asked himself the question.

Adjusting his new black Stetson from the reflection in the mirror, he strode from the room, down the short hallway and toward the front door.

"I beg your pardon, Mr. Henry," old persimmon face called after him. "Is your room satisfactory?"

"Passable," Matt replied over his shoulder as he pushed through the front door.

Wherever it was all those folks were going when he rode in, they must be coming back now because the street was still as busy as before. He wove around folks passing on foot, dodged buggies and finally made it across the street to the bank. Stepping around workers busy laying planks for a new boardwalk, he paused for a moment and swept a gaze around the busy town.

Like the old barber said, the place was a madhouse. Just from where he stood he could count a half-dozen buildings going up. Just down the street he even saw a tent set up with a hastily scrawled sign announcing the ALAMO SALOON.

Turning, he opened the stained glass door to the bank and stepped inside.

"May I help you, sir?" a nice-looking young fellow asked cheerfully from behind a caged, chest high counter.

"My name's Matt Henry, I'm supposed to meet Mr. McCoy."

"Yes sir, Mr. Henry. Mr. McCoy is expecting you. Right this way."

The young man hurried to a door, tapped lightly and waited for an invitation before opening it halfway.

"Mr. Henry is here to see you, sir."

The young fellow opened the door wide and stepped aside. Matt strode confidently into the office. Two men rose to their feet as he entered. One, behind a desk, Matt assumed was the cattleman, Joseph McCoy. Matt had no idea who the other man might be.

Everything Matt's concept of a cattleman would be was reflected in the man who hurried around the desk with a hand outstretched: Tall, broad-shouldered, deep chested. He had a clean cut, near handsome face. He was deeply tanned, like he had spent more time out of doors than in. His shock of light brown hair was close cut and well groomed with sprinkles of gray here and there. The wide, friendly smile put Matt at ease immediately.

"Matt, I'm Joseph McCoy."

"It's good to finally meet you, Mr. McCoy," Matt said, returning the firm handshake.

"Please, call me Joseph. I want you to meet P.D. Armour from Chicago."

Matt swung his attention to the second man in the room. He saw a businessman, pure and simple. A man that no matter where he might be, everyone that saw him would recognize him as such. He was of medium build, just shy of six feet, likely in his mid-fifties. Clean shaven of the face and a hairline that was scooting to the back of his head. His eyes were all business.

"Hello, Mr. Henry," the man said, looking Matt straight in the eyes. "It's good to meet you. Joseph has told me quite a lot about you, I must say, I'm quite impressed with what I hear."

At Joseph McCoy's suggestion they all took a chair and made get acquainted talk for most of a half-hour. They talked about the cattle business, the Texas fever scare, the trail blocker problem and politics. Then the subject gradually turned to Matt Henry.

They seemed genuinely interested in hearing about the loss of his family, about his quest to bring their killers to justice, about his relationship with J.R. Cunningham and how it came to be and about his recent marriage to the rancher's daughter.

It didn't take Matt long to figure out that the discussion was mostly about him and that these fellows already knew the answers before they asked the questions. He couldn't help noticing the fleeting glances between McCoy and Armour while Matt was talking. He couldn't put his finger on what was going on but they were sure asking a lot of questions.

Finally, after the best part of two hours, Matt saw Mr. Armour glance at McCoy and nod his head slightly. McCoy took on a relieved look and cracked a smile.

"Matt," McCoy said, "I hope you'll forgive us for asking so many questions but we had to be sure. What we're about to tell you must be held in the strictest confidence. We're going to lay our cards on the table face up and see if you want to play the hand.

"When I came up with the idea of moving out here in the middle of nowhere to build my cattle operation, a hundred miles from a railhead or the nearest town, folks thought I had lost my mind. They not only thought it, they said it to my face.

"I took my plan to the Missouri-Pacific Railroad to seek their help and they literally threw me out of their office. I went to the Kansas-Pacific Railroad and talked to their president. He listened politely and finally agreed if I would build it, they would then run a railhead to it, but they refused to provide any financial help.

"I talked to several banks but nobody was interested. Like a lot of men, I guess, I had a good idea but didn't have the money to make it happen. Well, to make a long story short, I heard about P.D. Armour building the largest meat processing plant in the country. To be honest, I figured it was another waste of time but I went to Chicago and talked with him. He not only listened, he saw the possibilities and agreed to back me with the funds I needed.

"Now Matt, again, I'll have to ask you not to repeat what you're hearing. For my operation here to be successful I need— no, I must have the other cattle buyers coming here. If they were to find out that Mr. Armour and I are partners in this venture, they would stop coming and if they stop coming, the Texas cattlemen would stop bringing their herds here."

Matt listened intently to all that was being said. He was not only absorbing the picture they were painting, his mind began to run ahead of the conversation. New ideas and possibilities were being born in his mind even as he sat there listening.

"You see, Matt," Mr. Armour joined in, "I recognized in Joseph here, a man much like myself. For whatever reason I have always been a dreamer, a risk-taker, an entrepreneur. My experience tells me most successful men are.

"I have made and lost several fortunes in my lifetime. I risked it all again when I decided to build the largest, most modern meat processing plant this country has ever seen. I did it because I could see the limitless market in this country for beef. Let me say it this way, I can sell whatever I can produce. Swift and Company saw it too, that's why they built their own plant within three months of my opening.

"To be honest with you, Matt, our problem wasn't selling our product, nor was it processing the meat. My plant alone has the capacity of processing up to six hundred beeves a day. That's eighteen thousand head a month.

"The packing industry's problem, indeed my problem, was obtaining a sufficient and dependable supply of cattle to keep my plant running and meeting my sales commitments. That's why, when Joseph approached me with his, so-called, hair-brained scheme, I immediately saw the possibilities of a source of supply for my plant.

"I had a talk with the railroad and between us, we were able to convince the Governor to make certain allowances to create a mile wide corridor so the Texas cattle could be brought across the Kansas line and directly to Abilene, despite the law prohibiting it."

"As you undoubtedly know Matt," McCoy took up the story, "after opening the yards last year we weren't able to convince either the Texas growers nor the buyers to come to Abilene. I was able to ship only a hundred carloads last year. I have the capacity to ship that many every day.

"That's why I hired Mr. Suggs and sent him to Texas, trying to convince the Texas growers to bring their herds to Abilene. Frankly, we were on the verge of abandoning the whole venture as a failure until you came into the picture with your daring proposal.

"You, Matt, provided that missing link to our plan, the last piece of the puzzle. That's why we questioned you so hard awhile ago. We had to be sure you were what we thought you were."

"It's a rare moment," Mr. Armour interjected, "when three men with the same characteristics, men with a daring spirit, men of vision, willing to risk failure in order to succeed, come together in one room.

"Joseph and I are convinced," Mr. Armour continued, "that you are not only a man of vision, but that you have the tenacity and fortitude to finish whatever you begin. But most importantly, we are convinced that you are a man of honor, even as we are men of honor."

CHAPTER XIX

Wisdom's Reward

If you are wise, your wisdom
will reward you." (Proverbs 9:12)

"We're looking for a man like you Matt," Mr. McCoy said, "A man that is both capable and willing to supply a steady supply of Texas beef. You've proved to the world that you could do what no other man has ever attempted before."

"So" Armour said, "here's what we are proposing to you. We will promise you three dollars a head above whatever the current market is for every head of beef you can deliver to us. If the market rises, your price will rise, if it goes down, of course your price will also go down.

"You may or may not know, the buyer for our competitor, Swift and Company is in town as well as several smaller cattle buyers. I suspect he will make you an offer, probably in the range of thirty to thirty-two dollars a head. Cattle right now on the Chicago market is going for forty-two.

"That means, Matt," Armour continued, "We'll give you thirty-five dollars a head for your herd and three dollars a head above our competition's price for every herd you can deliver here to Abilene.

"Joseph and I have our own arrangement worked out with the railroad and each other. He receives a percentage and my company pays the freight charges. The railroad pays Joseph five dollars for every carload he ships on their line.

"I've always believed the only good business deal is one where everybody involved makes money. In business we call it a win, win, win, arrangement.

"So, Matt," Armour asked, leaning forward in his chair and looking him straight in the eyes. "It all comes down to this. We need your answer to three questions. First, can you secure enough beef to provide us a dependable supply? Second, can you deliver it in a timely fashion. Thirdly, are you interested in our business proposal?"

"The answer to all three questions is yes," Matt said without hesitation, already anticipated where they were headed.

"Then let's shake on it," P.D. Armour said, smiling broadly and pushing to his feet. "I was raised to believe a man's word was his bond and your word is good enough for me. We have an agreement, sir. An agreement between honorable men."

They talked for another half hour. Deciding how many head Matt could supply, how soon he could begin delivering and the financial arrangements.

"I'm kind of looking for some shorthorn breeding stock," Matt told Joseph McCoy, "We're wanting to do some cross breeding on my ranch down in Arkansas. Thought you might know where a man could lay his hands on a small herd."

"As a matter of fact I might," McCoy told him, "There's a ranch southeast of here down on the Cottonwood River called the Bar-J-Bar. A fellow named Ben Jackson, real nice fellow, owns it. He did have a herd he was looking to sell, don't know for sure if he still does. If he does it's good stock."

"Thanks," Matt said, "I'll look into it."

"Ever hear of a man named Clay Ballinger?" Matt asked.

"Most everybody in these parts has heard of Ballinger," McCoy said, "Why? You know him?"

"Yeah, we met down the trail a piece. He said he was President of the Kansas Cattle Association. Is he legit?"

"He's a renegade bandit that uses his fictitious organization as an excuse to steal cattle," McCoy said bitterly. It was clear Matt had hit on a sore subject. "Him and his bunch are probably the single biggest factor in preventing herds from reaching the railheads. Ballinger and his men have shot down or hung at least a dozen men that tried to resist losing their herds."

Matt told them the story of their encounter with Ballinger's outfit. When he got to the part about stripping them and sending them off barefooted and in their long johns, both of the men reared back and laughed uproariously.

"I must say, Matt," Armour said, "you're quite an amazing man. I feel fortunate that we are associates rather than adversaries. I'm looking forward to a long and mutually profitable relationship. If I can ever be of help to you, please feel free to let me know. Joseph will settle up with you when you get the final tally."

"Thanks, Mr. Armour," Matt said, shaking his hand. "You're an easy man to do business with."

Later, walking back to the hotel, Matt could hardly keep his feet on the ground. Thirty-five dollars a head? He could hardly believe it—that was far more than had even hoped for. Better still, he had an agreement to supply twenty thousand head every month. The possibilities were unlimited, but so were the obstacles that had to be overcome. He couldn't wait to get back to the hotel and do some figuring and planning.

Sol Israel was waiting for him in the lobby. That huge smile that Matt couldn't say no to wrapped itself across the man's face when he saw Matt walk in. He'd forgotten all about promising to meet with the man. Oh well, he'd answer a few questions and be done with it.

"Sorry I kept you waiting" Matt secretly wished he hadn't promised to meet with the man. "Why don't we have a cup of coffee in the dining room while we talk?"

Only a few customers were scattered among the thirty or so tables in the large dining room. Matt chose one, drew back an empty chair and folded into it.

He motioned to a waiter as Sol withdrew a pad and pencil from his pocket.

"Would you like a cup of coffee?" Matt asked.

"Huh? Oh, yes, that would be good."

A waiter in black pants and white shirt hurried up and took their order and returned quickly with their coffee.

"Just what is it you'd like to know about the drive?" Matt asked.

"Well, would you mind just telling me the story of the drive? What it was like and difficulties you might have had, tell me about the good times, that sort of thing."

Matt didn't know where to start, so he started at the first, then, he couldn't find a stopping place. The better part of two hours later, he finally wound up the story. To his own surprise, he told the reporter most everything. He told of sitting around the campfires at night, some of the boys singing, sipping coffee and spinning yarns. He told about the rainy days and the sunsets and Spud Weber's snake bite. He told of the river crossings, the brush with the Indians and the stampede. His voice grew sad and broke when he told of burying the cowboys killed along the way.

Sol laughed so hard tears came in his eyes when Matt told about the encounter with Clay Ballinger's trail blockers and about them striking out into the prairie night in nothing except their long johns.

When Matt finished, the reporter leaned back in his chair, his eyes flashing with excitement and his fingers cramped from taking notes in his little pad.

"Mr. Henry, that's the most extraordinary story I ever heard. That's much more than just a newspaper story. That should be a book. Would you mind if, in addition to my story for the newspaper, I wrote one of those dime novels about the trail drive. I'd like to call it simply, 'The Trail Drive?'

"Don't know who'd want to read about a bunch of cowboys driving cows, but if you're a mind to, go ahead. Could I ask a favor?" Matt asked.

"Anything," the reporter said, "anything at all. If I can do it, I will."

"You reckon I could borrow a pencil and one of those little pads? I need to do some figuring."

Sitting in his room, Matt did the numbers three times and still came out with the same answer each time. Twenty thousand six hundred head, times thirty-five dollars a head, came out to seven hundred twenty one thousand dollars.

His eyes got as big as saucers. For a long time he just sat there staring at all those zeros. In all his planning before the drive he never dreamed on getting such a good price for his cattle. He had never even actually sat down and figured up what it would all add up to.

Of course he had to pay the boys their wages and bonus, but Mr. McCoy had said he would advance him whatever he needed for that and deduct it from payment for the herd. Starting on another clean page, he figured for another hour.

After paying off all of his expenses, he still came out with six hundred sixty seven thousand ,six hundred twenty five dollars. That was more money that he ever heard of, much less thought he would ever have.

Then it dawned on him for the first time, near that much would be coming in every month. He quickly flipped to another clean page and figured some more.

When he finally finished he sat back and shook his head in amazement. Even if he paid six dollars a head for his supply of cattle and he could most likely get 'em for four, after it all washed out, he'd wind up with over a half million dollars a month profit.

In his planning, Matt decided to give the young man at the bank a list of what he paid his men and let them collect their wages right at the bank. That way, he'd make sure all his men got what they had coming.

Matt ate a leisurely supper alone and turned in early. He slept like a log and was up before good light. He went to the dining room and found a table near the back. He was taking his first sip of coffee when Sol Israel hurried up to his table looking like a man that had some news so exciting he just had to share it with somebody. Matt guessed he was the lucky one that was gonna hear it.

"Good morning, Mr. Henry."

"Morning, Israel," Matt said. "Care to join me?"

The man looked grateful and quickly slid out a chair. Matt motioned for the waiter.

"Why don't you bring Mr. Israel one of those man-sized breakfasts like mine." He told the waiter.

He figured in his mind that Israel was most likely on a tight budget. From the looks of him, he could use some more meat on his bones.

"The book I told you about?" the reporter said. "You know, the trail drive? Well, I worked all night on it and I'm very close to having it finished. I predict it will be read all over the country. Mr. Henry, you may become famous after my book is published."

"Don't reckon I know what being famous means," Matt told him, taking a sip of coffee. "Unless it means everybody is talking about you and I ain't so shore that's something worth wanting. That train robber, Jesse James? Now, he's what you would call famous ain't he? All its gonna get him is a bullet in the back one of these days."

"Well, just wait until you read it. Of course, I had to exaggerate a few things here and there, you know, to add a little more excitement. You're going to like it."

After breakfast, Matt strolled up to the General Mercantile Store. He needed to pick up a suit of everyday clothes. All he had worth wearing was the suit Suggs had brought him. A right pretty young lady greeted him warmly.

"Good morning, sir," she said, real perky like. "How may I help you this morning?"

"Well, ma'am, to be honest, you already have. It just sorta starts the day off better running into someone as happy sounding as you are."

"Well, that's a nice thing to say. So, what else can I help you with this morning?"

"I was thinking I might need a change of clothes, something not quite so dressy," he told her, browsing around as they talked.

"I can't imagine you looking much better than you already do," she said brazenly.

She flashed Matt a big smile and lifted a hand to brush her long blonde curls back from her face. One thing for shore, if she was typical, these Kansas girls shore weren't shy. Matt looked away quickly, feeling guilty.

He found a stack of blue cord pants, selected a pair that looked like they might fit. He held them up to him, then exchanged them for a larger size. The lady sauntered over to a rack of shirts and fingered through them and selected a gray one.

"This would look good on you," she said, walking over to him and holding it up against him. "Are you settling down here or just passing through?"

"No, ma'am, I'll be leaving in a couple of days." he said, stepping back a step. "These will do just fine."

"Too bad," she said, faking a pout with turned down lips.

"What do I owe you, ma'am?"

She told him and he paid her and beat a trail out of there. He'd have to tell the boys about her. They might decide they need some new duds too.

Matt headed for the bank. He spent the next hour going over figures with the young man that worked there. His name was Jimmy Matthews. Matt liked the young fellow. Joseph McCoy came in just as they were finishing up. Together, they walked out to the edge of town and looked over the cattle pens.

"How many can your pens hold?" Matt asked as they leaned on the heavy wooden beams that made up the fence.

"I can handle three thousand at a time in the pens, we'll hold the overflow over north in the Smoky Hill Valley. We can load out a hundred rail cars a day. What size herds will you be bring up the trail once you start, Matt?"

"I been doing some figuring on that. We'll have to see how it shakes out, but right now my thinking is to keep the herds to ten thousand head and string 'em out two weeks apart.

"That's twenty thousand head a month. Mr. Armour said he could process eighteen thousand a month, that would allow a few for losses along the way and a few for backup inventory. What do you think?"

"I think it sounds like a mighty big job," McCoy said.

"I've got some mighty good men," Matt told him.

"When can we expect the first herd?"

"Don't see how we could get here with the first bunch until early October. But once we start they'll be coming in every two weeks."

"Good. Very good. That will allow me time to make arrangements for the cars. I'm excited about our arrangement, Matt. It wouldn't have happened without your historic drive."

"Somebody would have done it sooner or later."

"Maybe, but it would have been too late for me and Mr. Armour. We've both bet it all on this venture."

The day was far spent. The hot Kansas sun had done its worst and headed on its downward destiny with night as Matt rode out of town and headed south. It was less than an hour's ride out to the camp and he arrived before good dark.

Since there was plenty of graze and water whenever the herd felt the need, only the night herders were scattered about the herd, lazily sitting their saddles, playing nurse-maid to the contented cattle. The rest of the crew lounged about camp, playing poker, pitching horseshoes, napping, or sipping coffee. It was a peaceful scene.

Matt ate supper with his crew, answering many questions put to him by the boys about the town and what they could expect when they took the herds in the next day. After they ate, Matt asked his foremen to meet with him over by one of the small campfires, a ways away from the rest of the crew.

They poured themselves a cup from the blackened pot and squatted around the fire. In addition to his seven foremen, Matt had asked Shorty, Romano and Cal Murray to sit in. He filled them in on the plans for taking the herd in at first light the next morning.

"The whole town's busting at the seams, boys," Matt told his men. "I never seen anything like it. Folks have come in from all over creation to watch the herd come in. There's cattle buyers and newspaper people and plain old ever-day folks from no telling where. They've got a big circus in town with elephants and such that puts on a performance ever afternoon late.

"They're throwing a big welcome shindig for us tomorrow night with a pie supper and dance and lots of pretty ladies, so the boys might want to wash up and dig out their best britches. There's some mighty pretty gals hankering to get a look at a real live Texas cowboy. They're making a big deal out of it so we want to give 'em a good show when we take the herd in. Let's spread 'em out wide and drive 'em as close to town as we can so the folks can get a good gawk before splitting 'em in the middle, just be careful we don't tear the whole thing down.

"They've got cattle pens that'll hold three thousand, so let's fill those up for 'em, the rest we'll take north of town a couple of miles to the Smoky Hill Valley. Mr. McCoy's riders will take over the herd after that. They've got a big corral built like a funnel. It's big on one end and narrows down real tight so they can count as you run 'em through. It'll take a couple of days to push the whole herd through. Joe, I'd like you and Jess to help with the counting, they'll have their men there, too.

"Once we get the herd settled in tomorrow, the boys can go by the bank and draw their pay. Mr. McCoy is throwing a big supper for our whole crew. After that, the shindig will start."

Then Matt broke the big news to them. He explained the agreement he had made with Mr. McCoy to supply ten thousand head every two weeks. Like he had promised, he made no mention of P.D. Armour's involvement, other than to say that all of this herd would be going to the Armour Packing Company in Chicago.

"It's gonna be a mighty big job, boys," he told the shocked cowboys. "I'm gonna need all the good help I can get. The way I figure it, we're gonna need nine sixty-man crews to pull this off. We're gonna keep six herds on the trail all the time, winter and summer.

"We'll drive ten thousand head in each herd and start 'em from Texas two weeks apart. There'll be two crews riding back to Texas to our headquarters at all times. So we're gonna have a string of riders going and coming all the time up and down the trail. Joe will be in charge of the home crew and do all the hiring and buying. They'll make up the herds and have them ready to hit the trail every two weeks."

Matt paused and slowly swept a gaze around the circle. His men stared back at him, looking like he had just dumped the whole wagonload on them. He couldn't blame them none. What he had outlined was enough to scare anybody that any sense about 'em at all.

"I've told you the bad news, now let me tell you some good," Matt told them. "Like I said, we'll have eight crews on the trail at all times, six going, two coming home and another branding and making up the herds. I'm allowing three months to make the drive and another month to get back to headquarters.

"Every crew will get a week off with pay after every drive. That will let the boys spend some time with their families or just rest up for the next drive. We're gonna need near six hundred cowboys riding for the Double H, fellows, we want the best there is and we want to keep 'em happy.

"We'll pay drovers and wranglers a hundred dollars a month and keep, with a hundred dollar bonus for every herd they help deliver. Our cooks will draw two hundred a month, helpers a hundred. I'm hoping by paying more than double what other outfits pay, we can hire the best and keep the ones we hire.

"That brings us to trail bosses. I need nine of them. As far as I'm concerned, sitting right here around this fire are the best that ever forked a saddle. If you boys want the job, it's yours. Starting day after tomorrow, my trail bosses draw four hundred a month, plus a hundred dollar bonus for every herd you deliver."

Again he paused to allow what he had just said to sink in. The men looked stunned, glancing at each other, as if wondering if they heard right.

"Some of you might want some time to think about all this and that's fine, but I need to know what you decide by payoff time tomorrow. Anybody got any questions?"

They all looked at one another, seemingly waiting for the other one to ask their question first. Finally Shorty spoke up.

"Boss, did I understand you to say you're offering me and Ramano and Cal a job as one of your trail bosses?"

"It's yours if you want it," Matt said.

"Then I don't have to think about it," he said quickly, a big grin breaking across his face. "Count me in."

"Me, too," Cal said happily.

"Si, señor," Ramano said.

"Speaking for myself," Jess Tanner spoke up, then glancing quickly around the circle, "and I figure for the others too, I'm mighty proud our crew is getting to stay together. I never rode with a better outfit nor worked for a better boss."

Nods of agreement shook heads all around the fire.

"Boss," Joe said, hesitantly, "you said something about the headquarters. Where you thinking it will be?"

"Good question, Joe. Course I haven't talked to J.R. yet, but he's already told me we could use as much land as we needed on the north end of the ranch, up along the Guadalupe River. If you're wondering if there'll be a place for a house and new bride the answer is yes."

Joe's face flushed red with embarrassment then broke into a big grin. The other boys all joined in ribbing him about it.

"That's all I got to say boys," Matt told them. "You might want to spread the word among the crew and see who's willing to stay on with us. Joe, if you'd hang around a minute, I need to talk with you."

The others drifted off in groups of two or three, all talking excitedly, anxious to share the good news with their men.

"Joe," Matt said, after the others had gone. "This thing I've taken on scares me to death. We've put together a good crew. They're the best I've ever seen, maybe the saltiest that ever rode under one brand. A lot of the credit for that lays square on your shoulders. You've done a good job, Joe, better'n good.

"Hiring all the men, buying all the cattle and looking after the whole operation is gonna be a mighty big job. Joe, I'm asking you to be my Segundo, my boss of bosses. I'll be spending most of my time at the ranch in Arkansas. You'd be in charge of the whole she-bang. I'll pay you a thousand dollars a month and build you and Avianna a brand new house there along the river. What do you say? Will you take it on?"

Joe just squatted there by the fire, staring at the red flames licking toward the stars. He swallowed two or three times before he even tried to speak. Finally, he swiped at a tear with the back of his hand and continued staring into the fire as he spoke.

"Ain't it odd the way things happen sometime?" he said, his voice near breaking up. "I mean, sometimes the things that seem the worst, turn out to be the best. Back there in that silver mine work camp, I wouldn't a give you a spit in the wind for my future. Then I met you.

"Now I want you to just look. Here I am, fixing to ask the most beautiful woman I ever seen to be my wife, I got a job paying more money than I ever heard of and a new home to raise my kids in. I'm counting myself one lucky fellow."

I've heard it said the sun always shines in Kansas—well, that may or may not be true, Matt thought, one thing was for sure, it was proving true this day. He sat his saddle and watched the blinding red ball climb slowly into a crystal-clear sky. The sun's rays crept across the backs of the seemingly endless sea of multi-colored bodies grazing peacefully along the Smoky Hill River.

"Let's take 'em to town!" Matt hollered.

Double H riders yipped and yelled, swatting stubborn longhorns across their rumps with coiled ropes. Gradually, the herd moved back into the familiar routine they had known for the past five months.

Stretched out more than a mile wide, the great herd moved across the flat prairie like an invading army toward the little cluster of buildings off in the distance. As they plodded closer, one could see people standing in wagons, on rooftops and in the circus grandstand.

"Daddy was there," they could someday tell their children or grandchildren.

"Daddy was there in Abilene, Kansas on June 6, 1868 when they brought in the biggest cattle herd in history."

Matt raised high in his saddle and twisted a look over his shoulder to scan the herd. Everything looked good. His swing riders were positioned only a short ways apart along the ragged line of cattle. At his signal, they would move in and split the herd into two, bypassing the watching town on both sides.

Many stood for hours watching the endless stream of cattle. Most, however, tired after awhile and returned to their normal daily routine.

Once the pens were full, the rest of the herd was driven the two miles or so out to the Smoky Hill Valley and turned over to McCoy's riders. The counting started and would continue until dark and most of the next day.

Matt's riders rode in and headed in a long line toward the bank to collect their pay. Matt and Mr. McCoy stood nearby visiting and watched the cowboys' reactions as they left the bank waving all that money in the air. Shorty rode up and propped his arms across his saddle horn.

"Boss, Joe wanted to know what to do with the calves and young yearlings?"

"I saw they was building a new church over at the edge of town," Matt said, "maybe they might have a use for them. Ride over and talk to the Parson. If he can make use for 'em, they're his."

"That was a nice thing to do, Matt," McCoy said.

"Lookee here," a cowboy yelled, coming out from the bank waving a fistful of money. "That's five hundred dollars and it's all mine!"

"Looks like you've got a good bunch of boys, Matt," the cattle buyer said, leaning back against the fence. "They've done what few thought could be done."

"Yep," Matt said, "and their work is just now starting."

They drifted into the big dining room at the Drover's Cottage slowly, a few at a time. Extra waiters had been brought in for the occasion. When they were all seated the room was crowded.

Thick juicy steaks and all the trimmings were set in front of every man. There was lots of laughing, joshing and conversation among the happy cowboys.

"Shore didn't take long to turn them ornery critters into steaks," one man said loudly.

"Yeah," another shouted, "I think I just ate Old Bossy." Everybody split their britches at that one.

When everybody had finished eating, Matt climbed to his feet. Wanting to hear what the boss had to say, they quickly quieted down.

"Men, there's a fellow here I want you to meet. Him and the town of Abilene give this supper for all of us. He's the man that built and owns the whole town. He's the man that bought the herd and put the jingle that's in your pockets right now. Without him, none of this would have happened. How about giving a Double H howdy to Mr. Joseph McCoy?"

A loud applause amply mixed with yips and cowboy yells broke out and continued until Matt raised his hands.

"Now I know you boys have been looking forward to this time for a lot of miles and there's a heap of things you'd rather be doing than listening to me so I'll just say what I gotta say and be done with it.

"There's some things going on you need to know about. Now I know you've already heard all about all the herds that we'll be bringing up the trail and all, so I won't go into all that. I do want you to know who will be heading up them drives though.

"Now you boys all know my foremen like you know that little gal back home, maybe even better. I do want to tell you a couple of things. First off, I've hired my good friend Joe Doyle to be my Segundo, my boss of bosses. He'll be in complete charge of our whole operation.

"The next fellow is another that has been with me right from the start. He'll be going to our Fourche Valley Ranch in Arkansas and taking charge of the day to day operation there.

"I've promoted some of your own to foremen and we'll be looking for others. These fellows have proved themselves and will be heading up drives just as soon as we get back to Texas. Stand up...Shorty Shepherd...Ramano...Cal Murray."

If Matt thought the other outbreak was loud, this one near burst his eardrums. It was clear, the cowboys were proud that three of their own had been promoted to trail boss. Finally, Matt got everybody to sit down again.

"Just one more thing and I'll let you go. I just want you boys to know what a good job you've done. There ain't a better crew anywhere than the one sitting right here. I'm proud to have you riding for the Double H. Now, I think Mr. McCoy has something he wants to say."

"Boys, I'll make this short and sweet. All of us here in Abilene wanted to show our appreciation for all your work bringing the herd up here to Abilene. The town's put together a celebration in your honor.

"Right down the street at the circus arena, the single ladies of our town have put together a pie supper. They've decided all the money raised from it will go to help build our new church. While I'm talking about that, we want to thank Mr. Henry for donating all the young calves and yearlings that are too young for market.

"So, if you can outbid your saddle partner, you might just get to share a pie with one of our pretty ladies. Now you won't know who's pie you're bidding on, unless of course, some of those little gals cheat and let the cat out of the bag. Right after that, there'll be a big dance in the circus arena. Have fun boys."

It was a night every Double H cowboy would talk about all the way back to Texas. There were only forty pies up for bidding. That made for some spirited bidding among the hundred drovers.

Some of the ladies cheated though, especially when they had their eyes on a particular cowboy. They would giggle and drop their heads, acting embarrassed.

Matt and Joseph stood off to the side, watching the activities. Matt saw the pretty little gal from the store standing in the line of girls that had pies up for bid. It would have been plain to a blind man when her pie came up for bid. She giggled shyly, tossed her head, brushed her long blonde locks aside with a flick of her hand and fixed those big mooneyes directly at Ramano.

The Parson was serving as auctioneer and set her pie in at fifty cents.

One of Matt's drovers named Bret bid a dollar, another quickly raised the bid to two dollars. Bret shot a malevolent stare at the other bidder and shouted "three dollars."

"Three dollars. I have three dollars bid for this delicious-looking apple pie. Do I hear three-fifty?"

The girl from the store slowly raised her eyes and fixed a long, inviting and obvious look right at Ramano, completely ignoring the other two bidders. A smile slowly curled her lips that held promises few men could resist.

"Three dollars going once!" the Parson shouted, pausing a long minute. "Three dollars going twice!"

"Five dollars," Ramano said loudly, not even looking at the cowboy he'd just outbid.

"Five dollars!" the auctioneer shouted excitedly. "I have a bid of five dollars from this gentleman right here in front. Do I hear five-fifty? Five dollars going once...going twice. Sold!"

Ramano strode forward proudly and paid his five dollars. The pretty girl from the store stepped forward and lifted her pie, then flashing another of those looks, curled her arm through his as they strolled off somewhere to share Ramano's five dollar pie together.

Later on, after the band started playing, Matt sat alone in the grandstands watching the couples dancing happily. He curled a grin when he saw Ramano and the girl from the store dancing every dance together.

He remembered what he had said one time, that you could be alone, even in a crowd. He lifted a look up at the heavens, fixed a stare on the eastern star and thought of Jamie.

The long line of Double H wagons and riders stretched out from one end of Abilene to the other. It looked like everybody in town had turned to see them off.

The townspeople stood along the street waving. Several cowboys were on the receiving end of a kiss, blown on the wind, from a girl they had met the night before.

Matt saw Ramano turn his palomino out of line to ride close to the boardwalk in front of the mercantile store. He leaned far over in the saddle, his lips meeting those lifted to him by the pretty little gal from the store. Likely Ramano would be the first to volunteer to lead a herd back up the trail to Abilene, Matt figured.

The Parson and two helpers were putting the roof on the new church at the edge of town. They stopped hammering, stood on the rafters and waved their hats as the long procession moved past.

Rolling southeast, like Joseph McCoy had instructed, they came to the Lyon River near dusky dark and set up camp. It was a happy crowd of cowboys that sat around the fires that night. They joked, laughed and told each other tall tales of their exploits the night before.

By first light they were in the saddle and on the move. They made good time and by nightfall, camped on the Cottonwood River.

"This looks like a good spot," Matt told Joe as they pulled into a grove of trees from which the river was undoubtedly named. "Let's set up camp here. First thing in the morning me and you'll ride downstream and find the Bar-J-Bar Ranch."

By sunup they rode up to the well kept looking ranch house. An older fellow with graying hair and a limp in his get-along came out from the house to greet them.

"Howdy," the fellow greeted with a friendly sounding tone. "You gents are out and about mighty early. Something I can do for you?"

"I'm Matt Henry from the Fourche Valley Ranch down in Arkansas. "This here is my foreman, Joe Doyle. We're looking for Ben Jackson of the Bar-J-Bar."

Matt sat comfortably in his saddle, waiting, having not yet been invited to step down. He knew you waited for an invite before taking that liberty.

"You found him," the man said. "You fellows light down and join us for breakfast. The wife and I were just about to sit down to it when you fellows rode in."

"If you're shore you got enough we'd be obliged," Matt told him, swinging a leg over his saddle. "You shore got a nice place here, Mr. Jackson."

"We've been working thirty-five years to make it so." The fellow turned and headed back into the house. "You boys come on in."

A sickly-looking woman wearing a white apron over a flour-sack dress offered a friendly smile. She set a platter full of hot biscuits on a red and white checkered oil cloth covered table.

"This is my wife, Bertie," Mr. Jackson said, motioning them to sit.

"Howdy do, ma'am," both Matt and Joe said, shucking their Stetsons before they sat.

"You boys are a far piece from Arkansas," the old rancher said. "What you doing up in this neck of the woods?"

"We just trailed a herd from Texas up to Abilene," Matt told him. "We're on our way back to Texas now. Mr. McCoy said you might have some shorthorns you'd sell."

"Reckon I might. Say, you wouldn't be the fellows that brought that big herd up the trail would you?" the rancher asked, passing Joe a big platter of ham and eggs.

"Yes, sir."

"How many was it you had in that herd?"

"A little over twenty thousand," Matt told him, taking the platter Joe passed and sliding four eggs onto his plate.

"That's what I heard too," the old fellow said, hurrying a big slice of ham to his mouth. "Then you'd be the one that set a fire to that Ballinger fellow's tail feathers. I declare, that story's spread faster than a Kansas prairie fire. I'd a give a wagonload of corn to have seen that. That story's being talked in every bunkhouse in Kansas I reckon. Wife, pass the biscuits to that fellow, he gets 'em down right quick."

"These shore are good biscuits, Mrs. Jackson," Joe told her, taking two while the plate was close.

"I thought I heard you say your ranch was in Arkansas?" Mr. Jackson asked.

"Yes sir, it is," Matt said. "My ranch is down in Scott County, just below Fort Smith. We're trailing longhorns up out of Texas to Mr. McCoy's place in Abilene. That's why we rode by. I'm looking for some good shorthorn stock to do some crossbreeding with. Mr. McCoy said yours was the best in Kansas."

"How many you looking for?" the rancher asked, taking another helping of ham and eggs.

"That depends on the price," Matt told him. "How many you willing to sell?"

"My herd is just shy of twenty-one hundred head," Jackson told him, "but McCoy's right, they're the best shorthorn stock ever walked on four legs.

"McCoy's been after me to sell 'em to him, but we've worked hard building up our herd of prime stock. I don't cotton to seeing them wind up on some blue-belly's supper plate up in New York or someplace.

"Wouldn't even think of selling 'em, pass the biscuits please, but I got all boogered up when my horse fell on me. The wife is feeling poorly and our daughter in Kansas City has been after us to sell out and move up there. I'd rather take a whipping than sell, but I reckon that's best."

"I'd like to look at your herd if I could?" Matt asked, sopping his plate with a last bite of biscuit. "Mrs. Jackson, if any of our cooks could make biscuits like that I'd give them a raise."

"Much obliged," she said, the only words he heard her say.

"Thanks for the good breakfast," Joe told her, scraping out his chair, then reaching for one last bite of biscuit he'd left on his plate.

The nice woman just smiled, nodded her head and started gathering up dirty dishes from the table.

Matt noticed that Mr. Jackson had to use half of a wooden barrel turned upside down to climb up on his dappled gray. Now he rode with one leg stretched out to the side.

Two men looked up for only a moment from their work of replacing a worn out rail in the corral. Two more were pitching hay from a wagon into the loft of the barn. As they rode toward the distant herd, they passed three more men with shovels cleaning out a pond.

"How many hands you working?" Matt asked the old rancher, impressed at how hard the men were working.

"I'm down to a baker's dozen now," Jackson said. "I've already had to lay off all the late comers. The thirteen I got left has been with me a long time. Shore hate to have to let 'em go, they're good men, every last one of 'em."

"Good hands that will stick are hard to find, shore enough," Matt said.

Matt sure couldn't lay claim to being any kind of judge of cattle, especially shorthorns. But it didn't take an expert to recognize the quality of the cattle they saw grazing peacefully on the rich grass they were riding through.

Joe walked his horse among the cattle as Matt and Mr. Jackson reined up and watched. It didn't take him long to do the looking he needed to. Matt saw the slight nod of Joe's head when he rode back beside them.

"What are you asking?" Matt wanted to know.

"How many you talking about?" Jackson asked.

"All of them," Matt said, "I'd like to buy your whole herd."

"Well now," the old rancher said, swiping his hat from his head and sleeving his forehead. "That's a horse of a different color."

He studied for a long few minutes. His eyes clouded with sadness as he stared at the herd he had put a good chunk of his life into. Matt felt sorry for the old fellow. A man puts his whole life into building something, some bad things happen and it's gone and part of his life with it.

"I hear the market's gonna be strong this year. They're saying most anything that can walk will fetch thirty a head. What you're looking at here ain't eating cattle, these are breeding stock. I reckon they ought to be worth forty a head if they're worth a nickel."

"I reckon you're right," Matt told the old rancher. "I'll take 'em. What about your bulls?"

"I've got fifty of the best shorthorn bulls standing anywhere. I'll let you have 'em for a hundred a head. They's some young bulls that are coming on, but ain't quite ready yet. I'll throw them in with the cows if you're taking the whole herd."

"Sounds fair," Matt said. "How would you feel about me talking to your hands? I could use some more good men."

"Well now, that would shore take a load off my mind. I'd rather be horse whipped than have to lay them boys off."

The three men visited as they rode back to the barn. Mr. Jackson struggled to get down from his horse and called out to one of the men working nearby.

"Dan, gather all the boys and bring 'em down to the bunkhouse, we need to have a word."

Matt and Joe walked with the rancher up to the ranch house and sat down at the kitchen table. Matt pulled a paper from his pocket Mr. McCoy had given him and handed it to the old rancher. The man took his time and read it carefully.

"Looks like you come prepared, young fellow. That's McCoy's hand that signed it alright, I do my banking there and I'd know his signature anywhere. That bank draft looks good to me."

The old rancher reached for a Big Chief tablet and pencil from a drawer. He licked the end of the pencil and started figuring. He bent low over the tablet for awhile. Matt waited patiently.

"Like I said, young fellow," the rancher said, looking up from his figuring. "I'm a few head short of twenty-one hundred, no more'n fifteen or twenty. We can count 'em exactly if you're of a mind."

"Let's go ahead and call it twenty-one hundred," Matt told him. "Since you throwed in the steers and all."

"Then that's twenty one hundred, times forty dollars a head. Son, that's a wad of money ain't it?" the man said.

Mr. Jackson scooted the pad over to Matt. He looked at it for a minute then handed it to Joe, who went over the figures, then scooted it back to the old rancher.

"Then, we've got fifty bulls at a hundred apiece, that would be five thousand more. Let's see. All told, I come out with a hundred twenty three thousand. Is that what you come up with?" Mr. Jackson asked.

"Yes sir," Joe said, glancing at the figures. "That's what I get."

"Joe," Matt said, "why don't you go ahead and fill out that bank draft for that amount and I'll sign it? Mr. McCoy said to tell you he'd have your money waiting anytime you wanted to pick it up," Matt told Jackson.

The three men shook hands all around, then headed down to the bunkhouse. The thirteen hands were all there waiting, obviously knowing something was up. They stood around nervously, looking like they suspected the worst.

Matt swept the group with a long searching gaze. What he saw was pleasing to him. These were men used to hard work. Men who had spent their whole life either in the saddle or working with their hands.

He saw faces that were dark from long days in the Kansas sun. Turkey tracks lined the edges of their eyes. They were lean in the middle and wide in the shoulders with hands that were thick-skinned with calluses.

Mr. Jackson stood, his head bowed, his booted foot scraping a line in the dirt. Matt saw a silver tear creep from the corner of one eye and trace slowly down a sun-darkened, wrinkled cheek. He cleared his throat and swallowed before trying to speak.

"Men," he said softly. "We've been together a long time. Some of you might near growed up here on the Bar-J-Bar. You're like family to me.

"The wife and me ain't in good health and we're getting on up in years now.

"We've done a lot of thinking and talking about it and we've decided to move up to Kansas City close to Amy and her family.

"I've just got through selling my whole herd to Mr. Henry here. He's got a ranch down in Arkansas. He's asked me if he could talk to you boys. It's like I told him, I'd rather take a lickin' than have to lay you boys off, but I'm afraid that's what its come down to. Go ahead, Mr. Henry and say what you got to say."

"Men, I've found it's easy just to hire men, but hiring good men is something else again. Mr. Jackson tells me you're some of the best and I'm a mind to believe him.

"I'm needing some good men, so here's what I'm offering. I don't know what Mr. Jackson's been paying. He didn't say and I didn't ask. I've got two jobs to offer. You can pick which one you want or you might decide not to take either one, that's up to you.

"The first is a puncher's job on my ranch down in Scott County, Arkansas. It's called the Fourche Valley Ranch. That's where this herd is going. If you take the puncher's job, you'd be looking after the same cows you've been taking care of. You'd be putting the Double H brand on 'em when we get there. We expect our men to ride for the brand. We pay fifty a month and keep.

"The other job is trailing herds from near San Antonio, Texas to Abilene. We're driving herds of ten thousand head up the trail, spread out two weeks apart, winter and summer.

"Now I know not every cowboy is cut out of the leather it takes to work a cattle drive—and that's all right too—it's hard work, long days and short nights. That's why I pay a hundred a month and keep, plus a hundred-dollar bonus at the railhead. You get a week off with pay after every drive.

"I've made the offer, now it's up to you," Matt told the men. "Me and my trail boss will be waiting over by the corral. Anybody that's a mind to ride for the Double H, get your bedroll and saddle your horse. We'll wait there for half an hour before we ride on."

Having had his say, Matt and Joe turned and strode over to lean on the corral fence. They watched as, one after one, the cowboys walked over, said a few words to the old rancher, and shook hands for a long minute before disappearing into the bunkhouse.

Within minutes, thirteen cowboys threw saddles on their horses, cinched down bedrolls behind their saddles and stepped into the saddle. Ready to leave one life behind to begin another. They reined up in front of Matt and Joe, waiting orders from their new boss.

"Joe," Matt said, threading a stirrup with a booted foot and swinging into the saddle, "help the boys round up the herd and bring them up to the camp. I'll meet you there."

Wheeling his black stallion, Matt kneed him into a short-lope and headed back toward camp. Joe and the thirteen new Double H riders headed out to start the herd to their new home in Arkansas.

When Matt got back he found the men relaxing around camp. Several had a horseshoe game going. Some were splashing around in a deep swimming hole in the river, jumping in like a bunch of schoolboys. Others were stretched out in the shade of a big cottonwood tree, their hats pulled down over their eyes. It was a peaceful sight.

"We'll be having thirteen more for supper," he told Moses. "I hired some drovers. Them and Joe will be bringing a herd in I bought, too."

"Lordy, Lordy, Mr. Henry, we drives one bunch of cows to Kansas, then we drives another bunch back. Don't make no sense to me a tall."

"Yeah," Matt said, "it does seem kinda funny when you think on it don't it?"

Matt unsaddled his horse and tethered him so he could get good graze. He poured himself a cup of coffee and strolled down to watch the boys swim.

"Come on in, boss," they called.

"I'm afraid you boys might drown me," he called, squatting on the river bank and sipping his coffee. Hearing them splash around in the water took his mind back to a little mountain-top lake and to a beautiful lady splashing about, challenging him to come on in.

It was just before sundown when they sighted the new herd. They circled it well away from camp and were getting them settled down.

"Shorty," Matt called to his new foreman. "How about sending a few boys out to relieve our new men and let 'em come in for supper?"

"Sure thing, boss."

Just after supper he asked the whole crew to gather around. They crowded near, sipping coffee and waiting to see what the boss had to say.

"First off, I've hired thirteen new men today. I want you boys to make 'em welcome. At first light, Jess Tanner, Buck Wheeler, Ed Stovall, Ed Beaver, and Ramano will be taking eighty of you and riding hard for Texas. You'll take only packhorses with you so you can travel faster. As soon as you get there, I want you to put together two herds of ten thousand each and get 'em ready for the trail. Tell Mr. Cunningham I need twenty thousand head, I'll explain it all to him when we get there.

"When we get to the Canadian River, Joe, Julio, Juan and the new men will be turning east and heading to our ranch in Arkansas, then joining up with us later in Texas. The rest of us will bring the wagons and remuda on as soon as we can get 'em there."

The crew heading to Texas pulled out at first light. It was kinda sad to see them go, but it was the fastest way Matt could think of to save time.

Matt and the rest of the men and wagons stayed with the herd of shorthorns. He was pleased to see how well the new men were fitting in. He was also happy to learn the shorthorns trailed a lot easier than the stubborn longhorns.

They drove due south and averaged a good fifteen miles a day. They reached the Kansas line eight days later. Two more long days brought them to the Arkansas. They crossed without a whole lot of trouble and made camp on the far side.

Since they were now in Indian country they doubled the number of night herders. They also put ten armed nighthawks around the remuda of Mendoza blacks.

It was near midnight when shots woke Matt from a good dream about Jamie. It sounded like they came from the direction of the remuda. Leaping from his bedroll he scooped up his Henry rifle and raced barefooted to where Midnight was tethered. He swung aboard bareback and raced the stallion toward the remuda.

The first nighthawk he came to was Jim Bob, the former hide-peeler, now a first class wrangler. The boy stood beside his mount, his pistol pointed directly at the chest of a downed Indian. The Indian was graveyard dead.

"What happened?" Matt asked, as several more Double H riders reined up.

"There was six or eight of them, Mr. Henry," the boy said. "They just seemed to come out of nowhere. They made a run for the horses. Ain't nobody getting our horses if I can help it."

"All our boys are okay," Shorty rode up and reported. "Best we can tell there was ten of 'em. They made a run at the remuda, most likely trying to scatter 'em. Our boys dusted 'em pretty good, downed six we found so far. Could be others that crawled off in the bushes wounded. Want us to go looking for 'em?"

"No," Matt said. "Call the boys back. A shot up Indian in the bush is more dangerous than a wounded cougar."

CHAPTER XX

Vengeance is mine

> "For the day of vengeance is in my
> heart, and the time of my
> redemption is come." (Isaiah 63:4)

The crossing of the Canadian River went smoothly. The date was June 26. The boys were worn out from the crossing so they made an early camp on the southern side of the river.

Matt hadn't been sleeping good for the last week or so and knew it would be a waste of time to turn in early. He squatted by the fire alone, sipping coffee and staring forlornly at the hypnotic flames of the campfire. The camp was quiet except for the snoring of his crew.

He decided to ride out and check on the herd and remuda. He mounted and walked his horse slowly around the herd, chatting quietly with the night herders. He was there when Shorty found him.

"Boss, one of our nighthawks spotted lights from a campfire down river a couple of miles. Reckon I ought to roust out some boys and check it out?"

"Naw," Matt told him, "I can't sleep anyway, no use waking the boys, I'll ride down and take a look. Couldn't be anybody meaning us harm or we'd never seen their fire. I'll be back in a bit."

He found the camp on a high riverbank overlooking the water. As he walked his horse near and reined up, still a ways off, he sat his horse and peered through the darkness, searching for any sign of danger, for anything that might tell him who they were.

In the light from their fire, Matt could see the outline of an odd-looking wagon of some sort, though he'd never seen one like it before. His gaze revealed three men squatting on their haunches around the fire, sipping coffee.

"Hello the camp," he called out.

"Ride on in," a deep voice called back, "but keep your hands empty and where we can see 'em."

Matt thumbed back the hammers of both his Rattler and Widow Maker just to be on the safe side. He stepped his stallion slowly into the jagged circle of light.

His inquiring eyes showed him a wagon with four heavy freight horses, still harnessed, with feedbags strapped over their muzzles. Their reins were tied to the wagon wheel.

On the wagon sat a big cage made of heavy bars. In the wagon, sitting cross-legged, was an Indian. His hands and feet were shackled with leg irons and connected with a heavy-looking chain.

Tethered to a rope line stretched between two trees stood three riding horses. Three saddles lay near the fire, along with four bedrolls—but only three men were in sight.

"Climb down and pour yourself a cup if you're a mind," the deep voiced fellow said, raising his gaze only enough to search Matt with his eyes.

"Just finished one at my fire," Matt said, "but I reckon I could use another."

Matt slowly stepped down from the saddle, being careful to keep the three men in sight and his horse between himself and a dark clump of bushes off to his left.

"There's an extra cup there on the log," the speaker said.

The man motioned with the cup in his left hand, his right hand rested on his hip, uncomfortably close to the Smith and Wesson strapped low on his right leg.

"Kinda figured that cup belonged to the fellow out there in the bushes with his rifle trained on me," Matt said, picking up the cup and pouring it full from the blackened pot.

"You're a mighty observant fellow," the speaker said, chuckling. "I'm Charley Steele, I'm Deputy Marshal out of Van Buren, Arkansas. This here is Pete Lawson and Strobe Jessup. The fellow out there in the bushes is Les Brummit. Might just as well come on in Les, he knowed you was out there all the time."

Matt looked the men over again with renewed curiosity. These men were rock hard and tougher than boot leather. Men who, more than likely, had tread mighty close to the blurred line that separates the lawman from the outlaw. They were the kind of men you walk around if you got a lick of sense about you.

"I'm Matt Henry," he told them. "I'm from the Fourche Valley down in Scott County. You're a cautious fellow too, Mr. Steele."

"In our line of work, I've found a man lives longer that way. We saw your fires awhile ago. You either got a lot of men or you want others to think you do."

"That's what's left of my trail crew," Matt said. "We drove a bunch of longhorns up from Texas to Abilene. Now we're taking a few to my ranch down in the Fourche Valley."

"Heard there was a big herd went through the territory a month or so back, twenty thousand head somebody said, never heard of one that big."

"It was a passel, shore enough," Matt said.

He glanced up when the fourth man stepped into the circle of light, leaned his rifle against his saddle and squatted by the fire. His eyes were on Matt the whole time.

"I sent most of my crew on back to Texas to start another herd up the trail," Matt said.

"Say your name's Henry?" the marshal, asked.

He asked it real slow, rolling the name around on his tongue like he was tasting it to search his memory for the facts connected to a name like that.

"Oh, yeah," the deputy said, "it was your family that Trotter killed about a year ago. Somewhere down below Waldron wasn't it?"

"It was my family," Matt said, sipping the strong coffee and staring at the fire.

"Then you'd be the one they call the Man Hunter. The fellow that's might near wiped out the whole Trotter gang all by himself. The stories I heard said you tracked that bunch all over creation, plumb down in Mexico even. Said you dogged 'em and picked 'em off a few at a time. Said you wouldn't stop till the last one was gone."

Again the marshal let his gaze crawl slowly up and down Matt, pausing long at the weapons on both hips.

"From all the stories I heard, somehow I had you pictured a whole lot taller and wider and meaner looking."

"Well, you know how stories are, Marshal, they get bigger with the telling," Matt said. "Don't reckon you've heard any news about Trotter lately? Last I heard they came out on the short end of a shoot-out with some marshals down at Doan's store on the Red River a while back. I reckon that was you boys?"

"I reckon," Marshal Steele said. "Pete here just rode in today with some news, matter of fact. He said somebody spotted Trotter and some of his boys down the river a piece. Can't say if it's true or not."

"When was they supposed to have been there?"

"Yesterday, wasn't it, Pete?"

"Yeah," the one called Pete drawled. "A Choctaw friend of mine saw 'em down at old Honest Abe's place. He said there was five of 'em. It was Trotter, shore enough. He's a hard one to miss with that patch over his eye. That Mexican that runs with him was there, too."

"I suppose you'll be going after 'em then?" Marshal Steele asked.

"Hadn't planned on it. I'm on my way back to Texas. I figured you fellows would check it out."

"Nope, not this trip. If it's Trotter, he'll have to wait. We've got to get the Indian back to Van Buren."

"That's some contraption you got there," Matt said, glancing at the cage.

"Yeah," Marshal Steele said, looking over the rim of his coffee cup at the cage. "We call it the tumble weed. Shore makes hauling 'em back a lot easier. Lets a man sleep better at night."

"Who is he?" Matt asked, peering at the man in the cage.

"That there is the Kiowa Kid. He's a bad one. We've been on his trail four months. Finally cornered him up in the panhandle. We're taking him back to Van Buren to stretch his neck, though I been fighting the urge to save ourselves the trip. Old Judge Caldwell gets riled though when we don't bring 'em back still kicking. Don't know why he'd give a hoot, if you ask me, he's near as crooked as the ones he hangs."

"What'd the Indian do?"

"He murdered a whole family up near Fort Coffee. He raped the woman and little girl before he carved 'em up. Wasn't hardly enough left to bury when he got through with 'em."

"Mind if I take a look?"

"Just don't get too close, like I say, he's a bad one."

Matt rose and stepped near the cage, examining the Indian with a curious gaze. The dark eyes that bore back at Matt were cold, deadly eyes, unafraid, unemotional. They were the eyes of one that lived in a world of his own—a world without consequences, without values. One who placed no value on human life, not even his own. They were the eyes of a rabid animal.

Matt sipped his coffee and stared hard at the man inside the cage and saw, not a man at all, but an animal inside a man's body, just like Jack Trotter.

Suddenly Matt felt the fire of vengeance rekindle deep within him. The fire that he just now realized had all but gone out.

Standing there staring at the Indian, he knew what he had to do. He didn't want to but deep down, he knew he had no choice. His plans, his dreams, his future would all have to wait. He had to keep the promise he'd made on the graves of Amelia and James. He had to finish the job he had started. He had to do what had to be done. He could not rest until he did. His jaw muscles tightened and he looked away.

Having made up his mind, he threw out the remaining coffee in his cup and strode determinedly back to the fire with measured steps.

"Where is this place," he asked, his voice harsher than a moment before, "the place where Trotter was spotted?"

"It's on down the river maybe twenty miles or so. Old Abe's place is smack-dab in the middle of the horseshoe bend of the Canadian River. You can't miss it. Apts as not you'd be wasting a ride though. Even if Trotter was there, that old scoundrel ain't liable to tell you nothing. Only reason the Indians ain't already lifted his scalp, he's the only place they can get their whisky and plug tobacco. They know he'll keep his mouth shut.

"Even if he was to tell you something, I wouldn't put much store by it. Folks call him Honest Abe, though for the life of me I ain't figured out why. I wouldn't trust him no further than I could throw him and after you see him, you'll know that wouldn't be more'n a spit away. He's a big one, that fellow is."

"Think I'll ride down and have a talk with him anyway," Matt breathed, setting the coffee cup back on the log. "He might have a change of heart. Maybe I'll see you again."

"Maybeso. We're headed down that way on our way back to Arkansas."

Matt stepped into the saddle and reined Midnight around. He kneed him into a short-lope and headed back to camp.

Shorty was still riding nighthawk when Matt rode up beside

him. He filled the foreman in on what he had learned and that he was gonna ride down and check it out.

"You boys head on toward Texas," Matt told his foreman. "Get there as fast as these wagons will make the trip. Jess and the others will need them for the drives. Don't wait on me, I'll catch up. I'm gonna wake Joe and tell him what I'm gonna do."

Matt rode on into camp and dug his packsaddle out of the storage wagon. He rummaged around the chuck wagon, found a few leftovers and stuffed them into his pack. He tied his big Sharps buffalo gun on top and cinched the whole thing onto a packhorse, then he shook Joe awake.

In a hushed and hurried voice he tried to explain the unexplainable. He tried to tell his friend and Segundo what he must do and why he must do it. When he finished, he knew he had failed.

"Joe, I want you to take this herd on down to the ranch. Leave Julio there with his family to help J.C. with the ranch, then take Avianna and the rest of the boys on down to Texas as quick as you can.

"In this saddlebag is a lot of cash money and the bank draft from the sale of the herd. If something happens and I don't show up, use it to get the trail drives going and deliver the beef I promised I would. I give them my word.

"If...if this don't turn out right...tell Jamie....tell her I love her."

Without waiting to hear Joe's protests, Matt stood quickly and swung into his saddle, took up the lead rope to his packhorse and rode off into the night.

The trading post was there, right where the marshal said it would be. Matt reined up and peered through the near darkness of early dawn. The square log structure sat in a clearing, surrounded by a thick stand of sycamore trees, and overlooked the river.

A thin trail of smoke from a fresh fire lifted from the chimney and was bent sharply by a stiff breeze from the south and scattered into nothingness. The smell of fresh boiling coffee reached Matt's nose.

As he watched, a single square of light shot out across the bare ground as the front door jerked open. Then, just as suddenly, the escaping lamplight was all but blotted out by the hulk of a mountain of a man who pushed through the doorway.

He was a full two heads taller than Matt's six foot-three inches and would weigh at least three hundred-fifty pounds. He wore only boots, pants and wide red suspenders over filthy-looking red long johns.

"Just hurry and fix up some grub, squaw-woman," the man growled over his shoulder like a grizzly with a sore tooth. "It's mite near day and still there ain't nothing on the table. There better be breakfast ready and waiting time I get back from feeding the horses or I'll give you a beating you won't ever forget."

Matt sat his horse in the thick grove of willows by the river and watched the giant lumber his way to a small lean-to shed surrounded on three sides by a makeshift pole corral holding a half-dozen broom-tails. They nickered and trotted over to the fence anticipating the feed in the half-filled gunnysack the big fellow carried in his left arm. Matt quickly put his hand over his stallion's nose to prevent him from answering the whinny.

The big man dumped the feed into a trough and lifted two buckets turned upside down on some fence posts. He headed for the river to fetch water for the horses.

Figuring this would be as good a time as any, Matt quickly swung down, tied Midnight to a young sapling and grabbed a handful of rawhide pigging string from his saddlebag. Running crouched, Matt made it to the riverbank ahead of the giant.

He hid behind a heavy clump of blackberry vines beside the well-beaten path that ended at the water's edge and waited.

Waddling along wagging the two wooden buckets, the monster reached the water and folded his huge body over to dip the two buckets. That's when Matt hit him. It felt like the Rattler's barrel nearly bent double with the impact. The vicious blow landed just above where the giant's ear should have been, but which the long shaggy hair covered.

For a scary moment Matt thought the man had scarcely felt the blow. He remained unmoved. Then, like a felled tree, he slowly rolled onto his side. Matt hurriedly tied the giant's hands behind his back, thought about it, then double tied them. He sure didn't want this fellow's hands free when he woke up.

Lifting one of the buckets, Matt dumped the water into the big man's face. He sputtered, moaned and said some bad works Matt had never even heard before and he thought he'd heard 'em all.

"Who are you?" the man said, shaking his big head.

"Who I am don't matter," Matt said, "what I want, does. Now Abe, I want to explain something to you so you can understand it. Here's how this is gonna work. I'm gonna ask you some questions and you're gonna answer them. If I don't hear your answer in two heartbeats, or if I get the notion you're lying to me, real bad things are gonna happen to you. Do you understand?"

The giant hesitated, cutting his hate filled eyes up at Matt, saying nothing.

Like a striking viper, Matt's right hand swiped the big Bowie from its scabbard even as his left hand found the giant's ear. The razor sharp blade flashed out, severing the ear as easily as if it were hot butter.

A deep, rumbling roar settled into a long, pitiful moan, as Matt dropped the bleeding ear beside the man's head.

"I asked a question," Matt said through clenched teeth. "I don't ask but once. I said, do you understand?"

This time there was no hesitation. He interrupted his moaning long enough to nod his head and with the word.

"Yes."

"Who's in the cabin?" Matt asked.

"Nobody but my Choctaw squaw."

"Good," Matt said. "Now see, Abe, that was a whole lot easier wasn't it? Come on."

Grabbing a handful of shaggy hair he hauled the giant to his knees, then to his feet and shoved him ahead of him up the path toward the cabin. Reaching there, Matt shoved the door open and put a booted foot in the middle of the big man's back and shoved. The giant stumbled across the hard-packed dirt floor and sprawled into a makeshift shelf piled high with all sorts of furs, scattering them across the floor.

Matt quickly followed the man through the door and swerved to one side, pistol in hand. The nose of his weapon followed his sweeping glance of the room and revealed no one but the Indian woman. She stood by a pot-bellied stove in one corner, a black-burned skillet in one hand and a large spoon in the other. She barely glanced in Matt's direction, showed no emotion or reaction and went back to stirring whatever it was in the skillet.

"Don't mind us," Matt said, "We're just having a little talk."

The woman didn't even look, she just kept stirring. Matt walked over to the trader and grabbed a handful of hair. He half lifted the man from the dirt floor before pricking the soft skin just below one of those hate-filled eyes with the needlepoint of the Bowie.

"Next question. I hear there was some fellows come by yesterday or the day before. One was a Mexican. The other was a big fellow, red hair and beard, wears a patch over one eye. Most likely lost it the way you're gonna lose yours if I don't get the right answer. Where are they?"

Old Honest Abe liked his eye. The only hesitation was to take time to swallow hard and squeeze the answer in amongst the whimpering.

"There was five of 'em," he managed.

"Where are they holed up?" Matt demanded.

"They'll kill me if I tell you."

"I'll kill you if you don't, but not until I've hurt you real bad."

One heartbeat...two...

"Okay," the man shouted. "They're staying in an old trapper's cabin in a box canyon about ten miles southeast on the Muddy Boggy River. They been staying there awhile."

"Abe, they shore better be there," Matt said, dropping the man's head. "One more thing, I'm gonna ride back by before long. If I see even one scratch or bruise on that woman, it's gonna make me real mad. Do you understand me?"

The giant nodded and dropped his head. Matt flicked a glance at the heavy-set woman. Matt doubted the big man was gonna feel much like eating whatever the woman was spooning out into a tin plate on the table.

It was late afternoon before he found their hideout. It was well hidden in a narrow-mouthed little canyon. The entrance was overgrown with bushes and he would have ridden right past it if it hadn't been for the small piece of horse dropping that somebody had missed. He stepped down and squatted in the dirt, searching the area with a slow, sweeping gaze.

They had gone to a lot of trouble brushing out the hoof prints for fifty yards around the entrance. Somebody had even removed the horse mess, except for a small piece.

Peering through the bushes, he saw a well-used trail weaving through thick bushes that crowded the small canyon's floor. A low, dirt-roofed log cabin hugged the face of the little blind canyon. For whatever reason, the builder had built the small square structure flat against the sheer rock wall.

Figuring there might be a lookout, Matt stuffed a handful of extra shells into his pocket and untied the big Sharps long rifle from his packhorse. He climbed the brush-choked hillside that overlooked the canyon and found a vantagepoint from which he had a clear view of the cabin.

He slowly surveyed each wall of the canyon, examining every rock, every bush, every place that might offer cover for a lookout. Satisfied there was none, he turned his attention to the small enclosure that held five horses.

As far as he could see, the front door was the only way in or out. It looked as solid as a fort, sure enough, but a fellow trapped inside had a problem. It was quite a hideout. No wonder Trotter hadn't been found. An Army could wear out their boots and saddles searching for it and go home empty-handed.

He fed the hungry Sharps long gun. It held seven of the heavy shells in the tube and one in the chamber. He fed it until it was full, then settled down to wait.

He chewed on a strip of jerky and remembered how good it tasted back in the silver mine slave camp. He wondered how the boys were about now. He wondered about Jamie and what would happen to her if he didn't return.

His daydreaming was interrupted when the cabin door opened and the Mexican stepped through. The same bandoleers crisscrossed his chest. Matt could see a knife scabbard hanging at his waist sash. Most likely holding the same knife used to slit James's throat.

The Mexican killer casually looked around, lifted both arms high in a long stretch, yawned, scratched his bare head and stumbled around the corner of the cabin to relieve himself.

A flash of sudden rage burned white-hot in Matt's belly. Anger sweat beaded his forehead. He clamped his jaws tight shut. The veins in his temples bulged. The muscles in his neck corded and he tried to swallow back down the killing urge that welled up within him.

His mind's eye showed him a little tree swing moved by a gentle wind. A blonde-haired boy lying in a puddle of blood. A cruel smiling face. A bloody knife.

Matt stared through narrowed eyelids that tried—and failed—to hold back the tears that were suddenly born there. He blinked his eyes just once to clear the tears away . . .and pulled the trigger.

At that distance, the big slug from the Sharps reached its target before the sound. The impact lifted the Mexican cutthroat's body completely off the ground. He was dead before it dropped him. When the explosion boomed down the small canyon it bounced off both the walls and wallowed around a few times before dying down.

Slamming another shell into the firing chamber, Matt laid it squarely on the center of the open door and fired. He knew it was a wasted bullet, but he wanted to send a message.

As he watched he wondered what they would do. Would they burst through the door with guns blazing and try to make it to cover? Would they wait until dark and try to slip out under the cover of darkness? What?

The wind was getting up and the breeze of a half-hour before was now bursts of wind coming from Matt's back. A low far-off rumbling gave warning of an approaching storm. Dusky dark was spreading its cloak of darkness. Darkness would be his enemy.

Crawfishing, he eased backwards, then quickly climbed down the hillside.

At his horses, he retied the buffalo gun on his pack, slid the Henry from the saddle boot and entrusted his Stetson to his saddle horn for safekeeping.

A stiff breeze was whipping down the little canyon. Using the thick bushes for cover, he worked his way close to the little pole corral. Keeping an eye on the front door, he worked two poles loose and they dropped to the ground, opening one section. Picking up a couple of small rocks, he scared the horses and they bolted through the opening, galloping off down the canyon.

A fleeting figure darted from the front door. Matt whirled and fired the Henry rifle from the waist. The slug caught the man mid-stride. He let out a muffled cry, stumbled another step and fell face first into the dirt. Two down, three to go, Matt thought.

Watching the front door, he ran, crouched over, the twenty yards or so to the end of the cabin. He looked down at the Mexican. A hole the size of Matt's thumb squarely in the man's chest pumped a steady stream of blood. The exit hole was as big as his fist. Matt lifted a booted foot and stepped over the body.

Matt peeked around the corner just in time to see a man burst through the door, twisting and firing his pistol wildly in every direction as he headed for a clump of bushes.

"Stop!" Matt yelled, knowing it was a wasted breath.

In answer the fellow twisted toward the sound and threw a quick shot in Matt's direction. Matt's rifle barked. The man threw up his hands with the impact, flinging the pistol spinning through the air—three down.

Long minutes passed with no further sound or movement from within the cabin. Plastering his back to the rough-hewn logs of the cabin, Matt inched his way along the front wall toward the open door.

Six feet from the front door he paused and waited. Darkness had covered the little canyon with its black shroud. It was pitch black. Even the stars and thumbnail moon was barely visible around the edges of the heavy clouds. The storm was rolling in. Matt whiffed the smell of rain and the wind was now whistling through the bending bushes.

"You!" Matt shouted above the howling wind. "The man in the cabin. Far as I know, I got no beef with you. All I want is Trotter. Throw out your gun and follow it on your belly. Stay and you'll die with him!"

Long minutes passed. From inside Matt heard the sound of angry voices. The door swung wider. Matt braced with the Rattler in his hand, hammer back.

"Don't shoot!" someone shouted. "I'm coming out!"

A pistol flew through the open door. Matt heard it bounce across the dirt. The shadowy form of a man started through the door, bending to his knees. A shot rang out from inside the cabin. The man toppled forward to lay, half in, half out and face down. He had been shot in the back.

"Trotter!" Matt shouted, "This is Matt Henry. I've come for you!"

"Who are you?" a gruff voice snarled from inside the cabin. "I never heard of you."

"I was the farmer down in Arkansas. You and your men raped my wife and murdered her. That piece of garbage called a Mexican laying out here cut my boy's throat. I'm the man that caught your boy and saw him hang. I'm the fellow that set Miss Lilly free. I'm the man your friend, the El Capitan dragged half to death. Now, I've come for you.

"This is the end of the line, Trotter. This is where it all ends. Give up and you'll live a little longer or die right here. Makes no difference to me."

"I should have killed you when I had the chance!" Trotter growled.

"Yep."

"Well, I ain't coming out and you ain't crazy enough to come in and get me. Let's make a deal."

"The only deal you get is a quick bullet or a short rope. You decide."

Long minutes passed with no other sound from the cabin. Trotter was right, he thought, he sure couldn't go in that door after him. How was he gonna smoke him out? That's it!

Inching backwards along the wall he made it back to the corner of the cabin.

He quietly moved to a pile of kindling and firewood piled against the end of the cabin he had seen before it got good dark. Scooping up an armload, he headed back toward the front door.

It took three matches before he was able to shield them with his hands and get the dry grass started. He held it under the kindling, then laid on larger sticks and piled on more grass. Using his boot, he pushed it against the body lying in the doorway.

The howling wind caught up the smoke and carried every whiff right through the open door. It took only a few minutes before Matt heard a choking cough from inside. A few more minutes...

"Okay!" a choking voice shouted. "Don't shoot! I'm coming out!"

Deputy Marshal Charley Steele sloshed through the mud beside the tumbleweed wagon. The hooves of his strawberry roan splashed water with each step, buried fetlock deep in the soft mud and made a sucking sound when each hoof was withdrawn.

Deputy Brummit swung the ends of the long reins and lashed the rumps of the four sweating horses. A heavy layer of red clay had built up on the wide wheels and caused them to lunge harder against the trace chains just to move the heavy wagon forward.

Lawson and Jessup straggled along behind, grumbling out loud about traveling in this kind of weather.

"Whoa," Marshal Steele called out, lifting a hand to stop the procession. "What in tarnation is that coming yonder?"

The man he recognized from night before last as Matt Henry was riding toward them on that big black stallion. A packhorse sloshed behind and staggering along behind the packhorse at the end of a rope—his hands tied behind his back—was something resembling a man.

The man on the rope was unrecognizable. Mud covered his whole body, obviously from many falls and being dragged along in the mud. The man stumbled, went down to his knees, struggled up before the rope drew taunt. When Matt drew rein in front of them the man on the end of the rope collapsed into the mud and lay unmoving where he fell.

"Morning, Marshal,"

"Howdy, Mr. Henry. If I was a betting man, which I ain't, I'd lay odds that fellow under all that mud is Jack Trotter."

"Yep."

"Looks like he's had a rough trip," Marshal Steele said, something close akin to a grin lifting one corner of his lips.

"He made it pretty good the first couple of miles," Matt said. "He's had a hard time the last eight or so."

"Yeah, I reckon," the marshal said. "What you aiming to do with him?"

"I was kinda hoping you might have room in that cage. Don't know if he could make it all the way to Van Buren walking."

"What happened to the Mexican and the others?" Steele inquired.

"They'll have to skip the hanging party," Matt said. "They couldn't make it. See you later, Marshal."

Matt whirled the big stallion, lifted a hand goodbye and pointed Midnight's nose toward Texas.

EPILOGUE

My Cup Runneth Over

> "...my cup runneth over, surely goodness
> and mercy shall follow me all the
> days of my life...." (Psalms 23:5-6)

The aged old sheriff once known as the Town Tamer leaned back in his rocking chair. His booted feet were propped up on the porch railing. He took a slow sip of coffee. He squinted against the late afternoon sun and peered across the lush green pasture to watch the young boy on a beautiful black and white pinto.

His thick chest swelled with pride at the young boy's horsemanship. He himself had started teaching the boy when he was no taller than a jackrabbit. Now, at six, young Matthew Henry could ride as good as any man on the vast Fourche Valley Ranch.

Taking another swig from his cup, he cut his eyes to the man sitting beside him. He pinned him with a critical look.

"So?" he questioned in an impatient tone, "are you gonna finish the story or not? That's a thing that always riled me about you, Matt. You get a fellow all interested in a story and you just stop in the middle of it. Did you and Jamie ever go back up to that Saddle Rock Mountain after that?"

"J.C.," Matt said patiently. "If I've told you that story once, I've told you a hundred times."

"Well, is it gonna wear out your tongue to tell me again?"

"Yep," Matt told him, "we went back two more times as a matter of fact."

Matt sipped from his own cup and watched his son cutting calves expertly from the herd. He about busted a button every time he saw him do that.

"Well?" the old sheriff asked again. "What happened?"

"Same thing that happened after we spent our honeymoon up there. Nine months later Matthew was born. Nine months after the second trip, James Robert was born. Nine months after the third visit, Jeanetta was born. We ain't been back since."

For a long time they sat in silence, sipping their coffee and watching young Matthew.

"That shore must be some mountain," the old sheriff said, shaking his head. "You know, Matt, I was thinking. If it weren't so dad blamed far, me and widow Frost might just take a ride down and spend some time on that mountain."

~THE END~

About the Author

I was born and raised in eastern Oklahoma—formerly known as the Indian Territory. My home was only a half-day's ride by horseback from old historic Fort Smith, Arkansas, home of Judge Isaac C. Parker, who became famous as "The Hanging Judge."

As a young boy I rode the same trails once ridden by the likes of the James, Younger, and Dalton gangs. The infamous "Bandit Queen," Belle Starr's home and grave were only thirty miles from my own. I grew up listening to stories of lawmen and outlaws.

For as long as I can remember I love to read, and the more I read the more I wanted to write. Hundreds of poems, songs, and short stories only partially satisfied my love of writing. Dozens of stories of the Old West gathered dust on the shelves of my mind. When I retired I began to take down those stories, dust them off, and do what I dreamed of doing ever since I was a small boy—writing historical western novels.